The Son of the Morning

Jacob Peppers

This book is a work of fiction. Names, characters, places and incidents are either the product of the author's imagination or are used fictitiously. Any resemblance to actual persons, living or dead, or to actual events or locales is entirely coincidental.

The Son of the Morning

Copyright © 2018 Jacob Nathaniel Peppers. All rights reserved, including the right to reproduce this book, or portions thereof, in any form. No part of this text may be reproduced, transmitted, downloaded, decompiled, reverse engineered, or stored in or introduced into any information storage and retrieval system, in any form or by any means, whether electronic or mechanical without the express written permission of the author. The scanning, uploading, and distribution of this book via the Internet or via any other means without the permission of the publisher is illegal and punishable by law. Please purchase only authorized editions, and do not participate in or encourage piracy of copyrighted materials.

The publisher does not have any control over and does not assume any responsibility for author or third-party websites or their content.

Visit the author website:
www.JacobPeppersAuthor.com

*This one's for you, dear reader—
I might create these worlds, these characters
But you're the one that makes them breathe*

To stay up to date on new release info as well as upcoming promotions on Jacob's latest projects, sign up for the newsletter at http://jacobpeppersauthor.com/newsletter-sign-up/.

Or visit Jacob's website at http://www.jacobpeppersauthor.com/

CHAPTER ONE

ALESH STEPPED INTO THE BACK street of the city's poor quarter asking himself, not for the first time, why he was here. He could hear the distant sounds of merrymaking streets away, people laughing and drinking and living their lives beneath the summer's warm sun. But here, on this street, there was only the silence, solemn and ominous. The dead did not laugh, and they'd long since forgotten the feel of the sun on their skin.

He walked up to the two men standing watch in front of the small house. They wore the gold and white uniforms of the city guard, the golden torches stitched into their tunics marking them as followers of Chosen Olliman, Ilrika's ruler and protector. Though, in recent times, that last had been called into question more times than Alesh cared to think about. He noticed, as he approached, that their uniforms were in need of washing, and they were engaged in a quiet conversation, paying little attention to their surroundings. *Guards who guard the dead and do a piss poor job.* The dress and behavior of the men were shameful but, then, Alesh was not the man to tell them so. They would not have listened, even if he had.

The guards started when they finally noticed him despite the fact that it was broad daylight, and he'd made no attempt to mask his approach. Their faces wore the expressions of men roused from a nightmare and scared that any moment they might slip back into it. *And haven't they?* He thought as he approached them, *haven't we all?* After all, not all nightmares fled with the coming of the sun. Some held on despite the dawn, digging their talons into a man's soul and refusing to be moved. Alesh knew that better than most. He rubbed at the left side of his chest and his shoulder where the scar had begun to burn, as it often did when he was agitated.

"Who goes there? State your business." One of the men demanded in a growl that did little to disguise the tremble in his voice.

Alesh held up his hands in a gesture of peace. "I mean no harm. I have been sent by his Holiness, Chosen Olliman."

"Oh," the guard who'd spoken said. He leaned over and spat, "It's the *orphan*." The tone of his voice made it a curse.

The title kindled an old pain and anger that was always close to the surface, but Alesh forced it down and simply nodded. He'd been called worse things, after all. Far worse, and no doubt the man himself would like to say more. But, whatever the guardsman thought, he would not say it now, would not risk Olliman's displeasure.

As he drew closer, Alesh detected a smell that had become depressingly familiar in recent weeks. Death. It was a combination of things. The coppery scent of blood, the hot, cloying odor of meat left out in the heat to ruin and another smell, one that ran through the others, subtler but no less noticeable for all that. Fear. It was the cold, shriveled scent of a feaar so great that it could stop a man's heart. Most people wouldn't have believed that fear *had* a smell. Alesh envied them their ignorance.

He drew closer, breathing through his mouth, "How long?"

The second guard grunted, scratching at his dark beard, "Since he was found? Two hours. Maybe three. Poor old bastard's daughter came by to visit with her kiddies. Lucky for them, she went in alone when she saw the door knocked in. If those kids woulda seen i—"

"Has anyone been inside?" Alesh interrupted. He didn't want to offend the guard—he'd hate him anyway, of course, but there was no use in making it easier for him—but he was fairly certain he couldn't think about those kids walking in on their grandfather, not as he was. Children should not see some things. *And yet they do,* a voice whispered in his head, but he forced it into silence. He knew well what he would find inside—he'd seen it before.

The guard frowned and grunted, clearly displeased at the interruption,

"His daughter, like I told you."

Alesh was already looking past the two men, his eyes looking through the tarp that had been hung over the door frame, a temporary covering since the door that had set there was shattered to pieces. "Anyone else? Have either of you went in?"

The first guard seemed to startle at this then looked offended, "Course we ain't. The Chosen's said not to, hadn't he?"

A lie, but there was no point in pressing them. Whatever damage had been done was done already. "Alright," Alesh said and, without another word, he walked past the two men and into the house.

The smell was stronger here, much stronger, as if the dead were calling out, demanding to be known, and Alesh took a moment to take a few shallow breaths before looking around. He pointedly ignored the contents of the open room, choosing instead to walk to the bed chamber. The small straw bed had been turned over, and the room's single table lay on its side. Studying the ground, Alesh noticed a trail of blood that led back to the main room.

He did not die abed, at least. He swept the room with his gaze, taking in the details in case there was anything he'd missed then, reluctantly, he followed the trail back to the main room. The room was empty of furniture save for a wooden table at the center of it. Its surface, like the majority of the room, was splattered with blood. The crimson stains on its surface displayed in long streaks of spatter, indicating that the man had been slashed deeply, with significant power behind the attack. The weapon used most likely no bigger than a knife. *Or a claw.*

Anger and disgust roiled in him, and the scar on his chest and shoulder began to burn, as if someone were waving a flaming brand just over the surface of the skin. He rubbed at it absently, studying the pattern of blood in the room. Most people probably wouldn't have believed a man could bleed so much, had they not seen it before. But Alesh had. The last victim had bled as much. The one before him had. His *parents* had. It was as if men were little more than wine skins, ready to be punctured or cut, so that they could spill their contents out onto the earth.

He realized he was stalling, putting off gazing at the body, so he steeled himself, took another slow, deep breath and turned. He regretted it immediately as his stomach turned threateningly and bile gathered in the back of his throat.

The victim had been a man once, with his own hopes and dreams, with a daughter and grandchildren that came to visit him. He had been poor, true, his house little more than four rotting walls and a leaky roof, and he'd probably passed a lot of hungry days, but he'd been *alive* damnit. He'd probably spent his life working in the fields or in the city, providing for his family, had buried a wife, if the daughter was to be believed, and Alesh saw no reason for her to lie, and judging by the small figurine of a flaming torch lying on the floor of the hovel, he'd been a devout man despite all of that. He'd no doubt spent hours bent in prayer, asking the Father of Light, the Bringer of the Flame for a good life for his children maybe, for enough food to keep the worst of the stomach cramps at bay.

And for what? To end up lying in a pool of his own blood in his same shitty house, his body so torn apart that his own daughter probably hadn't actually recognized him. *Amedan,* Alesh thought, not for the first time, *if you exist, then damn you to the Depths.* Words he'd never speak aloud, of course. Not for fear of offending the Lightwielder—if the god did exist he was either too wrapped up in his own greatness to give a shit about the suffering of mankind, or he *was* watching and just didn't care. Either way, Alesh had no use for him. No, they were words he would not speak aloud not for fear or respect for some useless god, but for respect for the man who had dedicated his life to the service of that god. The same man who had saved Alesh's own life years ago.

The same man, in fact, who had sent him here. He had not wanted to come—as a servant at the castle, he had a modicum of skill in some areas, true, but they did little good here. The dead cared little for having their horse fed or their swords polished. Not that the poor soul that lay on the floor, broken and torn like some child's discarded doll had been able to afford either, of course. No, he had not wanted to come, but he had. Just as he had come the time before, and the time before that. To look, as the Chosen had told him, to *see*. Though he had yet to figure out *what* exactly he was supposed to be looking *for*. The only thing he saw on these occasions—growing disturbingly, frustratingly frequent in recent months—was more proof of Amedan's nonexistence or, at best, unforgiving cruelty. Neither of which, he was sure, the Chosen had in mind.

Stalling again, damn you. Get it done. Just get it done and you can go back to the castle. Swallowing back his rising gorge, Alesh stepped forward and knelt in front of the body. The man was on his left side, what was left of his right arm raised up as if in an attempt to cover his face, though it was hard to be sure since it was severed below the elbow, the dismembered limb lying beside him. His back was to Alesh, so that he could not see his face or the front of him. He knelt there for a second, taking in what he *could* see.

The victim had on no shoes or shirt, nothing except some faded, patched linen trousers that would have most likely served as sleep wear and day wear both. Alesh considered, recreating the scene in his mind. The old man had been in bed, sleeping. He'd heard something—the sound of the door crashing in, most likely—and had woken. Had he lay in bed for a moment, wondering what had wakened him, confused in his half sleep? Probably. Either way, he'd been standing when they came at him. He'd retreated into the main room, taking several defensive wounds—the trail of blood and the cuts on his arms and face indicated as much. Here, he had fallen. It was much the same as the other times, no surprises, nothing unusual. The nightlings were nothing if not consistent. *Darkness-cursed bastards.*

It should be enough, *Gods* how he wanted it to be enough. But it was not. The Chosen would ask him questions, would want to know everything. If Alesh didn't have answers, he would not be angry, there would be no reproving or scolding. Only the nod, and the apology for asking Alesh to endure such horror. But there, almost but not quite hidden in that blue-eyed gaze, would be something Alesh could not see, not in Olliman. Disappointment.

He was leaning forward when a twinkle in the corner of his vision caught his attention. He turned back to where the wooden table had been turned over and broken. At first, he saw nothing, then sunlight shone through the house's only window—a small, crookedly built frame—and the twinkle came again. Hesitantly, he walked toward the broken pieces of the table, careful to avoid stepping in any of the piles of blood and knelt down. Tentatively, he pushed some of the blood-soaked wooden debris out of the way and there, lying in a pool of blood, was a crude blade with a wooden handle wrapped in faded and worn leather strapping, the kind of knife a fisherman might use to gut fish.

Alesh saw at once that the blade was covered in blood—no surprise that, considering that it lay in a pool of it—but was surprised to notice that the handle, at least the side that faced him, had only a single drop of crimson staining its surface. Which left only one explanation. *At least you made the bastards bleed for their meal.* That was surprising, though. After all, the nightlings were said to be fast—incredibly so—with hides that proved difficult for even a sword swung by a grown man to pierce. How, then, had this old man managed to cut one with no more than a fish knife? He made a mental note to tell Olliman of the knife the next time he saw him. *Better still,* he thought, going to the old man's bedroom and returning with a piece of torn fabric. *I'll show him.* He wrapped the cloth around the dagger and put it inside his tunic then went back to the old man's body.

He hesitated, staring down at the corpse, his stomach roiling. "Come on, damn it," he said aloud, the sound of his own voice seeming strange, lifeless. He took a deep breath, knelt down, and grabbed hold of the man's shoulder. The feel of blood, sticky beneath his hand, sent a wave of revulsion through him, and he fought back the urge to vomit. Once he had himself under control, he turned the body over. The man was heavy, as all the dead were. It was as if the living possessed a will, a *need* to move, but when whatever mechanism that controlled the body left, it took that need with it, left only a desire to remain unmoved, a silent testament to their own tragedy. Alesh grunted, straining with the effort and, finally, the body flopped lifelessly onto its back like an abandoned marionette from some mummer's show for the damned.

Alesh knew what he would see. He *knew,* but that knowledge didn't keep the gasp from escaping his throat. The center of the man's chest had been ripped open, the bones of it sticking every which way like broken twigs.

Where his heart had once been, there was only an empty, bloody cavity. *The hearts. They eat the hearts. Gods have mercy.* It was all suddenly too much to bear, and Alesh jerked up, the sleeve of his white servant's tunic going to his mouth, then turned and stumbled toward the door.

He barely made it outside of the house before he found himself on his knees, heaving out that morning's breakfast. After a time, the heaving stopped, but the images that flashed in his mind did not. Would not, he knew, for some time. *If they ever did.*

"Reckon he's dead then?"

In his distress, Alesh had completely forgotten the two guards were even there, and he looked up from his place on the ground to see them looking at him, small, cruel grins on their faces. He clenched his jaw, ignoring the man's sarcasm and obvious meaning, that Alesh was useless here. How could it anger him? After all, he agreed. Slowly, he rose to his feet. "Chosen Olliman wishes this to be cleaned up, and the man to be buried in the graveyard on Noble's street."

One of the guards barked a harsh laugh, "Oh? Why that poor bastard didn't have two coins to rub together. Less'n he's got a pirate's ransom stashed under one of those rotten floorboards—which he ain't—he ain't left enough money to rent the shovel, let alone pay for space among the city's finest dead."

Alesh couldn't keep his top lip from snarling, "The Chosen will pay for it out of his own treasury. The man, as I've said, is to have a proper burial on Noble street." He turned to go, but he'd only taken a few steps when he heard the guard murmur something.

"Well, ain't that damned charitable of him. I 'spose that sack of meat in there ought to be thankful, then. Not that his Holiness could bother comin' himself, of course."

A red rage suddenly overcame Alesh, and his heart began to pump loudly in his ears. The scar on his chest was burning in earnest now, as if his flesh was on fire, but the pain was a distant thing, its voice drowned out by the roar of his anger. He turned and, the next thing he knew, he was inches away from the guard's stricken face, the man a head taller than him, much taller than he'd originally appeared.

He was confused by this until he realized that he was holding the front of the man's tunic in both hands, lifting him off the ground. "What. Did you. Say?" He asked, the words grating out of his throat with a sound like sanding paper on wood.

The man's eyes were wide with surprise and fear for a moment, then they narrowed, and Alesh saw what he was thinking in that gaze. "Go ahead." Alesh said, grinning. "Reach for the sword. Please."

The man met Alesh's stare, but he must have seen something there he didn't like, for he swallowed slowly and shook his head. "I didn't say nothing, sir. They ain't no reason for us to get bloody over it. We're all on the same side here."

Alesh felt a terrible disappointment as he realized the man wasn't going to reach for the blade, but his anger had been kindled now, and it was not ready to be put to bed. "Are we?" He rasped. "*Are we?*" He shook the guard roughly and shoved him backwards where he stumbled and fell on the ground. "The Chosen's not here," he said, looking between the fallen man and his companion, "because he's busy trying to figure out how this is happening, spending his hours trying to find a way to keep worthless pieces of shit like you alive."

"Hey, now—" the guard still standing started, but stopped when Alesh turned to him. "It's just that uh … we know he's trying. We know that. We're Chosen Olliman's men, the both of us. We believe in him, and we'll do whatever he asks, of course."

Alesh's anger was dying now, but it was not dead yet. He reached into his tunic, withdrawing a small sack of gold coins and threw it on the man on the ground where they spilled across his chest. "Then bury the fucking corpse."

CHAPTER TWO

THE DREAM CAME IN SNATCHES, as it did every night. Not memories, really, but the ghosts of them. *Shadows in the darkness on either side of the road, capering and watching the cart's passage with hungry eyes that glowed like the dying embers of a fire in the night. The rock and bounce of wood beneath him as the wagon's wheels shook and rattled across the dirt path. The fitful pale glow of the lantern as it rocked precariously on the wagon's front, its light seeming weak, frail against the darkness surrounding t. A scream, his mother's, shrill and terrified, and then they were flying through the air, Alesh bouncing end over end in the wagon's back as they flipped. Then the darkness. His mother's screams, his father's prayers to a God who would not or could not help, growls and shrieks of triumph that could issue from no human throat, the sound of something—claws maybe, or teeth—entering flesh, and then ... silence.*

It was the first time he felt that silence, the empty silence of the dead, and the only sound that of a little boy's breathing, low and afraid. Then, the moment passed, and now the sound of wood snapping, tearing as if under some great force. A shower of splinters, red eyes staring at him in the darkness, something warm and hot—blood, he thinks—dripping onto his face as he looks up at those eyes, eyes that have never known compassion or love, but know only the thrill of the hunt, see only blood and death. Movement in the shadows, reaching, pulling ... and then only the darkness.

Alesh awoke sprawled on the floor of his small room, gasping for breath, his arms raised above him as if to ward off a blow, a scream dying on his lips.

Slowly, he let his arms drop and brought one hand to his face, unsurprised to find it wet with tears. The scar on his shoulder and chest felt warm, and the coarse linen of his night shirt rubbed against it uncomfortably. He rose on shaky legs and slowly, carefully removed the shirt, wincing as it rubbed along the scar.

The memory of his father's prayers and his mother's screams still fresh in his mind, he looked down at the scar in disgust. A black puckered hole the size of a coin with black, vein-like lines stretching out from it for two or three inches. And was it any wonder that the other servants of the castle whispered behind their hands when he passed, whispered things like, "Devilspawn," or "Nightling slave." Was it any surprise, really, that they hated him? Cursed they called him, and he always argued with them on that, told them they were wrong. But were they? Really? Cursed. With bad dreams, that was true enough. Cursed to relive his parents' deaths every night. Cursed with a scar that never healed, no matter how many unguents he applied, no matter how many prayers the priests said over it—and had those lines of darkness grown longer? Had they?—he couldn't be sure, but he thought maybe they had.

But the scar was not all, nor the dreams. Alesh also possessed a temper that, when kindled, took control of him, consuming him, as it had the day before when that guard had spoken against Olliman. And what if he hadn't come back to himself when he'd been holding that guard off the ground? Would he have taken the man's blade? Would he have used it on its owner? He couldn't be sure, but he thought maybe he would have. Maybe. Cursed, they said. And they were probably right. His anger had gotten hold of him before. Not bad enough to kill a man, maybe, but enough to break a little boy's nose and one of his arms when he'd been a child himself. Break the arm so bad that the boy had spent months with a cast around it and still, almost fifteen years later, he could perform only the most rudimentary tasks with that hand. And did it matter that that boy had attacked him first? That he'd called him a night-spawned orphan with Dark worshippers for parents—it had been this last that had set Alesh off. He didn't think so. He didn't think that mattered much at all.

After that, the taunts stopped coming, though he thought it was more the doing of Abigail, the castle's head cook and self-appointed guardian and moral guide of the castle's children, than anything he'd done himself. After all, Abigail did most of her "guarding" with a long wooden spoon, the sight of which made even the castle's guards—the best warriors in the city—tread lightly.

Still, Abigail or no Abigail, the children had treated Alesh as an outsider, and he'd grown up without any friends. No friends, that was, except Abigail herself, Chorin and, later, Sonya.

As if on cue, there was a quick, familiar knock on his door. "Just a second!" He said, hurrying over to his small closet and withdrawing his servant's tunic, pulling it on over his head. As soon as the scar was out of sight, he found that he felt better. He'd only just managed to get the shirt on before the door burst open, and a young girl ran in, her blonde hair flying out behind her as she rushed forward and jumped on him. Alesh caught her and, despite the fact that she could have weighed no more than forty five or fifty pounds, he stumbled a step before getting his balance. She hugged him, and he hugged her back before setting her down. "Good morning, Alesh!" She said, smiling widely.

Alesh took in that smile, the earnest, innocent joy in it, and the last vestiges of his dream fell away. *Until tonight then.* "Light, Sonya, what are you so excited about? You about flattened me you know and besides, if your grin was any bigger, you'd be chewing on your own ears."

The little girl giggled, "That's silly. People can't chew on their own ears."

"Oh, come now," he said, mussing her hair, "I believe in you. You can do anything you put your mind to."

She laughed again, darting out from under his reach, "Alesh, don't you know what tomorrow is?"

He made a show of considering, "Hmm … let me think … oh, I've got it. Laundry day!"

She sighed, a long-suffering sound that she'd picked up from Abigail. "It's *Fairday,* silly," she said as if talking to someone who wasn't quite all there.

"Oh?" He said, sitting on the bed and reaching for his boots, "Is that right?"

She nodded, "It is, and Abigail said she'd take me." She paused for a moment before launching into an excited ramble that was almost too quick for Alesh to follow, "It's going to be great, Alesh. Thomas says that there might be jugglers and sweet meats and bards and actors and even *magicians.* Tom is Lord Gustan's servant, and *he* knows. He says that his master always goes to the Fairday because he likes to go to something called …" her young face screwed up in thought for a moment, "he called it … oh, I remember, a *cathouse."* Her eyes grew wide with delight, "I've never been to a cathouse before, Alesh, have you? I bet they're wonderful. I asked Abigail if we could go and maybe I could get a kitty, but then she got that look she gets sometime, you know the one"—*The Gods know I do,* he thought—"and she asked me who told me about it. I told her Tom did, and she said she was going to talk to him about it. I guess maybe to ask for directions, but she seemed mad." She leaned forward, her expression suddenly deadly serious, "Does Abigail not like kitties, Alesh?"

Alesh laughed and held up a hand, "Easy there, Sonya. Take a breath." Yes, Abigail would be mad alright. Lord Gustan was an elderly nobleman who was known for his appetites for the fairer sex—particularly the kind that charged for a night's company. Gustan's servant, Tom, was young, no older than nine or ten summers himself, and he probably didn't know what a cathouse was any more than Sonya did, but he'd catch the rough side of Abigail's tongue regardless. Ever since three years ago when Sonya's parents had abandoned her outside of the Chosen's castle—a girl of no more than five—the head cook had fretted and worried over her like a mother bear over her cub. Abigail was a sweet lady, one of the few who treated the young servants like equals instead of slaves, but her temper was legendary around the castle. Unfortunately for Tom, Alesh knew from experience that, if anything, the legends fell far short of the reality.

The little girl frowned, "You're getting the same look that Abigail had. Did I do something wrong, Alesh? I didn't mean to, honest I didn't." Her bottom lip began to tremble, "Abigail's not going to get mad and not let me go, is she? I'll be good, Alesh, really. We don't have to go to the cathouse if she doesn't want to."

Alesh smiled reassuringly, "No, Sonya, you didn't do anything wrong. I'm sure Abigail will still take you to Fairday, but I don't think you'll be visiting the cathouse. Abigail is … *allergic,* you understand? It means that … well, she can't stand to be around them." Which was true enough. If she had her way, the head cook would no doubt round up all of the women working at the place and set to them with her long-handled wooden spoon. Abigail was of the opinion that there were few things that a good whipping couldn't cure, and Alesh had to admit that, from what he'd seen, she was usually right.

The little girl considered this for a moment, "You mean it, Alesh? She'll really let me go? I didn't know that she was acerbic."

He fought down a laugh and nodded, "I'm sure, but if I was you I'd go and give her a great big hug, and tell her that you didn't know she was, uh, acerbic to kitties."

"I will, Alesh," she said, rising and rushing toward the door, "I'll tell her right now, thanks!"

Alesh watched her go, a smile on his face as he thought of how much her time at the castle had changed the little girl. When she'd first arrived, she'd been half-starved, covered in bruises, and terrified of pretty much everything. A raised voice or too many people enough to send her skittering away like a frightened hare, not to be found until hours later, hidden in some pantry or unoccupied room of the castle.

She'd been great at hiding then, and though the kindness of the Chosen and many of the servants—older women mostly, who spoiled her and treated her as if she was their own child—had done much to bring her out of her shell, she had not lost that talent. Abigail often complained about the girl's whimsical nature and ability to seemingly vanish at will, but she was never able to hide the glint of amusement in her eyes, or the love that showed through when she spoke of the girl.

For her part, Sonya had latched onto the kind, if sometimes gruff Abigail more than she had any of the other servants, and the woman was more of a mother to her than Alesh suspected her own had ever been.

As he tugged on his other boot, his thoughts turned back to Fairday and he felt a twinge of foreboding. The shows and performers would attract crowds in large numbers. Farmers and tradesmen from the outlying areas would come to town to sell and trade their wares and others, peasant and noble alike, would come to take part in the celebration.

It was a time of laughter and celebration, when even the most self-absorbed or cruel of men could be found sharing ale and a joke with strangers. Alesh *should* have been excited, but he was not. With that many people in the city, that many ears to hear and eyes to see, the Redeemers would be out in force. They would march through the main street, as they had so often of late, their red and black armor shifting in the sunlight like blood and shadows, their expressions grim as they proclaimed their allegiance to Shira, Goddess of the Wilds, denouncing Amedan, her husband, the God of Light and patron god of all of the Chosen. The thought made him uneasy.

It wasn't the fact that the Redeemers worshipped another god that bothered him. As far as Alesh was concerned, all the gods, major and minor both, were equally useless. After all, neither Amedan nor Shira, nor any of their children had raised a finger to save his parents or to save Sonya from hers. Amedan was not Alesh's god, but he *was* the Chosen's god, and the Chosen had taken him in and given him a home when no one else would. Besides, he didn't like the cold, hard gazes of the Redeemers. There was something hungry, something feral about them. He'd told Abigail once that he'd thought they were dangerous, but she'd only laughed and patted his hand in that motherly way of hers, *"All fools are dangerous, Alesh,"* she'd said, *"but even the Redeemers would not be so foolish as to do anything against Chosen Olliman."*

She was right, of course. Olliman was the leader and most powerful of all the Chosen, a man who, by all accounts, had slayed Argush, the king of the nightlings, single-handedly. It was said that his god's favor had granted him the strength of ten men and magic powerful enough that, during the war, he'd laid waste to dozens of the night's creatures with no more than a wave of his hand. But Olliman, like the other Chosen, was getting old, well over a hundred in fact, his long life—another of his god's gifts—stretched out behind him. Most people seemed to think he'd live forever, as eternal as the sun or stars themselves, but they did not see him as Alesh did. They were not the ones summoned to the Chosen's chambers late at night with a special tea to help him sleep, and they did not see the weariness, the aching exhaustion that showed in his eyes in his few unguarded moments or the painful memories that etched themselves into his wizened face when darkness reigned and the sun was yet hours away. Perhaps, he thought, that was why men didn't live forever. For unlike joy and happiness—which could be forgotten—a man's deepest pains never left him, accumulating instead the way a lifetime soldier's wounds will, slowing him down more and more until he cannot rise beneath the weight of them. Dark, maybe, but true. Alesh was in a position to know that more than most.

He sighed. If Chorin—the only friend he had close to his age—was here, he'd chide Alesh for worrying like an old maid, and he'd be right to do it. Fairday was a time for happiness, not a time to look for shadows in the sunlight. Pushing his dark thoughts away with a will, he rose and headed for the door. It wasn't that he didn't have enough in the present to worry about without looking for problems in the future. After all, it would soon be time for his training session with Kale. Why the Chosen had picked Alesh to be his apprentice's training partner was beyond him. Abigail told him that he should feel honored, that he was lucky to have been chosen, but his training sessions rarely left him feeling honored. Bruised and sore maybe, but rarely honored. But the Chosen had picked him, for whatever reason, and a few bruises and aches were a small price to pay a man who'd taken in an orphan who'd stumbled into his city covered in dirt and blood.

He was headed for the Chosen's personal training grounds—a place only Kale, the Chosen, and himself were allowed to go—when he turned a corner and saw a large familiar form patrolling the corridor. "Good morning, Chorin."

The thickly-muscled castle guard turned and regarded him with a grin, "Alesh, how are you?"

Alesh walked up and clasped his hand, wincing at the strength in the man's grip, "Oh, you know, same as always." He frowned, "You know, you should really start working out. It doesn't look good for one of the Chosen's guards to be so out of shape. It's embarrassing really."

Chorin laughed, his massive shoulders and chest shifting like boulders beneath his jerkin as he did. He clapped Alesh on the shoulder hard enough that he nearly stumbled, "Is this gallows humor?" Chorin asked, still smiling, "You *are* headed to a training session with Kale, aren't you?"

Alesh frowned, "Well, aren't you just a funny bastard."

The big man nodded, "One of the many gifts his Grace Amedan has given me along with my devilish good looks and abounding humility."

Alesh laughed despite himself. Chorin was the largest of the Chosen's guards and only half a head shorter than the Chosen himself. He was in his late twenties—a few years older than Alesh—and had been a soldier before he was given the much sought after honor of guarding the Chosen; an honor which spoke volumes about his skill with the blade sheathed at his side. Many would have seen the guard's size and the long, jagged scar that cut its way across his face and thought him an unthinking brute who spent his spare time picking fights in bars and crunching rocks in his teeth, but they would have been wrong.

The truth was that Chorin was one of those people who everyone seemed to take an immediate liking to. Especially women. The bastard. Rarely did a day pass when Alesh didn't hear groups of them—nobles and servants alike—whispering about the big man when he passed. When he was off duty, Chorin could always be found with a different woman or *women* under his arm and, for reasons Alesh couldn't fathom, they never grew angry with Chorin himself, choosing instead to compete with each other for his attentions. Alesh thought about his own romantic experiences to date and frowned. It was a short thought. "It must be a tough life," he said, unable to keep a touch of bitterness from his voice.

His friend's expression grew serious for a minute, then he smiled, "Hey, why don't you come to Fairday with me tomorrow? Uriel and I were going to go, and she mentioned bringing her cousin along."

Alesh gaped despite himself, "Do you mean *Lady* Uriel? As in Uriel of the house Tarland?" Uriel Tarland who *also* just so happened to be a member of the second richest family in the city.

Chorin nodded, apparently not seeing anything strange about one of the most powerful noblewomen in the city spending time with a common guard. Alesh groaned wondering, not for the first time, if the man had any idea how blessed of a life he led. Chorin was his best friend, had been for years, and he loved him like a brother, but he could think of a few things he'd rather do than spend the day watching noblewomen fawn over his friend. Being hanged, for instance. "Look, Chorin—"

The big man held up a hand to stop him, "No excuses, Alesh. We both know that the Chosen gives the people in the castle Fairday off. Now, come on out with us. It'll be fun."

"I appreciate the invite, Chor, really I do, but I'll probably just go to the library. There's a book there—"

"That will be there *next* week," interrupted Chorin. "Now listen, I've seen the cousin Uriel was talking about. She's real pretty. Nice too. Much better company than a bunch of dusty old tomes."

Alesh sighed, "What's her name?"

Chorin considered for a moment, "It was uh … oh yes, Isabelle, Lady Isabelle. Uri says that her family's from Latlia, but they've come to the city for Fairday."

Uri, Alesh thought, amazed. *Not Lady Uriel, not Mistress Tarland. Uri.* "This Lady Isabelle," he said, struggling to keep his teeth from clenching, "Is she smart?"

Chorin hesitated, frowning, "I … I'm sure she is."

Alesh nodded, "Then she won't waste her time with a castle servant."

The guard's face twisted in an almost comical annoyance, and he started to speak, but Alesh held up a placating hand, "Alright, Chor, alright," he said with a sigh, "I'll go but don't knock the books. At least *they* don't care that I'm a servant." *Or think I'm cursed.* "Besides, as far as I'm concerned, people should learn more about the nightlings. It seems that everybody—"

"Oh, Light blast me," Chorin said, slapping his hand to his forehead, "I nearly forgot. Have you heard?"

Something in his friend's tone sent a shiver of dread racing up Alesh's back. "Heard what?" He asked, scared that he already knew the answer.

"There was another attack last night," Chorin said, his voice grim, "This one was on the Street of Lords." He looked around at the empty hallway then leaned closer, speaking in a barely audible whisper, "Lord Simion was killed."

Alesh gasped, feeling as if someone had just punched him in the gut, "You can't be serious. The nightwalkers have never attacked the royal quarter before. Why, there's so many guards that someone would *have* to see them and sound the alarm. I mean ... how would they even *get* that far?"

Chorin shrugged uncomfortably, "I don't know, but no one saw anything."

Alesh frowned, his mind racing. There'd been several attacks over the past months, but they'd all been in the poorer districts of the city. Places where there were fewer guards and the only lights were those maintained by the City Watch under Olliman's orders in order to protect the people as best as he could. Nightlings hated the light, were hurt and eventually killed by it. The lights should have been enough to keep them away, to keep the people of the city safe. But they kept dying anyway. Still, for such a thing to happen among the well-lit manors of the nobles was unheard of. Unlike the commoners, the nobles that lived on the Street of Lords could afford to buy and maintain their own lights in addition to the city's regular ones.

Since the attacks had started nearly a year ago, many nobles had spent small fortunes hiring men to install lanterns and torches and others to constantly maintain them as well as patrol the grounds of their family homes. Had anyone asked him before today, Alesh would have said that the night never touched the wealthy district, and that it would have been impossible for any of its creatures to venture into that part of the city. Apparently, he would have been wrong. "Was anyone else hurt?" His voice sounded numb, dazed, even to his own ears.

Chorin shook his head, "One of his servants found him this morning in his bed."

"Well," Alesh said, "maybe ... maybe it wasn't a nightling. Maybe they just *thought* it was. After all, the attacks have everyone on edge. One of the other nobles could have had him assassinated—it wouldn't be the first time." A faint hope, tempered by the knowledge of Lord Simion's death arose in him. A noble feud could be dangerous, true, but it was better than the alternative. If the nightwalkers actually *had* somehow managed to attack into the Street of Lords then no one in the city was safe.

"No," his friend agreed, his expression grim, "You're right. It wouldn't be the first time. Some of the nobles would wish a man dead for no more than wearing the same hat as them in public. Thing is, royal assassins don't eat the hearts of their victims."

Oh, Alesh thought, fighting back his rising gorge, *right*. "But how? How could it happen? After the other attacks, the Chosen has tripled the guards throughout the city and the Street of Lords already had more than anywhere else."

Chorin shrugged, "I don't know how only that it did. Captain Valen said that we'll be working double shifts after Fairday, and he's even enlisted Lightbringers to accompany the patrols along the city wall. A friend of mine that's posted on the wall said that a section of the east wall was broken in—a large section. Apparently, it was a big bastard that came through last night."

Alesh frowned, "You're sure it was the eastern wall?"

"I'm sure."

"Well, see, that doesn't make sense either," Alesh said, frustrated, "Why in the world would a nightwalker break in on the *east* wall, then sneak all the way through the poor quarter, through market square, and into the *west* side of the city where the Street of Lords is to murder," he stopped, suddenly unable to finish. Lord Simion had been one of the Chosen's closest friends among the nobles, and Alesh had served him many times when he'd attended one of the castle feasts or a private dinner with the Chosen. The lord had been an old man, gray-haired and unable to walk without the help of a cane, but he'd always made it a point to visit the servants in the kitchen and thank them for the meal. He'd been the only noble who'd treated Alesh and the others with respect, one of the few who obeyed Olliman without trying to wheedle anything from him. He'd been a good man, a kind man. Now he was a dead one.

Chorin put a hand on his shoulder, "Who knows why the creatures do what they do, Alesh? Better to guess at the thoughts of a lightning strike than to try to figure out the way one of those bastards' mind works."

"Does the Chosen know?" Alesh asked, hearing the hollowness in his voice.

His friend nodded, "Of course."

Alesh felt a pang of sympathy for the Chosen. For all his power and renown, Olliman was a man like any other and more sensitive than most. On more than one occasion since the attacks had begun, Alesh had seen him kneeling, his face haunted, his normally bright blue gaze dim and tortured, as he prayed to Amedan for help protecting his people. The god, as far as Alesh knew, had never answered.

"I have to go," he muttered, struggling to keep the worry out of his voice, "If I'm not there for Kale to beat up on he's liable to start chewing on the practice swords." In truth, he wasn't thinking about the Chosen's apprentice at all, but Olliman himself. Simion had been a friend, Olliman's closest, and Alesh knew that his murder would hit the Chosen hard.

"Do you think he'll be okay?" Chorin asked, and Alesh could see his own worry mirrored in his friend's expression.

"I don't know. I'll see you later, Chorin." He started away.

"Alesh?"

He turned back to his friend, fighting down a sigh of impatience.

"Don't forget about tomorrow, alright? It'll do you good to get out. I'll meet you in market square over at *The Dancing Maid* at First Bell. You know the place?"

Alesh nodded distractedly, "I know it. See you then."

CHAPTER THREE

SERVANTS OF THE CASTLE MOVED through its many corridors, busily going about their chores. Several marked his passage with the familiar stares of disgust and suspicion, but Alesh didn't give them a thought as he sped toward the Chosen's quarters, his mind working over what Chorin had told hm.

Most scholars believed that the nightwalkers were unthinking beasts, little different than other predators like wolves or bears. Even during the war, when the nightling king Argush had led the creatures against mankind, the books described them as more of a mob than an army, a dangerous mob to be sure, but one that spent no time considering tactics or strategy. Alesh wasn't so sure. After all, was it just coincidence that they'd killed the Chosen's most powerful and loyal supporter among the nobles? True, others had been killed, but to travel all the way across the city risking the guards and the light of the torches and lanterns that were regularly maintained just to kill someone at random? It didn't seem likely to Alesh, and he was considering how truly little anyone actually *knew* about the creatures when he turned a corner and let out a cry of surprise as he ran into something as solid as a wall of stone. Hands shot out, impossibly fast, and caught him, keeping him from falling. "Good morning, Alesh," a familiar voice said.

Alesh stared up, a feeling of dread building in him, and saw that it was Chosen Olliman who held him, Chosen Olliman who he'd went rushing into like some foolish child. Looking at him then, half a foot taller than Alesh's own six feet two inches, his hair long and white, his eyes a piercing blue that didn't seem to miss anything, Alesh understood why people thought of the Chosen as eternal, almost a god himself. He swallowed hard, "Good morning, Chosen Olliman."

The Chosen took in Alesh's panting, sweaty form, and frowned, "Is the castle on fire somewhere, and no one's bothered telling me?"

"Uh … no sir."

"Ah. Then, have we been invaded?"

Alesh felt his face grow hot with embarrassment, but he shook his head.

"Then relax, boy," the Chosen said, a small smile on his face. "If Abigail caught you this way, I imagine she'd be reaching for her spoon, grown man or not."

Alesh coughed, "I um … I didn't want to be late, sir."

"That eager for your training session, are you?" The Chosen asked. His smile would have fooled most, but Alesh could see the sadness, the pain lurking just under its surface.

"No sir … or … yes, I mean—"

"Oh, I think I know what you mean." He said, "Well, it seems that you have a respite. Kale has not yet arrived. Apparently, some pressing matter has demanded his attention elsewhere." His expression grew contemplative for a moment, then he shook himself and gave Alesh a wink, "I suspect it is drink or women. Most likely both."

Alesh shifted uncomfortably. He had known the Chosen since he was a child. The man had always been kind to him, always treated him far better than a servant had a right to be treated, but that didn't change the fact that Alesh always felt inadequate under his gaze. Somehow, he felt as if those eyes were always testing him, searching within him for something of worth and now, like always, he felt that he was destined to disappoint them. "You've heard about the attack?" The Chosen asked abruptly.

"Yes sir," Alesh said, "I'm … I'm sorry about Lord Simion, sir."

The Chosen sighed heavily, running a shaky, leathery hand across his face, "As am I, Alesh. Everett was a good man and a better friend."

"Sir …" Alesh ventured hesitantly, "they say … they say it was a nightwalker."

The old man nodded, a strange, unfamiliar look in his eyes, "So they do, and you are wondering—as I suspect much of the city is—how that is possible. After all," he said in a suddenly bitter voice Alesh had not heard come from the man before, "it is my job to protect the people from such things, is it not?"

Alesh thought it best to remain silent. The Chosen's mouth worked for a moment as if in anger or grief then he waved a hand dismissively, "I have lived a long time, Alesh," he said in a voice that was little more than a whisper, "Too long, I often think, and if there is one thing that the years have taught me, it's that things are not always as they seem." His eyes grew cold and distant then, and they no longer looked like eyes at all, but chunks of some frigid glacier, cold and implacable. He glanced around them, as if expecting someone to be listening, "Simion was a good man," he continued, voice still low, "a righteous man who followed the precepts of our Lord Amedan faithfully all of his life and my strongest supporter among the nobles. Now, he is a dead man." He paused, meeting Alesh's gaze, "I wonder why that is."

"Sir—" Alesh began, wanting to say something of comfort but unable to think of anything.

The Chosen held up a hand, silencing him, "I assume you've also heard that the creature broke in through the eastern wall?"

"Yes sir."

"Good," he said, his voice business-like once more, "I have sent out some workers to rebuild the hole before the new night comes. I would like for you to go there and ensure that it is done … properly. I would go myself, but I'm to meet with the Merchant's Guild today, and, knowing Guildmaster Balen and the others, I don't expect to be done until late tonight."

"Sir," Alesh said surprised, "I don't know anything about masonry. I wouldn't know if they were doing it wrong or not."

The Chosen smiled, "That's alright, Alesh. Just go and do what you can and let me know if you see anything … out of place."

"Out of place, sir?"

Olliman started to speak, paused, then seemed to change what he'd been about to say, "Just see that the wall is finished and done well. If it's not repaired before sundown, we'll have the creatures prowling the streets of the city in force."

Judging by the past few months, Alesh thought that they probably already did, but he wouldn't dare say so. "Yes sir. I'll go now." He started away, but the Chosen stopped him with a hand on his shoulder.

"Are you happy, Alesh?" He asked. The question caught Alesh off guard, and he turned back to look at the Chosen. There was a sad, almost desperate look in the man's eyes. In that moment, he wasn't the ruler of the grand city of Ilrika and its outlying provinces, or one of the priests of Amedan, magically endowed with a portion of his god's power. He was an old man, a man with his own doubts, his own fears. A man who had just lost his closest friend.

"I am, sir," Alesh answered. "When my parents," he hesitated at the pain the memory brought, "when they died, I didn't think I'd ever be happy again. I felt ... I felt as if the world had ended, and I wanted to die too. It still ... it still hurts, and I miss them all the time, but thanks to you I have another life, one with friends and duties and responsibility."

The Chosen nodded sadly, "That is good. I know that you blame Amedan for the deaths of your parents, for not saving them," the Chosen held up a hand to forestall his objections, "You have never told me as much, nor would you, but it is true just the same. I just hope that one day you'll grow to understand that although we must sometimes weather pain, and even death, it is not without purpose. No, do not speak, son. I ask only that you think on it." He paused for a moment then, his gaze growing distant, "I am glad that you like your duties, Alesh. I think that, in the days to come, you will have more yet."

Alesh was still trying to figure out what *that* meant when the Chosen draped an arm across his shoulders and began guiding him toward one of the castle's windows, "Now, do you know of a tavern called *The Full Tankard?*"

Alesh shook his head, still not trusting himself to speak. "Nor would I expect you to," the Chosen said. "It is one of the cities more *colorful* inns. The kind of place where the nobles you see in the castle wouldn't frequent," he winked conspiratorially, "or at least wouldn't *speak* of frequenting." They stopped in front of the window, and despite the fact that he'd seen the view for years since living in the castle, Alesh was still impressed.

The Chosen's castle sat on a hill in the center of the city and was high enough so that depending on which window a person stared out of, he could see an entire section of the city laid out before him, all the way to the massive stone walls that surrounded Ilrika. From this height, the buildings, shops and businesses, looked like a child's toys, the people like ants as they traveled through the finger-wide roads that wove through the city. This particular window looked out upon the poorer, eastern part of the city. Olliman gestured out the window, "What do you see, son?"

Alesh squinted, sure that there was something specific he was supposed to notice, but having no clue as to what it as. It seemed to him that the Chosen was always giving him tests, asking him questions or riddles that would often keep him awake at night. He would have thought nothing of them if not for the questing, searching look that always accompanied the questions. Finally, he sighed, feeling, as always, like a failure, "Nothing. Just the people and the buildings."

Suddenly, the hand on Alesh's arm grew warmer, and he turned, letting out a small sound of surprise. The Chosen's other hand glowed a soft, muted gold like sunlight reflected off of a forest lake. Olliman smiled and flicked his hand at the window. The sparkling light drifted from his hand in a small golden cloud, passing through the window as if it wasn't there and flowing onward out into the air until it disappeared out of sight.

Alesh stared after it in awe. He'd lived at the Chosen's castle since he was a child, but he'd only ever seen the man use his magic once before, healing a guard that had been badly wounded in a training exercise. Once, years ago, he'd asked Olliman why he didn't use his gift more. After all, what was the point of having all that power if you never used it?

At first, Olliman didn't answer and when he finally did, he did so in a voice almost too low to hear, "All power carries burdens, Alesh" he'd said, his gaze growing distant, as if he was remembering a different place or time, "and magic more than most. A man must not wield it lightly, for it has a way of twisting in his grip, like a serpent, and hurting those he meant to protect."

Alesh had wanted to ask him more, but something in the Chosen's eyes had stopped him. He did not ask again. It was enough to know that the Chosen didn't use his power frivolously but only when he saw no other way. Alesh couldn't help wondering why he'd chosen to use it now. "Now what do you see?" The Chosen asked in a whisper, his voice sounding strained.

Alesh turned and regarded the city once more. At first, it seemed the same as before but then he saw it. In the distance, not far from the eastern wall, a building glowed the same golden hue as the Chosen's hand had. "But how?" Alesh gasped. "It ... it's beautiful." The building shone like a small sun, the golden light swirling and dancing around it like millions of dust motes engaged in some intricate, never-ending dance.

When the Chosen spoke, Alesh could hear the laughter in his voice, "Yes, yes, it is, isn't it? Mark the place well, Alesh, for that is *The Full Tankard*. On your way to the wall, I would like for you to stop there and deliver something for me."

He reached into one of the deep pockets of his white robe and withdrew a letter sealed with a golden torch. The torch was the symbol of Amedan, and as one of the god's priests, Olliman's as well. Alesh took the letter reverently, handling it the way a man might hold a priceless jewel. "You must take this there and deliver it to a woman by the name of Katherine Elar," the Chosen said, leaning close and holding Alesh's gaze, "Her and no other."

Alesh swallowed hard at the sudden seriousness in the Chosen's voice and nodded, "I will, sir, but ... forgive me, why ...." He hesitated, suddenly unsure.

"Why didn't I just tell you directions or get someone to lead you there?"

Alesh *had* been thinking that and something about his expression must have given it away because the Chosen laughed, "Perhaps it is too long since I have used Amedan's gift and wanted only to feel it once more." He shrugged, "At least now you will not have to ask for directions."

And why does that second bit feel more important than the first? Alesh thought, but Olliman was speaking once more, "Thank you, Alesh. Oh, and see Abigail about a change of clothes."

"Sir?"

The Chosen looked out at the city, a frown on his face, "News of the attack will have already spread into the city. People will be angry and scared and looking for someone to blame. It's best that you don't wear your servant's whites; I don't want them taking their anger for me out on you. I've had Abigail set some clothes aside, see her before you leave."

"But sir," Alesh said, startled, "they can't blame you. You've done everything—"

"I've done *nothing*," Olliman growled, and Alesh recoiled in shock at the sudden fury in the man's tone.

He'd never seen the Chosen lose his temper before, and he was suddenly terribly aware that he was talking to the most powerful man in all of Entarna, a man who had, if the stories were to be believed, slain hundreds of the night's creatures with his bare hands, who had defeated even the nightling king Argush in single combat. "I'm sorry, sir," he managed, the words coming out as a croak from a mouth that had gone impossibly dry, "I didn't mean to offend you."

Olliman sighed, "No I'm the one who's sorry, Alesh. It's not your fault. But the fact is that I *have* failed them. It is my job to keep the city safe, yet the attacks keep coming." His face twisted in sudden fury, his eyes flashed a brilliant gold, and he slammed a fist against the stone wall. There was an ear-splitting *crack* and the stone spider-webbed like glass beneath a hammer. "Simion was a good man," the Chosen growled, "a good friend, and I could not protect him."

Alesh stared at the cracked stone in shock, desperately wishing that he was somewhere else, *anywhere* else. Several tense seconds passed and finally Omidan took a slow, deep breath, "Please, forgive me, Alesh," he said in a weary voice, "Sometimes I think Amedan was a fool to choose me."

"S-sir?" Alesh asked, his blood going cold in his veins. In all the time Alesh had known him, Chosen Olliman had always seemed to be all-powerful, a man who had all the answers, who could do anything he wished. Alesh had never before seen the man so full of doubt, and it left him feeling helpless and terrified.

"Never mind," the Chosen said, "I'm just tired, boy, that's all. It has been a trying few months. Still, do not be angry with the people. They are right to be upset; I *have* failed them. If it helps them to have someone to blame, then that, at least, I can do for them."

Distant shouts rose up to them from the street and Olliman glanced out the window, "Ah. It seems that Par is at it again; I wonder how that man ever gets any sleep."

Alesh followed the Chosen's gaze and was only half-aware of his muscles going rigid. A procession of what looked to be about two dozen men and women in black and red marched down the street in front of the castle. The Redeemers had been around for years, but since the attacks began, it seemed that they were in the streets nearly every day, parading and urging the people to forsake Amedan, God of Fire and Light, and put their faith, instead, in Shira, Goddess of the Wild and Amedan's wife. Alesh's lip curled in anger. No doubt they were, even now, using Lord Simion's death as a means to show Amedan—and Olliman's—ineffectiveness.

"You don't like them, do you?" The Chosen asked.

They're dangerous, Alesh thought, *why can't you see that?* But he said, "There's something … strange about them, sir. I guess they just make me nervous. Why do they all carry weapons, anyway?" What he really wanted to ask was why the Chosen *allowed* them to carry weapons, but he would not. Servants did not question their masters.

The old man smiled knowingly, as if hearing Alesh's thoughts, "They would tell you, I suspect, that the weapons are to protect themselves and others from the night's creatures." He shrugged, "I doubt that half of them know how to use them, anyway, though I am sure that there are those among them who do."

Alesh nodded dubiously, "Yes sir. So … they're harmless then."

"No," The Chosen said, "They are far from harmless, as I believe you've already guessed, but their danger is not in the weapons they carry, It is in their words. With a blade or a mace, a man can slay another, Alesh, but with words, with ideas, he can slay a nation."

Maybe, Alesh thought, *but I'd rather get hit with an idea than a mace any day.* "Forgive me, sir, but … why let them stay then?"

"Because they are mine to protect," the Chosen said grimly, "as well as I might. Tell me, are you excited for Fairday tomorrow?"

Again, the abrupt change of topic. "Yes sir," he said, knowing it for a lie as he said t.

"That is well, then." They stood in silence for several moments then, gazing out at the city spread out before them, at the thousands going about their daily lives. Alesh found himself imagining what it would be like to be the Chosen, to be the one that all of those thousands looked to for protection, and he felt a sudden wave of guilt. While he complained about being a servant or having to spar with Kale, the Chosen spent his hours looking after a people who, at best, feared him, and at worst despised him. No wonder the man seemed so lonely sometimes. And now the one true friend he'd had was dead. Alesh felt an overpowering compassion for the man beside him, this man who had sacrificed so much for his people without ever asking for anything in return.

He opened his mouth to speak, not sure of what he was about to say, but the Chosen spoke first, "I suppose it's time you were off," he said, not looking away from the view, "You'll have to hurry back in time for your training session with Kale as it is."

Alesh stood there for a moment, wanting to say something, but the words would not come and finally he nodded, "Yes sir." He turned and started away.

"Oh, and Alesh?"

He stopped and looked back. The Chosen was watching him intently, his blue eyes flashing like chips of ice, "Remember, Katherine Elar and no other. *Before* you visit the wall."

"Yes sir." He waited in case the man would say anything else, but he'd already turned back to the window. In that moment, with the sunlight illuminating the deep lines of his face, his shoulders slumped under a weight too heavy for any man to bear, he looked impossibly old and frail, like a man close to death. *Don't be a fool,* Alesh told himself, *he's lived this long, and he'll live a long time yet.* The thought gave him little comfort though, and he turned and hurried away, not daring to look back.

CHAPTER FOUR

ALESH WAS CHANGING INTO THE clothes Abigail had laid out in his room for him when a bundle fell from his tunic, and he realized with a shock that he'd forgotten to mention the knife to Olliman. *Idiot,* he thought. He slid the cloth-wrapped knife underneath his bed then turned back to his new clothes. *Nobleman's clothes,* he thought, examining the finely-made black trousers and the white silk shirt. These clothes would have cost more money than Alesh owned, as fine or finer than many of the tunics and breeches he saw adorning visiting nobles and dignitaries. Why, then, had the Chosen asked him, a servant, to wear them? *Never mind,* he thought, *he has his reasons.* But the thought gave him little comfort, and he couldn't help feeling like an impostor as he walked out of his quarters, the tightness of the clothes an unpleasant change from the loose servant's garb he normally wore.

He'd only just arrived in the city streets when he saw the Redeemers. One of them—a handsome man with long dark hair and a too-wide grin—stood in the street, preaching on the greatness of Shira. Even as Alesh approached, the man raised his voice in condemnation, "Do you not see, people of Ilrika, the *folly of your ways? How many must die before you realize that Amedan has forsaken you? Either that, or he and his* chosen," the man spat the word contemptuously, "*are powerless against the creatures of the night. But do not be afraid, for the Holy Goddess Shira, in all of her glory—*"

Alesh glanced around him, despair welling up in his chest. A crowd of about thirty had gathered and were nodding along as the man spoke, shouting out their agreement. Not many, perhaps, but more than there had been a month before, that was certain. Alesh's hands knotted into fists at his sides, and he forced his way through the crowd, gritting his teeth in barely suppressed anger. He finally made it through and let out a breath as he turned a corner in the street.

"Spare a coin, my lord?"

He turned at the sound of the voice and saw a woman in a ratty wool dress, a too-thin young child clinging to her side. He glanced around for a moment, confused, before he realized that she was speaking to him. "I-I'm sorry," he said, "I have no money."

She nodded as if she'd expected such an answer and started down the street. The young boy glanced at him with large, vacant eyes, before hurrying after her.

Alesh frowned at the clothes he wore, checked to make sure the letter the Chosen had given him was secure in his tunic, and continued on, feeling more and more like a fool with each step he took. As he walked, he saw several people who'd apparently decided to get an early start on the Fairday celebration staggering drunkenly down the sides of the street. Carts laden with various goods clogged the main thoroughfare and drivers shouted at horses and people alike, demanding room that just wasn't there.

Along the sides of the street, tailors, smiths, jewelers, chandlers, and merchants of all types were busily setting up stalls and unpacking their goods. Already, the streets were alive with the sounds of their shouts as they hawked their wares to the passersby. Children darted between the crowds, laughing and chasing each other and pausing occasionally to stare at the stalls and decorations with wide, eager eyes.

Despite the recent attacks—or perhaps because of them—everyone seemed determined to have a good time. Alesh wished he could share their excitement, but all he could think about was how old Olliman had looked standing in the window's light, how weak, like a man at the end of his strength.

And what of the errand he'd given Alesh? Who was Katherine Elar, and why had Olliman asked him to deliver the letter? After all, there were plenty of message bearers who he could have sent. The thought made him feel at once honored and more than a little uneasy.

"Watch out, my lord!" Someone shouted. Distracted by his thoughts, Alesh had wandered into the street, and he let out a cry of surprise as he jumped to the side, barely avoiding being run over by a horse-drawn cart. The driver shouted an apology, but Alesh heard him mutter a curse about drunken noblemen as he passed. Apparently, the upcoming festivities hadn't infected everybody after all. He took a minute to let his racing heart calm and then, suddenly frantic, he reached into his tunic for the letter, sure that it would be gone. For a moment, his questing fingers found nothing, and he was just about to run into the cart-filled street in search of it, when he felt the paper in his hand and withdrew it, breathing an audible sigh of relief. *Idiot*, he thought, *less than an hour way from the castle, and you've already nearly failed at the Chosen's task.*

Alesh gripped the letter tightly and once more began winding his way through the crowds. In time, he came to the building Olliman had shown him, and for several seconds he stood in the street staring at it, sure that he'd went to the wrong place, after all. The golden glow was still there, but faded, draped across the place like mist, though if any of the passersby could see it, they gave no sign. What had given Alesh pause, however, was not the golden glow, but the run-down, dilapidated state of the place. The front door of the inn sat askew in its frame, and the sign hung crookedly above its door. He was sure that it had once said *The Full Tankard*, but either kids or the worst vandals of all—weather and time—had defaced it, so that it read instead, *h Ful kard*.

Alesh took a deep breath, tucked the letter carefully into his tunic once more, and went inside. Pipe smoke drifted through the common room of the inn like a thick fog, obscuring the faces of the people who sat at the crowded tables, and making his throat instantly scratchy and raw. After a moment, the smoke parted like a curtain and a heavy-set woman in her forties seemed to materialize in front of him. Her dress was scandalously low cut, and the thick coating of face paint she wore did little to conceal features that were homely at best. "Well, hello there my lord," she said. She looked him up and down then gave him a lecherous wink, "My, well you're a big fella, aren't you? I bet your woman is mighty pleased."

"I don't have a woman, ma'am." He replied, and immediately realized it had been the wrong thing to say.

The woman grinned displaying a row of crooked, yellow teeth, "Surely, it can't be true, my lord? Well," she said, stepping so close that her massive bosom pressed against him, "how would you like to change that?"

Alesh felt his face heat, and the woman laughed. "Aw, now, don't you tell me you're a first timer, honey. Not with that face, surely." Her hand ran across his chest, down toward his stomach, "And not with this *body*, why, Amedan be praised it's like running my hand across rock." She drew closer still, and it was all Alesh could do to keep from taking a step back, "Why, I wonder if all of you is so hard," she breathed, her sour breath hot on his face, and he caught her hand just as it was slipping below his waistline.

"I'm sorry, ma'am," he said, struggling to regain his composure, "but I'm here on business."

The woman apparently wasn't accustomed to rejection—the gods knew why not. She frowned, all traces of her good humor gone, "What, are you a boy lover, is that it?"

"I'm no boy lover," he said, resisting the urge to say that he was no troll lover either, "But I *am* here on behalf of my master. I wonder, ma'am do you know—"

"Your *master,* huh?" She spat, her chest heaving grotesquely as she raised her voice, "Well, take it somewhere else. We don't want any of it here."

Alesh noticed that some of the tavern's nearby patrons, hard, angry looking men, were beginning to gaze at him with hard, angry looks. "I'm sorry, ma'am, you must have misunderstood. If you could just tell me where to find—"

"Hey, you!" Alesh turned to see a giant of a man rise from one of the nearby tables. His arms and chest were powerfully built, though the effect was ruined somewhat by a bulging stomach that was no doubt a product of too many nights spent in places such as this one. He ran a hand through his black, filthy beard, and stalked forward, weaving in what Alesh took to be a sign that the alcohol was doing its work. "Are you giving Martha a hard time, or are you just hard of hearin'? She done told you we don't want your kind around here."

Alesh forced himself to take a deep, slow breath. He was here on behalf of the Chosen, and the last thing he wanted to do was get into a fight. "Listen, sir, I'm not trying to give *anyone* a hard time. I'm looking for—"

"The door?" The man interrupted with a growl as he grabbed a hold of the front of Alesh's shirt and jerked him forward, "Don't worry, princess," he hissed, his breath rank with the smell of liquor and rot, "I'll show you, but first I think you need to be taught some manners."

Enough, Alesh thought. Dimly, he was aware that the scar on his shoulder had begun to burn, but it was a small, inconsequential thing next to his rising anger. He needed to find the woman the Chosen had told him about, and he didn't have time to spend on some drunk that wanted to show just how big his balls were. The man was considerably larger than him, and almost certainly stronger. Once, he might have even been dangerous, but time and drink had done their work, and after years spent training with the Chosen and his apprentice, it was easy enough to see the blow coming.

The man swung at him with a meaty fist, and Alesh ducked the attack casually then struck the man in the stomach. The drunk's belly yielded beneath Alesh's fist like uncooked dough, and he staggered, belching out the sour odor of alcohol, gasping for air. Before he could gather himself, Alesh pivoted and hit him again, harder. The man's breath left him in a gurgling wheeze, his knees buckled, and he crumpled to the ground in a heap. The sight of the man struggling for air on the ground did little to pacify Alesh's anger, and he stood there, fists clenched at is sides, trying to force his raging heart to slow.

The man choked out something unintelligible, and Alesh leaned down, putting his ear close to the man's face, "I'm sorry. What was that?"

"B-bastard," the man croaked. Fresh anger welled up in Alesh at the man's words, at the uselessness and idiocy of this man who would start a fight in an tavern with a stranger while the city came unraveled around him. The anger turned to rage as he met the man's hateful gaze. The scar burned feverishly now, but Alesh took little notice. He felt the rage building and building, an unstoppable river pressing against a dam too weak and frail to stop it and then, inevitably, the dam broke. And then there was only darkness.

When Alesh came to, someone was screaming. He was still standing, his chest heaving, his knuckles aching and covered in blood. He looked down and saw that the man still lay at his feet. His nose was broken, twisted grotesquely, and blood covered his face. One of his eyes was swollen shut, and his bottom lip sported a bloody cut. What's more, he seemed to be unconscious. *What in the night did I do?* Alesh thought in shock as he stared at his bloody, shaking hands.

He glanced up and saw the two men the drunk had been sitting with standing up at their table. Alesh met their eyes and they swallowed, glancing nervously at each other before easing back down into their seats.

Alesh felt hot with disgust and shame, but when he turned to the wide-eyed, frightened servant girl, some part of him felt a dark satisfaction, and he found it was all he could do to keep from grinning. "Now then," he said, allowing the politeness to enter his tone once more, "I wonder if anyone can help me. I'm looking for a woman named Katherine Elar."

"She's…"

"Mister, Katherine Elar is…"

"I can tell you where…"

He held up a hand, and their mouths snapped shut hard enough that Alesh heard teeth clack together, "I only need one person to tell me where she is. I can't understand when everyone's speaking at once. How about you," he said, jabbing a finger at the serving maid.

She jumped as if he'd pointed a dagger at her, "She's … uh … the thing is she's … busy right now." she said in a whiny voice. She must have seen something in Alesh's expression because she raised her hands as if to ward off a blow, "I can go and fetch her, of course, if you want, sir, but she won't be long now."

Alesh considered for a minute and shook his head, "No, that's alright. I'll just sit over here and wait." He started toward a nearby table and then the dark side of him made him turn back, "That is, of course," he said, eyeing each person in turn, "unless anyone has a problem with that?"

People at the tables closest to him began studying their drinks as if trying to divine the future from their murky depths, and the serving girl suddenly realized that someone on the far end of the room needed her help. Nodding, a warm, almost animal-like thrill of pleasure racing through him, Alesh walked to the table and sat.

After a few minutes, the giant's friends went to him, lifted his unconscious form between the two of them, and started for the door, snatching looks at Alesh over their shoulders as if he was a lion that might pounce at any moment. He watched them go, feeling more in control, more *powerful* than he ever remembered having felt before.

He hadn't been in a real fight since he was little, and as much as Alesh hated being Kale's practice dummy, he was forced to admit that he'd grown a lot stronger from his time spent in the role.

He hadn't realized how much, in fact, until the big man had attacked him. For years, he'd only ever fought in practice bouts against Kale, and it always seemed to him that the Chosen was intent on watching him get beaten. Rare were the times that Alesh arrived at the bouts without having just finished a long day of labor that left him so exhausted he could barely stand and when he did the Chosen inevitably decided to make Kale practice sword fighting against an unarmed opponent, or—one of his favorites—archery against a moving target. The arrows were blunted, of course, and the thick padding Alesh wore kept him from getting seriously injured, but it also slowed him down and though the arrows might not be lethal, they hurt plenty, leaving big, ugly bruises that ached for days afterward.

True, he'd blacked out—as he had yesterday—a thing he hadn't done since he was a child and that was worrying, but the fact was that after years of losing to Kale, it felt good to actually win, for someone else to be the one limping away for a change. For a moment, when he'd fought the man, all of the uncertainties of the day, all of his worries and fears had vanished. For once in his life, he'd been in control, and it had been a good feeling.

No, a voice in his head corrected, *that's not it, or not all of it anyway. It wasn't just the control; you liked hurting him, liked watching him lying there, gasping for breath. And the others ... you liked the way they looked at you, the way they were scared of you. And what about the black out? Nothing for years and then two in as many days? And your scar, why did it burn as if—*

"No," he whispered, his voice harsh, "I'm no monster." But even as he said it, a part of him remembered the feel of the man's stomach beneath his fist, remembered the frightened looks the others had given him, remembered and reveled in it. Several of the people nearby turned to eye him warily, but Alesh ignored them. Let them think what they wanted; Alesh hadn't asked for trouble, and the man had got what he'd had coming to him. And if Alesh had gone a little farther than he had intended ... well, people got hurt in fights. After all, the man had *tried* to hurt him, hadn't he?

He looked away from the wary stares, studying his hands. He was surprised to find that they were knotted into fists so tightly that his knuckles were stark white where they weren't' covered in blood. He forced them to relax and, as they did, the crumpled letter fell onto the tabletop. Alesh grunted in surprise. In his anger, he'd forgotten all about the letter. He laid it on the table and saw to his dismay that several drops of blood stained the fine white parchment. He tried to wipe the blood off, but succeeded only in smearing it, and had to content himself with smoothing the paper as best he could on the flat tabletop.

Staring at the letter made him think of the Chosen, and he felt a fresh stab of guilt. The High Priest never would have used his power to hurt someone because of something as selfish as pride. *But, then, he'd never have to, would he?* Alesh thought bitterly. He was the *Chosen*, after all. Sure, merchants might complain, nobles might whine, and the members of the Council might try to manipulate him, but no one would ever be stupid enough to attack one of Amedan's Chosen, let alone Olliman, the most powerful and leader of the Six. What did Olliman know of being chased by children with rocks because of a scar he couldn't remember getting, or of waking up to find his mother and father gone, dried pools of blood on a dusty road the only evidence that they'd ever existed at all.

But that wasn't fair, and he knew it. Olliman hadn't *asked* to be Chosen, after all, and the man had dedicated his entire life to protecting and providing for the people of his city, even taking time out of his pressing schedule to speak with a lowly servant like Alesh. Besides, Alesh didn't envy Ilrika's ruler his place as Amedan's most favored priest, not really. He never fantasized about being chosen by one of the gods—even the lesser ones—like many men did. As far as he was concerned, the best gift the gods could ever give him would be to forget he existed at all.

The common room suddenly grew completely silent, and Alesh glanced up, half-expecting to see someone else—one of the drunk's friends, perhaps—standing at his table. He felt a small flash of disappointment when no one was there, and he followed the gazes of the people around him to a small, slightly raised platform at the back of the common room. A woman in a blue dress stepped out from behind a curtain onto the stage, and Alesh's breath caught in his throat. She was the most beautiful woman he'd ever seen, more beautiful, even, than the Lady Uriel who Chorin was taking to Fairday, and Lady Uriel was known throughout Ilrika for her beauty and grace.

The woman stood on the platform, her long blonde hair hanging around her smooth, unblemished face. She glanced shyly around the room from under long, dark lashes, her eyes like emeralds, flashing in the lantern light. *No*, Alesh thought, unable to take his gaze away from her, *on their best day, emeralds don't come close.* Unlike the popular style among many of the city's noblewomen, the woman's dress didn't feature a plunging neckline or a slit in the side to reveal her legs, yet Alesh felt his face heat just the same.

After a few seconds, two men walked onto the small stage. One carried a stool, the other a large harp case, and they gazed at the woman with undisguised lust as they sat them down in front of her. Alesh felt a stab of jealousy at their roaming eyes and had to fight down the urge to shout at them. *Stop acting like a fool*, he thought to himself, *you've seen beautiful women before*, yet even as he thought it, another part of his mind disagreed. *Not like this you haven't. Not like her.*

The two men turned to go and Alesh heard the woman thank them in a quiet, almost timid voice. The men turned back with looks of surprise then turned and started quickly away, though not quickly enough to hide the grins that spread across their faces like children who'd been praised on their cleverness.

Once they were gone, the woman took a deep breath as if to gather herself and opened the case, withdrawing a wooden harp. Unlike its owner, the harp was nothing remarkable. Alesh had seen musicians come to the Chosen's castle to ply their trades during feasts and celebrations. They always brought richly designed instruments, often decorated with gems and golden inlays that would have cost a small fortune. The woman's own harp, in contrast, was of a light, faded wood and displayed no such engravings or jewels, yet she treated it with more care than Alesh remembered any of the castle musicians showing, cradling it gently, like a child, as she brought it to her lap.

A moment of expectant silence passed and then the woman's fingers began to move, gliding gently over the strings of the harp. The melody was slow and soft at first, so low that Alesh found himself leaning forward in an effort to hear, despite the stillness of the tavern. The smooth music of the harp flowed across the listeners, a river gliding over rock, seeming to smooth out the rough edges of those in the room, of the room itself, and Alesh felt as if he, and those listening with him, were being transported to some simpler, some better place, by the song. For all of the musicians he'd heard at the Chosen's castle, Alesh had never heard anything as achingly sweet. Until, that was, the woman began to sing.

Her voice was soft, yet strong, quiet yet insistent, and Alesh thought that if the music of the harp had been a river, then the woman's voice was one of the great oceans itself, a thing so wide, so deep and soothing, that it could swallow a man before he knew it. Her voice served at once as a melody and a counterpoint to the gentle thrums of the harp. Alesh sat, spellbound, as he listened to the song, as he watched the lantern light lay, almost lovingly, across the woman's skin, watched it glimmer playfully in her green eyes. He was so engrossed by the beauty of the song that it took him over a minute before he realized he'd heard it before.

It was the legend of King Leantrian and Queen Parenia who were said to have lived and reigned before the first coming of the nightwalkers. The two had been greatly loved by their people and had loved them in turn, but it was their love for each other that was the true legend. The two, it was said, never left each other's side. Even in times of war, before the nightlings came, when

King Leantrian led his armies against the barbarian king from the north, Parenia would not be kept away, traveling with him even when in the field.

Alesh had thought he knew the story, but as the woman played and sang, it seemed to him that all of the other performances had been no more than impartial accountings, cheap summaries that lacked the burning passion and truth he now heard, not a fire themselves, but the scorch marks left to mark its passing.

The woman's fingers danced across the harps strings in a slow rhythm, and as she sang, Alesh found himself there, among the court of that ancient kingdom, listening to the king speak as the queen sat beside him, the love that connected them almost a physical thing. Later, he was walking behind them as they made their way through their private gardens, talking and laughing together as they planned how to lead their people to prosperity and peace.

The song continued to weave its spell. The woman's voice grew stronger, more insistent, and the harp's play grew faster and faster until her hands were nothing but a blur on the strings and, as if brought forth by her call, the first nightwalkers appeared out of the shadowy veil of the night, and Alesh felt fear. There were only a few at first, then more and more until they spread across the whole of Entarna like a plague, leaving nothing but corpses and grief in their wake.

Leantrin was at council then, trying to bring an end to the war with the barbarians. His wife, newly with child and overcome with the sickness it sometimes brings, had—at the pleadings of the court's healers and Leantrin himself—left his side for the first time since their marriage to rest. It was there, seated among his most trusted advisors, that news first reached Leantrin of shadows given form, of monstrous creatures appearing out of the night and laying waste to his people and their homes. His counselors, terrified, begged him to tell them what to do, to protect them, but Leantrin could think only of his wife and unborn child, and he left a group of frightened, confused men and women behind him as he rushed to his beloved's side. He was too late.

Alesh wasn't surprised to feel a hot tear course its way down his cheek as he stood behind the king, watched him gaze down on the broken body of his wife. He felt his own answering rage as Leantrin, mad with grief and fury, ignored the entreaties of his counselors and servants and charged into the night alone, sword in hand, his dead wife's name on his lips. He did not return.

The story ended with the people of the kingdom mourning the loss of not only their queen, but their king as well. Alesh listened to every word, every note as if they were not about strangers out of legend at all, but funeral words spoken at the death of his closest family, his dearest friends and, as the townspeople mourned, so he mourned with them.

Then it was over, the woman's singing drifting into nothingness, and the ghosts of the past once more vanished into memory as the final note of the harp hung in the air. A long moment passed and, as one, the crowd seemed to take a breath, and the spell was broken. The common room erupted in applause and raucous talk, men elbowing and chiding each other good naturedly even as they wiped at the tears in their own eyes.

The woman eased her harp back into its case and stood amid the thundering applause. She bowed, hugging the case to her body like a shield, her blonde hair shimmering in the lantern light, then turned and disappeared through the curtain. Alesh was suddenly struck with an almost overpowering desire to go and talk to her, and he was half way out of his seat before he paused. *Yeah, sure,* he thought, bitterly, *because a woman like that, a woman who could pick any man she wanted, why she's been waiting all her life for an orphaned castle servant who people believe to be Night-cursed. Why, you're a dream come true.*

He sighed and sank back into his seat, deciding that he would wait for the crowd to calm down before trying to find the person Olliman had sent him to find.

He was thinking of the woman, of the way her hands had played so gracefully across the harp strings, of the small, sad smile that her red, painted lips had formed as she played, of the way they'd parted delicately, like one of the flowers in the castle gardens, wondering what it would feel like to kiss those lips, when a hand touched him on the shoulder. He tensed and jerked around, sure that the drunk had come back for more. His eyes widened in surprise and something like guilt as he saw who had sat down beside him.

She'd rubbed off her face paint, and traded the blue dress for a pair of leather trousers and a ratty brown cloak, the hood of which served to cover her long blonde hair. "Y-you're," he stumbled, suddenly unable to find words. He felt his face heating, half-convinced that she somehow knew what he'd been thinking.

The woman raised an eyebrow and waited for him to continue. He swallowed hard and tried again, "You're ... the sin—"

"I'm *no one,*" she interrupted sharply, casting a glance around them, "and *you*—judging by your show from earlier—are an overgrown bully who's always gotten through life on his looks and the size of his arms."

He was so surprised and disoriented by the harshness in her voice that he actually sputtered. "W-what are you talking about?"

She frowned then, taking him in with her green eyes. They didn't look bright anymore, like emeralds on fire. Instead, they reminded him of lonely pools deep in some hidden forest, deep and mysterious, and somehow foreboding. "I saw what you did," she said, voice accusing, "is it your idea of a good time to beat up on men so drunk they can barely stand? Is that how noblemen find their amusement these days?"

Alesh stared at the woman, his mouth hanging open in astonishment. "You can't be serious," he managed, "That man is the one who tried to fight *me.*"

She rolled her eyes, "Oh?" She asked, "I'd like to see *you* act any better after losing your wife to one of those *creatures.*" She shrugged, and despite the anger in her expression and his own bewilderment, Alesh couldn't help noticing what the movement did with her the curves of her breasts beneath the tight-fitting shirt she wore, "Not that a pampered nobleman's son like you would know anything about real loss."

Alesh stared at her, incredulous, his growing anger working its way past his surprise, "Look, lady," he said, his voice hard, "I don't know who you think you are, but you don't know a torch-burning *thing* about me. I'm about as far from a noble as—"

"Oh," she interrupted in disgust, "and a blasphemer too! Your parents must be very proud of you."

"I don't *have* parents," he growled, "and I don't need some puffed-up woman who thinks she's Amedan's perfect creation needling me over something she knows nothing about! Now, I didn't *know* that the man had lost his wife, how could I? And what business of it is yours, anyway? I don't remember asking for your opinion on it."

"Well," she said, "if you didn't want my opinion, then maybe you shouldn't have been walking around shouting out the name Katherine Elar to anyone who would listen, should you, dandy?"

"Wait a minute," he said, his anger fading in his surprise, "you don't mean to say that you're—"

"You must be stupid even for a noble," she interrupted, "I've already told you; I'm *no one*. The woman who you heard sing is Elizabeth, the woman who you're looking for is Katherine, and I'm none of your *damned business.* Now, is there a *reason* you're looking for Katherine, or is it your habit to burst into taverns, pick fights, and shout names at random?"

Alesh took a long, deep breath, struggling to keep his anger in check. The woman might be beautiful, but she was also more annoying than weeding the castle garden, and more difficult than shoeing a horse in heat. Suddenly, he found himself almost looking forward to his training bout with Kale. "Look, Mrs. *No one,* I'm about as far from a dandy as you can get, and to answer your question no, I'm *not* in the habit of picking fights and shouting names at random. I was sent here by my master to find a woman named Katherine Elar and deliver this letter." He withdrew the paper from his cloak and flapped it in front of her.

The woman's eyes widened at the gold seal that flashed on its surface, "*Fool,*" she hissed, grabbing for it, "keep that hidden!"

Alesh jerked the letter back, away from her grasp. "Now, look lady," he said with a smile, "I'm not normally a bully, but since that's what you've decided I am anyway, I think I need to be clear that this letter was to be delivered to a *Katherine Elar,* certainly not a Mrs. No one. My master was very clear on that."

The woman made a growling noise in her throat, "Fine," she grated through clenched teeth, "I'm Katherine, now will you give me the letter or not?"

"Oh?" He asked in mock surprise, "Well, I had no idea. Why, of *course* I'll give it to you, ma'am." He grinned, smugly satisfied at the reddish spots of anger that crept into her cheeks. He held the letter out, and she tore it from his grasp.

"Is this all you were given?" She asked, in a suddenly business-like voice, all traces of anger gone.

"Yes," he said, with a nod, "That's all. Now see, was that so hard, being polite?"

She grinned back, "Of course not. Thanks." She looked him up and down for a moment, a considerate expression on her face, "You look pretty fast."

He frowned, "Fast? What does that have to d—"

Before he could finish, the woman burst out of her chair, knocking it over and backing away from him, her hands held out as if to ward him away, "I said *don't touch me!*" She screamed, "Just stop it, I told you no!"

Alesh's eyes went wide in surprise once more as he reached for her, sure that she must be having some sort of fit, "What? Look, I don't know what you're—"

"Don't come one step closer!" She screeched in a terrified voice as she stumbled away, both of her hands coming to her chest and fluttering nervously. "Please, someone help me, please!"

Alesh suddenly became aware that a dozen men had risen from their spots in the room, all of them watching him with murderous stares and, more importantly, with murderous knives or clubs gripped in their fists. "Look," he said, rising from his chair and backing away, his hands held up, "I didn't do anything, she … she—" His voice trailed off as he realized that the men were much too far gone to listen to any explanation he might give. The woman had seen to that. He shot a glance at her, and though her mouth was covered with her hand as if in fear, he could see the laughter sparkling in her green eyes once more.

He started to say something sharp and cutting, something meant to take the mockery, the laughter out of her eyes, but as one the men, apparently having decided that they didn't dare let the woman's virtue go unavenged any longer, let out shouts and charged toward him like a stampede. Alesh swallowed hard and did something he'd done almost every day since he'd been picked as Kale's training partner—he ran. He weaved in and out of men and women too stunned or confused to do anything, dodging them when he could and knocking them aside when he couldn't. He jumped a table, bellowed in pain as his shin cracked against a chair, stumbled and rushed through the door, slamming it shut behind him. *The woman's insane,* he thought wildly, rubbing at his smarting shin. Angry shouts and curses rose from inside the inn, coming closer, like a chorus of snarling wolves tracking their prey. Alesh cursed, took a deep breath, and ran.

CHAPTER FIVE

KATHERINE WATCHED THE ARROGANT NOBLEMAN flee the tavern followed by a group of angry, drunken men, a small smile on her face. She was sick and tired of nobles always treating the common people like they were animals, and it was good to finally see one get what he deserved. That made her think of the letter, and she glanced down at it, swallowing hard. This was why she'd come, spending two weeks in travel and another singing in some broken down inn where men would as soon stick a knife in you as say hello. She looked around to make sure no one was watching her then folded the letter and slipped it into a pocket sewn into the interior lining of her cloak until she could find a more private place in which to read it.

Movement at her side caught her attention, and she turned to see Darl standing beside her. In the weak lantern light of the tavern, his dusky-hued skin looked almost black, and his bushy black eyebrows were drawn into a frown that matched the one on his lips, "What?" She asked, annoyed, "He deserved it. You saw the way he was acting."

The man's expression did not change. "Oh, come on," she said, rolling her eyes, "He's just some self-loving noble that thinks he can treat people however he wants. It'll do him good to learn that not everyone's prepared to bow and scrape for him just because his family's got money."

Darl continued to study her with eyes so brown that they were nearly black. She stared back at him in challenge for several seconds then finally gave up, sighing heavily and looking away. She'd been traveling with the man for over a year, and she knew him well enough to hear the reproach in his silence. Apparently satisfied that his point had been made, he sat down beside her at the table, and Katherine turned to look at him again, considering, not for the first time, how little she really knew of her companion.

His dark skin marked him as a Ferinan—the nomadic people of the southern deserts who, it was said, could disappear into shadows, hiding even from the nightwalkers themselves. Of course, that was no more than conjecture. Little was known about the Ferinans beyond the fact that they kept to themselves, and that they were said to possess grace and agility akin to the large, predatory sand cats that supposedly roamed the deserts of their homeland. Katherine couldn't say whether or not they could hide from nightwalkers, but if Darl was typical of his people, then she could attest to their dexterity and physical poise. Even when doing something as simple as walking, the wiry-muscled man made each step seem like a part of some elaborate dance, and she'd long since lost track of the times she'd turned around to find him beside her without hearing so much as a single footstep or breath.

It was unnerving at times, how silently the man could move, but even more unnerving—and frustrating—she thought wryly, was his unflappable calm. Ferinans, perhaps because of their reclusiveness, were considered savages by most people, but she'd never once seen the man angry or sad, had never heard him laugh or cry or shout. He greeted every situation, from a sunny morning to a gang of muggers in search of coin with the same calm, blank expression, as if he was waiting for something specific and wasn't particularly interested in anything that came before it.

In their time together, she'd seen Darl overcome a group of scraggly highwaymen, scale a rocky mountainside, and endure the taunts of ignorant people with no more change in expression than he now showed. Yet, the man still seemed to somehow let her know that he was disappointed in her. "Alright, alright," she said, "stop looking at me like that. Maybe I *was* a little too hard on him. I'm just nervous is all, Darl. Something doesn't feel right about this. It's like … it's like a melody that doesn't sound right, but I can't figure out *why*."

His expression didn't change, but he grunted in what she decided to take as agreement. "Anyway," she said, talking mostly to herself, "why him? Who is he anyway?"

The Ferinan shrugged, and she fought the urge to sigh again. Another one of the vexing things about Darl was that he never spoke. In fact, Katherine wasn't even sure that he *could* speak. At first, she'd thought that his tongue had been cut out and that was the reason why he remained silent, but knew from observing him while he ate that it wasn't the case. She'd asked him about his silence on more than one occasion, but, perhaps unsurprisingly, she'd received no answer. "And why now, why like this?" She said, continuing her thought, "Wouldn't it have been better, safer, to have just called us to the castle for an audience?" She frowned, pushing a stray hair out of her eyes, "I don't like it, Darl, any of it."

The dark-skinned met her eyes, and she wondered, not for the first time, how he could seem to say so much without speaking a word. "Of course, I'll do what Chosen Alashia asks," she said defensively. "It's the least I can do after … after what she did." At her words, memories rushed unbidden, crowding into her mind.

A dream, it seemed now, thinking back. Surely that little girl sitting in the street with a faded lute that had once belonged to her mother wasn't *her* was it? That little girl who watched her father spend his fortune on healers and priests, who watched her mother shrivel and shrink despite their attentions, who cried herself to sleep each night, who'd brought breakfast to her mother only to find her long gone, nothing left but a corpse and a madness that would claim her father. That little girl who'd braved the streets of Valeria's poor district, playing her music in hopes of making enough to feed her father and sister for the day, always wondering if the next person to pass would want what little she had: her money, her lute … something worse. And then an old woman, stepping out of a carriage, one of her legs withered and wasted, an arm twisted and bent, the hand at the end of it retracted into a constant claw, but feeling comfort for all that. For here, *here* was a good one.

Months on the street made a person a good judge of character, a good reader of faces, of eyes, and in that face, only kindness, in those eyes, only compassion. And though the years had come and gone since then, and Katherine was no longer that little girl with the tears in her eyes and the faded dress that had been patched so much that its original color couldn't be guessed at, she remembered those words as if she'd heard them only yesterday. "*You have played for beggars,*" the woman had said, bending over Katherine, her hands on her cane, a smile on her wizened face, "*and you have sung to empty streets. I would see you play for kings. I would see you sing to the world.*"

Darl's comforting hand on her shoulder pulled Katherine from the depths of memory, and she wiped a hand at the tears gathered in her eyes. Because of the Chosen's kindness, Katherine and her family were alive, and the money Katherine made was more than enough to see that her sister and father no longer had to worry about where their next meal was coming from. She would take the letter to the Chosen; she'd walk through fire for the woman, if she asked it of her. Still, it *was* strange for Alashia to send her on weeks of travel and post her in a place such as this for something as simple as a single letter. After all, as the ruler of Galia, Alashia had dozens of messengers, men and women who'd been to Ilrika many times before, who knew people in Olliman's city and were granted easy access to the castle. What possible reason could she have to send Katherine instead?

"I don't like it," she muttered again, more to herself than Darl. She glanced at him and felt a pang of shame. Ferinans were treated poorly everywhere, even in the southern cities of the realm where they could be seen, if rarely. Ilrika was much farther removed from the southern stretches of desert than Katherine's home city of Galia and many of its people had never seen one of the dark-skinned Ferinan before. For all of her complaints about their mission and about the small tavern they now found themselves in, it was Darl who truly suffered. It was Darl who was forced to endure murmured curses and open hostility, and he did so without complaint. *Still* a stubborn voice in her head insisted, *that doesn't explain the letter.*

Whatever Alashia's reasons had been, they must have been good ones. She would not have sent Katherine so far without good reason. That could only mean that she believed the contents of the letter were very important, maybe even dangerous. *No. Not maybe. Dangerous and for a certainty.* Suddenly,

Katherine felt eyes on her back. She turned, but those few that remained in the tavern after the nobleman's abrupt exit didn't seem to be paying her or Darl any attention for the time being. Still, the feeling of being watched, of being *hunted,* only grew stronger. "Come on," she said, tucking the letter inside her pocket, "let's get out of here."

CHAPTER SIX

Alesh's chest was heaving, his legs burning by the time the last of his pursuers finally gave up the chase. It was a good thing he *had* done so much running as Kale's training partner. Otherwise, he supposed he'd have spent the last hour getting the shit kicked out of him by a mob of drunken fools and that if he were lucky. *Damn that woman,* he thought, yet even as he thought it another part of him remembered that small, crooked smile, still wondered what it would be like to feel those lips, soft and full without being pouty like so many of the noblewomen's were, on his own. *I must be out of my mind,* he thought as he propped his back against the wall of a building and struggled to slow his breathing, *smarter to wonder what it would be like to kiss a nightling. Shit. Probably safer too.*

After a moment, he headed toward the wall once more, glancing over his shoulder from time to time to make sure none of his pursuers had found him. As he walked, he thought of how strange of a day it had been. First the conversation with the Chosen, then his meeting with the girl … so much had happened so quickly that he felt as if his head was still spinning. If things kept up at this rate, he thought maybe he'd set a fire in his boots and try to outrun it, just to slow things down a bit.

He was thinking of the girl, not of the cruel trick she'd played on him, but of the way her hair had seemed to glow in the lantern light, when he saw a vaguely familiar form walking through the crowd on the other end of the street. He turned and for a moment the passing people obscured the figure.

He stopped, waited, and was just about to decide he'd imagined it when the crowd parted, and he saw Kale striding down the avenue. The man was dressed plainly, unlike his usual rich, ostentatious garb, and Alesh could only catch a glimpse of him here and there as he moved through the crowd, but he knew it was him just the same. He'd recognize that walk anywhere. It was the walk of a man who thought he owned the city and everyone in it. The problem, of course, was that considering Kale's family was the richest in Ilrika, he wasn't far wrong.

But what is he doing in the poor district? Alesh thought. For as long as he'd known the Chosen's Apprentice, the man had always treated peasants and commoners as if they were little more than cattle—had even called them such on more than one occasion. What possible reason would he have to be in the poor district when he was supposed to have been training with the Chosen?

The idea was so ludicrous that Alesh was tempted to believe that he was wrong despite his certainty. But … no. It was the Chosen's apprentice, alright. Not many other people besides the son of Lord and Lady Leranian, the wealthiest and most powerful nobles in the city, could mimic the scowl and arrogance in the apprentice's face.

And who was that walking beside him? There was something naggingly familiar about the man, but right when he thought he had it, several horse-drawn carts trundled past, the drivers shouting people out of the way in loud, angry voices that somehow managed to rise even above the loud buzz of the city streets. One of the teamsters paused to slash a whip at a dirty, shirtless youth who was filching one of his melons. A loud *crack* filled the air, and the youth cried out as the whip struck home, but he did not let go of his prize, and he was taking a mouthful of it even as he disappeared into the crowd.

The driver threw a couple of curses after the boy then took his whip to the nags pulling his cart, and the wagon trundled forward. As it did, Kale and his companion came into view once more. The man was as tall as the Chosen's Apprentice, but thinner, almost gaunt, but, if anything, he looked more dangerous than Kale. Both men wore their anger, their hatred of the world for all to see, but where Kale's was the hot, ready kind—the kind that, Alesh knew from experience, often meant a trip to the healers for anyone who got in his way, the other man's was different. The look he gave those around him wasn't full of threat but promise, not disgust, but hope. Looking at that man's gaze—one that seemed to dare someone to do something of which he could take offense—Alesh got the distinct impression that the objects of this man's anger didn't end up at the healer. They ended up at the cemetery.

He wore a simple linen tunic and breeches, as many of the people of the poor district did, but only a blind man could have mistaken him for just another merchant or day laborer going about his life. He walked with too much purpose, like a man on an important mission. Again, Alesh was struck with something familiar about him, but his mind was already awhirl with so many thoughts, all jumbled together and confused, that it wouldn't come to him. He considered following the pair, did follow them for a short distance, in fact, then glanced up to where the sun had risen surprisingly far in the sky. "*Night,*" he cursed softly.

He was already late on the Chosen's errand, and the two men were walking in the opposite direction of the wall. He turned and rushed away, the incident all but forgotten as he hurried through the crowd.

CHAPTER SEVEN

IT WAS ALMOST MIDDAY BY the time Alesh reached the breach in the wall and despite all of the books he'd read about the nightwalkers and what they were capable of, he was still shocked by the extent of the damage. The hole was as wide as six men standing abreast and at least ten feet high. *It'd take ten men with hammers and chisels the better part of a night to cause such damage,* he thought wonderingly.

A crew of workers and masons coated in gray stone dust with handkerchiefs tied around their mouths and noses carried stones to the hole, watched over by a short, stocky man who barked orders and curses at them as they worked.

Alesh approached the man, "Sir?"

"Not now," the man snapped without turning, "can't you see I'm working? Go beg someone else, boy."

Alesh started to speak but coughed as a gust of wind blew stone dust in his face, quickly making him understand the need for the handkerchiefs. He spat in a useless effort to rid his mouth of the dry, clinging taste, then tried again "Sir, I'm not—"

The headman swung around angrily, "Listen, damn you—" He took in Alesh's fine, though disheveled clothes and frowned. "Just what kind of night-cursed street urchin are you, boy? Listen, if you really want some pay why don't you help the lads there bear those stones over to that big damned hole in the wall? Big bastard like you shouldn't have any problem with the work, and we've got to get the blasted thing patched up before night fall, else those fucking devils'll pass through it as easily as Jake there," he gestured at a skinny worker, "passes through a whore's c—"

"*Sir,*" Alesh interrupted before the man could finish, "I'm no beggar. I was sent here to make sure the work was done well by my master."

"Your *master,*" the man sneered, "and who might that be? No, let me guess, that damned Osgard. Well, you just tell the *Official Inspector* that he's not cheating me on this deal unless he wants to be inspecting an army of nightlings instead of stuffing his face with cakes and sweetmeats. Shit, I'll show them the way. Fact is, we've already agreed on the price, and I mean to have it even if I have to carve it outta his fat ass."

The crew leader turned back to the workers, Alesh already forgotten, "Get it moving you lazy louts! Why, I could have hired a few good street girls and had it done in half the time with twice the fun!"

Alesh could have made a point of that; there *were* other masons, after all, and the crew leader could bluster as much as he wanted. That didn't change the fact that, if Osgard chose to, he could make the man's life difficult in the future. But he didn't. Partly because he wasn't there to trade threats with the man, only to see the work was done properly, but mostly because he was right. Osgard *did* love his sweetmeats and cakes—the bulging stomach that caused the castle tailors such grief was proof of that—and, what's more, the man *was* a bastard. When he stayed at the castle, the Official Inspector always complained about the servants and the food—though that didn't stop him from eating it, of course, or from goosing the serving girls when they brought him his meals.

"Look," Alesh said, grabbing the crew leader by the shoulder and turning him back, trying to keep his tone cordial despite his rising annoyance. It had been a long damn day, and this man wasn't making it any easier, "I wasn't sent here by the Official Inspector. Chosen Olliman sent me."

He saw at once that it was the wrong thing to say. The man's eyes shrank to narrow slits, and his lips compressed into a thin, white line. "Ah. It's the nightling orphan. And just what does our honorable *protector* want with a couple o' simple stoneworkers?" He asked with a sneer. The emphasis on 'protector' was slight, but it was enough to make it plain what he thought of the job Olliman was doing.

Alesh started to speak but bit back the scathing words before they came. There'd been a time—not long ago—when men like the bullying crew master would have thought themselves lucky and thanked the gods if given a chance to clean the Chosen's boots. *But that was before the nightlings came. Before people started dying.* Alesh took a slow deep breath, then, "I was sent to make sure that you didn't need any help."

"Is that so?" The man asked. He smiled, but there was no humor in it, "Well, I suppose we do at that. You see, lad," he said, gesturing to a cart that had been stacked high with large stones, "that there is a lotta rock."

Alesh glanced between the man and the pile. *Just see that the wall is finished and done well,* the Chosen had said. He reflected bitterly how, once again, the Chosen had managed to find a way to have him completely exhausted and worthless before his training session with Kale.

"Well?" The man asked, "You goin' to help or not?"

Alesh sighed, "I'll need a mask."

CHAPTER EIGHT

HE STUMBLED THROUGH THE CASTLE hallways, too tired to care about the strange looks the guards and the other servants gave him. His arms and legs felt like lead weights, and his clothes and skin were so covered in dust that he looked like some corpse freshly risen from the grave. He'd thought to clean himself first, but upon arriving at the castle, one of the other servants had told him—in between frowns at the state of his clothing—that the Chosen wanted to see him immediately. He'd put off going only long enough to take a drink of water in a wasted effort to clear some of the stone dust out of his mouth. Mask or not, he felt as if he'd spent the last hour gargling the stuff and with each swallow his throat felt as if it was coated in sanding paper.

Still, despite his fatigue and having spent the better part of the day being chased by a mob of drunks or shouted at by the crewmaster in ever more creative—and confusing—curses, he felt good. The wall was repaired and, surely, once he saw his condition, the Chosen would call off training for the day. After all, he'd performed the man's errands, hadn't he? Had gone out of his way, in fact, to do so. If he'd needed any reminder of that, then the sharp pain that lanced up his back with each step would have served admirably.

Eventually, his legs shaking and threatening to give out underneath him, Alesh arrived at the enclosed courtyard that the Chosen reserved for his own training as well as that of his apprentice. Two guards were posted on either side of the door, and they grinned when they saw him. "Ah, it's Alesh," one of them said, "almost didn't recognize you."

Alesh frowned at the man, too tired to speak, and, after a moment, the guard opened the door, and Alesh stepped past the grinning men and into the courtyard. The Chosen and Kale were seated on the ground, their eyes closed as they both performed the meditation exercises the Chosen was so fond of. "Ah," the old man said, his eyes still closed, "I see that you have decided to join us after all, Alesh."

"Yes sir," he said, panting, "I'm sorry I'm late."

"That's enough meditation for now, Kale," the Chosen said, opening his eyes and rising to his feet with a fluid grace that belied his years. The nobleman mimicked him, studying Alesh from behind the Chosen with a cruel grin.

"I'm sorry I'm late, sir," Alesh said, doing his best to ignore the apprentice, "but I did as you asked. I gave the le—"

"How does the wall fare?" The Chosen asked, cutting him off.

"I-it's finished, sir."

"That is good. Now, I believe that we will train your hand to hand combat skills today, Kale."

The nobleman's grin grew wider, "Sounds good to me." The Chosen frowned and turned to regard him with an icy stare, "sir," Kale added with a frown, darting an angry look at Alesh as if he'd done something.

"Very well," the Chosen said after a moment, "Let us begin. Alesh, come forward."

"But sir," he said. The Chosen turned that cold stare on him, and he swallowed hard, "In truth, I don't think I'd be much help in his training just now. I can barely stand."

"Nonsense," the old man said with a smile, "you appear to be getting along well enough to me, now come. There isn't much time left in the day."

Alesh fought down a sigh and shuffled forward, wondering if maybe he wouldn't have been better off if the Chosen had left him in the street that day so long ago. Probably dead, but maybe better off. Kale strutted toward him with his familiar, arrogant walk, and Alesh watched him come with a weary resignation. He was so tired that he could barely stand, and he was about to spar with a man who murderers would have said was "a little rough for their tastes."

Alesh supposed he should be grateful. After all, at least the Chosen had picked hand to hand training instead of deciding Kale needed to work on his strikes—an exercise that left Alesh frantically struggling to keep a wooden practice sword at bay with a shield without having any weapon of his own, forced to dodge and block without being allowed to strike back.

"Remember," the Chosen said, regarding Kale, "we are only here to practice." The nobleman nodded quickly, eager to be about it. *And so he would be,* Alesh thought bitterly, *he hasn't spent all day in the poor district hauling stones like a damned pack mule.*

No, a voice inside him said, *he hasn't, but he* was *in the poor district, wasn't he? And just what was all that about, and who was that man with him? You know him from somewhere, don't you?*

I don't know, and I don't care, Alesh thought back. He was too tired to care. Whatever Kale had been doing in the poor district could wait for tomorrow, for when his body didn't feel like he'd been run over by a horse-cart instead of only *almost* run over, and his mind didn't feel full of cotton, his thoughts fuzzy and unclear.

"Begin!" The Chosen barked, and Kale waded forward in a flurry of lightning-fast blows. The years of training had left Alesh with more bruises and aches than he could count, but they *had* made him good at avoiding being hit. It was more instinct than anything else that allowed him to dodge the man's first strike, and block the next several. Kale stepped forward again, pressing the attack, and Alesh moved to the side, but his left leg threatened to buckle from exhaustion, and the nobleman's fist took him hard in the stomach. He let out a grunt and fell to one knee as the air left him in a *whoosh*.

He saw the apprentice moving closer, his fist drawn back. "*Kale!*"

The apprentice stopped reluctantly, gazing at Alesh with a feral expression reminiscent of a half-starved dog gazing at a plate of freshly-cooked roast. All well enough if you were the dog, maybe, but certainly not the way the cow had planned on his day turning out. The Chosen came to Alesh, grabbed him by the shoulders and pulled him to his feet. "I know you're tired, Alesh," he whispered, "But evil will not wait for you to be rested. It will come when you least expect it, from *where* you least expect it." He paused at that, and his eyes got that distant, far-off look that he seemed to get more and more of late. After a moment, his gaze snapped back to the present, "You must try harder," he said in a voice so low that Alesh could barely hear him, "They are all counting on you."

Alesh frowned at that, sure that the words hadn't been meant for him, but for the Chosen himself. How far gone to grief must the man be if he was talking to himself without realizing it? The thought of all that the Chosen had been through, all that he had sacrificed, made a fresh stab of pity and guilt go through Alesh, and he nodded, forcing his weary back to straighten. "I'm ready."

The Chosen met his eyes, studying him intently. Then he nodded in return. "Yes. You are." Then, louder, "Again!"

CHAPTER NINE

Alesh lay awake in his small bed, his various aches and pains competing for his attention. He'd done the best he could against Kale, which, was to say, that he had tried his best to keep the time between when the apprentice knocked him down, and when he stood up so that he could do it again to a minimum. He supposed he could take some consolation in the fact that Kale's fists would probably be sore in the morning from all the abuse they'd taken.

His mind drifted back to the girl, to the soft melody she'd played, to the way it had seemed, after a time, that he hadn't heard the music at all, but *felt* it in the way a man could feel a cool breeze against his face, or the warm kiss of sunshine against his skin, of the way her eyes had glowed in the lantern light … shone like emeralds. He felt his eyes close almost of their own accord. Her and the music … so soft and warm.

Darkness, rushing past. The horses panting in fear and exhaustion. His mother's voice, screaming. A shock, the sound of wood cracking and the feeling of flying, toppling end over end in the cart, his head striking the inside of the wagon hard enough to make stars dance in his eyes, then again, and again, pain in white, hot starbursts, and then another hit, harder this time, and only darkness.

Waking to the taste of blood in his mouth, his head throbbing. Silence, at first. Then a faint, scrabbling that grew louder until it wasn't scrabbling at all but clawing. Tearing.

A growl so deep, so powerful that it seemed to run through him. The sound of wood splintering and being torn apart. The door of the compartment flying free in a shower of splinters that struck his face and arms. The stars overhead, distant and weak. Then the stars are blotted out and something is reaching through the opening. Then not reaching through at all but through already. A claw, grabbing him, trying to tear him out of the wagon, and he's fighting. Fighting against it— "Alesh! Relax, son!"

"F-father?" He asked, his voice thick and muddled. He opened his eyes and saw that he was no longer in the darkness, no longer in that tomb-like cart along the roadside, but back in the servant's quarters, lying in bed and covered in the cold, clammy sweat of his own fear. Not his father, standing over him, but the Chosen himself.

A lantern burned weakly on the room's nightstand, and the Chosen's eyes seemed to blaze in the fitful light, twin orbs of blue fire dancing in the near-darkness. The Chosen standing over him, with the dream still clinging to him so close and so real, nagged at his memory. He was transported to a time, long ago, reminded of a boy, half-mad with grief and pain, shuffling, deaf and dumb to the world around him. He felt again the hard slap of a soldier as he drew too close to a procession working its way through the streets, witnessed, once more, as a man stepped down from the carriage, scolding the soldier, then turning to him, crouching low, asking him his name.

The same man, the same eyes, but where once those eyes had held confidence, had held faith, now they held grief. Doubt. And there ... so deep as to be nearly hidden ... madness? *Gods, no. Please, not that.* "Sir? Is it you?"

"You still dream of them." Not a question. In the glow of the lantern, the Chosen looked shrunken, somehow, beaten, and more than any other time since Alesh had known him, Brent Olliman looked all of his ninety eight years. It was as if the gift of Amedan, the gift that had endowed him with a longer lifespan than normal mortals, had been stripped from him. Alesh took in the Chosen's weary expression, the dark circles under his eyes, the way his hands, always so sure, so graceful in their movements, now shook with small but perceptible tremors.

Before him was not the great warrior who had led Amedan's Six into battle against the nightling hordes, nor the living legend who had met Argush in battle, casting him down and slaying him with the power of his god, but a man whose death was so close that he could taste it, could smell it, a smell like rotting roses and dust, like the memory of fine things turned to ash. Alesh hadn't yet been born during the War of Darkness, but he'd heard the story a thousand times, how the man had glowed with a golden light, how even his breath had come out in vapor the color of the sun. It was said that the night's creatures had cowered and fled at the approach of High Priest Olliman, leader and greatest of Amedan's Chosen. Now, the man looked as if he could barely keep his head upright and in his face Alesh saw something that sent chills running through him. Fear.

"S-sir," He asked, a knot of uncertainty coiling in his stomach, "has something happened?"

"Something," the old man muttered, staring at the small window, "but what? *What?*" The last word came out as little more than a growl, and Alesh swallowed hard. Since he'd known him, the Chosen had always seemed in complete control but now ... not madness. *Not* madness. "I have called," the Chosen growled, "but he hasn't answered. *Why?*"

"Sir?" Alesh asked, sitting up in bed.

"*Why?*" The Chosen demanded, but he wasn't speaking to Alesh anymore. His eyes had got that distant look, as if he stared into a world only he could see, and Alesh felt goosebumps rise on his arms and chest.

"Sir," he said, "I don't understand."

Suddenly, the Chosen's eyes snapped back into focus and he turned back to Alesh. "It's started," he said, with a ringing finality that made the knot of fear in Alesh's stomach grow bigger. "I thought that there was more time. Amedan help me I thought there was more time. Oh, Simion," he moaned, his voice so low that Alesh could barely make out the words, "what have I done?"

Alesh was just about to rise and go for a healer, sure that the Chosen was having some kind of fit, when the old man spoke again, "We have been fools. *I* have been a fool." He sighed then, "Never mind that. Tell me, my son, did you deliver the message?"

He nodded, "Yes sir."

The Chosen nodded, "Good. That's good." Alesh was relieved to see that some of the old surety had come back into the man's voice. "There might still be time yet."

"Time, sir?" Alesh asked uncertainly.

The old man nodded thoughtfully, now fully back to his old self, "Thank you, Alesh, for listening. I am sorry for disturbing you so late at night. It is just that it is a burden at times … such a burden." He paused, then shrugged as if it didn't matter, "But it remains my burden still. At least for a time. Good night, Alesh. Sleep well."

As if I can sleep now, he thought as he watched the Chosen grab the lantern and head for the door, "Good night, sir. Amedan watch over you."

The Chosen turned back and smiled at that, but there was little humor in it, "Amedan watch over us all." He stood there for a second, without speaking, then, "You have become a good man, Alesh. Your father would have been proud of you. *I* am proud of you."

Alesh opened his mouth to speak, but his throat was suddenly impossibly tight, and in another moment the Chosen was gone, and he was alone. He lay awake for some time, disturbed and more than a little afraid but eventually the toils of the day took their toll, and he drifting toward sleep once more. It wasn't until sleep was nearly upon him that he realized he'd once again forgotten to tell Olliman about the bloody knife he'd found. *In the morning,* he thought to himself, his mind already foggy with sleep, *in the morning.*

CHAPTER TEN

"—SH! ALESH, WAKE UP!"

He groaned and turned on his side, covering his head with his arm. He'd spend most of the night lying in bed worrying over the Chosen's words like a dog with a bone before exhaustion had finally had its say, and his eyes felt heavy and grainy.

"Come on, already," the voice insisted, "Abigail is waiting on us!"

The owner of the voice tugged insistently on his arm, and Alesh finally decided that he'd slept all he was going to and sat up. Sonya stood watching him, fidgeting excitedly. "Woah, alright, I'm up," he mumbled, "What's all the excitement about?"

The little girl rolled her eyes, "It's *Fairday* Alesh, remember? Chorin told Abigail that you were planning on going, so she said we could all walk into the city together." Her face bunched up in thought, "She also muttered something about men only thinking with their business ends, but I don't think she was talking to me. Why does your face look like that, Alesh? Does your tummy hurt?"

Here, in the daylight, with Sonya dancing from foot to foot in excitement, the late night conversation with the Chosen lost some of its hold on him. The cold, creeping fear that had been building in him faded like morning mist, and he found himself struggling not to laugh. "No, little one, my tummy is fine. Uh … just let me get dressed."

The little girl fidgeted restlessly as he pulled on a shirt and his boots. "Can we go now, Alesh? Can we, please?"

He nodded, "Alright alright. Let's go."

Abigail was waiting for them in the hallway. The short, squat woman wore a blue dress instead of her usual white cook's one, and her brown and gray hair hung loose, one of the few times Alesh had ever seen it so—both concessions for the holiday. "Mother Abigail," he said, giving his best imitation of a nobleman's courtly bow, "You look enchanting this morning."

Sonya giggled and Abigail frowned, though he could see the smile in it, "Don't you tease me, boy. Not unless you fancy the idea of spending tomorrow scouring pots and mopping floors."

Alesh grinned and bowed again, "I am, of course, at madam's service."

The head cook rolled her eyes, "Well, come on then. Let's get this over with." She turned grimly, one hand holding Sonya's, and marched down the hall like a woman heading toward her own execution and determined to meet her end with as much dignity as she could muster. Feeling better than he had in days, Alesh followed after. It wasn't until they were outside, in the courtyard, that he came to an abrupt stop.

"What is it, boy?" Abigail asked.

Alesh winced, remembering that he'd meant to tell the Chosen about seeing Kale in the poor district. *And the knife. The damned knife.* "I forgot, I need to tell the Chosen somethi—"

"Oh no you don't," the woman interrupted, one hand on her hip as she wagged a finger at him, "You're not going to find an excuse to spend the day in that library with your head stuck in a book. You know as well as I do that Chosen Olliman would want you to have some time for yourself. Besides, he hasn't been out of his quarters yet, and you know what that means."

Alesh nodded reluctantly. As High Priest to Amedan, the Chosen often spent hours praying to his god. Sometimes entire days would pass without him ever leaving the private altar connected to his quarters. "Still," he hesitated, "it wouldn't take lo—"

Abigail frowned at him, "Now you just listen to me, Alesh. You might be a grown man now, but if you don't stop acting a fool, I'm going to walk right back in the castle and come back with my spoon. You *do* remember my spoon, don't you?"

Alesh swallowed, "Yes ma'am."

She nodded, satisfied, "As well you should. You've always been a good boy, Alesh, a smart boy, but there have been times when I think Amedan himself would have lost patience with you."

He smiled and they started forward again, Sonya skipping ahead of them, full of excitement and expectation as only the young can be. *Not me though,* Alesh thought as he watched her. His childhood had been shorter than most—the creatures had seen to that. "Was I really so difficult?" He asked of the head cook as he watched the young girl playing in her own world, a world of magic and enchantment, one where good men never grew old and old men were never murdered in their homes, their hearts torn from their chests.

She snorted, "As a noble with a tooth ache."

He laughed at that and was surprised to find that, despite his misgivings, he was excited for Fairday. Excited, at least, until he remembered that he'd promised Chorin he'd meet Lady Uriel's cousin. And with such a meeting looming, he thought that the day could only end in disaster. He had no idea, then, just how right he was.

CHAPTER ELEVEN

ONCE IN THE CITY, ALESH was amazed at the crowds that surged around them. People of all ages, from all walks of life, flooded the streets, examining the wares at the dozens of merchant stalls lining the street. Shopkeepers and vendors shouted to be heard over the din, advertising wares ranging from the practical to the ludicrous, and the smells of dozens of foods and spices drifted in the breeze, almost thick enough to touch. They walked for a time, Sonya gawking with wide eyes and frequently tugging on Abigail or Alesh's sleeves, guiding them to some new marvel or trinket that caught her eye. Abigail scolded her for acting like a chicken with its head cut off, but Alesh saw her smiling after the little girl when she thought no one was watching.

They passed merchants selling jewelry and clothes ranging from plain, inexpensive tunics and trousers to those—if the sellers had their way—that were worth a small fortune. They walked by another stall where a heavyset woman was selling a tonic that she swore would keep a woman thin no matter what she ate, and Alesh was still marveling at the irony of it when they came upon a thin man that looked to be in his fifties who was currently engaged in assuring an elderly woman that the charms he carried would ward off any nightling, great or small. And hers, today, for the paltry price of a single gold Sun! A paltry sum, he claimed, when held against one's life or the lives of her loved ones.

Alesh glanced at Abigail and saw that the head cook's hands worked as if she wished she'd brought her wooden spoon with her and before he could consider stopping her, she stepped up to the thin man, a scowl on her face. Alesh groaned inwardly. He recognized the look on her face; any of the castle's children would have and, seeing it, they would have known that the only course of action was to run. The poor man, though, had not seen the look before and did not know what it portended. "Charms, are they?" Abigail asked, interrupting the man mid-sentence, "guaranteed to frighten off the night's creatures?"

The man smiled revealing sharp, badger-like teeth as he saw the opportunity for another sale, "That's right, ma'am," he said, nodding reassuringly, "Why, one of those big old nasties wouldn't think to come close to you if you were wearing one of *these*, and you can have one for the *paltry* sum of—"

"I wonder," Abigail said, "just how many of those "big old nasties" you've faced down with one of those trinkets? Just how many nights have you spent outside the walls, sleeping peacefully while the nightwalkers cowered in their holes, scared to come near you?"

The man fidgeted uncomfortably, "Well, ma'am, only a fool would spend a night outside the city on purpose, but things happen." He glanced back at the old woman with the cane, apparently deciding his time would be better served there, "Why, sometimes I like to visit my grandchildren, you know? They live in Dale with their mother, and I'm not ashamed to admit that I can't always afford to hire a Lightbringer for the journey. So instead, I always carry one of my charms to protect—"

"What are their names?" Abigail interrupted.

The man frowned at her, "Names, ma'am?"

The head cook nodded, crossing her arms over herself, "Your grandchildren. What are their names?"

"Err .. they're uh … listen, ma'am, I don't really see what that has to do with—"

"No, you wouldn't, would you?" Abigail said, shaking her head, "You ought to be ashamed of yourself, boy, making a living off of people's fear." Despite the fact that the man looked of an age with Abigail herself, his face turned red, and his gaze fell to the ground like any scolded kitchen servant.

"Abigail?" Sonya asked, as she walked up, returning from a nearby stall with two honey-cakes in her small hands. "What's wrong?"

The head cook's scowl disappeared immediately, and she turned to the little girl with a smile, "Nothing's wrong, sweet one. Come on, I hear there's to be a show in the Town Square. Doesn't that sound nice?" She turned and frowned at the merchant, "I think I've had my fill of shopping for now." The old merchant didn't bother trying to hide the relief on his face.

The little girl's eyes lit up, "A show? Can we go, Abigail, please can we—"

"Of course, child, of course. Come on, why don't we head there now? I imagine it'll be starting before too much longer." She turned to Alesh, "And you'd better be going to meet Chorin, if you've a mind to."

Alesh glanced at the sun and winced. He'd been so distracted by the crowded streets and all of the different things going on around him that he'd nearly forgotten. "You're right," he said with a sigh, "I need to go. You two have fun; I'll see you later." He turned to go, and Abigail stopped him with a hand on his arm.

"Have a good time, Alesh," the old woman said with a smile, "and try to keep that Chorin out of trouble."

"I'll try, ma'am; you know how he is."

She sighed, "Yes, I do. I know how both of you are." She pulled him into a quick hug, then turned and headed down the street, shouting after Sonya.

Alesh watched her go, her bun of gray-hair already coming undone, the hairs trailing behind her as she pushed her way through the crowd, her face set in its usual no-nonsense expression, and he couldn't help from grinning. She'd only gone a short distance before she looked back, saw him still standing there, and waved him on with a shooing gesture. Alesh grinned and waved back, but the head cook had already disappeared into the sea of people. It was the last time he saw her alive.

CHAPTER TWELVE

First Bell had come and gone by the time Alesh arrived, out of breath and sweating, to *The Dancing Maid*. It didn't take long to spot Chorin and the two women. The tavern was close to the poor quarter and was filled with a loud, boisterous crowd of commoners dressed in plain linens and homespun. The two noble women, in their bright silk dresses, their ears, fingers, and neck adorned with expensive jewels, their hair done up in a way that Alesh thought must have taken at least two or three sets of hands, stuck out like peacocks among chickens. Which, he supposed, was the point.

He looked down at his own servant's whites and felt his face heat. *Gods, what am I doing here?* He was just about to turn and leave when Chorin glanced over, saw him, and waved him over with a grin. Alesh bit back a curse and walked to their table, clasping Chorin's hand. "I didn't think you were going to make it," the big guard said.

Alesh shrugged, "Abigail insisted. She said that someone has to keep you out of trouble."

Chorin sighed, "Poor man," he said, winking at Lady Uriel who giggled behind one white-gloved hand, "You were doomed from the start."

They all laughed at that, and Chorin slapped himself on the forehead, "Where are my manners. Alesh," he said, indicating the noble lady sitting beside him, "this is the intoxicating Lady Uriel, and this," he said, nodding his head at a thin, delicate looking woman sitting across from them, "is Lady Isabelle, Lady Uriel's radiant cousin."

The two women giggled, blushing prettily. *How does the bastard do it?* Alesh thought, sitting down at the table. If he'd said something like that, he'd have been lucky to get away with a curse and a red cheek and just as likely to get the city guards called on him, "It's uh ... a pleasure to meet you both."

"Tell me, Alesh," Lady Uriel said, fingering a diamond necklace that hung at her throat just in case anyone had missed it, "is Chorin always so charming?"

His friend's grin widened, "Yeah, Alesh, am I?"

Alesh considered having to suffer through another night of being told how great his friend was then an idea occurred to him, and he only just managed to keep himself from grinning. Instead, he leaned forward, a serious expression on his face, "Yes ma'am, most always. Except when he wakes from one of his nightmares."

Chorin opened his mouth to speak, but the noblewoman beat him to it, "You have nightmares, sweetling?" She asked, running a hand down the big man's cheek, "Why that's so terrible."

Alesh nodded, ignoring Chorin's scowl, "It is indeed, my lady. Has them most every night, in fact. I'm sure he would have mentioned it but ... well, you know how brave our Chorin is. He doesn't like to make a big fuss over himself."

The noblewomen both looked at Chorin, something like adoration in their eyes, and Lady Uriel nodded, "He is the bravest man I've ever met. Still," she said, waving an admonishing finger at him, "you should have told me about this, Chorry. Maybe I could help, somehow. Are they about your time as a soldier? I'm sure it must have been terrible all that—"

"No ma'am," Alesh interrupted, "He never dreams about that time—at least that's what he tells me. No, his nightmares are about something far ... stranger."

"Look," Chorin said frowning, "I don't—"

"Hush now, sweet Chorry," Lady Uriel said, putting a delicate finger over his lips, "let your friend tell us. I know that you would never admit to any weakness, and I don't think you any less of a man for having nightmares."

"Now," she said, turning to Alesh, "tell us, please, Akresh. What terrible dreams plague him so?"

"Yes, do tell us," Lady Isabelle said in a soft, not unpleasant voice. Alesh noted that the two noblewomen were leaning forward in their seats now, their breath held in anticipation.

"Forgive me, my lady," he said, "but it's *Alesh*. Anyway, it is terrible. Truly. You see, our Chor—*Chorry* here," he had to pause for a second at that, fighting the laughter down, "well, he does not dream of his time as a soldier, *or* of the nightlings as so many people do. No, he is plagued by dreams of," he paused for effect, and the two noblewomen looked as if their eyes would pop out of their heads in expectation, "*dogs*."

A pause then the slightest raising of a perfectly trimmed eyebrow, "Dogs?"

Alesh nodded, his expressions solemn, "Well. Puppies, really."

The two women recoiled for a moment before they realized what he'd said, then they frowned. "Forgive me," Lady Uriel said uncertainly, "it sounded as if you said puppies."

"Oh yes," Alesh said gravely, noting the murderous glare his friend was giving him out of the corner of his eye, "but not just *any* puppies. No, these puppies are more dangerous than any blade or tourney spear could ever be. Sure they *look* cute and cuddly, but that's only a disguise, a clever ruse that they use to lure people in."

"Oh, I see!" Lady Isabelle exclaimed, a self-satisfied smile on her face, "they aren't *really* puppies at all, are they? No, they're actually," she leaned forward, whispering the last in the hushed tone a child might use, "they're *nightlings*."

Alesh considered this for a moment then shook his head, "No, my lady. At least, I don't believe so. Still, I woke him up one time while he was having the dream, and that was about as close to death as I care to come. Why, he about strangled the life out of me before he came fully awake, and you *know* how strong our Chorry is."

The noblewoman frowned and ran a delicate hand through her long black hair, "Then why—"

Chorin cleared his throat, "I think it's about time we got going, don't you all? Otherwise, we'll miss the entire Fairday. Why don't you two ladies wait outside? *Alesh* and I will settle up with the barkeep for the drinks."

The two women glanced uncertainly to each other. Finally, Lady Uriel nodded, "Of course, Chorry." She patted him softly on the arm as if she'd just heard he'd been the victim of some terrible accident and was scared to hurt him. "Come, Isabelle."

The women rose and left, leaving Chorin scowling at Alesh across the table. "That was a bastardly thing to do."

"Bastardly? What do you mean?" Alesh asked innocently, "My friend, I'm *here* for you, alright? We're *all* here for you in your time of need."

Chorin frowned at him for a second longer then broke into a loud fit of laughter. After a moment, he wiped his hand across his face and sighed, "I told you I'm not *scared* of puppies. I just don't *like* them."

"*Oh,*" Alesh said, "my mistake," he paused then, "explain to me again how anyone doesn't like puppies? That's like saying you don't like sunshine or happiness."

"As far as I know, happiness doesn't shit and piss everywhere and leave me to clean it up."

Alesh nodded at the four empty tankards sitting on the table in front of Chorin, "The way you drink, I'd think you'd be used to that."

Chorin rolled his eyes and stood, swaying slightly. "Come on, you bastard, let's go and pay for the drinks. I've got a lot of work to do if I plan to rob Lady Uriel of her virtue tonight after your help."

Alesh grinned and clapped his friend on the back as they headed toward the bar, "If what I hear is true, I'm surprised she has any left."

Chorin barked a laugh at that, "Well," he said as he counted out two Dawns to the bored-looking barkeep, "there's only one way to find out. That is, if I *can* now, thanks to you."

"Aw, quit your complaining. If anything, you should be thanking me. This way, you won't have to look for a reason to get her to leave. I seriously doubt she'll want to stay over and risk you having one of your puppy dog dreams."

"*Night,* you're a bastard," his friend muttered, "still, you're probably right. Come on, let's try to show the women a good time."

Alesh nodded with a smile, "Lead the way, *Chorry.*"

CHAPTER THIRTEEN

THEY SPENT HALF OF THE day walking through the city, stopping here and there to watch jugglers or musicians plying their trades along the sides of the street, or to let the two noblewomen browse the racks of dresses, scarves, and other garments at some of the tailors' booths. Lady Isabelle was pretty, as Chorin had said, and she seemed smart enough, she even tried to initiate several conversations with Alesh, but he found himself distracted with thoughts of the woman from the night before. *Katherine. Her name was Katherine.*

Stop being a fool, he told himself, *you saw what she did. She damn near got you killed, and all you can think about is the way her lips moved while she sang and the way her dress fit her.* Stupid, useless thoughts. Still, the dress *had* fit her well. There was no denying that.

He was still thinking about the singer when they rounded a corner and came upon a procession of grim-faced men and women in the red and black uniforms that had become all too familiar in the past months. Alesh peered over the heads of the gathered crowd, and gasped in surprise as he recognized the leader of the procession.

The man wore a rich crimson tunic with a sable cloak and trousers, and he looked straight forward determinedly, as if he was prepared to walk through anyone or anything stupid enough to get in his way. Falen Par. The leader of the Redeemers.

"Alesh?" Chorin asked, "Are you okay? You look as if you've seen your own ghost."

"I *knew* he looked familiar," Alesh breathed.

"What are you talking about?" Chorin asked, grabbing one of his arms, "Alesh, what's wrong?"

But what would Kale be doing in the poor quarter with the leader of the Redeemers unless... "Chorin," he said, his eyes never leaving the thin man, "I'm sorry, but I have to go."

"You have to go? Why? Alesh, is everything okay?"

He shook his head, "I don't think so, Chor. I really don't." He forced his gaze away from Falen Par and turned to his friend, "Something's not right. I have to talk to the Chosen. I have to—" He swallowed hard, "Chorin, can you do me a favor? Abigail and Sonya have gone to the market square for the show. Could you go and get them, make sure they're safe?"

His friend frowned, "Of course they're sa—"

Alesh grabbed his friend by the shoulder, and Chorin must have seen something in his expression because he stopped midsentence. "Please, Chorin. I've got a really bad feeling."

The big guard opened his mouth to speak, then shut it again. Finally, he nodded. "Alright, I will, but you're going to tell me what all of this is about later."

"Of course," Alesh said, nodding impatiently, "I'll tell you all about it." His friend started to say something else, but Alesh was already gone, pushing his way through the crowd, cursing at how slow he was forced to move. He wasn't sure why, but he got the distinct feeling that time was running out. If, that was, it wasn't out already.

CHAPTER FOURTEEN

BY THE TIME HE MADE it to the castle, Alesh's fear had taken such hold of him that he was half-surprised not to find a pile of burning rubble where it had once stood. He had spent the last hour and a half trying to tell himself that everything was okay, that he was overreacting, but every time he did he remembered the Chosen's face from the night before, old and haggard, the desperate, almost lost look he'd seen in his eyes, and the lie showed itself for what it was. As he ran, ignoring the sharp ache in his side, he became more and more certain that something was terribly wrong, had, in fact, been wrong for some time now. He rushed through the servants' hallways, oblivious of the surprised castle workers and furious nobles he shouldered past in his haste.

He stopped by his room first, wanting to grab the small bloody fisherman's knife that he'd hid under his bed to show Olliman, but he was shocked to see that it wasn't there. Someone had taken it. His sense of foreboding growing with each passing second, Alesh left his room and hurried through the castle toward Olliman's chambers.

As he approached the Chosen's quarters, he finally allowed himself to slow, and he glanced around the empty hallway with surprise. Apparently, Olliman had ended his prayers quicker than normal. If he'd still been in his rooms, there would have been guards posted at his doors, but there was no one, and the hallway was silent. He started to turn away, thinking to search for the Chosen elsewhere, but stopped as he noticed that the door to Olliman's personal quarters stood ajar.

Apparently, some of the servants had taken the opportunity afforded by the Chosen's absence to clean. Alesh breathed a sigh of relief. They would know where to find him.

"Excuse me—" he began as he stepped inside the door then froze in shock. The first thing he noticed was the blood. It covered the walls, the floor, and the white sheets of the bed like red paint, a red brighter than he would have thought possible. *A man could never hold so much,* he thought wildly, *not a dozen men.* He wanted, *needed* to close his eyes against the terrible sight, close them before it was too late, but he could not and, against his wishes, his gaze shifted to the figure lying on the bed.

Lord Olliman, High Priest of Amedan, ruler of Valeria and leader of the Six, was still dressed in the white robes he'd worn the day before, though they were barely recognizable. The normally clean, immaculate cloth was covered in gore and blood, so thick that it looked as if the Chosen had waded in a river of it.

The old man's face was peaceful, as if he were merely sleeping, his blue gaze locked on the ceiling as if even now he sought his god. Alesh prayed that he'd found him, for he was not sleeping, and whatever the outcome of his searching, it was over now. The large, gaping hole that had been ripped in his chest was proof of that. *His heart,* he thought, too shocked to move, his hands trembling at his side, *they ate his heart.*

A noise came from behind him, and he spun, his breath catching with terror. The sound had come from the Chosen's personal sanctuary, a place where no one—not even a servant—was allowed to enter. The door was closed. *It's them,* he thought in a panic, *It's the nightlings. They've killed the Chosen, and now they're going to kill me too.*

It can't be, some desperate part of his mind insisted. Everyone knew the creatures only came out at night, that they were powerless in the day. *Just like everyone knew that no nightwalker could ever slay Olliman,* Alesh thought. "H-hello?" He'd meant to ask the question aloud, but his voice came out in a raspy whisper.

He told himself he should run, *needed* to run. After all, someone had to tell the castle guards what had happened. But even as he thought this, he found himself moving toward the small, unadorned door, felt his hand grasping its latch and, in another moment, the door was swinging open.

He winced in anticipation of the sharp claws and fangs that were certainly about to tear into him, at the evil that was waiting on the other side, but the door pulled wide, and it was not a nightling waiting on him, but Kale, the Chosen's apprentice. The nobleman stood, facing the altar above which hung a golden torch, the sacred symbol of Amedan. "Kale?" Alesh asked, shocked and more than a little outraged to find the apprentice here, in Olliman's personal sanctuary.

The nobleman jerked around in surprise and looked at Alesh. After a moment, the surprised expression faded and he nodded once, solemnly, "So," Kale said, his voice hoarse as if he'd been shouting or crying, "You have seen it. You know."

"Know what?" Alesh asked, his thoughts scattered at unexpectedly finding Kale here.

"Our Master. He is dead."

Thoughts tumbled through Alesh's head too quickly to grasp but he finally managed to hold on to one. "I saw you," Alesh said, "in the poor district with Falen Par."

Another surprised look from the nobleman—and was that guilt?—but it was gone in another moment. Kale nodded, "I had not meant for you to see that."

Alesh braced, expecting the nobleman to attack him at any moment. If he'd been plotting with Falen Par to overthrow the Chosen, he wouldn't, *couldn't* leave any witnesses. But Kale only stood there, his expression one of a deep, terrible grief. "I was trying to make a deal with him, Alesh. Hoping that I could get him to see reason, to come back to Amedan's grace or, at the very least, to take his Redeemers elsewhere."

Alesh frowned, not just at the nobleman's words but also at his use of Alesh's name. He could not recall him ever having used it before—asshole, servant, peasant, sure. But his name? "That doesn't make any sense. Chosen Olliman tried to negotiate with Falen Par. The man would hear none of it. What hopes could you have possibly had of doing better?"

The nobleman sighed, "None, I'm sure. But I thought ... well, that if I somehow *did* manage to come to some terms with Falen Par and his Redeemers, perhaps the Chosen would deem me ready to take his place."

Alesh considered this. That last *did* sound like the Kale he knew, ambitious, hungry for power. Still, something was bothering him. "Why are you here?" Their training session hadn't been scheduled until later in the day, and the Kale he knew would have been spending his time chasing after women or power, maybe a peasant whose life he could make a living hell, not coming to check on the Chosen without being called.

Kale shrugged sadly, "I came to tell him that Falen Par has agreed to meet with him. I know, I know," he said, holding up a hand to forestall Alesh's arguments, "it probably wouldn't have done any good, but I had to *try*. You've no idea what it's like, Alesh, having parents that always expect more than you can give, having a father who looks at you as a failure no matter what you do." The Chosen's apprentice paused, his teeth clenching, as if in the grip of some great emotion, and Alesh saw a tear run its way down the nobleman's face, "I thought that, maybe, if Olliman stepped down and made me the new Chosen ... maybe I could make him proud."

You're right, Alesh thought, *I don't know what it's like at all. I don't even know what it's like to have a father.* He glanced back at the room in which the Chosen lay dead. *At least, not anymore.* With that thought, he felt his own throat clench with sadness and despite the fact that yesterday he would have thought it impossible, he felt compassion for the nobleman. "Then ... how?" He asked.

He wasn't able to say more, but apparently Kale understood his meaning because he shook his head sadly, "Nightwalkers, Alesh. How else?" He took a step toward him, and Alesh gasped. He hadn't noticed before because of the low light of the altar room, but Kale was covered in blood, almost as much as Olliman himself. The nobleman noticed his stare and nodded sadly, "I ... I tried to save him, but I was too late." He gestured to the altar, "I've been praying to Amedan, Alesh, praying that he grant me the strength, the wisdom to be worthy of taking Olliman's place."

"His place?" Alesh asked, his grief making him incapable of understanding what the nobleman was saying.

The dark-haired man nodded, "I know, brother," he said, coming up to Alesh and placing a blood-stained hand on his shoulder, "Our master's death is more than any man should have to bear, and I fear Ilrika will suffer for it." He sighed then, and it was the sigh of a man who has taken up a great burden that he does not expect to put down soon, "I am no Olliman. His wisdom, his kindness will be sorely missed in the days to come, but I will do my best, that I promise you."

Kale gripped his shoulder firmly for a moment, then walked to the bed and knelt beside where the Chosen lay, the look of grief and pain on his face so great that Alesh was suddenly ashamed of every cruel thought he'd ever had about the nobleman. The Chosen's Apprentice grasped Olliman's lifeless hand where it hung loose over the side of the bed and kissed it tenderly, heedless of the blood that covered it. "I am sorry I was not here, master," he whispered, though not so quietly that Alesh couldn't hear, "I will try to make you proud."

Alesh stood, his feet rooted to the spot, oblivious of the hot tears that wound their way down his face. After a moment, Kale rose, "He was a leader to us all," he said, "I'll go and tell the others." Then he turned and left.

No, Alesh thought, *he was more than that.* When Kale was gone, he walked to the other side of the bed and stared into the Chosen's eyes, the eyes that had known him the second they'd seen him, had tested and measured and loved. He let out a choked sob and fell to his knees, his legs suddenly too weak to hold him. "How?" He asked those blank, lifeless orbs.

"Why?" He asked, but this time not of the body of his master but of the god who had let him die. "He followed your tenets," he hissed, anger and hate mixing in his words, "He did everything you asked of him. If you can't protect him, if you couldn't protect my parents, then what good *are* you?"

There was no answer. But, then, there never was. Amedan, it seemed, if he existed at all, cared nothing for the people who wasted their lives following his teachings. "*Damn you,*" Alesh growled, his hands knotting into fists at his sides, "*Damn you!*" He shook with the hate, the rage that roared through him. But as quickly as it had come, his anger vanished, leaving behind a grief too great to bear. He closed his eyes and wept, and it wasn't the man he was whose tears fell onto the bed linens, but the boy from so long ago, the boy who was left lying broken among the wreckage of his life, broken and alone.

After a time, he rose and turned to go, but a glint of light caught his eye. He turned back and saw that something was gripped in the Chosen's hand. Gently, he unfurled the cold fingers and saw that it was the Chosen's medallion, the symbol of the High Priests of Amedan, a golden torch inlaid in a golden circle, its fire burning a brilliant white.

Clutching the medallion by its chain, so tightly that it hurt, he walked back into the altar room. A small window sat at the back of the sanctuary, and he made his way toward it. He reached for the latch but found that it was already unhooked and that the glass pane had not been secured into its fastening but left loose. He pushed it the rest of the way open and stared out at the city below, full of people who believed that the Lord of Light would protect them, would keep them safe. "Not me," He said, his voice shaking with barely contained fury, "never again." He stared at the amulet in his hand for a moment then dropped it out the window, watching as it fell out of sight, then he turned and walked away.

CHAPTER FIFTEEN

Alesh wandered the castle hallways aimlessly. He felt as if there were things he should be doing, but he couldn't seem to bring himself to care. The news of the Chosen's death spread through the castle ahead of him, and the wails and weeping of the castle's servants seemed to surround him, echoing off of the walls, as if he trod through the underworld itself, each step carrying him past the tortured screams of the dead and the dying.

He didn't know how long he wandered that terrible landscape, a revenant living in memories of the past, oblivious of its present, but eventually he turned a corner and saw a pale-faced noblewoman leading her young daughter by the hand as they hurried through the castle, porters carrying their bags behind them. Something about the image pulled him out of his stupor, and he frowned. Since the recent attacks, the Chosen had allowed some of the more faint-hearted nobles to come and stay in one of the castle's many guest rooms, but in the wake of Olliman's death, the woman had apparently decided to seek safety elsewhere.

Watching the little girl drug past by her mother, Alesh thought of Sonya, and *that* made him think of the reason he'd come back in the first place. Kale and Falen Par walking through the poor district. Despite what Kale had said, they hadn't seemed like two men negotiating to him. They had seemed like two men on a mission, two men with a lot on their minds. Besides, if Kale's intention had been to win the leader of the Redeemers over, as he'd claimed, wouldn't he have chosen a wealthier side of town? He knew the Chosen's apprentice well enough to know this would be true. He would have wanted to host Par in his family's manse, with servants scurrying to and fro at his every command. So why, then, would he have met him in the poor district? Alesh could think of only one reason—to hide. He decided that he wanted to ask the Chosen's apprentice a few more questions. If nothing else, it would give him something to do, something to keep the grief back for a little while longer, at least.

CHAPTER SIXTEEN

He asked a passing servant where he could find Kale, and the man, wiping at his eyes and sniffling loudly, managed to tell him that Kale was preparing to give a speech in the audience room. Once again, Alesh was overcome with the feeling that he was running out of time, that some invisible clock was ticking down to ... *to what?* Ridiculous, of course. The Chosen was dead and no amount of hurrying could change that.

He hurried anyway. Four guards wearing the white and gold colors of Olliman were positioned outside the massive double doors, and one of them, a bearded man with eyes so dark they were nearly black held up a hand as he approached. Alesh noticed, absently, that it was bandaged. "Stop where you are."

Alesh glanced up at the man and was surprised to find that he didn't recognize him. In fact, he only recognized one of the four guards. Strange considering that he'd been living at the castle since he was a child and had thought he knew all the guards by name. "I'm sorry," he said, "But is Kale in there? I have to talk to him. It's important."

The man sneered, "The Chosen ain't got time to waste on servants. In case you haven't noticed, boy, the city's in a state of crisis—or soon will be once the commoners find out what's happened."

"But I have t—"

"Leave, boy," another of the guards growled, "Before we make you. You wouldn't like that, believe me."

Alesh turned to the guard he recognized, an older man with a short, neatly trimmed gray beard. "Erwin?"

"Best do what they say, Alesh," Erwin said in a gruff voice, "You'll have a chance to talk to Leranian," he paused at a look from one of the guards, "To *Chosen* Leranian after he's finished giving his speech."

Alesh stared at the man in surprise. "But Erwin—"

"*Go!*" Alesh took an involuntary step back at the anger in the man's voice. He'd known Erwin for years, since he'd first come to the castle, had often sat and talked to the older man about his daughter and his grandchildren. Erwin had always been kind to him, in the past. What had changed? Never mind that. "Chosen Olliman's throne room is always open to any who wish to speak with him."

The first guard who'd spoken stepped forward, reaching for the truncheon hanging at his side, "I've had about enough of this boy's blather, now—"

Erwin stuck out an arm, forestalling him, "I'll handle this," he growled. The man frowned at the hand on his chest, but made no move. "Olliman's dead, boy," Erwin said, meeting Alesh's eyes for the first time, "dead and gone, and there are going to be some changes. If I was you, I'd get out of the castle; we don't need you here now." He took a step closer, a grim expression on his face, "Do you understand, boy? You need to *go*."

Anger ran through Alesh, anger at these men who dared to counteract Olliman's ordinances when his corpse was not yet cold, and, a wild, almost irrepressible urge came over him to charge them, to *rend and tear and rip, to see their blood bright and red and*—he swallowed hard, shaking his head as if to clear it. Where had *that* come from? He forced himself to take a slow deep breath, rubbing absently at his shoulder where the scar had begun to burn uncomfortably. "Fine," he managed through gritted teeth, "I'll go."

He glanced once more at the entrance to the audience chamber before turning and stalking off. He wouldn't be getting to Kale through *that* door. *But, then,* he thought, smiling grimly as he turned the corner, *servants rarely take the main entrance.*

In a short time, Alesh was in the servant's corridors, the tunnels that ran throughout the castle like veins through a man's body, only these veins didn't carry blood, but men and women going about their masters' errands. Here, no expensive rugs lay on the floor, no elaborate tapestries and paintings adorned the walls, and no guards stood watch. Such things were reserved for nobles and visiting dignitaries, not servants. The plain stone beneath his feet and on the surrounding walls was covered here and there with thin layers of dust—those who would have cleaned them much too busy doing the bidding of their masters to worry about the cleanliness of a corridor only they used.

Footprints in the film of dust on the floor showed where servants had traipsed back and forth in answer to their masters' bidding. Alesh, himself, had used the corridors nearly every day for the past fifteen years, running errands for his own master. *But not now,* he thought bitterly, *my master is dead, and I will find out what Kale knows of it.* His jaw set, he started down the hallway.

A short walk brought him to the door he was looking for. The servants' marking above it assured him that it led to the Chosen's audience room. He hesitated with his hand on the knob to what, he supposed, was Kale's audience room now, and had a moment of doubt.

Kale *was* the Chosen's apprentice, after all; he was *supposed* to take his place if something happened to Olliman, had been training for years for this very eventuality, and so what if Kale *had* been speaking with Falen Par? It wasn't as if the man was a criminal. The Redeemers had been around for some time, as long as Alesh could remember, and just because they advocated the worship of a different god didn't make them evil, Olliman himself had practically said as much. They claimed that the God of Light and Fire was worthless, that he did nothing for the people, true, but how could Alesh fault them for such a thought when he believed it himself?

Of course, they also worshipped Amedan's wife, Shira, and Alesh had no use for the Goddess of the Wilderness either. Neither Amedan or Shira, nor any of their children, had bothered to show themselves when his parents were killed. His hand on the latch, he wondered—as he had so many times before—why his father and mother had been on the road that day. His memories from before that night were nothing more than vague snatches of a life which wasn't his anymore: his father's laughter, his mother's soft voice, singing him to sleep. The truth was, they didn't feel like his memories at all, but those of some other boy, a boy whose biggest concerns were his chores and when the next minstrels were coming town. That wasn't him, and if it ever had been, that part of him had died with his parents. After all, he didn't even know his father's name. It was lost to him, somewhere behind that scene of blood and death.

Some days, he thought that if he only knew the reason why his parents had risked the darkness, maybe he could find some small measure of peace, of understanding. But all he had was the memory of their screams, of the buck and sway of the cart as it tipped over and over, and the sound of the screech and growl of the shadows in the darkness. And, of course, the scar. A reminder—if ever one was needed—of all that he had lost, of all that had been taken from him.

And, just as he didn't know the reasons behind his parents' death, neither did he understand how the nightlings could have snuck into the Chosen's castle, his stronghold, and killed him without so much as rousing a guard. *And speaking of guards,* he thought, *just who were those three men with Erwin?*

The fact was, he didn't know. He didn't know why there were new guards, he didn't know why Olliman had died, didn't even know his father's name. He decided that he'd had enough of not knowing. He reached out, swung the door open, and stepped inside.

CHAPTER SEVENTEEN

"—MUST GO ON AS BEST we can," Kale was saying from where he sat on the Chosen's throne. Two guards flanked him and several others stood at the sides of the room. Alesh glanced at them for only a moment, long enough to realize he didn't recognize any of them, before his gaze drifted back to the Chosen's Apprentice.

Kale had changed into a rich golden doublet and black trousers and there was no trace of the blood that had covered him. Alesh found himself thinking that blood should be harder to hide than that. So much harder. He looked at the nobles and the city's wealthiest merchants cowering in the room, huddled close together like children in the darkness. Compassion and confidence mingled in the apprentice's strong, handsome features, and Alesh was forced to admit that Kale looked noble, sitting in the throne, looked as if he'd been made for it. Which, of course, wasn't far from the truth. After all, Olliman, a man who many believed to be the wisest person who'd ever lived, had *chosen* him for the task. It was his duty, what he'd been groomed for. But why, then, did a cold dread run up Alesh's spine at the sight of the man sitting on Olliman's throne?

"But *how* could this happen?" said Lord Carlyle, a heavy-set noble, in what was nearly a shout. Judging by his red sweaty face, he had been partaking heavily of the Welian wine which he favored.

"If they can kill the Chosen," wailed a noblewoman who Alesh didn't recognize, "Then they could get any of us. None of us are safe!"

The crowd broke into nervous chatter then, the merchants complaining about what news of the Chosen's death would do for business while nobles demanded protection for their families, and Alesh's upper lip pulled back from his teeth in a silent snarl. Olliman was dead, murdered in his own castle, and all these selfish fools could think about was themselves and their own profits.

Kale raised a hand for silence, an amused expression on his face, "Aren't you *listening* to us?" Lord Carlyle shouted, bursting out of his chair, his face so red that he looked as if he might explode, "Do you think this is *funny?*"

He stalked toward the throne, waving a meaty fist in the air, screaming curses, but he only made it a few steps before Kale nodded to one of the guards. The man stepped forward and struck the nobleman over the head with one of the weighted truncheons they call carried. There was a sickening, meaty *crack*, and the noble dropped to the ground like a puppet with its strings cut.

The tirade of the nobles and merchants cut off in an instant, and they gawked at the unconscious nobleman, one of the most powerful of their number, in mute shock. Alesh stared, disbelieving, as blood began to leak from the wound, pooling on the pristine white marble floor. Calmly, as if nothing had happened, Kale motioned to several nearby servants, and they hurried forward, two of them straining to lift the lord and carry him out of the room while a third wiped at the blood-stained floor with a rag. Once they'd departed, several seconds of tense silence passed before Kale spoke, "My people," he said, into the sudden quiet, his voice solemn, "I can assure you that I find nothing humorous about what has happened. Ilrika has lost a great leader, a great man."

"But how?" One of the noblemen ventured cautiously, "How could the creatures make it into the castle and attack the Chosen?"

Kale seemed to consider for a second then, "It is my belief that Lord Olliman was betrayed."

There was a collective gasp from the crowd at his words, and they broke into whispers again. Kale held up a hand for silence. This time, the whispers cut off immediately, and the apprentice smiled. Perhaps, it was meant to be reassuring, but to Alesh he looked like a cruel boy who has just finished beating a dog into silence, "It is true that Chosen Olliman was gifted with divine power from our Lord Amedan, but even the Chosen must sleep. I have reason to believe that some of the castle guards betrayed him, letting the nightwalkers into the keep while he was defenseless."

The crowd began to glance suspiciously at the guards standing on the outside of the room. "Do not fret, my children," Kale continued, "I have already seen to the matter. The guards who I believe responsible have been detained, and I have brought in good, loyal men to take their places. You need not worry about them."

Alesh glanced at the floor where, moments before, Lord Carlyle's blood had stained the white marble. *And what of you?* He thought. "Now," Kale said, "the Chosen will be buried, his body dedicated to the god he served." The way he said it niggled at Alesh's mind, but the man was already moving on, "Though it is hard, let us shed no more tears for him, for he has gone to be with Amedan, and even now must be basking in his divine presence. The dead are dead and beyond saving. Let us, instead, care for the living."

"And how are we to do that?" A woman asked, her hand to her chest, "The attacks are worse now than they've ever been!"

Kale nodded, "Yes, but I assure you that measures will be taken to remedy that." He scowled then, a dangerous glint in his eyes, "And you may believe me when I say that these *creatures* will be punished for what they have done to us. One way or the other, they will suffer for the pain that they've caused. This I promise you." His eyes sparked as if on fire, "Olliman was like a father to me, and he *will* be avenged."

Kale was just opening his mouth to say something else when the doors opened and a gray-haired man in tattered peasants' clothing rushed inside. The nobles frowned at him, and murmured to each other, apparently not scared enough to ignore a peasant acting above his station, "Chosen Olli—" The man paused uncertainly when he noticed Kale sitting on the throne.

"Yes?" Kale asked, frowning. Apparently, he didn't appreciate his speech being interrupted by some commoner.

The man looked around, confused, as he wiped sweat from his brow, "My lord ... where is the Chosen?"

"I am sorry to tell you this, sir, but Lord Olliman was killed last night in a nightling attack."

The man recoiled as if shocked and fell to his knees, stricken.

"Yes, yes, enough of that," Kale snapped, "What is your name?"

"T-the name's Bremblow, my Lord, Dannet Bremblow. Is it true, is the Chos—"

"And what have you come to report, Master Bremblow?"

"I-it's the Redeemers, sir," the man stumbled, "T-they've taken over the city square and the poor district. Folks s-says they even killed the guards on the walls." There were gasps in the crowd, and Alesh felt his own stomach clench. Surely the man was wrong, the Redeemers wouldn't dare. Then he remembered Falen Par, the commander of the Redeemers, remembered the man's eyes, so cold and lifeless yet so ... eager.

Kale studied the man for a moment, "Are you certain of this, Master Bremblow?"

The man nodded, gulping air heavily, "I am, my Lord. I'm a chandler, you see. Well, I'd slept late and had just gotten to the square and was setting up my stall when it happened. First off they was just walking through, marching and preachin' like they always do, but then they pulled their weapons and started forcing folks into buildings. They was taking folks captive and blocking off the streets, killin anybody as resisted." *Sonya and Abigail,* Alesh thought with a shock. They were in the square. With Chorin.

"And how is it," Kale asked, "That you managed to escape capture, I wonder?"

"Luck is all, my lord," the man said, bobbing his head, "Amedan's luck and nothin' more. You see, by the time I got to the square, it was so chock full o' folks that I weren't able to bring my cart all the way in. Had to tie the horses at an inn a few streets over and carry everything myself. I was just now leavin' the square to go back for more when I heard folks screaming. I looked back and saw the Redeemers hacking into the crowd of people, forcing them together. One of 'em chased me, told me to stop, but I ran as fast as my old feet could carry me and here I am. I remember thinkin' how bad my luck was, getting' to the square late," he paused, wiping at his eyes, "Seems maybe I'm the lucky one, after all."

"Yes," Kale said with a single nod, "You're the lucky one. Thank you, Master Bremblow. You may go now."

The man looked confused, "S-sir?"

Kale motioned and two of the guards detached themselves from the wall, grabbing the peasant by either arm. "Make sure," he said as they led the old man out, "That he is well taken care of."

The two men nodded and led him out of the room, practically carrying him between them. The old man shot a confused, frightened look over his shoulders then the doors closed behind him, and he was gone.

Alesh burst forward, unable to hold his tongue any longer, "Kale, you have to do something!"

The nobleman turned to look at him, his expression one of surprise, "Alesh?" He asked, his surprise slowly turning into a frown, "What are you doing here?"

"Never mind that," Alesh said, stepping toward the throne, "Sonya and Abigail are in the square. You have to help them. You have to!"

Kale sighed sadly and turned to address the crowd, "A moment, please, my people. Alesh here was a personal servant of the Chosen, and he is overcome with grief." The crowd immediately burst into conversation, whispering to each other about everything that had transpired.

"Kale, send the soldiers, please! Abigail and Sonya—"

Kale stood and walked forward, draping a hand across Alesh's shoulders, "Alesh, of *course* I'm going to do something, but we have to remain calm. We can't let our grief over the Chosen's death keep us from—"

"*Night*, Kale, the Redeemers are taking over the city. We have to move now!"

"*We?*" The nobleman asked in a sudden angry hiss, "*We?* Perhaps you forget yourself, Alesh, but you are nothing but a servant, one who the Chosen, in his kindness, took in off the street." One of the guards moved forward, gripping his truncheon, but Kale forestalled him with a hand, "Do not presume to tell me what *we* must do. Now, if you'll excuse me, I'm currently trying to quell a panic." He started away then turned back, "Oh, and Alesh? Your services will no longer be required in the castle." He motioned to two nearby guards, "See him out."

Immediately, the two guards stepped forward and grabbed him by the arms. Alesh fought free of them and started toward Kale again, "You weren't trying to negotiate a peace with him, were you, Kale? You were planning o—" Something dull and hard slammed into the back of his head, and Alesh's vision erupted into bright white light, the words dying on his lips. He teetered drunkenly, latching onto the front of Kale's silk tunic, "I ... I saw—" Something struck him again, harder this time, and he felt himself falling down, down, down. Down into the waiting darkness.

CHAPTER EIGHTEEN

ALESH JERKED AWAKE, HIS HEAD aching like jeweler's glass that had been set at with a smith's hammer. He tried to sit up and gagged, nearly vomiting, as a wave of dizziness swept over him. He lay there for several seconds, his eyes squeezed shut, moaning softly at the sharp, throbbing pain in his head and taking slow cautious breaths in an effort to quell his churning stomach. Once he didn't feel in immediate danger of retching out his last meal, he eased his eyes open.

Weak orange light splashed around him, illuminating a room so small that he could almost have reached out his arms and touched both walls at once. The floor was hard packed dirt, the door a row of iron bars with a key hole. *The dungeons,* he thought wildly, *they've thrown me in the dungeons.* Slowly, not daring to move too fast for fear that the throbbing in the back of his head would become too much to bear, he craned his neck to look out the door. The light, he saw, came from a lantern hung on a hook outside of the cell. Somewhere in the darkness beyond the orange glow of the flame, he could hear a man's voice. *"Help me. Help me. Help … me."* Over and over again the words came, a hoarse, desperate litany, a plea for mercy that would not come.

From somewhere further away in the darkness came the sound of a man screaming to be let out in a rough, cracking voice that held no trace of sanity. Soon, other voices joined the chorus, and, though they all used different words, their meanings were all the same. *Help me. Kill me. Save me.* The disembodied voices seemed to drift to him out of the very air itself, the ravings of lost souls, the whispers of ghosts. *How long?* Alesh wondered. *How long before I, too, am just another ghost? Just another voice in the darkness, begging the shadows for mercy, though even a child knows the shadows have no mercy in them?*

The thought sent a surge of panic through him, and he tried to rise but something tugged at his leg. He stumbled and fell, his head slamming into the hard-packed earth. He gasped as pain seared through his head and body, and flecks of blackness began to dance at the corners of his eyes. Clenching his teeth so hard that they felt as if they would crack, he fought against the urge to pass out.

Once the darkness receded, he glanced down and saw what had pulled him up short. His ankles and wrists had been manacled together. Carefully, conscious of the small amount of slack his bonds afforded him, he worked his way to his feet. As he rose, a fresh spike of agony lanced through his head, and he grunted, stumbled forward, and barely managed to catch himself on the cell door. Using one of the bars for support, he gingerly probed at the back of his head, wincing as he did. Just how hard had the bastard hit him? He brought his hand back and saw that his fingers were wet with blood. *His* blood. "Hey!" He shouted, adding his own voice to the din, "Let me out of here! I've done nothing wrong!"

He told himself he needed to remain calm, to think of a way to escape, but instead his mind turned to the chandler's words, to Abigail and Sonya, going to the market square to hear the singers, to Chorin, his friend, who he'd sent after them, and before he knew it, he was screaming until his voice was hoarse, his head throbbing with each rapid, heavy pulse of his heart. He yelled and threatened, begged and pleaded. And no one came. It was only him and the other prisoners. Only him and the ghosts.

Finally, exhausted and overcome with dizziness, he stumbled to the corner of his cell and collapsed. He sat, listening to the disembodied voices from the darkness, begging, demanding, promising. Time passed—he did not know how long, it could have been minutes or hours—and despite his fears and his worries, an exhaustion more complete than any he'd ever felt swept over him, and he went away for a time.

CHAPTER NINETEEN

THE CITY BURNED. FLAMES CRACKLED and roared, like some great storm breaking and thick serpents of smoke rose into the sky. Timbers crashed and snapped all around him as the fire ate its fill. He knew he needed to run, to get out, but his feet wouldn't obey his commands, no matter how hard he tried. His skin burned as if it was on fire, and his throat was so full of smoke and heat that he could not draw a breath. He thought that, at any moment, he would die, that surely he *must* die, but he did not, *could* not and so he stood and watched his city, his home, burn, watched its ashes float and swirl around him like soot-gray snow.

Smoke was everywhere, obscuring his view, but he could make out vague, human shapes running through that churning grayness, there one moment and gone the next, like restless phantoms in the world of the dead. It covered everything, that shifting sea of darkness and mystery. Or, at least, almost everything. It did not cover the screams. They were all around him, shrill and desperate and bereft of hope or humanity. There were other voices too, other sounds. Sounds not unlike the baying of wolves, savage and cruel and alien.

Alesh started awake to a rasping, metallic sound, and he raised his head, the sounds of those screams, those hungry, demanding screams, still fresh in his mind. Four men were filing into his cell and locking the door behind them. In the flickering light of the lantern one of them carried, he saw that it was the guard from the audience room, Barek, and the others who'd stood watch with him.

"Erwin?" He asked, confused and half-sure that he must still be dreaming.

But the older man avoided his gaze, and it was Barek who answered, "I told you you'd regret fucking with me, boy." And, as he spoke, he and the others—even Erwin—withdrew the truncheons from their belts.

Alesh's weariness vanished in an instant, and he jerked to his feet, backing away from the four guards until his back fetched against the stone wall of the cell. "Erwin," he said, his voice hoarse and scratchy, "You don't have to do this."

The old man met his eyes then, and Alesh was surprised at the sadness he saw there. "Yes, I do. I'm sorry, Alesh." Then the men began to spread out around him, their truncheons raised. Despite his words, Erwin hung back, watching the other three.

Alesh watched them come, noting the swords they had sheathed at their waists. If he could get hold of one of those—his thoughts were cut off as the men charged him, their truncheons swinging at him in vicious arcs. He ducked under one man's wild swing, and caught the wrist of the second man before his blow connected. He just had time to see the man's eyes open in surprise before he punched him hard in the stomach, and the guard doubled over, gasping for breath.

He caught movement out of the corner of his eye, and he jumped to the side. The truncheon, which had been aimed at his head, struck his shoulder instead. He shouted in agony, lashing out with his other arm and hitting his attacker in the face. The guard's nose snapped under his fist and blood and snot fountained out. The man stumbled backward with a muffled cry, his truncheon falling to the ground as he cupped his broken nose in both hands.

The guard named Barek growled a curse and swung his own truncheon. Alesh caught his hand and slammed it against the wall. The big guard grunted in pain and the truncheon clattered to the ground. Alesh took the opportunity this afforded him, kicking the guard in the stomach and sending him rolling backward. He took a step toward the fallen man, reaching for his sword, a flash of hope going through his mind. If he could only get that sword—but before he'd grabbed the handle he was jerked back as thick arms wrapped around him from behind.

He struggled to break free, but his left arm was numb and weak from the blow he'd taken, and he was still struggling when Barek stood and punched him in the face. Alesh grunted as his head rocked back from the force of the blow. He kicked out desperately, but the big guard dodged it easily and waded in to him, striking him in the stomach and the face with savage, cruel blows. After what felt like an eternity, the guard holding him let Alesh go, and he doubled over, falling to his hands and knees and heaving in painful gasps in an effort to get his breath back.

Every part of his body screamed in pain, but he knew that if he didn't get up, these men would beat him to death. He hacked and spat out a gob of blood and was starting to his feet when one of the guards kicked him in the stomach. The air left him in a *whoosh,* and he fell onto his side, gasping in pain. "Stop your sniveling!" Barek said, kicking the guard with the broken nose who was sitting up, moaning as he cupped his face in crimson hands. Barek drew the sword at his waist and stalked toward Alesh, his expression grim, "Time to die, boy."

Alesh blinked in a vain attempt to clear his blurry vision. He watched the guard raise his sword, but was too tired, too hurt to do anything about it. He winced in anticipation, but instead of the kiss of steel on his neck, something wet and warm splattered on his face. The grizzly guard's eyes widened in surprise, and his own sword fell from his hands. He looked down, as surprised as Alesh, at the foot of exposed, blood-streaked steel protruding from his chest. Alesh was still trying to figure out what happened when the blade was pulled free, and the dead guard crumpled on top of him.

He grunted as the man's dead weight fell on him. He tried to push the corpse off, but his body ached terribly, and he could have no more lifted the man off of him just then than he could have lifted a mountain.

He grunted, trying again, but the effort took too much out of him, and the darkness which, until then, had been lurking at the corners of his vision, surged forward in a rush and, for a time, he knew nothing.

He started awake with hands gripping his arms, shaking him. "Get up!"

Alesh grunted, his eyes fluttering open. Barek's corpse had been thrown off of him and a blurry, gray-haired form stood over him, holding out a hand. "*Erwin?*" He asked in a croak.

The older man nodded, "It's me, Alesh." The guard helped him sit up, then walked to the cell door and looked out.

Using the wall for support, Alesh struggled to his feet, one hand cupped to his side where Barek's boot had struck him. He looked at the three corpses sprawled on the floor of the cell. "You killed them." He said, knowing it was foolish even as he said it, but too hurt and confused for anything else.

Erwin turned back, glanced at the three corpses, and nodded. "I did. Now, come on. There's not much time." He knelt by one of the corpses and retrieved a set of keys then walked to the cell door and unlocked it.

"Not much time for what?" Alesh asked uncertainly.

"For you to get out," the guard said, unlocking the manacles at Alesh's wrists and ankles. He studied Alesh with a critical eye. "You're covered in blood. You'll need to get new clothes as quick as you can then get out of the city."

"Leave the city?" Alesh asked. Since stumbling into Ilrika as a child, half mad with grief and hunger, the dried blood of his parents coating his face and clothes, he had never left and the thought left him cold.

"Damnit," Erwin said, "Don't you get it, Alesh? The city's gone mad. Kale's denounced Amedan, claiming Shira as his goddess, and the people have followed him." He spat, "It's made them like animals, as like to kill you as look at you. You *have* to get to Valeria. Of the Great Cities, it's the closest. Tell Chosen Tesharna what's happened. She'll send help. Get *help* Alesh."

Shira ... the Goddess of the Wilds. No, he couldn't think of that now. There were more pressing things to worry about. "Valeria's weeks away," Alesh said. Valeria was the second largest of the six cities of the Chosen, and although he'd never been there, he'd seen maps in the Chosen's library that depicted the Six Cities of the Dawn. "I'd never make it. The nightlings—"

"There's no choice, Alesh," Erwin hissed, glancing again out the corridor, "If you stay here, you'll be killed along with the others. You must hurry." He reached into his pocket and produced a short cylinder of dark metal about half the length of Alesh's forearm. "Take this."

Alesh inhaled sharply at what the man held. He hesitated but finally reached out, almost reverently, and took the cylinder. It was heavier than he'd thought it would be. The intricate golden runes that were etched deeply into its surface felt warm beneath his fingers. "An Evertorch," he breathed, "but how did you—"

"Never mind," Erwin said. "There's no time."

Alesh swallowed hard as he gazed at the cylinder. The Evertorches were priceless artifacts, remnants of the War of Darkness, created by Chosen Larin to help in the fight against the night walkers. Larin, whom the texts commonly referred to as the Shaper was probably the least well known of the Six, but he had created many weapons and defenses during the war, none of which were greater than the Evertorches that were said to produce a light as damaging to the night's creatures as the sun itself.

None of the scholars knew what happened to Larin after the war, only that he'd disappeared after Argush and his armies had been vanquished, never to be seen again. Some argued that he'd been kidnapped and killed by Argush, or that he and Olliman had argued—though about what, no one seemed to know—and that he'd left in a fit of rage. Of course, this seemed unlikely to Alesh considering that the northern city of Larindale had been created in memory of the Shaper. Still others contended that he'd used up the magic Amedan had given him in the creation of the Evertorches, thereafter becoming a normal man, assuming a different name and fading into obscurity as a normal, though exceptional weapon smith.

Alesh ran his finger wonderingly over the tiny *L* inscribed at the base of the cylinder. Whether or not Chosen Larin had truly used up his gift in the creation of the Evertorches, there was no question that they displayed a craftsmanship and magic unsurpassed by anything else before or since, and that they'd been of great aid during the war. Some scholars even went so far as to say that without the advent of the Evertorches, the war itself would have been lost.

"A last resort," Erwin said. "Take this too." He held out a small pouch that jingled as Alesh took it. He opened it up and looked inside, gasping again. The inside of the small bag was filled with golden Suns that didn't seem to reflect the lantern light so much as absorb it. "Hire a Lightbringer before you leave the city and show no one the Evertorch unless you absolutely have to.

The things will attract more attention than you'll want and if word gets around of someone being seen with one, it won't take Kale long to put it together."

Alesh stared wide eyed at the bag of coins in his hand, more money than he'd ever seen in one place and most likely several year's wages for the castle guard. "I can't take this, Erwi—"

"You *will* take it," the man interrupted gruffly. "You have to bring word to the other cities of what's happened here, Alesh. You have to. And remember, find a Lightbringer. It shouldn't take as much coin as that to hire one, but these are uncertain times. You hire one even if it takes every single coin, you understand? You've got a trip ahead of you and a Lightbringer is more important than food where you're going."

The darkness, Alesh thought, *he means the darkness.* The thought of leaving the city made his blood run cold, but he managed a nod. The Lightbringers were men who hired out their services in escorting travelers safely across the breadth of Entarna. Alesh had seen several of the men as they brought dignitaries or nobles to the Chosen's castle, and from what he'd seen, they were a grim lot. Men with hard, cold eyes, men who had seen what waited in the darkness when the lights went out, who had seen the worst evil the world had to offer and expected to see more before they were done.

The Lightbringers often carried large rucksacks slung over their backs. These bags contained common light-producing objects such as torches, flint and tinder, and lanterns, but they were also said to hold more exotic items such as an herbal ointment that, when rubbed on the skin, made it glow with a bright, but temporary luminosity, and others that were a secret kept only for guild members. About their person, hung from their belts and jerkins, the Lightbringers carried small torches, dangerously flammable herbs and roots, and other objects, the purpose of which Alesh could only guess. They also, more often than not, sported burns on their hands and arms, sometimes even their faces. The other servants of the castle had sometimes made mock of the Lightbringers and their strange appearance, but never Alesh. He had seen what the darkness held and there was something, in his mind at least, almost sacred, almost holy, about those men and women who braved its dangers.

He was reminded of a book he'd once read in the library titled *The Night Wars: Bringing the Darkness to Light*. The author, a Bishop of Amedan, had primarily focused on the Chosen and their role in the Night Wars, but he'd confessed to little knowledge of the Lightbringers or their origins, noting only that there was said to be a time, thousands of years ago, before the nightlings first vanished from the land of Entarna, that every girl and boy were taught their ways from a young age.

Whether or not it was true, the author hadn't known, but he'd went on to say that when the creatures reappeared so, too, had the Lightbringers, though in far fewer numbers and with far less knowledge than it was said they once possessed.

Carefully, Alesh slipped the Evertorch into the pocket of his trousers and turned back to Erwin. "Why are you helping me?" He asked, "You're supposed to serve the Chosen."

The guard nodded, rubbing at his short beard, "And so I do. I have served Olliman for fifteen years, and I will serve him always, but I will not forsake Amedan no matter what Kale says." He paused for a moment. "The Chosen cared for you, Alesh. You were like a son to him, I think. Now go."

"Come with me."

The guard shook his head, "I cannot. My family—" he frowned, waving a hand dismissively. "There's no time. There are no guards at the entrance right now, but it won't be long before the others come for the shift change." He drew a dagger from his tunic and gave it to Alesh. "Take it and go."

Alesh nodded, swallowing hard. "Thank you, Erwin."

The man waved a hand dismissively, "Find Chosen Tesharna, Alesh. Tell her what's happened."

Alesh swallowed hard, nodding, "I will, Erwin. I promise." He stepped into the shadowed hallway, walking into the darkness. "Damn you, Kale," he whispered fiercely, "You'll pay for what you've done. I promise you, you'll pay." He glanced back once more at Erwin, standing pale-faced in the lantern light, then he tucked the dagger into his belt and, ignoring the throbbing aches that riddled his body, he ran.

CHAPTER TWENTY

ALESH ASCENDED THE STAIRS AND was relieved to see that no guards stood watch. Cautiously, he peered out of the door then slipped into the hallway, making his way through the servant's corridors.

At his room, he crept inside and eased the door shut behind him. Then he stripped out of his bloody, soiled clothes and was shocked to see the dark purple bruises covering his body. He hurried to dress in fresh trousers and a linen shirt then he wrapped the Evertorch in a strip of cloth and slipped it into his pocket. This done, he grabbed a bag and stowed away a change of clothes as well as the dagger Erwin had given him. He gave one final look to the room which had been his home since he was a child then he turned and walked out.

As he made his way out of the castle, he was surprised again by how empty the servant's hallways were. He supposed he should have been grateful, but instead the silence, the absence of the usual bustle of hurrying servants, seemed ominous, and with each step he took, the air within the corridors grew more and more oppressive, until he felt as if he couldn't breathe for the stillness, the silence.

He gasped a sigh of relief when he finally emerged in the stables. He crept past the stalls, wincing as some of the horses snorted and nickered, and slid through a crack in the stable doors.

Outside, Alesh froze, all thoughts of stealth, all worries of being caught swept away in shock. Ilrika was burning. Flames shot up high in the air, pillars of smoke grasping like huge, vapory fingers. Even from where he was, the smell of ash and cooked meat filled his nostrils, and he gagged. *It's burning,* he thought, *just like in my dream. The whole city's burning. No,* he thought, struggling to get control of his galloping heart, *not the whole city. Only parts.* In fact, the vast majority of the fires seemed to be happening in the poor quarter and the town square; the town square where, earlier that day, minstrels and jugglers were supposed to have put on a show. The town square where Sonya and Abigail had gone. *Chorin, I'm coming,* he thought desperately as he broke into a shuffling run, *keep them safe.*

The streets were alive with screams. The same street that had, that morning, been filled with people going about the business of living, hoping to make a profit or have a good time, was now a place of death from which all hope had faded. The smoke hung over the city, a gray veil, so that Alesh could only see a few feet in any direction, but it did nothing to block out the screams that seemed to come from all around him. Alesh stuck to the shadows as much as possible, his eyes studying the gloom around him as he uneasily made his way through the city street. He came upon two men thrashing on the ground, clawing and biting at each other, both of them bloody and snarling like animals as they fought. He made his way quickly past and was thankful when, in moments, the gloom swallowed their struggling, manic forms.

He passed by several shops, the windows and doors of which had been broken out and even now men and women were climbing out of them carrying away goods ranging from food to clothing to jewelry with no apparent concern for *what* they looted, so long as they stole something. As he watched, a middle-aged woman dropped an armful of precious jewels and necklaces and, with a savage, inhuman scream, rushed at a man twice her size who was carrying an armful of cheaply-made linens. The man bellowed in feral rage and, for a moment, faltered under the viciousness of the woman's attack. When he finally managed to push her off, he streamed blood from his arms and chest where she'd clawed him, and one of his cheeks hung in a bloody ruin where she'd bitten it. She charged again, but this time the man was ready for it, and he used his superior strength to stop her charge then he grabbed the woman by her tousled, lank hair and slammed her head into the cobbles of the street with a wet *thump*. The woman's body seemed to deflate as she went still, but the man wasn't finished, continuing to smash her face into the cobbles as he growled and grunted like some hateful beast.

Alesh fought back his rising gorge and turned, hurrying away. *We were worried about the night walkers,* he thought, wiping a hand across his eyes, *when we should have been worried about ourselves.*

He continued on in a numb haze, hopelessness settling heavy on his shoulders. Even if he *did* somehow manage to reach Valeria and speak with Chosen Tesharna what good would it do? How could you save people from themselves?

Further on, he came upon overturned carts and carriages their contents—what little the looters and thieves had left—spilled out onto the stone cobbles like so much garbage. Necklaces and bracelets that would have cost an average worker a year's salary lay broken and discarded as if of no worth, hand-made dresses and clothing that some tailor had spent hours of labor on lay in dirty, soiled heaps. Alesh thought that he had never seen anything quite so sad, so solid a proof of civilization's fragility. But then he saw the bodies.

They lay under and around the carts, their expressions slack, their gazes dead and still, just another broken thing in a street full of broken things. At first, the dead all seemed to be merchants, men and women who'd toiled throughout the year and come to the city in hopes of making a profit, and instead finding only death, gaining only the silence, the peace of the grave.

As he drew closer to the city square, however, he began to see the bodies of men and women of all ages, some dressed in the simple homespun that marked them as peasants, others in the fine accoutrements of noblemen and women, their status and money scant protection against the madness that gripped the city.

Staring at one broken, bloody form after the next, Alesh felt some belief he'd had about the world, about its people, bend then finally break under the strain, a frost-laden limb snapping under winter's unavoidable truths.

He'd looked away from the street and its grizzly decorations when something on a nearby building caught his eye, and he gasped in disgust and horror. The man hung from the building, his hands and feet nailed to its wooden surface. His stomach had been ripped open, and his guts hung out like pink vines, dangling in stringy, bloody ropes. His skin was charred in places, as if he'd been burned, and a gaping gash had been carved in his neck, the front of his ragged shirt covered in dried blood. Alesh wanted to look away, but his eyes wouldn't obey his commands as a dark fascination took him. He'd seen the man before, hadn't he? Yes, of course he had. It had been hard to tell at first, what with the blood and the burns, but the corpse was that of the man who'd been selling nightling charms in the marketplace, the man who Abigail had scolded.

Alesh's stomach lurched and the next thing he knew he was on his knees, spewing his guts out onto the ground in rasping heaves. The man had been a fraud, but he hadn't deserved this. No one did.

When his stomach finally stopped convulsing, Alesh wiped at his mouth with the sleeve of his tunic, stood on wobbly legs, and pressed on, each step taking him further into nightmare. The further he went, the worse the defilement got, as if the city had been overtaken by disease, some cancer, and the heart of it was at the town square. The bodies grew in number until finally they were stacked on one another in small gruesome piles. A group of what appeared to be at least twenty dead lay in a line against a wall, their throats slit. Not random killings, not this. An execution.

Suddenly, he felt exhausted, was overcome with the almost irresistible urge to collapse in the street, to wait for his own death to find him. But fear for his friends drove him on, and soon he came upon the square itself. In the center, the statue of Amedan stood as it always had, the god depicted as an older man in a white robe, a torch held high in one hand, the other grasping the hilt of a sword scabbarded at his side. Amedan. The Light Maker. The statue had been defaced by vandals. Both of the god's eyes had been hacked out, his marble ears sheared off. Blood and what looked like human waste had been smeared all over the statue's surface.

A blind, deaf god, Alesh thought, feeling light-headed, *at least some things don't change.* The statue was ringed by the corpses of men, women, and children, some of their hands still clasped in silent prayer to a god with no eyes to see and no ears to hear.

Alesh shuffled around the square, searching the corpses for signs of his friends, oblivious of the tears that cut lines through the dirt and grime on his face. He was halfway around when a group of corpses caught his eye. There were five in all and, unlike the others, these wore the black and red uniforms of the Redeemers. One of them was short an arm, another a leg, and all of their faces were twisted in hate and rage, as if even death was not enough to quell their thirst for violence.

Then he saw him. Chorin sat with his back against the corner of a nearby alleyway, standing sentinel over its entrance even in death. His sword, covered in the blood of the Redeemers he'd slain, was still clutched in his fist, his blank stare turned not to where the Redeemers were, but instead toward the alley. Two more dead men in red and black uniforms lay near the big guard. His friend was covered in dozens of bloody slashes, several of which would have been mortal wounds, but his face, even now, wore a grim, crimson mask of determination. Gone was his knowing smile and his easy charm. Instead, he'd become just another corpse in a city full of them, some still walking and breathing, but corpses just the same.

Alesh fell to his knees beside his friend. "Gods, Chor," he rasped, "I'm so sorry." He decided then that the children had been right; he *was* cursed. If not for him, Chorin would be safe, alive and well, most likely tucked away in bed with the Lady Uriel. *Find them,* he'd said, *keep them safe.*

The Redeemers may have done the work, but with those words, he'd killed his friend. He looked at the blood-slicked blade in his friend's hand, thought of how easy it would be. A quick slice, a little pain, and then nothing. After a time, Alesh withdrew the scabbard from Chorin's belt and clipped it onto his own. He reached for Chorin's sword, the short, double-edged sword given as an honor to any man deemed worthy of guarding Amedan's Chosen and his people, but his friend gripped it stubbornly as if even in death he was reluctant to relinquish that honor, that duty.

Finally, Alesh managed to pry the blade from the cold stiff fingers. It felt impossibly heavy in his grip, as if he hadn't taken just the sword at all, but had taken upon himself the burden of duty that went along with it. He considered it for a moment, studied the blade, the sharpness of it. A minute passed, then another. Finally, Alesh shook his head like a man emerging from a dream and looked away from the blade and its deadly promise. The handle was in the shape of a torch, the cross-guard formed by the flames that came out of it. It was the mark of Amedan, the sword a tool of his servants, and the thought was almost enough to make Alesh throw it to the ground. *It's only a blade,* he told himself, *no different than the ones you trained with during your bouts with Kale.*

But that wasn't true, was it? Before, when he'd been given one by the Chosen, it had been only for training, for practice. Now, he was faced with the definite possibility that he would be forced to use the sword to defend himself, possibly even to kill another person. He wondered if the blade would grow heavier as the days drew on or, worse yet, lighter, so that eventually a man would grow used to that length of steel and its deadly purpose. The thought made bile rise in his throat. He swallowed hard, walked to a nearby corpse of one of the Redeemers and wiped the blade clean before tucking it into its scabbard, feeling a wash of relief when the blade was out of his hands.

In the distance, someone screamed, but he paid it scant attention. Given time, he decided, a man could grow used to anything. It was not a pleasant thought. He examined the corpses of the Redeemers and Chorin again, the numbness that had settled over him lending him an almost clinical detachment. Apparently, Chorin had fought them off here then retreated to the alleyway. He must have been dreadfully outnumbered, but instead of turning to run, he'd fought on, taking injury after injury until finally he'd fallen.

Why didn't you run, Chor? Alesh thought sadly, *Why wouldn't you run ... unless.* His eyes widening with realization, he hurried forward and glanced down the alleyway. Shadows and darkness. No way of knowing what might lie beyond it, but he felt all too certain that he *did* know. A cold knot of dread building in his stomach, Alesh grabbed a torch from a nearby body, lit it using the guttering flames from one of the buildings and stepped into the darkness.

He didn't have to go far before he came upon Abigail. Her face was so badly battered that it was unrecognizable, but the dress was the same she'd worn only the day before. An arrow stuck out of her back. Alesh sank onto the cobbles of the street, oblivious of the blood and the biting flies that roused and landed on him. He sat there for a time—how long, he would never know—then, he screamed. He screamed out his own rage, his own hate, let it blend into some dreadful harmony with the song of the dying city around him and, for a time, he knew nothing more.

When he came to, he was hunkered over Abigail's body, gripping the hilt of the sword so tightly that his hand ached. "There's nothing left," he whispered harshly. "No one. Night take you," he growled, staring at the sky, glaring into that star-covered vastness where it was said Amedan sat enthroned, watching over his people, "Why can't you help us? *Why?*" Nothing. Only the silence and the dead.

He again considered the sword at his side, thought with something almost like relief about the sharpness of it, about how quickly it would do its work. *But what of Sonya?* A voice in his head that didn't seem like his own asked, *What of her? She might still be alive.*

"She's dead," he muttered, "Just like all the rest. She has to be."

If that's true, the voice said, *then where is she?*

Reluctantly, he rose. It took more effort than he'd ever thought it would, but he rose just the same. She *might* still be alive. It was doubtful, almost impossible, but she *might* be. And Kale. Alesh's face twisted into a snarl at the thought, though he wasn't aware of it. Yes, Kale was alive. Him and the Redeemers, Falen Par, and the rest. The men and women who'd brought Ilrika to this. *They'll pay,* a voice inside of his head assured him, and this time the voice was entirely his own, *I'll kill them all, every night-cursed one of them.*

CHAPTER TWENTY-ONE

HE'D DROPPED THE TORCH AND had to relight it before continuing on. If the Chosen had been like a father to him, Abigail like a mother, then Sonya had been his little sister, so full of life and innocence ... so vulnerable. The finding of her corpse would, he did not doubt, push him over the edge, would make of him even less than the savages that now wondered the city, killing and looting. Still, she was out there and, one way or the other, he would find her.

He saw no sign of her as he walked and, after a few minutes, the alleyway emptied out onto another street, another tableau of death and fire and madness. Grimly, he examined the dozens of bodies that littered the street, and with each small, child's body he turned over only to find that it wasn't her, with each desperate feeling of relief that struck him, a little of him died.

He searched on, taken by a sort of fatalistic madness, turning over the mutilated corpses and peering into their faces until he'd checked every body that littered the avenue, until his hands were covered in the blood of innocents, then he shuffled to the next street and began again.

The distant screaming had stopped during his search, and the only sounds were that of his own hoarse breaths, the crackling of fires throughout the city, and the almost imperceptible wheeze let out by each corpse as he moved them, as if the dead were trying to speak to him. But if they spoke, it was in a language he did not know. Not yet. After a time, a shout broke the near-silence. Alesh turned and saw five Redeemers approaching on the other end of the street, watching him the way one might watch a wild animal that has escaped its pen.

His hand was on the hilt of his sword before he knew it. His chest heaved not with fear, but with a sudden, implacable fury, demanding vengeance. The men must have seen something of the madness lurking in his gaze, for they hesitated as he turned to them, a silent snarl twisting his face, the blood of the city's dead covering him.

He took a step toward them, his mouth twisting into a cruel grin then a single thought broke through the red haze that had settled on his thoughts. *Sonya. You have to find her.* He teetered, shaking with the anger, the hate that begged to be released. *She's counting on you,* the voice told him, *Erwin's counting on you.*

Alright, he thought, *alright.* He would wait. For now. But when it was done, he promised himself he'd butcher every man that dared to wear that red cloak. Pain like fire lanced through the scar on his shoulder as he stared at the men, but he ignored it. The Chosen had thought you could reason with some men, but he had been wrong and people had died for his trust. Alesh would not make the same mistake. Men like these had killed everyone he cared about, and he would make them pay. But not yet. He had promises to keep, first.

One of the men held his sword uncertainly and stepped forward. Alesh growled, and the man froze. "Not yet," he grated, his voice harsh, "but soon." The men glanced at each other as if he was mad, and that was alright. Maybe he was. Maybe they all were. He turned his back on them and slowly stalked away. The soldiers watched as he disappeared into the darkness of a nearby alleyway, fading like some phantom of blood and shadow. They did not follow.

CHAPTER TWENTY-TWO

RION TIRINIAN WATCHED THE DICE chase each other across the table with the same rapt attention husbands reserved for their lovers or priests for their gods. *Let the priests have their worship and the nobles their mistresses,* he thought as he studied the tumbling dice. To Rion, no woman's touch was ever as enchanting, no god ever as mysterious, as divine, as a card not shown, a gamble not yet won, or, as was now the case, dice on the move.

Motionless, they were nothing but small, crudely-made wooden cubes with symbols etched into their sides, but, once thrown, they transformed, tumbling through a world of possibilities, of chance, the depth and complexity of which sometimes left Rion nearly breathless.

After what felt like an eternity, the dice came to rest showing two ones and that moment of excitement ended. Suddenly bored, Rion leaned forward, his thin, delicate hands dragging the coins across the table to his own growing stack. "You torch-burning, cheat," Jorin growled, "no one throws the god's eyes three times in a row. No one wins that much."

Rion sighed. Jorin was a big man, at least twice Rion's own size, with meaty arms and a meatier gut, compliments of the large quantities of ale he drank. Said gut was pressed tightly against the table as he leaned forward, scowling at Rion through narrowed-eyes. He'd once been a soldier in Tesharna's small standing army until he'd been discharged from service. The stories people told—always out of Jorin's hearing—disagreed on the manner of the big man's dismissal from the army, but Rion suspected he knew well enough.

The man had a temper like a gelded bull. He was a brawler and a drinker, but Rion didn't believe it was any of these vices that had led him to being forced to hire himself out as a guard to the merchant's guild. After all, of all the things that Jorin was, he was a gambler more than anything else. In Rion's estimation, it was this quality, this vice that kept him from being a complete bore. "You know I never cheat, Jorin," he said, his voice soft and cultured despite the simple linen trousers and ragged shirt he wore.

"He's right, Jorin," The chubby merchant's son Mikael ventured from the other side of the table, wincing as if in anticipation of a blow, "Rion doesn't cheat. He's just got a Chosen's own luck, that's all."

Gods forbid, Rion thought. Who wanted to spend their lives ruling cities, responsible for protecting and looking after people too stupid to protect themselves? Who wanted to mediate disputes between pampered nobles who spent their time arguing over ownership of this foot hill or that wheat field, or to listen to grieving peasants complain about their cruel masters or being cheated on their wages? He wondered, not for the first time, how humans had survived as long as they had. Creatures prowled the night, killing anyone foolish enough to be out when the sun went down and, by all accounts, it was getting worse, yet people couldn't see farther than their own shitty little place in the world.

Not that Rion often concerned himself with such matters. In his estimation, the Night Wars had seen no victory, only a delay of the inevitable extinction of mankind, and his bet—if bets were taken on such a thing—would have been that one day the nightlings alone would rule Entarna. But that day was not yet, not now. It sat somewhere in the distant future, on the other side of many dice throws and card hands, and he made a habit of giving it no more thought than necessary.

After all, he had his own shitty little place to concern himself with. He smiled at the thought and realized it might not have been the most politic response as Jorin scowled, balling meaty hands the size of dinner platters into fists. Mikael swallowed nervously, and Rion stifled a yawn as he waited. The fact that the ex-soldier felt cheated held little interest for him. Either he would decide to do something about it, or he would not, and either way presented its own possibilities. Subtly, Rion shifted so that his hand was close to the blade concealed beneath his tunic, confident that his cloak, a tattered, frayed thing that he had bought from a homeless man, would hide the movement.

Jorin studied him for another moment then sat back in his chair with a grunt. "Carry on, Mikael, you useless bastard. It's your throw." Rion let a small smile crease his lips and leaned forward in anticipation as the chubby man obediently picked up the dice. He didn't win another throw, but that was alright, since he was still far ahead for the night. Winning too much attracted attention, attention that a man like him couldn't afford. He knew, deep down, that he needed the money, but when the dice were rolling, when the cards were landing with ringing finality, the final product of chance determined, he always lost interest.

Since he was little, it had never been the money that had interested Rion— he'd lost far more money than any of the men around him had ever owned. Perhaps, then, what intrigued him were the possibilities, the seemingly random throws of fate and chance, like some grand abstract in which a man could glimpse a deeper purpose, a deeper meaning. After all, what was life except a random throw of fate and chance? *Shit,* he thought as he waited eagerly for the next throw, *maybe I just like to gamble.*

It wasn't until several hours later that he left the tavern and stepped out into the shadowed streets. By Chosen Tesharna's order, large, slow-burning lanterns hung at regular intervals from poles erected for the purpose, but even the light of so many flames could not chase away the shadows that clung to the sides of the shops and the edges of the street. The Chosen had claimed that the lights were to ward off nightlings, but as far as Rion knew, none of the creatures had ever breached the imposing walls of Valeria to enter into the city itself. Perhaps, the news of attacks in Ilrika, the realm's largest city, had made the Chosen nervous, and though he wondered how the night walkers managed to break through the walls of a city that was said to have even more formidable defenses than Valeria, he suspected that the lights were intended to ward off the evil of men more than any creature of the night.

In truth, the Chosen's efforts to eradicate crime in the city had been less than a complete success. For all her efforts, she had only really managed to widen the gap between normal criminals and the true lords of the underground. Men with wits as well as ruthlessness, men who were always long gone before the city guard arrived. Personally, Rion didn't mind. The crime bosses served a purpose; criminals ranging from petty pick-pockets to thugs even to assassins could all find work and a family, of sorts. As long, of course, as they were willing to contribute a percentage of their earnings to the boss in question. Sure, Valeria's crime lords might not be what attracted visitors to the city, but they had their uses. Their constant in-fighting and the accompanying deaths helped to check any possible population problems the city might face in the future, and a man who was able to use his wits could make a fortune playing one side against the other.

Besides, Rion thought as he turned down a dark alleyway, pretending not to notice the two shadows that separated themselves from the wall behind him, *They make life so much more interesting.*

The men were good at their work, masking the sounds of their footfalls by timing them perfectly to his own, and had he not been looking for them, he doubted he ever would have seen them coming. Of course, Rion *always* watched the shadows, always calculated the odds, considered the possibilities in everything. He'd done so since he was a child, and years spent gambling in back alley card games and dice rolls where a man wagered not only his coins, but often his life as well, had only sharpened that natural tendency.

The only light in the alleyway came from a lantern from the wall about halfway down. He kept his eyes turned away from it as he drew closer in order to maintain his night vision. He judged it had been a quarter hour since he'd left the tavern, long enough for his eyes to have adjusted as much as they would to the night's shadows.

He continued on slowly, as if he was a man with no worries or cares in the world as the men stalked behind him. When he drew parallel with the lantern, he lunged toward it, careful to keep his eyes away from the light, and in one motion turned and threw it at where he thought one of the two figures was.

There was a shout of surprise and the lantern shattered in a shower of bright, fiery light as one of the men swatted it out of the air with a weapon that had no doubt been intended for Rion. He kept his eyes low to the ground until the last spark of the light faded and the men cursed. "Where did the bastard go?" One of the men asked.

Slowly, soundlessly, Rion crept closer to the vague shapes of their shadowed outlines. "How the fuck should I know?" The other man growled back, "I can't see a damned thing."

"It's the light," Rion said from beside the second man, "it wreaks havoc on the night vision."

The man gasped in surprise swinging something that, in the darkness, could have been a blade or a club. Rion ducked the clumsy, blind blow then smashed the hilt of his dagger into the man's head. The thug let out a grunt and crumpled, Rion gliding away before he hit the ground. The other man gave a cry and lunged forward, swinging wildly, and Rion stepped smoothly to the side, keeping his breathing shallow and quiet. There was a chance the man would hear him, that he would turn and stab out and that would be the end of it. But, then, the chance was what made things interesting.

Instead of swinging again, the man paused, his breathing ragged, "Pellam? He asked, his voice a whisper, and in the darkness Rion could see him turning left and right, holding his weapon in front of him uncertainly, his eyes not yet adjusted to the darkness around him, "Pellam, are you there? What in the name of the Light is going on?"

"Pellam's not able to talk just now," Rion said, side-stepping the man's panicked swing. The man swung again, and this time Rion stepped forward, drawing the blade from his tunic and slashing at the man's exposed hand.

The thug cried out, and his weapon clattered to the ground. Before he could recover, Rion skipped forward and kicked him in the shin, hard. The man howled and fell over backward, at once trying to comfort his aching leg and wounded hand. "Now then," Rion said, as he crouched down and let the bloody steel of his blade rest against the man's throat, "I get the feeling you gentlemen wish a parley."

The man froze at the feel of the cold steel against his neck. "A ... what the fuck are you talking about?" He asked through gritted teeth, his bloody hand cradled against his chest.

Rion sighed, "You wanted to talk?"

"My hand ... You'll pay for that, prick. I'll see you dead."

Rion smiled in the darkness, "We all die sooner or later," he said, "It's the one bet even a fool could win. Now, why were you following me?"

"Night take you," the man growled, the pain clear in his voice.

Rion lowered the blade, and the man hissed as the steel kissed his neck drawing a thin line of blood, "Alright, alright," he sputtered, "Sigan sent us. We was supposed to remind you about the money you owe him."

Rion rubbed wearily at his temples. The thing about borrowing large sums of money from crime lords is that they always wanted it back. "*Were*," he corrected.

"Huh?" The man asked.

Rion waved a hand dismissively, "Forget it. So what?" He asked, not withdrawing the dagger, "You were supposed to rough me up a little bit, scare me into bringing his money to him?"

The man grunted, as still as a statue under the cold steel. Oh yes, he was a professional alright. "Something like that. Sometimes folks forget what they owe, so Sigan sends us out to refresh their memory. We weren't goin' to kill you or nothin'."

"No, I don't suppose you were," Rion agreed. "Still, I consider it bad manners to sneak up on a man while he's out for a stroll, don't you?"

The man swallowed hard, his fists clenching and unclenching at his sides, "I was just doin' my job, friend. Nothing personal."

Rion nodded slowly, reaching his other hand out and grasping the short, crude club the man had carried, "I understand. You were just doing your job, the same as a dockworker or a whore. Still, a man—like a whore—has to take responsibility for his actions, wouldn't you say?"

He felt the man tense beneath the blade, "I'm not su—"

Rion brought the heavy club down, and the man screamed as his fingers snapped and broke like dried twigs. He jerked as if to sit up, but the blade stopped him, and he fell back down, panting heavily, his face pale and damp with sweat. "You stupid bastard," he hissed through clenched teeth, "We were just going to rough you up before, scare you a little. After this, Sigan will make sure you're a long time in dying."

"If that's the case," Rion said, leaning forward, "then I don't suppose there's much point in keeping you alive, is there?"

"W-wait. Okay, okay. Just tell me what you want."

"How about an apology?"

"You've got to be kidding me," the man snarled.

"If this is a joke," Rion said quietly, "then you really don't want to hear the punch line."

"Fine, okay, man, whatever you say," he spat, "I'm sorry, alright? I'm real fucking sorry."

Rion nodded, suddenly bored. The dice had landed, and he'd won. *No one wins that much*, Jorin had said, and he'd been right. A man couldn't always win—he just had to win when it mattered. He withdrew the blade and rose, "You tell Sigan, when you see him, that the next time he sends someone after me I'll send him back a corpse, you got it? And after that, I'm coming for him."

The man's eyes widened, "You must be out of your damned mind he'll ki—" He must have seen something in Rion's eyes because he stopped, took a deep, shuddering breath, and nodded, "I'll tell him," he grated.

"Good, now get your friend and get out of here."

The man rose, cradling his ruined hand against his chest, his eyes never leaving the blade. Then he turned and stumbled toward his partner, kicking him to rouse him. The unconscious man mumbled something incoherent then the other kicked him again, harder. He sat up then, speaking in a slow, slurred voice, "W-what happened?"

"Come on," the first man growled, "get on your feet. We're gettin' out of here."

The man stood unsteadily, "What about the mark?"

"Never mind the fucking mark. Move your ass."

Rion watched them shuffle back the way they'd come. Once he was satisfied they weren't turning around, he tossed the cudgel onto the cobbles, sheathed his dagger, and started away.

He prowled the streets aimlessly for a while, taking roads and alleyways seemingly without purpose and always watching to see if anyone was following him. When he was satisfied that he was trailed by nothing but his own shadow, long and thin in the light of the street lanterns, he turned, leaving the beggars and petty criminals of the poor quarter behind and headed toward the northern part of the town, to the expansive mansions and elaborate houses of the noblemen and women of Valeria. He took several other roundabout paths, stopping once to get a drink at an inn before continuing on in order to make absolutely certain no one was trailing him.

Because of this, the trip took over twice the time it normally would, but it was necessary. Rion the gambler was known in many parts of the poor district for his quiet demeanor, his cultured speech, and his almost unbelievable luck in any gamble. The few who cared enough to guess assumed that he was either a fallen priest—shunned for his inability to resist the temptation of a wager—or a failed scholar suffering from the same affliction. What they didn't guess, what Eriondrian Tirinian would do almost anything to *keep* them from guessing, was that he was actually the only son and heir of one of the city's most powerful noble houses.

Rion didn't know what would happen to him, or his family, if the entire city—the other nobles, not to mention Sigan and the other crime lords—discovered the truth about his identity, but it was one gamble he wasn't prepared to take.

CHAPTER TWENTY-THREE

ONCE HE WAS IN THE rich quarter, Rion headed toward *The Golden Torch*. The inn wasn't a particularly good one—the ale was watered down and the serving girls too fat for his tastes—but it had the distinct benefit of being the closest place to the poor district. Strictly speaking, it wasn't illegal for members of the poor quarter to travel the finer roads of the northern parts of the city, but patrol guards grew bored sometimes, as any man did, and legalities didn't mean a whole lot, if they decided some uppity beggar needed to be shown his place.

He went through the back entrance and made his way to his rented room. Once there, he changed into clothes more fitting his station: a rich, blue doublet, black trousers, and a pair of fine black leather boots. He traded his tattered cloak for a full length one of black velvet lined with fur, and fastened it on one side with a silver brooch.

He studied himself in the mirror. A thin man—his mother would have said too thin—with black hair tied in a ponytail that reached past his shoulders, and a face that, he thought, could have almost been handsome if not for the sharpness of it. Still, handsome or not, there were women enough to be had if he wanted them; his family's fame and their believed fortune attracted them like bees to honey.

He slid the bed aside, pulled up a loose floor plank, and peered inside. Coins ranging from the small, drab Dusks to the larger Dawns and a dozen or so golden Suns glittered back at him. He took the night's winnings, a handful of Dusks a few Dawns, and a Sun, and put them with the rest, wondering idly how many of the noblewomen who asked after him, who batted their lashes and whispered as he passed, would still do so if they knew that his family's fortune was no more real than the affection they claimed to possess, but he didn't wonder long. A man could catch bees with honey but without it? Well, it was a big world, wasn't it?

He replaced the board, slid the bed back into place, and headed out of the inn, taking the front entrance this time. Mistress Aberdine, the owner of the inn, didn't speak or glance up from her place at the counter as he strode past her and through the nearly empty common room. *As well she shouldn't,* he thought sourly. The jewels the heavy-set widow so loved to wear, as well as the dresses with plunging necklines that would have appeared too forward on a woman half her age and a third her size, were paid for by that silence, by that disinterest.

A short time later, he strode down the stone pathway of his family's manse, in between the rows of finely-trimmed hedges, past the marble carving of several swans whose mouths acted as fountains, perpetually fluting out water. They were beautiful, but every time he looked at them, Rion could almost feel his purse growing lighter. The damned statues might spit out water, but, as far as he was concerned, they drank money. Still, some facades had to be maintained and there was no use worrying over it.

The house was dark except for the light of a lantern, spilling into the hallway from the open door that led to his father's study. Stifling a yawn, Rion hung his own cloak—Fermin, their manservant—having been in bed for hours gone, and started toward his room. As he tread along the richly-embroidered rugs covering the floor, his mind automatically began to calculate how many dice throws, how many hands of cards, each was worth, but he cut those thoughts off with a will. He had enough worries already without depressing himself further.

He was just slipping past his father's study when a voice came from inside, "Eriondrian? Is that you?"

He hesitated in the shadows, weary beyond belief and wanting nothing but to crawl into bed and fall into a deep sleep. Finally, he reluctantly walked inside. His father was seated in a cushioned chair, the book he'd been reading draped over its arm. "Son," the old man asked with a smile, studying him from behind the thick spectacles he wore, "you're in late."

Sight was not the only thing age had taken from the patriarch of Rion's house. It was said that years ago, before Rion was born, his father, Albert, had been a handsome, well-built man, and he held many trophies from his wins in tournament games. Looking at him now, a small, shriveled old man that seemed to be swallowed by the chair in which he sat, with a few wisps of grey hair on his nearly-bald head, and liver-spotted hands that never ceased their trembling, Rion, almost couldn't believe it. "Hello, father," he said, forcing a smile past his weariness, "I apologize for the hour. There was some pressing business with the latest shipment that I had to attend to."

"Oh?" His father asked, "Is it anything I can help you with, my boy?"

Sure, if you can find us another fortune. Know where one might be lying about? Rion shook his head, "It's fine, father. Just a small matter and easily dealt with. I can handle it."

"I don't doubt that, my boy," his father said, smiling, "Since you've taken over the business, you've done better than I ever did." He met his eyes then, the rheumy, nearly sightless orbs looked milky and foggy behind the spectacles he wore, "I'm proud of you, son."

Rion felt a stab of guilt. When his father had been a young man, nearly fifty years ago, he'd taken what was a small inheritance and invested it in trade, buying caravans and hiring merchants and guards to oversee land trade to other cities. Under his father's leadership, the business had prospered, and in time Albert Tirinian had turned his meager inheritance into a kingly fortune. Ten years ago, when Rion turned twenty, and Albert's sight had grown so bad that he wasn't able to read the ledgers anymore, he'd given over management of the business to his son.

For a time, things had gone smoothly. Rion had always had a head for numbers and risks, but when the nightlings began to reappear a few years ago the business had begun to lose money despite his greatest efforts. Few were the merchants who would travel the roads with such dangers waiting in the night, and by the time Rion paid for a Lightbringer escort, he barely broke even on the trip. That, of course, wasn't considering the cost of food, guards, and the inevitable looting by bandits in the woods. The truth was, the business had hemorrhaged money for years until finally Rion had stopped trying. He still sent caravans out from time to time, so that his father and anyone else who had a mind to look would see them, but they were always empty, their guards paid well to look busy and keep their mouths shut.

He'd refused to tell his aging father and mother about the truth, and he'd busily tried everything he could, investing what little money they had left in the best way he knew how, but nothing had worked. Nothing, that was, until Rion the gambler was born. "You do me too much honor, father," he said quietly, "I will never be the man you were, the man you are."

His father's gentle laughter turned into a cough. He withdrew a silk handkerchief—*two dice throws? Three?*—from his tunic with shaking hands and, for a time, the only sound was that of him hacking into it.

Rion frowned, struggling not to let his anxiety show, "You shouldn't be up this late. The physicians said that you needed your rest."

His father grunted, "It's easy for them to say. I find that the older I get, the harder it is to sleep." He waved a hand dismissively, "Anyway, we were speaking of you. You must not spend so much time with the business, son. You're young. You need to enjoy yourself, find a good woman. If there's one thing I regret about my life it's how much time I wasted working instead of spending it with you and your mother. Now," he said, leaning forward, "Promise me you'll find time to enjoy yourself. You know how your mother worries."

But I do *enjoy myself, father. More than I should.* "I promise, father. Now, it's late. Why don't you go to bed?"

Lord Tirinian sighed, "I may as well try. I don't doubt I'll spend all night staring at the ceiling, but if I fall asleep in here again your mother will have my head." With that, he rose and headed toward the door. Before he walked through he turned back, "Are you sure everything's alright, son? You seem troubled."

Rion smiled, "I'm just tired, father, that's all. Sleep well until the Light returns."

His father nodded, "Until the Light returns," he said, then turned and shuffled out the door.

As soon as he left, a frown creased Rion's face. Despite the small fortune they spent on treatment, his father still seemed weak, and sometimes he forgot things. Still, the medicine that the latest, a man from the western reaches, prescribed *did* seem to help, some at least. Thinking of the expensive elixir, Rion rose and glanced out a nearby window. The moon sat almost in the center of the sky. There was still some night left, time for a few more throws, maybe a few hands of cards. He rubbed at his burning eyes and headed for the door.

CHAPTER TWENTY-FOUR

ALESH SANK DOWN AGAINST THE side of a building and draped his hands over his knees, exhausted, numb. He'd been searching for Sonya for over two hours and had found nothing. His throat was scratchy and hoarse from shouting her name, and he'd lost count of the amount of corpses he'd looked at, the amount of dead eyes that had met his gaze.

He noticed that his hands were shaking and no matter how hard he tried he couldn't make them stop. They were covered in blood from his efforts as were the clothes he wore. If someone saw him now, they'd probably run screaming, but what difference did that make? He hadn't seen another living soul since the group of patrolling Redeemers. He supposed that the people who hadn't gone insane in their worship of Shira, the goddess of the wild, were even now hiding in their cellars and basements, cowering behind locked doors and waiting for someone to bring order to their lives once more, waiting for the city to wake from its terrible nightmare of blood and death.

A mongrel dog slunk by in the street, eyeing him warily. Something bloody was clutched in its mouth. It stopped, watching him for a moment as if trying to decide whether or not Alesh meant to steal its hard-earned meal. Then it growled and walked away, disappearing into the haze of smoke that covered the streets like fog. "She isn't here," he muttered to himself, his voice sounding as if he'd gargled broken glass, "can't be. Maybe she made it away … maybe."

Screams sounded in the distance, one or two blocks over, but he ignored them. He'd heard plenty this night, and he'd no doubt hear more before it was through. *You have much to answer for Kale,* he thought as he looked around at the bloody streets, the broken windows and broken bodies. "And answer you will, damn you," he snarled, "I'll make sure of it."

Still, he suspected that things must have gotten even more out of hand than Kale had wished. After all, there wasn't much point in being the ruler of a city of corpses, was there? *He'll send troops in the morning,* he thought, and even as he thought it he knew it was true. Glancing up at the sky, he judged that there were only a few hours left before sunrise, a few hours left before the Redeemers would march into the streets in force, reinstating order at the point of their swords.

That meant that Alesh had only a few hours to make it out of the city. But to do that meant leaving Sonya alone. *Don't be a fool,* he told himself. The fact was, he could spend days searching through the corpses and still not find her. It was pointless. But, then, what was the point in any of it? He had as much chance of making it to Valeria alone as he did of taking on the entire army of Redeemers by himself. And if somehow he *did* make it, what did it matter? The Chosen was dead. Abigail, Chorin, all dead. *But Sonya...* no. That was a fool's hope. He sat, his arms propped on his knees, and considered waiting until sunrise. The Redeemers would come, and he would kill as many as he could before he died. And how many would he get? Two? Three, maybe? No. It wasn't enough. Not nearly enough.

He climbed wearily to his feet and looked around. It took him a moment to get his bearings—in the smoke-filled, wasted landscape one street looked much like any other—but finally he decided that he must be closest to the eastern gate. Indeed, he wasn't far from the place where he'd gone what felt like years ago to oversee the rebuilding of the hole in the wall on the Chosen's behalf.

He headed toward the gate. After a few minutes, he turned a corner and was confronted with four men in the uniform of the Redeemers. They were gathered around an old man in a gray robe who lay curled in a ball in the street, his arms covering his head and face. They were laughing as they spat and kicked at the man, too preoccupied with their fun to notice Alesh standing a short distance away from them. He started to turn and walk away but stopped. *I should leave him,* he thought, *if I try to help, we'll most likely both be killed, and then who will warn the Chosen?*

He'd taken a few steps away when an image of Chorin, his friend, lying dead with his back against the wall, his body covered in his own blood, came to him. Then he thought of Abigail, the woman who'd been like a mother, lying in the street like a discarded child's doll, beaten so bad as to be almost unrecognizable. Something stirred in him then. His scar began to burn but it was a distant thing, the feel of the sword's hilt much nearer. He drew the blade from its scabbard and stalked forward on the balls of his feet.

The Redeemers were still beating on the old man and didn't notice him until a foot of steel exploded from the chest of the first, showering the others in blood. They cried out in shock and surprise and were reaching for their blades when Alesh's blade hacked into the neck of the next closest. Blood fountained from the wound, covering him, as the man's head flew from his body and rolled several feet before finally coming to a stop on the cobbled street.

Alesh brought up his blade, barely managing to deflect a strike that had been aimed at his own head. The man started to pull back for another swing, but Alesh lunged forward, calling on all of the speed and strength he'd gained from countless hours of training under the Chosen's tutelage, and slammed his fist into the man's throat.

The soldier's blade clattered to the ground as he grabbed his throat with both hands, his eyes bulging. Faintly, Alesh could hear someone screaming, but he didn't spare it any thought as he stepped forward and unceremoniously rammed the blade through the man's heart. He jerked the sword free in a spray of blood and turned to the last man.

The soldier, a youth of no more than eighteen years, watched him with wide, frightened eyes. As Alesh moved toward him, the Redeemer dropped his weapon and held both of his hands up before him, "P-please," the youth stumbled, his face pale, "I didn't m—"

His words cut off as Alesh's sword licked out and in seconds another head rolled along the cobbles. Alesh swayed on his feet, staring at the corpses, and the screams continued to echo in his ears. It wasn't until his throat began to burn as if it was on fire that he realized the screams were his own. He stopped then, expecting the guilt, the shame of what he'd done to overwhelm him. It did not come.

Four men who'd been breathing moments before, who'd laughed and talked and had lives, men with mothers and fathers, sisters and brothers, and he felt nothing more than the rawness in his throat and an ache in his hand where he held the handle of the sword in a white-knuckled grip. *Later,* he told himself, though he didn't believe it, *I'll feel it later.*

He wiped the blade clean on one of the red cloaks and slid it back into the scabbard at his waist. Then he shuffled to the old man and rolled him onto his back, but instead of the dead, vacant gaze that he'd expected, the man's eyes, a blue so dark that they were almost black, stared back at him through a mask of blood. *No,* Alesh thought, *not at me, but at something.* The man's gaze was distant, clouded, and he didn't seem to see Alesh at all. It was as if he was instead staring into some other world, some other place where, perhaps, there were no streets that smelled of smoke and death, no bodies of children littering the alleyways.

The man's gaze was so steady, so level, that Alesh started to think he was dead after all, and it wasn't until he noticed the almost imperceptible rise and fall of the old man's chest that he was sure he was alive. "Are you okay?" As soon as the words were out of his mouth, he realized how stupid they sounded. Of course the man wasn't okay; he'd been nearly beaten to death by four men for no other reason than they happened across him in the street.

"*W-why?*" The man asked. Alesh started to ask him what he meant when he realized that the man wasn't speaking to him at all. Perhaps, he spoke to someone in that other world upon which he looked.

Alesh glanced around at the corpses that littered the street then back at the old man, "Listen, you'd best go home. Sooner or later, someone else is bound to come along and … well, it's just probably best that you go home."

"*You're wrong,*" the man croaked. "P-please," he said, his eyes filling with tears, "it isn't too late … please."

Alesh was surprised by the sympathetic clutch in his chest, and the tears that gathered in his own eyes as he watched the man's suffering. He'd thought himself incapable of anymore sadness; he'd been wrong. Perhaps the gods' greatest cruelty was that no matter how much suffering men endured, they still felt each new hurt as if it was the first.

Taking in the man's distant, absent stare, and the way his hands groped for something that wasn't there, Alesh was reminded of a time, a few years ago, when there'd been a tournament in Ilrika and one of the knights had caught a hard, square hit on his helmet with a lance during a joust. He'd lived, after a fashion, but he'd never been right in the head, always talking to people who weren't there in sentences that were as nonsensical as the old man's. He wondered if this man, too, had been made a simpleton by one of the blows he'd taken.

It won't matter one way or the other if you let him bleed to death, he scolded himself. The man didn't seem aware of his hurts, but he was still bleeding freely from a deep gash on his forehead, and one of his thin arms was clearly broken. "I'll be right back," he said, but if the man heard, he gave no sign.

Alesh shuffled to one of the nearby Redeemers and tore strips from the dead man's cloak before walking back to the old man. He used one of the make-shift bandages to wipe the blood away from the old man's face then tied a strip tightly around the man's forehead.

The old man was silent while he worked. Even when Alesh used several of the long strips of linen to wrap around his shoulder and arm in a makeshift sling, even when he forced the man's arm back into place, he did not cry out. *He's farther gone than I realized,* he thought, as he finished tying the knots together. When he was finished, he glanced up at the sky and saw that the moon had sunken considerably. *An hour. Maybe two.* Listen," he said, "I've got to go."

He waited several seconds, but still the man didn't answer. Alesh had been forced to pull him to a sitting position to put on the sling, and the old man sat there unmoving, as dead to the world as if he *had* been killed. *I should have left them to their work,* he thought, *it would have been a mercy.* "I-I'm sorry," he murmured. "I have to go ... I have to tell Tesharna what happened to Olliman."

The man's eyes snapped into focus then, and his gaze whipped to Alesh who recoiled at the intensity, the gravity of that gaze. "Olliman," the man rasped, "he's dead."

Alesh froze at the words. How could he know that? Then, *of course he'd know, you fool. News travels fast and bad news fastest of all as Abigail used to say.* Thinking of the head cook made his throat grow tight, and it was all he could do to nod.

The man let out a heavy sigh, his head and shoulders drooping. He sat that way for so long that Alesh became convinced that he'd fainted. Just when he was considering whether or not to leave the man unconscious in the street, whether or not he *could*, the man spoke, "Then ... it has begun."

Alesh felt a chill at the words, the same words that Olliman himself had used only the day before. Coincidence? Surely. It *had* to be, but suddenly, he didn't want to be here, talking to this man. For reasons he didn't fully understand himself, he was terrified of what the old man might say, yet he could not stop himself from asking, "What do you mean?"

The old man gave no answer, and his gaze grew distant and unfocused once more. "What has begun?" Alesh asked again, "Damnit, what do you mean?" The man gave no sign that he heard, and Alesh sighed heavily. *And what did you expect? He's half mad from his injuries, that's obvious. He's just spouting nonsense, nothing more. And while you're wasting time here, sunrise is coming.*

Judging by the man's gray robes, Alesh suspected he was one of Amedan's priests. With the Redeemers patrolling the streets, it wouldn't be long before they found him and then ... *You can't help him,* he told himself, *you can't even help yourself.* Everyone that Alesh had cared for—except, perhaps, for Sonya—had died, and it was his fault. If he'd have told the Chosen about seeing Kale speaking with Falen Par, if he hadn't have told Chorin to go to the town square, they might still be alive now.

He rubbed at the scar on his shoulder. Abigail had told him that he wasn't cursed, that it was only a foolish thing said by foolish people. She'd been wrong. "I'm sorry," he muttered again, "I can't help you." *I can't help anyone.* With that, he turned and started down the street. He did not look back.

CHAPTER TWENTY-FIVE

He'd only gone a short distance when he heard the sound of footsteps behind him. He turned and saw that the old man was limping after him, his face showing no sign of the agony he had to be feeling.

He waited, curious, as the old man shuffled up beside him then stopped, staring at him with an expectant expression. "You don't want to follow me," Alesh said, unable to keep the bitterness from his voice, "Whatever you do, you don't want to do that."

Though the man's expression didn't change, something about his eyes did, and for a moment Alesh was reminded of the Chosen himself, of those looks he'd given on those occasions when he'd scolded him. He waited, expecting the man to say something, but he remained silent. "I mean it," he said again, his voice little more than a whisper, "You're better on your own."

He took a few more steps and was annoyed to find that the man was following him once more. "Damn you," he said, stopping and turning to face the man, "Why won't you leave me alone? Look, if you think you owe me something for saving you, you don't. I didn't do it for you. I did it ..." he paused as the faces of the dead flew through his mind. *I did it because I wanted them dead. I want all of them dead.* The Chosen would have said that there was good in all men, that they only sought the opportunity to show it, and Abigail would have taken her spoon to him, grown or not.

But Abigail was dead. The Chosen was dead, and everything that he'd built had died with him. *And I'm left, alone. Always alone. Fine,* he decided. *If he wants to follow me, let him. What difference does it make?* He thought of Sonya. What chances did a little girl have when the whole world had gone mad? What chance did anyone have? And what had Erwin expected? For Alesh to be a hero? For him to save the city? He couldn't even save a little girl who had depended on him.

He noticed that the old man was still watching him and he grunted angrily. "Do what you want," he said, "It doesn't matter anyway." He started off in the direction of the eastern gate, concentrating on nothing but putting one foot in front of the other. In time, the path on which he traveled would lead him to Valeria or, more likely, to his death. He found that, at that moment, he didn't care much which.

CHAPTER TWENTY-SIX

S͟OMEONE SCREAMED IN THE DISTANCE, and Sonya tensed, hugging her knees tightly to her chest. Fresh tears gathered in her eyes, and she rubbed at them with an angry fist. Abigail had told her to be brave, and she *wanted* to. She really did. But her back and legs hurt and even though she knew that the inn in which she hid was empty, she kept thinking she heard the footsteps of the men in the red cloaks, kept thinking that one was sneaking up on her where she hid under the bar's counter. She was being dumb. Of course she *knew* that, just as she *knew* that there wasn't anyone in the inn except her. She'd been here for hours, after all, and if someone *was* here, they'd have already got her. She knew she was alone but … but what if she wasn't? What if the men were sitting at one of the tables maybe, or standing at the counter, just waiting for the dumb little girl to come crawling out so they could grab her?

She whimpered as a cramp began to spread in her leg and rubbed at it furiously. She knew she needed to get up, to stretch her legs and aching back, but every time she started to, she remembered the men in the square, remembered the way they'd climbed onto the stage, swinging their swords, remembered the actors screaming as blood—real blood, not the red ribbons they used on their play—flew across the stage in great big streaks, like paint. She'd stared, unable to believe what was happening, until Abigail had grabbed her up and started running away from the square. But everyone in the crowd was trying to run too, bumping into each other, knocking each other down. She saw several people disappear underneath the feet of the crowd but no one stopped to help them up. After what felt like *years* they made it to the edge of the crowd, but the men in the red cloaks were there, too, hitting people with their swords.

Two of them came toward her and Abigail but then Chorin was there, swinging his own sword and knocking both the men down like a knight out of one of the stories Abigail told her when she couldn't sleep. *"Get out of here!"* He'd shouted, swinging his sword at some other soldiers that had come to help their friends. Sonya wanted to stay and help, but Abigail had grabbed her again, and they were running down an alleyway when something hit Abigail, and she fell over. Sonya looked and saw a stick poking out of Abigail. She went to grab it, but the head cook had screamed at her. *"Sonya, you have to run baby. Be brave and run!"*

So she had—she'd always been good at running. Alesh said she was as fast as a rabbit when she wanted to be. She ran until her chest burned and her legs ached and then she'd ducked into the same inn she was in now and hid under the counter. She'd been there ever since. She knew she should do something, but she didn't know what. Abigail had told her to run, and she had, but she thought even rabbits couldn't run all the time. She wished Alesh was here—Alesh always knew what to do. He was brave, too. Alesh wouldn't have hidden under a counter like a 'fraidy cat chicken, too scared to crawl out and stretch his legs and back. Besides, she was hungry and if she didn't get something to eat soon, the men in red cloaks would find her just from hearing her stomach growling.

But she didn't know if there was any food in the inn and, if there was, where to find it. And what if one of the men found her when she was looking? She let out a whimper of frustration. Abigail always said that nothing got done until you started doing it. But what was she supposed to *do?* In the stories, the princesses *always* knew what to do. If you saw a toad wearing a crown, then you kissed him, and then he became a prince, and then you kissed *him*. Of course, kissing a toad was *gross* and kissing a prince didn't seem much better, but at least the girls in the stories did *something*. The stories always talked about how wise and brave and smart they were, about the wise and brave and smart things they did. As far as Sonya knew, there were no stories about little girls who hid under counters until they were old little girls with gray hair and warts on their noses.

Be brave, Abigail had told her. And she would be. She took a slow, deep breath and was just beginning to work her way out from beneath the counter when she heard the sound of approaching voices. Holding her breath, she crawled back into the shadowed corner. Moments later, the door swung open and the fitful light of a lantern chased shadows across the walls over Sonya's head.

"I *told* you we shouldn't have come here," a woman's voice said. "The whole city's gone insane! Oh, don't give me that look. Anyway, at least we've lost them for now, I don't think—wait. What is it? Where are you going?" There was the sound of soft, measured footsteps, and Sonya's breath caught in her throat.

A moment passed, then another, and she was just about to dare to breathe when a face, wreathed in shadow, appeared only inches in front of her. She screamed as hands grabbed her and pulled her out of her hiding place.

"P-please don't hurt me," she stammered, telling herself to be brave but crying anyway.

The stranger sat her on the counter and in the dancing light of the lantern he sat down beside her she saw that his skin was a light brown, like chocolate. The man smiled a smile that reached all the way to his eyes and despite her terror, Sonya found her sobs slowing then stopping altogether. "Darl?" The woman asked as she walked over to stand beside the man. "What's going on?" She looked at Sonya and her eyes went wide with what appeared to be concern, "Oh Light save us, honey, are you alright?"

Sonya looked at the woman and her breath caught in her throat again, not with fear this time but with wonder. The woman was beautiful. Her skin was smooth, her eyes green like the grass in the castle courtyard. She had long blonde hair that tumbled around her head as she leaned in to wipe away Sonya's tears. "A-are you a princess?" Sonya asked breathlessly.

The woman laughed. It was a lilting, musical laugh, and Sonya smiled hesitantly. "No, precious, I'm not a princess. In fact, I guess I'm about as far from one as you can get. My name's Katherine, but you can call me Kat. How about you? A little girl as beautiful as you are, why if you're not a princess then the world's gone crazier than I thought."

Sonya felt herself blush, "I'm Sonya. I'm not a princess, but I do live at a castle." She paused then, swallowing past a lump in her throat, "Or I did before …."

"I know, honey," the woman said, running a gentle hand through Sonya's hair, "I know. Listen—" She cut off at the sound of someone shouting in the street. "*Night take them,*" the woman breathed as she turned to the man, "They must have heard her scream. It won't be long before they check here. We have to go."

"P-please don't leave me," Sonya blurted, surprising herself. Abigail had told her to never go anywhere with strangers, but suddenly the thought of being alone again, of being left behind by this man with the smiling eyes, and the woman with the voice like music terrified her. "I-I'll be good, I promise, I do-"

"Oh, honey," the woman said, hugging her in her arms and picking her up, "of course we're not going to leave you."

"Really?" Sonya asked tentatively, "You promise?"

The woman smiled, "I promise, sweety." She turned to the man, Sonya still in her arms, "We've got to go. What do you want to do?"

The man pointed at the two of them then to the door at the inn's back entrance. The woman nodded and started toward the door. "W-wait," Sonya stammered, suddenly scared, "h-he's not coming? But the mean men will get him. They got Chorin and … and Abigail."

The woman smiled, "It's alright, sweet one. He'll catch up soon enough. Darl has a way of dealing with mean men."

The dusky skinned man, Darl, smiled and winked at her. Another shout came from outside, much closer than the first had been, and he looked at Katherine and raised an eyebrow.

"Right," the woman said, "We'll head toward the southern gate."

The man nodded and started toward the door. The shadows seemed to shift and stir around him as he moved, then he opened the main door of the inn and disappeared into the night.

"Alright, Sonya," The woman, Kat, said, "I need you to be brave and quiet. Can you be brave?"

Sonya didn't want to go outside. The men in the red cloaks were outside. But Abigail had told her to be brave. She nodded against the woman's shoulder, not trusting herself to speak.

The woman hugged her tightly for a second then sat her down. "Don't you worry, Sonya," she said, holding her hand, and leading her toward the back door of the inn, "Everything's going to be fine."

CHAPTER TWENTY-SEVEN

ALESH BREATHED A WEARY SIGH of relief. Finally. The smoke wasn't as bad here, closer to the edge of the city, and he could make out the western gate in the distance. He'd been forced to take several back alleys and side streets, avoiding groups of soldiers as well as one group of bloody, disheveled townsfolk who ran and growled like animals on the hunt.

He turned to look behind him and shook his head in disbelief. Somehow, despite his injuries, the old priest had managed to keep pace with him and, if anything, seemed to be in better shape than Alesh himself. He waited as the old man came to stand beside him. "We need to find a Lightbringer," Alesh said, mostly to himself. "That is, if there are any left who haven't gone mad or fled the city."

The old man cocked his head to the side, "Torchbearers?"

Alesh sighed. The Torchbearers had been the elite troops of the Chosen during the Night War, the toughest, most skilled soldiers of their time. That time, of course, was long past and by now they were all dead and gone, but he didn't have time to try to explain that to the old man. Not that it would do much good. The man might be surprisingly fast for an injured old priest, but it was obvious that the beating he'd taken had left him without his wits. "Come on," Alesh said, not bothering to see if the priest followed as he started down the street.

This far from the center of the city, the streets were empty of the living, but the dead were there in their multitudes. They lay scattered across the road, their mouths slack, their faces twisted in expressions of terror and agony so intense that even death had not quelled it. A sharp twinge of pain went through his hand, and he glanced down, surprised to see that he held the bare sword in a white knuckled grip. He started to put the blade away but decided against it. There didn't seem to be anyone around, but a person could never know when their death was coming. The dead, were they able, would have no doubt said as much. Slowly, stepping carefully so as to avoid disturbing the sprawled corpses, Alesh began making his way toward a large building on the side of the street.

The Lightbringer's Guildhouse was a plain, unassuming wooden building, differing from the humble dwellings of the poor district surrounding it only in its size. It was a sprawling two story structure, several times larger than an average inn. Not surprising, really, considering the fact that it was said to house the majority of Ilrika's Lightbringers while, at the same time, providing a shelter for those from other cities whose profession brought them to Ilrika.

Some of the city's Lightbringers lived in homes of their own, with families of their own, but such men and women were the minority. The life expectancy of a Lightbringer was about what one might expect of men and women who spent their days handling chemicals and herbs that could set a man on fire in an instant and their nights surrounded by nightwalkers with nothing to keep them at bay but their own skill. This, coupled with the fact that a Lightbringer's fortune, however large or small, always reverted to the guild upon his or her death, and it was no wonder that so few of them had families.

Still, the guild members did enjoy certain privileges, and those they enjoyed equally. No matter a man's status in society, commoner or noble, he resigned it upon entering the guild and not even the most arrogant of noblemen was foolish enough to offend the Lightbringers. After all, a man could never be certain when he might need to seek their services. The guild house was a place of equality, a symbol of man's fight against the darkness, a beacon of hope for those who looked out at the darkness with dread in their hearts. Or, at least, it had been. As Alesh drew closer to the building, he saw that the massive oak doors had been smashed in and what was left of them lay heaped in the entrance like kindling.

Inside, the guild hall was silent and shrouded in shadow, as if it had finally succumbed to the darkness that its members had fought for so long. The only light in the room came from the weak moonlight shining in through the broken door. Ahead of him, Alesh could just make out the entrances of several hallways that led to the living quarters of the Lightbringers but no sounds came from them. There was only the quiet, deep and suffocating and somehow malevolent.

Alesh took a few hesitant steps forward, then felt, more than heard, someone behind him. He turned, expecting to see the old man climbing over the rubble of the doorway. Instead, he let out a grunt of surprise as a knife blade appeared out of the darkness, stopping less than an inch from his throat. "Who the fuck are you?"

The man's voice was rough, as if his throat had been burned. He was a head shorter than Alesh, and even in the weak light of the moon, Alesh could see that his dark beard was patchy where scars covered his chin and cheeks. "My name's Alesh," he said softly, not daring to move a muscle as he felt the tip of the blade at his throat.

"And your family name?"

Alesh felt the familiar twinge of loss, "I ... don't have one."

"That so?" The man asked, "Just another bastard in a city full of 'em, eh? Well, where are the rest of your friends?"

"Friends?" Alesh asked uncertainly.

"Don't play stupid, boy," the man said, and Alesh thought he detected a slur to the man's words, "The other Redeemers."

"I'm no Redeemer," Alesh said, "We're just trying to get out of the city."

"We?" The man growled, moving closer, so that Alesh could smell the sour whiskey stink of his breath. "And just who the night is *we?*"

Alesh frowned, "Me and—" he paused, glancing over the man's shoulder to the empty street beyond. "Never mind," he said, "I guess it's just me, after all."

The man barked a cruel laugh, "Friend run out on ya, did he? Well, looks like it's just you and me, boy, so how about you just step nice and easy out into the street where I can see you better. I'll be right behind you, and if your friend *is* out there, you'd best hope he keeps his distance. Otherwise, you'll be smiling out of your throat come tomorrow, you follow me?"

Alesh started out of the building, painfully aware of the blade at his back. Once outside, he looked around at the corpse-strewn street and was surprised to feel a twinge of disappointment at realizing that the old priest really was gone. He'd been crazy, that was sure, and his mad ramblings had been annoying to say the least, but Alesh found that he'd grown used to having him around, if even just to reassure himself that there was at least one person in the city who *didn't* want to kill him.

Alesh grunted as the man slapped him in the back of the head. He spun angrily but came up short as the knife came to rest at his throat. "I didn't tell you to stop, boy," the man said, "Now get movin' before I give you some incentive."

Alesh gritted his teeth and started forward again, stopping in the middle of the street at a word from the man. "Now turn around." Alesh did, slowly. The bearded man studied him with shifting, unfocused eyes and frowned, "You don't look like the other bastards that came around earlier. Where's your uniform?"

Alesh fought down a surge of impatience. Each second he wasted here was a second he wasn't spending trying to figure out a way to make it out of the gate. Kale or Falen Par would have no doubt reinforced the guards there, and his best chance to make it by them was under the cover of darkness. "I don't have a uniform," he said slowly, struggling to keep his voice even, "because I'm not a Redeemer."

"You don't look like one of those assholes, that's true enough," the man admitted grudgingly, taking the knife away from Alesh's throat, "You look like a different type of asshole." He barked a laugh at his own joke then frowned again, "Still that doesn't explain why you came here."

Alesh took a slow, deep breath before he spoke, "I came here because I'm traveling to Valeria, and I need to hire one of the Lightbringers."

The bearded man grunted, "You picked a bad time to be looking for one, boy. As for the Lightbringers … well, you're looking at them."

Alesh frowned, confused, "What do you mean?"

"What I *mean,* boy, is that I'm the only one left. Those Redeemer bastards showed up earlier today and took the others. We fought, sure, but we're trained to defend ourselves against nightlings not soldiers." He hocked and spat, "Several of the others were killed and the rest were led off in chains."

Alesh stared incredulously, "You can't be serious." What possible reason would Kale or the Redeemers have for taking the Lightbringers as prisoners? No one would *dare* do such a thing. It was the Lightbringers who maintained the rows of torches that lined the city's walls, who kept travelers safe when their business took them to one of the realm's other cities.

Why would Kale take them prisoner? What possible purpose would it serve unless.... Alesh's heart sank as realization came. By imprisoning the Lightbringers, Kale had effectively trapped everyone in the city. Even if someone *did* manage to slip past the guards at the gates, they'd never survive a night alone in the darkness. The nightlings would see to that. There were tales of lone men surviving a night without a Lightbringer, true, but they were few and far between, and Alesh suspected that most of them were outright lies.

Any man could build a fire, sure, but the fact was that all men slept, and all fires, sooner or later, went out. Not to mention that, though nightlings were hurt by the light, the erratic illumination given off by a campfire, with its shifting shadows and flickering darkness, allowed them to get close—often too close. Only the Lightbringers were able to create the secret blend of herbs and minerals that made fires burn several times hotter—and brighter—than normal as well as lasting much longer.

Of course, imprisoning all of the Lightbringers had a second added benefit as well; it forced the citizens of Ilrika to rely exclusively on Kale, his men, and, of course, their new goddess, Shira, for protection. By neutralizing the Lightbringers, Kale had assured the peoples' obedience. A thought struck Alesh then, and he glanced back at the Lightbringer. "If all of the others were rounded up and taken into custody, why are you still here?"

The man frowned and raised the dagger again, "You calling me a coward, friend?"

Alesh was out of patience. He raised his hands, as if in acquiescence, then took a quick step forward, chopping the man's wrist and sending the knife clattering to the ground. The Lightbringer let out a howl and snarled, starting toward Alesh, but he only managed a step before Alesh had retrieved the dagger and held it at his chest. Their gazes met for a moment, Alesh's determined, the Lightbringer's surprised, afraid and, for the first time, focused. Several tense seconds passed then Alesh tossed the blade away. "There," he said, "now maybe we can talk like normal people. How did you not get captured?"

The man glanced between Alesh and where the knife lay, rubbing his wrist with one hand. Finally, he grunted, "It's none of your damned business, boy. Now, do you need a Lightbringer or not?"

Alesh fought down his anger—it wasn't as if he had a lot of options. Slowly, he nodded, "Yes. And my name's Alesh, not boy. What's yours?"

The man hesitated then shrugged. "I'm Garn. Now, where did you say you were headin' to, *Alesh?*"

Alesh sighed, "Valeria."

Garn snorted, "Valeria's weeks away."

"I know."

Garn glanced around at the corpse-littered street then shrugged, "What the fuck. Bout time I tried out a new city anyway. This one's went to shit. I'll need half an hour to prepare." He turned and staggered back toward the guild house. Alesh watched him go, frowning. How *had* the man avoided being captured? He must have hidden. Alesh didn't relish the idea of spending the next few weeks in the company of an angry drunk who just also happened to be a coward in the bargain.

"Not a good choice," he mumbled to himself, "Not at all. But the only one."

CHAPTER TWENTY-EIGHT

"What of you, Eriondrian?"

Rion barely heard. He was too busy staring at the cards as the dealer shuffled, watching as they flipped and blurred their way through thousands of possible outcomes. Observing the intricate dance, he felt as he always did, like a man on the verge of some immeasurable discovery. *No,* he thought, *that's not right.* It was more like what he imagined a baby might feel in the instant after it emerged from the darkness of its mother's womb, but before it opened its eyes, before the world asserted itself and decided what it was. He felt hope, despair, felt that anything was possible, but most of all, he felt alive.

"Eriondrian?" The voice asked again, just as the dealer began to pass out a new hand of cards. Rion turned to see Armiel staring at him, a concerned expression on the young nobleman's face.

"Sorry, what was that?"

"I was just asking which you would choose." The young man said, grinning in a slightly embarrassed way as he indicated the group of female dancers performing on stage. Rion noticed that the noble's face was red from drink, though he suspected that wasn't all that made the young man blush. He, like most of the others gathered at the table, lived a pampered life and no doubt felt as if he was balancing on the very knife's edge of scandal by even *being* at the gentleman's club. Rion wondered, idly, how the man would fair in some of the shady inns and taverns he himself had frequented of late. He suspected not very well. Not well at all.

He struggled to keep from wincing as he noticed that Armiel had spilled some wine on the rich, gold and blue striped tunic that he wore. *That tunic would be enough to pay for the upkeep of my family's manse for a week,* he thought. Armiel was the youngest of the five seated at the table, but he was also the wealthiest. His father, Lord Landon Hale, owned several shipping ventures and regularly financed trading expeditions that traveled as far as the distant land of Welia, returning with exotic and rare spices that he sold at an incredible profit.

"Well, Eriondrian?" Another voice asked, interrupting his thoughts. As always, Sevrin had his raven black hair slicked back on his head, a style that only served to accentuate his pointed nose and sharp chin, making him look more like a bird than a man. His lips were twisted in the knowing, contemptuous smirk he habitually wore. It was a look Rion had come to hate, one that implied that he was always slightly bored, and that those around him should feel privileged by his company. It was a look that someone—possibly Rion himself—would have wiped off the young nobleman's face years ago if nor for two reasons. One, Sevrin happened to be the son of Lord Alrick, another of the city's richest and most influential nobles a hard, unforgiving man who was not to be crossed lightly. Secondly, and more important to Rion, at least, Sevrin was too busy being smug to care about the coins he lost in cards. He was rich and careless with his money, and that, in Rion's mind, made up for a lot. Of course, he was also a complete ass. "Are you going to answer Armiel or must we sit here all night in anticipation?" Sevrin asked, smiling like a man who was speaking with a bunch of simpletons and couldn't help but be amused by it.

Rion tried to force a smile of his own, an effort made easier by the fact that his own stack of coins had grown several times larger over the last few hours. The truth was that he'd been much too focused on the game and winning to pay the dancer's any attention. His family wasn't wealthy like the others at the table—though none of them knew it. To them, the dancers, the club, the money, even the way they spoke with each other, was all a game, and it was a game in which Rion had no interest. A man in such a game could win influence or bragging rights, even respect, if he was lucky, but in Rion's experience, creditors tended to prefer coins. Still, the thing about games—whether or not they were interesting—was that all men played them, and if they said they didn't, that just meant they were losing.

He glanced at the eight women on stage. They *were* beautiful, certainly, and the way their bodies pressed against the tight fitting silk outfits they wore as they swayed and danced languidly to the music was enticing. But such women, if they were to be had, were never to be had cheap. After what he deemed an appropriate amount of time, he turned back, "The blonde."

Bastion guffawed loudly his right hand resting on his ample belly as he wiped grease from his mouth with a ring-bedecked left. "Why, Eriondrian, that's an easy enough guess. They're *all* blonde."

If they'd seen him now, in his food and wine-stained tunic, a small thread of spittle hanging from the corner of his mouth, many would have found it hard to credit that Bastion was in training to become a priest and, with his father's connections, would no doubt move up in the Brotherhood of Amedan quickly. It wasn't out of the question that the fat nobleman would wind up being the Archbishop of Valeria in another ten or fifteen years. He was disgusting, a lecher and a pig, but he was also a terrible card player who always gave away a bluff by nibbling at his lower lip, and, no matter how poor his manners or his hygiene, his coins spent as well as any. "Well then, my lord," Rion said, as he glanced down at the cards the dealer had given him, "I suppose I will take them all."

The nobleman broke into a fit of snuffling laughter that again put Rion in mind of some farmer's prized pig, and he busied himself taking a drink of his wine for an excuse to look away from the man. "And you, Odrick?" Sevrin asked, eyeing the other man at the table with a sneer, "Which would you choose?"

Out of all of them, Odrick was the only one that approached Bastion's size, but whereas the nobleman's bulk was fat, Odrick's large frame consisted of thick slabs of hard muscle on his arms and chest, tokens from hours spent working in his father's blacksmith shop. Despite this, he squirmed visibly under the nobleman's gaze like a child whose tutor had asked him a question he should have known but didn't. As was characteristic of the blacksmith, he took several seconds to deliberate the question before he finally shrugged uncomfortably, "I'm not sure. I suppose I'd have to get to know them first."

Sevrin rolled his eyes and the other two noblemen snickered. "How very *noble* of you, *lord* Odrick." He said, his dark eyes glittering in malicious amusement. The big man's face flushed red, but he did not speak. Odrick was the only commoner among them, and Sevrin took every opportunity to remind him of that fact. Odrick's family was rich, but instead of being born into it as the others, his was the only one that had *earned* instead of inherited their fortune. His father had gained his money through years of hard labor during which he earned a name for himself as the city's finest blacksmith and, if what Rion heard was true, Odrick was at least as good as his father if not better. But such things meant little to nobles. To them, he was a commoner, money or no, and little else need be said. As for Rion, he liked the blacksmith's son and not just because he played too cautiously and was easily bought out of a hand even when he had the better cards. In fact, if Rion was being honest with himself—a practice he tried to avoid whenever possible—the blacksmith's son was the closest thing to a real friend he had, and he didn't like listening to Sevrin belittling him.

"Oh, there now, Sevrin," he said, "let's not wish nobility on him. Why, the next thing we know, he'll spend all of his time greasing back his hair or trying on new shirts, and he'll be of no use at all."

Sevrin frowned and the other two nobles looked uncertain for a moment, but Rion didn't miss the quick look of relief and gratitude that washed over Odrick's face. *A rich commoner and a poor nobleman,* Rion thought, and was only just able to avoid laughing. *What a pair we make.*

"Yes, well, are we here to play cards or aren't we?" Sevrin asked in an annoyed voice as he slid a stack of coins into the pot without so much as checking his hand.

Rion smiled, as he glanced at his own hand, then matched the wager. It was going to be a good night. It was said—and he did not doubt it—that Jaevin, the God of Chance and Luck, son of Amedan and Shira, was a fickle deity, but a man didn't need a god to get lucky. He settled back into his chair, glanced at the men sharing the table with him, and smiled wider. Sometimes a man made his own luck.

CHAPTER TWENTY-NINE

RION WATCHED WARILY AS BASTION rose ponderously to his feet, his bulk swaying dangerously, as if at any moment he might topple over, crushing anyone unfortunate enough to be caught beneath him. "Well. Eh. Well, gents" the fat man slurred, "I'm off. I've got a uh … a date with a certain please … pleasant … *pleasure* woman that I don't," he paused to burp grotesquely, "that I d-don't want to miss."

Rion was too tired and disgusted to even match Odrick's mumbled, weak goodbye. The fat man stumbled into a nearby table, knocking several glasses over where they shattered on the floor, then waddled away, a stupid anticipatory grin on his face. Rion supposed that it didn't matter if you had to pay for your women, if your family had the kind of money that fat bastard's did.

He yawned and glanced around the large common room of the Gentlemen's club. Armiel and Sevrin had left much earlier, slinking off in search of their own favorite vices, their own favorite whores. The dancers had long since left the stage, and, aside from a few drunks who'd apparently decided that a tabletop would serve just as well as a bed, he and Odrick were the only customers left in the club. The truth was, Rion himself could barely keep his eyes open, but losing a few hours of sleep was well worth the amount of money he'd won off of the other noblemen and, to a much lesser extent, Odrick. He even entertained the scant hope that, for once, what sleep he did get wouldn't be troubled with the guilt that usually accompanied it, the shame he normally felt for resting when his family was only a month or two away from poverty.

The thought dampened his mood considerably. His mother and father, he knew, would not blame him for the loss of the family's fortune and somehow that made it worse. The thought of his father being forced to pawn the rare books he'd spent over half of his life collecting, or his mother having to sell the jewelry his father had so often given her as a token of his love, all the while both of them telling him it was okay, that it wasn't his fault, was enough to make him want to scream with frustration. Something of his thoughts must have shown on his face because Odrick leaned forward, concern etching his features.

"Are you alright, Eriondrian?" The big man asked, "You look like you just ate something that had gone off."

Rion forced a smile for his friend's benefit. "I'm fine, Odrick, just tired is all."

The big man considered this for a time, eyeing Rion steadily. "You're sure there's nothing else?"

Rion nodded, inwardly cursing himself for letting so much of his worry show. Because of his size and his slow, careful way of speaking many people thought the blacksmith simple, but the truth was that he was one of the smartest people Rion knew. "I'm sure, my friend." He said, hating himself for the lie even as he said it.

Odrick studied him for several seconds then finally nodded, "Alright well, I suppose I need to go. We've been getting a lot of orders recently and father will want to open the shop early." He rose from his chair and picked up the pieces of shattered glass left from Bastion's departure, put them on top of the table then nodded to Rion. "Sleep well, Eriondrian, and may the Light find you safe."

"And you as well. Odrick?"

The man turned back, "Yes?"

"You grew up poor, didn't you?"

Odrick frowned as if he was expecting to be the target of another joke but finally he nodded, "Yes."

"And now your father is one of the richest men in the city."

Another slow, cautious nod.

Rion hesitated, "What was it like ... before?"

The big man grinned, "Easier," he said. "It was easier." And with that, he turned and walked away.

Easier, Rion thought as he watched him go. *Were that it could be, my friend.* He sat there for a while longer, his good mood gone, sipping carefully at his wine. After a while, a serving girl in a skimpy, tight-fitting outfit walked over to the table, and began to stack the empty glasses of his friends on a silver tray, "You need anything else, hon?" She asked, a weary but practiced flirtation in her voice.

How does a thousand Suns sound? "No, thank you," Rion said, forcing himself to smile. It seemed that he'd been doing a lot of that lately.

"Well, you just let me know if you change your mind," she said, winking before turning and walking off, swaying her hips back and forth in a motion Rion didn't doubt was contrived to increase her tip rate dramatically.

"And why not?" Rion muttered as he drew a golden Sun from his purse, "She's earned it from being forced to deal with Bastion's pawing, and Sevrin's comments, if nothing else." He studied the coin in the orange glow of the table's lantern. Such a small thing, really, yet large enough to crush families, to topple kingdoms. On one side of the coin was an engraving of a brightly shining torch, Amedan's symbol, and on the other an engraving of the face of Lady Tesharna herself, her eyes full of compassion, a small, almost melancholy smile on her face.

So small a thing, he thought, toying with the coin, *to control so many lives.* Still, it was the world in which they lived, the game which they all played. *It may be true, what the priests say,* he thought. *Money might not buy happiness. Then again, for the price of a high priced whore or a fine meal, it can certainly rent it for a time.*

He tossed the coin idly on the table, and as it left his hand he felt a familiar tingle of anticipation. It was the same feeling of chance, of *possibility* that he felt with each throw of the dice, or with each shuffle of a deck of cards but stronger, more intense. The coin hit the hard wooden surface of the tabletop and began to spin. Rion watched it, suddenly entranced. A face flashed by, but in the glow of the lantern, it didn't look like Valeria's ruler at all. Instead, it appeared to be the cruel, twisted visage of some nightwalker, bearing its teeth in a hungry grin.

He tensed in shock and surprise, but in another instant the coin spun away and in its revolutions the flames of the torch seemed to come to some kind of sporadic life, blazing brightly one moment, and then dying to little more than weak sputters in the next. Rion watched it with a growing sense of both wonder and dread, unaware of the fact that he was clenching the tabletop in both hands so tightly that his knuckles were as white as sun-bleached bone. *A trick of the light, nothing more,* he told himself, but he did not, *could* not look away.

Which will it be, he thought, holding his breath, *the smiling Chosen of Amedan, or the laughing nightling, the bright torch, or the sputtering flame?* Each spin of the coin seemed to take hours, and he was struck by the thought that if only he could look a little harder, a little closer, he would have seen in its graceful dance secrets to which only the gods were privy and some perhaps even they did not know. When the coin finally slowed to a stop, Rion let out the breath he'd been holding in surprise. The coin had not fallen on either the torch, or the face, had shown no victor between the Chosen or the laughing nightwalker that had chased her round and round, but had instead came to rest standing on its side.

"Impossible," he muttered breathlessly, the hairs on the back of his neck standing up.

"Everything alright, hon?"

Rion jerked at the sound of the serving woman's voice and slammed his hand down on the coin before turning to her, "I'm fine," he grated, the words coming out harsher than he'd intended.

The woman stared at him as if seeing him for the first time, all pretense of flirting gone. "Uhuh," she said in a humoring tone before turning and walking off, her swaying walk nowhere in evidence.

Rion waited until she was gone then snatched his hand away from the coin as if burned and stared at it. A coin, nothing more. *It's just sleep,* he told himself, *that's all. You just need sleep.* He'd been pushing it hard the last few days, getting only a couple of hours of sleep when he got any at all. It was no wonder he was seeing things.

But that *face*. It had been *laughing.* He rose, his eyes not daring to leave the coin, backed away from the table slowly then turned and hurried out of the club, ignoring the serving woman's half-hearted goodbye.

Outside in the fresh air, amid the familiar surroundings of the city, *his* city, it became easier and easier to tell himself that the leering face on the coin had been a trick of the light and a weary mind, nothing more. And what of the coin coming to rest on its side? These things happened. Didn't they?

Soon, he made it to his family's manse, and as he lay in bed, he thought again of how the coin had stood on end, rigid and refusing to fall. *There was no nightling,* he told himself, *no sputtering torch. I'm tired that's all. It would have fallen, if I'd let it.* He repeated these words over and over in his head, so that, after a time, he almost believed them. Almost.

CHAPTER THIRTY

"Impossible," Alesh murmured, glancing around at the deserted city gate.

"What?" Garn asked. He'd changed out of the soiled shirt he'd been wearing and now wore a leather tunic etched and pocked with burn scars. Half a dozen miniature torches were strapped to the front of his tunic with leather thongs, and a large one was sheathed at his back like a sword. The belt he wore was full of pouches containing special mixtures of herbs and powders the creation and use of which was known only by Lightbringers.

At any other time, Alesh would have been dying to ask the man questions about his equipment, but now he was too disturbed to care. "It doesn't make sense," he said. "Obviously Kale doesn't want anyone getting out of the city, so why aren't there guards posted?"

The Lightbringer shrugged, "Who gives a shit? Maybe the bastards are too busy killing each other."

"Maybe," Alesh said, "but all of them?" He gestured at the dozens of corpses that lay scattered around the gates, many of them still oozing fresh blood from their wounds, "They were here recently, that's for sure. What possible reason could they have to abandon the gate?"

The bearded man grunted, "Why don't you go find one and ask him, boy? I'm sure they'd be more than happy to answer all of your questions." Despite his words, Alesh noted that the man kept casting nervous glances around them, and that the fingers of one of his burn-scarred hands toyed with the hilt of the dagger tucked at his side.

Alesh raised an eyebrow at him then shrugged and headed toward the gate. Behind him, the Lightbringer hissed a curse and followed after. Alesh crept into the guardhouse half expecting to be struck down by someone waiting inside, but it was empty. Feeling like a man in a dream, he reached toward the crank that controlled the gate.

Garn caught his wrist, "*Wait,* you crazy bastard," he snapped, and Alesh wasn't surprised to hear the terror in his voice, "Do you want to get us killed? They'll hear that damned gate from a mile away."

Alesh turned to him, strangely calm, "Do you have another idea of how to get out of here? Would you rather try to climb the wall?"

The Lightbringer's brows drew down in thought, and his eyes shifted nervously in their sockets, but he did not answer. Alesh shrugged then took hold of the crank and began to turn it. The creak of metal filled the night, loud enough to almost completely drown out the panicked curses of the Lightbringer at his side, but Alesh kept going until the gate was high enough to allow him and his companion to crawl under. Garn grabbed his shoulder roughly, "Are you out of your damned mi—"

"Quiet!" Alesh hissed, knocking the man's arm aside. *They'll come now,* he told himself, *there's no way they didn't hear that.* They'd come and cut him and the Lightbringer down, and that would be the end of it. He found that the idea didn't bother him very much. At least no one could say he hadn't tried. Several seconds passed in silence as he waited, expecting at any moment to hear shouts of alarm, but the only sounds were those of the distant screams and Garn's ragged breaths beside him.

Alesh walked back to the entrance and glanced out of the guardhouse. The street was empty. "Come on," he said, starting toward the gate.

They'll get us now, he thought, *before we make it to the gate.* But no one came, and after a moment the Lightbringer appeared at his side, his breathing harsh and shallow as if he'd just ran several miles. "What," he panted, "do you want to die, you damned fool, is that it?"

Maybe, Alesh thought, *maybe I do.* But he said nothing, and soon they came upon the gate. He hadn't raised the gate as much as he thought, and they were forced to wiggle under it on their bellies. Each second he spent crawling under the heavy wrought iron gate, he expected to hear alarmed shouts, to feel the prick of an arrow in his back, but nothing happened and in a short time, they were on the other side, the road laid out before them and stretching on into the darkness.

They walked for a time until the road sloped upward and they came to the top of a hill. Before he lost sight of the city altogether, Alesh turned and glanced back, gazing—most likely for the last time—upon the place he'd called home since he was a child. In the wan light of the moon and the flickering of the fires all around it, Ilrika seemed somehow insubstantial, as if it were no more than a memory of a dream he'd once had. *And that's exactly what it is*, he told himself. He tried to recall some of the good memories he'd had there, but he could think of nothing but the faces of those he'd loved as they lay butchered in the street. He turned and started away.

The road grew steadily darker as they got farther away from the city wall and the glow of its torches and after a few minutes, Garn stopped and withdrew two forearm-length torches from his tunic. He proceeded to take two lengths of cloth from one of the pouches on his belt and wrap it around the head of each torch. Though the strips of cloth looked like nothing more than simple linen, there was a strong herbal smell to them that Alesh didn't recognize.

Garn handed one of the torches to Alesh, "Here. A man's a fool that travels in the darkness even with torches, but we need to put some more distance between us and that damned city. Unlike you, I don't plan on getting my head lopped off by the red cloaks anytime soon." He waited as if expecting a response. When he didn't get one, he grunted and withdrew a piece of flint from a pouch at his belt. He struck it against the torch Alesh was holding, and Alesh cried out in pain at the blinding white light that suddenly burst in his eyes.

"Yeah, you never want to stare right at a Lightbringer torch," Garn said, his gruff voice tinged with cruel amusement, "You'll burn your eyes out like that."

Alesh gritted his teeth as he struggled to blink away the white spots in his vision, "Maybe that would have been something to tell me before you lit it."

"Look at it this way," the Lightbringer said, gesturing at the dark woods lying on either side of the road, "If it hurts us, imagine how *they* like it. Not that the bastards usually come this close to the city, anyway, but better safe than sorry." With that, the man began walking again.

Alesh sighed and reluctantly followed. Erwin had told him he needed to hire a Lightbringer and Alesh knew it to be true, but he still didn't like the idea of traveling alone with the man. There was something about his eyes that Alesh didn't trust. *I'm just tired,* he assured himself. *Just because Kale was a traitor doesn't mean everyone is. After all, the man has a right to be upset considering the fact that all of his friends were either killed or taken prisoner.*

They continued on, deeper into the night. The shadows of the trees loomed over their heads, their branches reaching, curling, as if at any moment they would snatch up the two men who dared venture into the night and make them pay for their foolishness. Silence hung over the woods, thick and full of deadly promise, and it was all Alesh could do to put one foot in front of the other, to fight the urge to turn and run back to Ilrika as fast as his feet could carry him. Kale and the Redeemers might be evil men, but they were *men*. If he was caught, he'd no doubt end up with his head decorating a pike or hung from a noose until his face turned black, and his eyes bulged like overripe fruits. Terrible, true, but at least those things he understood. If the creatures that waited in the night caught him ... no. Better not to think of it.

I have to keep going, he told himself over and over with each step he took, *I promised Erwin.* It was a good reason, but it was not his. He would make Kale pay for what he'd done, and if that meant braving the night and its creatures then he would. He would see the deaths of his friends paid for. "It's quiet," he said, more in an effort to break that muted, waiting silence than anything else.

The Lightbringer smirked, his eyes flashing orange in the torchlight, "Give it time, boy. Give it time."

CHAPTER THIRTY-ONE

SOMETHING STRUCK HIM IN THE side, and Alesh awoke with a start, expecting to find a nightwalker towering over him ready to tear out his heart and feast on his blood. He was only slightly relieved to find the scarred Lightbringer frowning down at him instead. "Time to go."

Alesh sighed and struggled to his feet, wincing. His body was not accustomed to sleeping on the hard forest floor and apparently had no intention of suffering in silence. He glanced over and saw Garn scattering a handful of crushed Pralentia leaves on a fire that was so hot it appeared white instead of red, so bright that it brought tears to your eyes if you looked at it. Alesh had watched the man do the same thing for the last three days, but he was still amazed by how quickly the fire began to die down.

The small leaves of the Pralentia plant, so dark green that they were nearly black, fluttered down into the blinding fire. The leaves began to lighten and swell and the fire shrank, sputtering and popping in weak protest. The Lightbringer had been growing increasingly taciturn and moody the farther they'd gone from Ilrika, but Alesh had questioned him until he'd finally given in with a curse and explained that the leaves of the Pralentia plant—a bushy, aquatic plant found only in swampy regions—absorbed the fire's heat. Alesh had asked him how, but the Lightbringer had cursed again and said that he was no scholar, and that he could care less *how* they worked, just so long as they did.

That they worked there was no denying. The leaves went from black to orange to red and finally a bright white, growing as large as a man's fist before bursting in a shower of white and red sparks. The whole process had taken no more than a matter of seconds and when it was finished nothing remained of the powerful blaze except for scattered remnants of ash, not even so much as a wisp of smoke to mark its passing.

Two days ago, in a more talkative mood than usual, Garn had complained of the expense of the herb, claiming that merchants sold it at exorbitant prices because of the Lightbringer's need for it. After all, he'd explained, a Lightbringer fire burned too hot to be doused with water or smothered in dirt, and only the gods' greatest fool would try to stamp one out. The dangers of such a fire getting out of control and causing massive amounts of damage to fields, forests, or even homes was very real—after all, it had happened before. It was the reason the Lightbringers guarded their secrets so carefully.

And so they do, Alesh thought as the Lightbringer checked the pouches of his belt and tunic, scowling as if he'd caught Alesh stealing something, then, apparently finished, he started off without so much as a word.

Alesh grit his teeth and followed after. A few days' worth of traveling with Garn had shown the Lightbringer to be even less likeable than he'd first appeared. Still, there was no denying his usefulness. It was his skill that had kept the nightlings at bay each night and, so far at least, out of sight.

Alesh rubbed at his burning, grainy eyes as they paced along. He'd slept little in the past three days. Though he hadn't seen any of the nightwalkers, he'd heard them, and that had been bad enough. Their screeches and hungry growls always seemed just out of sight beyond the cover of trees, and he'd spent his nights whipping around at every groan of a tree, tensing at every rustle of leaves, sure that one of the monstrosities was creeping toward them despite the intense light of the fire.

The forest sounds had been bad, terrible, in fact, but the cries of the creatures in the darkness were enough to drive a man insane. Traveling merchants—who spent their nights in covered caravans with a dozen guards and a Lightbringer to protect them—sometimes told stories about being terrified in the darkness as something approached the light of their fires only to discover that it was a squirrel or chipmunk, or that the angry growl they'd thought they'd heard had been nothing more than a lone, starving coyote. Dangerous, sure, but easily dealt with by a dozen armed men.

After three nights spent in the darkness, Alesh doubted them. Only a fool could mistake the sounds of nightlings for anything but what they were; the furious, hungry cries of creatures who didn't just want to eat, but who wanted to *kill*. Creatures who dreamed of blood and death and darkness. Even if Alesh had liked the Lightbringer before, the sound of him snoring while Alesh himself lay awake, the handle of his sword clasped in a white-knuckled grip, would have been enough to ensure that they would never be the best of friends.

The road through the forest was wide and judging by the tightly-packed dirt and evenly spaced furrows marring its surface, Alesh suspected that it was, in normal times, a well-traveled road. No doubt the one used by merchants and farmers heading to Ilrika to trade. But news of Ilrika had traveled the countryside ahead of them and today, like the days before it, the road was empty save the two of them. The merchants and farmers of the outlying areas having decided it was better to be alive than rich, better to stay in their own homes and fields than brave a night filled with nightwalkers, or a day filled with madmen seeking blood. Alesh couldn't blame them, but with Olliman dead and Kale now in power, he thought that they'd be pulled into the city's madness sooner or later, whether they wished it or not.

They trudged on and, after a while, the trees and bushes of the forest gave way to large fields of corn and wheat. Here and there, men walked their lines, tending the harvest and watching the travelers with suspicious stares, shying farther back into their fields as the two men passed as if Ilrika's destruction was a disease that could be passed from man to man. Alesh thought about the men he'd killed, how he'd enjoyed it and even now felt no sorrow at the act, and decided that maybe the men were right to keep their distance.

When the sun was high in the sky, the world dimming around them and beginning to fall in shadow, they came upon a small town. It was a simple place, the homes nothing more than small wooden cabins, the street little more than a dirt trail. The Lightbringer started to walk faster, with more purpose, and Alesh thought that he meant to leave the town behind, was already preparing himself for another night spent in the darkness when Garn came to an abrupt halt in front of a building that was larger than the rest. The sign above the door named it *Nature's Bounty Inn,* and Alesh smiled, barely able to suppress a sigh of relief. He glanced at Garn, expecting the man to share his own excitement at staying in doors for a change, but if anything he appeared even grimmer than usual. Garn drew a flask from his tunic, took a long pull as if to brace himself, wiped his mouth on his sleeve, and stepped through the doors with the determined walk of a man who has some nasty business ahead of him and wants to finish it as quickly as possible.

Alesh followed him past several empty tables and sat next to him at the bar. The bartender, a wide-shouldered man with a thick, barreled chest, turned from where he'd been cleaning a glass, his smile souring as he saw Garn, "And just what in the night do you think *you're* doing here?" He asked, his eyes narrowing to thin slits.

The Lightbringer barked a laugh but there was no humor in it, "Well, come on now, Tassin, that's no way to treat an old friend is it? Besides, what do most people come to an inn for? Why, rooms and ale, of course"

The man frowned, folding his massive arms across his chest, "You're no friend of mine, and I told you not to come back here, Garn, not after the last time. Now, why don't you hit the road before it hits you?"

Garn smiled as if the man had just told a joke, "Now, now, Tassin. Surely, you wouldn't turn away a 'bringer in need, not with night coming on? Besides, I'm sure that whatever's bothering you ain't nothin' but a misunderstanding, though I can't say as I remember it."

The big innkeeper grunted, "If you don't remember, that's because you're a boozing bastard who never met a drink he didn't like or a waitress he didn't paw like some half-brained mutt. I want you gone."

Garn sighed dramatically, "I'm sure you can't be serious, Tassin. As I understand it, Guildmaster Merik pays you a good wage to shelter passing 'bringers. Why, I wonder at what the others would say—the master too, of course—if they knew you were turning them away."

A hunted, uncertain look crept into the innkeeper's gaze, and he glanced at the two of them as if they'd just sprouted fangs. Alesh felt sorry for the man, and he hated the thought of being grouped with the Lightbringer in the innkeeper's mind, but he remained silent. Garn was a trial, sure, but the man would only have to put up with him for a night, while Alesh was forced to endure him for weeks. Besides, truth be told, the thought of sleeping indoors was too tempting to pass up.

The innkeeper seemed to be considering, but judging by Garn's greasy smile, the Lightbringer already knew what Alesh had just realized. Save for a single barmaid and the three of them, the inn was completely empty. Judging by the lack of customers, the innkeeper was probably only able to keep the place because of the money Merik paid him and if that well should run dry .... *Of course*, Alesh thought, *there's no guild left to pay him, but he won't know that*. No doubt the man had heard rumors, but if he'd known the extent of what happened he would have finished considering long ago and kicked the two of them out the door. "Damn you," the big man muttered finally, "haven't you any shame?"

Garn laughed again, "Not last I checked."

Tassin studied the two of them for a minute then finally gave a grudging nod. "Alright, two rooms, but you'll not get a touch of drink, not under my roof, and if you so much as look wrong at Belle, I'll have you out on your ass in the street, and Merik himself can come down and bitch about it if he likes. If he's got the time that is. From what I hear, Ilrika's not a very comfortable place to be just now. Shit, it must be even worse than I heard if he's letting you take jobs again."

Alesh glanced between the two men, "What do you—"

"It was nothing," Garn growled, glaring at the innkeeper, "just a misunderstanding, that's all."

The big innkeeper smiled widely, a victorious glint in his eyes, "Aye, if that's what you want to call it, but it seems to me that you're having a lot of those of late. You see, good sir," he said, turning to Alesh, "your guide here has a problem with his drink. In fact, if the Lightbringers didn't need everybody they could get, I reckon he would have been kicked out a long time ago."

Garnn's face twisted in rage, and he jerked out of his stool, his body rigid with anger. He glared at the two men then spat on the floor, "Night take you both," he snarled before turning and heading for the stairs. Alesh watched him go wishing, neither for the first or last time, that he'd found a different Lightbringer to serve as his guide.

CHAPTER THIRTY-TWO

"Mistress Elizabeth." The inn's proprietor was a thin, sickly looking man, but he smiled warmly as he watched Katherine and her companions walk inside. "It is great to see you in Leran once again, but I did not expect you so soon. Is everything alright?"

Katherine smiled back, "Everything's fine ... Islin, isn't it?"

The innkeeper beamed widely, "Yes, Mistress, just so. Still, you're sure that everything is okay? I've been hearing strange rumors of late."

"In truth," Katherine said, "I found that city life was not as much to my liking as I would have thought, and left only a short while after arriving." She hated herself for misleading the innkeeper, who had treated her kindly when she'd passed through Leran only weeks ago on her way to the city, but she didn't want him to associate her with anything that had happened in Ilrika if he thought of it later. Better for him to suppose she left the city before it ever happened. After all, a spy—and though she disliked the title, there was no denying that it was the primary function she provided for Chosen Alashia—was nowhere near as useful if people began to suspect her. "And you?" She asked the man, "How have things been? I hope that your wife, Matilda, is well?"

The man's grin widened further, so that it threatened to swallow the rest of his face, "The missus is good, thank you. She's still weak from the fever, but the physicians say that she's over the worst of it. She'll be glad to hear that you asked after her, my lady."

Katherine smiled. She was no noblewoman, but since she'd been given the golden horn by Chosen Alashia, a symbol of a musician's prowess as well as proof of the Chosen's favor, she was often treated as such. Of course, Darl, with his predatory grace and imposing presence might have also had something to do with that. After all, any noblewoman that was traveling alone would be expected to be accompanied by a bodyguard. She could have corrected the man, but she found it easier to let people believe what they wanted to believe. *Of course,* she thought to herself, *it's not exactly as if you mind being pampered and treated like someone important is it?*

"I wonder, Islin, if we might rent a room for the night?"

The man nodded, glancing at Darl and Sonya, "Of course, my lady," he said, "I have two very nice rooms available that will suit your needs per—"

"One will suffice, thank you, master Islin."

The man's smile twitched at this, but was back in place a moment later, "Yes, my lady, and it will be free of charge, of course, but I wonder … might it be possible for you to play us a song or two before you retire for the evening? Folks here are still talking about your last performance; some of them convinced that Deitra herself has come down to the world of men."

Katherine smiled at the man's attempts at flattery, "I am no Deitra, master Islin, and normally I would love too, but it has been a trying couple of days and—"

"Oh, please, Ka—Elizabeth," Sonya said, barely remembering to use the name they'd agreed on in her excitement, "Please won't you play? Just a few songs? It's so beautiful."

"My little mistress is quite wise," the innkeeper said, nodding his head so vigorously that Katherine thought it a wonder it didn't fall off, "Why, my lady, if you don't mind me saying so, I do not think I have ever heard anything so beautiful."

And of course it doesn't hurt that your custom will increase dramatically tonight when people hear that a Golden horn-bearer is performing in your inn, Katherine thought, but she forced a smile. There was a time, not so long ago, when men like the innkeeper would have thrown her out if she'd so much as dared to set foot in their establishment, when they sneered and spat as they passed her in the street, sometimes deigning to toss her a dusk while they complained to their fellows about what the poor were doing to the city.

But let men think you a noblewoman, let them see the golden horn hanging from your neck, and suddenly your music is a thing of magic. The thought of those days, so long ago, when she often went to bed with her stomach aching from hunger, was enough to make her want to turn the innkeeper down out of spite, but she glanced over at Sonya and saw the girl's hopeful eyes. "Alright," she said, "but only a few songs, and then we need to get some rest. We've got a long road ahead of us before we make it back to Galia."

"Wonderful," the innkeeper said, clapping his hands delightedly, "I will go get someone to prepare the stage and, of course, your rooms—err room. I will be back in a moment." He hurried away, shouting at one of the serving girls, all pretense of kindness gone.

"Katherine," Sonya said once he was gone, "are you sure you're not a noble? All of the innkeeper's we've met have thought you were."

Katherine laughed, "I'm sure, sweetness."

The little girl's eyebrows furrowed in confusion, "Then why do you let them think that you are?"

"For the same reason I give them the name Elizabeth," Katherine said, "it is easier to let men believe what they want to believe than the truth, sometimes."

Sonya frowned at that, "Abigail says that it's wrong to lie."

"It isn't a lie, honey," Katherine said, running a hand through the girl's hair, "it's just … well, not telling the truth, that's all."

Sonya considered this for a moment, "That seems like a lie to me."

Katherine glanced at Darl for help, but the dusky-skinned man only smiled, raising an eyebrow as if to say that she was on her own. She scowled at him for a moment before turning back to the little girl, "I know it might seem like that, Sonya, but when you get a little older you'll understand the difference. Sometimes, it's better to not tell *all* of the truth. After all, if I went around talking about how big Darl's nose was, it might hurt his feelings, don't you think?"

The little girl giggled, "Darl doesn't have a big nose." She turned to the man and hugged him, "I think it's perfect." Katherine shook her head in wonder. In the few days they'd been traveling together, the girl had latched on to the silent Ferinan as if she'd known him for all of her life, laughing at the faces he made from time to time, and having long conversations with him on their travels despite the fact that he never spoke a word. The dusky-skinned man met Katherine's gaze, and although his expression hadn't changed, she thought she detected a certain smugness in his face.

Katherine sighed good naturedly, and was about to point out that even if his nose *was* normal size, his ears were certainly the funniest-looking she'd ever seen when the innkeeper returned. "Mistress," he said, bobbing his head so low that it was a wonder he didn't scrape it on the wooden floor, "the stage is ready for you."

Katherine winked at Sonya as she turned and headed for the small, slightly-raised platform at the back of the room, Darl removing the harp case from where it rested on his back as he followed after her.

CHAPTER THIRTY-THREE

"KATHERINE! KATHERINE!"

Katherine snapped awake and turned to see Sonya standing beside her bed, "Sonya? Is everything okay?"

The girl nodded, "Yes, but Darl says it's time to get up."

Katherine rubbed at her grainy eyes, yawning heavily, then the girl's words made it past her sleep-muddled mind, and she turned to her, smiling tiredly, "He said that did he?"

"Well, he didn't *say* it," Sonya admitted, "but he got that face that he gets sometimes." She screwed her face up in an imitation of Darl, and despite her exhaustion, Katherine couldn't help but laugh.

Darl was waiting in the hallway when they emerged, Katherine still rubbing at the sleep in her eyes. "Sending her to do your dirty work?" She asked with a scowl, "You should be ashamed of yourself."

The Ferinan grinned and winked at the girl who giggled in return. Katherine sighed, "Alright then, we'd best be on our way."

"Ah, Lady Elizabeth!" The innkeeper exclaimed in a voice that Katherine thought was much too loud for so early in the morning, "I trust you slept well?"

Katherine fought back a frown. The truth was that she'd barely slept at all. The common room of the inn had grown busy later in the evening, and Islin had kept begging her for "one more song" flattering her shamelessly and not completely succeeding in hiding the twinkle of greed in his eyes as he watched the common room fill up with people. In a small town like Leran, news traveled fast, and it wasn't long after she'd began to play that the crowds had jostled in. They'd all acted excited about the prospect of hearing a golden hornbearer perform, but Katherine suspected that, for most of them, her performance had really just been a handy excuse for them to drink themselves into a stupor.

As always, when she played the music seemed to take over, coming not just from the harp's strings, but from *her* as well, as if her body and her soul resonated along with each note. She never felt more at peace, more whole, than when she was playing and before she knew it, she'd spent hours on the stage. Finally, so exhausted that she could barely sit up straight, she'd went to bed despite Islin's insistent flattery, but she'd only been asleep for a matter of hours before Sonya had come and woken her up.

Darl had stayed in the common room with her the entire time, his back propped against a wall, as still as a statue, only rousing when she finally walked down from the platform and headed toward her room. The dark-skinned man had slept no more than she had, but he appeared as alert as always. "We thank you for your hospitality, master Islin," she said, ignoring the man's question of her sleep—who said she couldn't be politic?—" but we really must be going."

"Oh, mistress," he whined, his thin, stick-like fingers rubbing together anxiously, "Must you leave so soon? Surely, you might stay with us one more night?"

"I'm sorry, but we cannot."

The innkeeper sighed, "Well, at least stay to break your fast. Surely, you can spare that much time, at least."

Katherine hesitated, considering. Darl had traded for two horses at the first town they'd come to once leaving Ilrika and for the last few days they'd been hurrying, trying to put as much distance between themselves and the doomed city as possible. Although they'd stayed at several inns, their meals had been hurried, half-hearted things consisting mostly of hard bread and water, and Katherine found her mouth watering at the thought of a real cooked meal. But she knew that, if she stayed any longer, the crafty innkeeper would find some way to talk her into playing again, and by the time they finally *did* leave, she'd be an old maid with fingers as wrinkled as prunes and a back that was permanently bent from strumming her harp. *Just one more song,* she thought sourly, and shook her head, "I thank you for your offer, but I am afraid we must regretfully decline it, as we have pressing business elsewhere."

The man's mouth, opened in preparation to no doubt issue another protest, but Katherine continued without letting him speak, "Rest assured, however, that should my travels take me this way again, I would be most happy to stop by and direct any friends who come to the area to do so as well."

Immediate greed and the potential for future profits warred in the innkeeper's expression for several seconds but finally he nodded. "If you are sure, my lady," he said reluctantly. "Truly, it has been an honor to have one of your skill and stature grace my lowly inn."

Katherine accepted the compliment with a nod, grabbed Sonya's hand, and headed toward the door.

"Oh, my lady," Islin said, hurrying up beside her, an apologetic expression on his face, "I'm so sorry, but I … that is … I just remembered that I have a message for you."

Katherine paused, confused, "A message? For me?"

The skinny innkeeper nodded, wringing his hands as he withdrew a folded piece of parchment from the pocket of his stained tunic, "Yes ma'am. I should have remembered it before now—Matty tells me that I wouldn't remember to dress if she wasn't there to remind me—and with the excitement of your visit and the music you were so kind to grace us with, I must confess that it completely slipped my mind."

"When did this arrive?" Katherine asked, taking the letter.

The innkeeper swallowed and stared at his feet, refusing to meet her eyes, "It umm … that is … I received the letter two night's past. Truly, my lady, I had not intended to—"

Katherine silenced him with a wave of her hand. She doubted very seriously that it had slipped the shrewd innkeeper's mind. More likely, he'd been concerned that the contents of the letter would force her to hurry away, taking with her his opportunity to make a few coins. Still, there was no time to worry about that now. *Who could possibly know I was going to be here?* She thought, suddenly nervous. She was reminded of her father telling her, once, that a man had to look for good news, but that bad news always found him, whether he wanted it to or not.

"It is an important letter, mistress?" The innkeeper asked, leaning over to look at it as if he hadn't had it only a moment before.

"Yes, I believe it is," she answered breathlessly, noting the seal on the letter. The stamp was a golden, stylized picture of a hand holding a sun, and few indeed were the people who would know it for what it was; the secret mark Alashia used to contact her agents or the one used when one of her agents intended to contact another. The Chosen had shown it to her not long after taking her into her service, but Alashia's agents rarely contacted each other—the Chosen preferred them to stay as autonomous as possible—and Alashia herself had never before needed to contact Katherine outside of the appointed times. Katherine had not seen the golden seal since that first day in the Chosen's private chamber.

For someone to try to contact Katherine in such a way, trusting the letter to the hands of the greedy innkeeper, meant that he, or she, was desperate indeed, and it was all Katherine could do to keep from tearing the letter open right then. Instead, she slid it into her bag that was draped over Darl's shoulder. "On second thought, I doubt that it is of any great importance. Thank you," she said to the disappointed looking innkeeper. "Still," she said, sparing a glance for Darl, "we really must be going."

It wasn't until they were on the road outside of town that Katherine reached inside the pack hanging from her horse's side—a placid, kindly mare that Sonya had taken to calling Brownie—and grasped the letter. "How difficult of a time do you imagine our Dear Islin had resisting opening it?" She asked, turning to Darl.

The dusky-skinned man met her gaze with his own eyes, so dark that they were nearly black and without seeming to change his expression at all, his message was clear enough. *You're stalling,* those eyes said, and, of course, they were right.

"Alright, alright," she said, "I suppose there's nothing to do but open it."

She took a deep breath then slowly, carefully, as if she was handling some poisonous snake instead of a letter, she peeled it open, a growing knot of unease settling in her stomach.

Katherine,

I hope that your travels find you well, and that you are taking time to enjoy yourself. Darl is a kind man, and I would trust him above all others, but he isn't much for conversation. Katherine snorted at this, and continued to read.

I am writing to tell you that Tesharna has asked me to visit her in Valeria on a matter of utmost importance and, by the time this letter finds you, I should already be well on my way. I ask that you meet me there with the ... item that you have procured as soon as possible. I look forward to seeing you. My attendants are kind enough, and although I love them all dearly, Amedan has, in his wisdom, seen fit to give them the personalities of a flock of geese.

May Amedan grant you safety and blessings in your journey and keep you always in the light,

Signed,

Chosen Alashia, Humble Priestess of the Great Lord Amedan.

P.S. Please, bring the girl, Sonya, with you. Hers is a kind, innocent soul, and I would very much like to meet her. Watch over her, Katherine. I have reason to believe that she may be important.

Katherine glanced around in surprise as if expecting to see the Chosen sharing the road with them, then caught herself. Amedan's blessing manifested itself differently in each Chosen. Although all of the Six were granted longer lives than normal mortals as well as greater strength and magic, Alashia was the only one that had ever shown any ability at foretelling. No matter how much time she spent with the Chosen, she couldn't get used to the idea that the woman could know what was going to happen before it ever did or, in this case, know what was happening hundreds of miles away.

She'd asked Alashia about it once, and the old woman had claimed that, for the most part, that manifestation of her gift was like trying to guess a man's identity by seeing his outline cloaked in shadow, or trying to read a book when four words out of five were missing. Rarely, she'd said, did she receive anything more than nonsensical fragments, and Katherine couldn't help her own surprise that the Chosen had apparently seen Sonya so clearly.

She handed the note to Darl who read it in silence, his face showing no emotion until the end when he turned to Katherine with one eyebrow raised, the only indication that he, too, had been surprised by the Chosen's words about the little girl. She met his eyes for a moment then nodded, "It looks like our plans have changed."

CHAPTER THIRTY-FOUR

ALESH BIT BACK A SIGH of exasperation as he watched Garn stumble up from the ground for at least the sixth or seventh time in an hour. Since leaving the inn the day before, the Lightbringer had been drinking even more than normal which, was to say, he'd drank enough alcohol to drown an army in. Alesh couldn't imagine where the man got it all, but he didn't like it. The day before, when night had been coming on, Garn had stumbled into the woods and fallen asleep without so much as lighting a single fire, and no matter how hard Alesh had tried, he'd been unable to rouse him. Luckily, he'd paid enough attention to the Lightbringer's use of the herbs he carried that he'd been able to gather wood and make a fire to keep the nightwalkers at bay.

It had been a terrifying night, listening to the snuffling, slinking sounds of the creatures in the woods around them and knowing that the only thing keeping them from tearing him and the bearded man apart was a fire *he'd* created with herbs he didn't even know the name of. The wind had been strong, gusting against the fire as if guided by the hand of some malevolent god, and he'd sat with his sword in his hands, sure that at any moment the flame would go out and the nightlings would charge in to claim their prize, the prize they were cheated out of so many years ago.

And had Garn shown any appreciation that he was still breathing this morning? Of course not. In fact, the man had been even surlier than usual—an achievement Alesh would have thought impossible until a few hours ago.

He'd asked the man what was wrong, but his attempts at conversation had been met with grunts or outright silence. After a time, Alesh had given up. The man wasn't going to talk to him no matter how hard he tried, and he had things of his own to worry about.

Things like making it to Valeria and warning Chosen Tesharna of Kale's betrayal. Things like finding Sonya. Every time he thought of the girl, so young and innocent, he felt a stab of guilt. He was sure that, once he told her what was happening, the Chosen would send an army to cast Kale and the Redeemers down, knew that he stood a better chance of saving Sonya that way than searching an entire city for her, dodging soldiers with each step, but that didn't change the fact that he felt like he was betraying the girl, the girl who'd trusted *him* to keep her safe.

"Come on. We'll make camp over there."

Alesh started at the sound of the man's voice, staring around in surprise. He'd been so lost in his own thoughts that he hadn't been aware of the deepening gloom.

He glanced to where Garn had pointed and blinked to be sure he was seeing it right; a circular crater that was at least a hundred feet in length sat in the middle of the trees. There was no grass, and the hard-packed soil looked black. There were no trees inside that ring of devastation, no plant growth at all, and those few stubborn specimens that stood at the crater's edge were twisted and bent outward, as if they'd preferred escape from whatever force had been unleashed there even more than they did the vital light of the sun. To Alesh, it looked like some giant had smashed his fist into the ground in a fit of rage. "W-where is this place?" He asked.

"Don't you know anything?" Garn asked with a sneer, "This is Shyler's Fell."

Alesh's mouth dropped open in surprise. Of course, he'd heard of Shyler's Fell. Everyone had. But he'd never expected to actually *see* it. There had been a point, about midway through the war, when it had looked as if the humans were going to lose. No matter what the Chosen did, Argush and his army were always ready to counter it, always lying in wait to ambush the armies of men when they weren't prepared, to attack them at their weakest point and no one could figure out how.

Amedan's Six had, of course, been the leaders of the army, and Olliman first among those, but they'd been priests and priestesses, not generals or military strategists. Even Tesharna, who would later become known as the greatest tactician the world had ever seen, had known nothing of warfare in the early days, and the Six had needed a man with experience to command their armies.

They found what they needed in a man named Shyler Aledrian, by all accounts a gruff, but incredibly cunning general, and, as it happened, Olliman's closest friend. According to the books Alesh had read, the man had been a nearly peerless swordsman but, more importantly, he was also one of the greatest generals the world had ever seen, and, at first, he validated the Six's faith in him by pulling the human armies out of near certain defeat again and again, winning victory after victory despite his army being significantly outnumbered. In the early days of the war, his name was whispered with almost as much reverence as Olliman himself, and it was the two of them, more than anyone else, that were considered the saviors of humanity. Now, however, he wasn't known for being a master swordsman or an extremely intelligent and capable general but, instead, as what he was, the world's most famous traitor, singularly responsible for the deaths of thousands of soldiers and very nearly the defeat of the human armies.

The stories claimed that Olliman learned of Shyler's treachery, and he and a few scouts confronted the traitorous general at the same spot that Alesh now stood. They came upon Shyler meeting with a small delegation sent from Argush's army. An eye witness account from one of the scouts claimed that upon finding Shyler so engaged, the Chosen went into a rage. He drew deeply on the power of his god, and his very eyes shone a gold so brilliant they were painful to look upon and that when he began to tear into the nightwalkers like some avenging god himself, thin wisps of golden light trailed from his body.

With the smoking corpses of the creatures lying about them in grotesque heaps, Olliman and his friend fought into the night. The Chosen, too, had been a renowned swordsman, and the scholars said that the fight lasted the rest of the night, both men drawing on all of their skill and training, fighting to the point of exhaustion, and then past it. Then, with the first light of dawn rising in the sky, Olliman smote Shyler with his sword and, once his friend lay writhing on the forest floor, defeated and dying, the Chosen called upon the power of his god, and fire and lightning blasted Shyler's body and the landscape surrounding it. Olliman cursed the ground on which he'd fallen, so that never again would it be given the gift of life, but would lie dead and useless forever, the unmarked grave of a man who had betrayed his people. To this day, no one knew why Shyler had did what he had, and his name was a by-word for traitors all over the kingdom.

Being at the site of the Chosen's betrayal, Alesh felt an almost unbearable sadness for Olliman. Despite the many blessings given him by Amedan, or perhaps because of them, Olliman had suffered more than few men ever had. Standing there before that crater of scorched earth, Alesh found himself unable to speak. Reading of the place was one thing, but seeing it, seeing the blackened ground, tasting the dead air that permeated the area around the clearing and staring at the warped trees struggling away from the desolation in their midst, was quite another.

He followed Garn into the woods nearby, stumbling over a tree root and almost falling because he couldn't seem to pull his eyes off of the burned out crater. Night had almost completely arrived by the time they were finished setting up camp and, without a word, Garn lay down to sleep. Alesh sat by the fire, staring into the darkness toward where he knew the crater lay, and a deep melancholy overcame him as he thought of those he'd lost. What was the point of all of it? Olliman had defeated Shyler, but in the end, it seemed that everything he'd spent his entire life building was falling apart just the same. A man could hold a light up to the night, could venture out to meet it and push the shadows back, but sooner or later all lights died, and the darkness was nothing if not patient.

After a time, Garn turned and looked at him. The firelight reflected in the Lightbringer's eyes gave them a sullen orange glow, but when he spoke his voice was almost sympathetic, "It's a bad place, boy, I know that, but we'll only have to suffer it for a night. Here." He reached into his pack and tossed Alesh a flask, "Take a drink. Sometimes, the world is sharp enough to cut, but a few drinks will soften the edges a bit, and you need your sleep." He glanced away into the darkness then, in a voice barely loud enough for Alesh to hear, "*A man can stomach anything, if he has to.*"

Alesh had never been much of a drinker—he only had a small amount of control in his life, and he didn't like the idea of giving that bit up to drunkenness—but just then, there were a lot of hard edges that needed smoothing, so he took a large pull from the flask, wincing as it traced a line of liquid fire down his throat, and tossed it back to the Lightbringer. "Thanks," he said, and meant it.

The man grunted and put the flask away before lying down again, the small kindness apparently taking its toll. Alesh wondered that the Lightbringer could sleep in such a place. The trees made it impossible to see the crater, but he could *feel* it out there just the same, festering like some great blight on the face of the land.

I'll be lucky if I ever sleep again, he thought, and he was preparing himself for another long night spent listening to creatures in the darkness, thinking of smoke and fire, of blood and corpses, when his eyelids suddenly felt impossibly heavy. He lay down and thought of his friends, of Olliman, and his parents, and the nightlings and, in another moment, nothing at all.

CHAPTER THIRTY-FIVE

His mother's scream was muffled by the wagon's compartment, but he could hear the fear, the hysteria in it. A moment more and his father's shouting joined hers, ragged cries of rage and despair. There was a bone-jarring impact, and Alesh's head slammed into the slat of wood that enclosed the compartment. He bit his tongue, tasted the coppery tang of blood, and then they were flipping through the air, end over end, each revolution slamming him against the inside of the wagon and sending sharp lances of agony through his body.

The wagon crashed to the earth, wood snapping and shattering with the force of its landing. Alesh's head struck the side of the wagon again and white light flashed in his eyes. He lay, dazed, feeling as if every bone in his body had been broken. Outside, something growled in what sound like satisfaction, then other voices joined it, growling and shrieking in maddening, terrible cries that sent a shiver of terror through him. "Get away from her, you bastards!" His father's voice, almost as feral, as bestial as the others.

"Torrik!" His mother screamed, "Watch out!"

His father answered in a wordless howl of fury and pain that seemed to go on forever. Then there was a violent *ripping* sound, and abruptly his father's cries cut off. His mother screamed, her voice breaking into heart-wrenching sobs that could be heard over the cacophony of growls and snarls that seemed to come from every direction. "*Amedan, Father of Light, ple—*" That terrible tearing sound came again, and then she, too, was silent.

Inhuman voices howled and cried out their triumph, a blood-curdling chorus that was, by far, the worst sound Alesh had ever heard. Until they began to feed. *Please no,* Alesh thought. *This isn't how it happened. I wasn't awake.* But the dream did not stop, and he laid there, his body crying out in pain, and listened to the wet slurping noises until, finally, they ended. He felt a wash of relief when the noises stopped but, in another moment, a snuffling came from outside the wagon, a sound that reminded Alesh of a dog searching for a scent. *They can smell me,* his fear-addled mind had time to register. Then the wagon gave a violent lurch, the wood creaking in protest as something jerked at the compartment door. Alesh's cry of fear was answered by an ear-splitting roar and the wagon gave a lurch even more powerful than the first. Wood cracked and a chunk of the compartment's door came free in a shower of splinters.

Alesh watched the finger-length claws tearing at the wood with something almost like relief. He would be with his parents again. Soon. *My father's name is Torrik,* he thought, then he closed his eyes and waited for the end.

Alesh, A strangely familiar voice spoke inside of his head, *you must awake.* He pushed the voice away, tried to ignore it. He'd been alone for too long. This time would be different, this time, he would be with his parents. *Wake up,* the words came again, more insistent this time.

He watched as the remnants of the doorway were torn free and thrown aside. An impossibly large form stared down at him. He could see little more than its shadow in the darkness, and its eyes. Glowing a deep red, like blood, a gaze that held no hint of compassion, no understanding of mercy or kindness. Eyes that knew only death, only blood and the screams of the dying.

Alesh felt hands on him, tugging at him. He expected at any moment to feel those claws, so long and sharp, but the grip that held him was almost gentle. *Alesh,* the voice said again, *you have to wake up.* He felt himself being pulled, and he fought against it, struggled to tear free, but though the grip was gentle, it was powerful, and he might as well have been a child struggling against a grown man. *Alesh, WAKE UP NOW!*

Alesh jerked to his feet, his hands pressed tightly against his temple as the dying echoes of the shout faded. He felt as if his head might explode but, in another moment, the pain was gone. Suddenly, he was overcome with the feeling that he was in some terrible danger, and he had the almost irresistible urge to run, to get *away*. *Relax,* he told himself, taking slow, deep breaths, wiping hair lank with sweat out of his face, *it was just the dream. That's all. Everything's fine.* Still, the feeling wouldn't go away.

He glanced at the fire that was still burning brightly, pushing back the darkness. The sight should have reassured him, but for some reason it didn't. He decided then that, foolish or not, he'd feel better with the sword in his hand. He walked to where he'd left it and found, to his surprise, that it was gone. He was still looking for it when he heard footsteps behind him.

"Looking for this?" Asked a voice he didn't recognize.

Alesh whipped around. In the firelight, the man's face looked hard, severe. A jagged, bone-white scar traced its way down one cheek. It was a soldier's face, and the cruel smile the man wore did nothing to soften its hard lines and edges. The man, like the five that stood behind him, was dressed in a suit of midnight black armor and a long red cape hung from his back. "Redeemers?" Alesh asked, confused, "but how—"

He backed up a step and started as he bumped into something. Turning, his hands coming up to defend himself, he nearly lashed out before he saw that the man behind him wasn't one of the soldiers, but the bearded Lightbringer. "Garn," he said, grabbing the man by the arm, "quick, we have to get out of here."

Garn shook his hand off and took a long pull from the liquor flask that had become all too familiar in their days on the road. "It's no use, boy. Where can you run? If you try to escape, the nightwalkers will get you."

"*Come on,* we can make it" Alesh said, grabbing the man's arm again and suddenly freezing as realization rocked him. You. He'd said *you*. He met the Lightbringer's gaze, a terrible calm settling over him. "You betrayed me," he said, a statement, not a question.

Garn's face twisted in sudden fury, "*I'm no traitor, boy!*" He shouted. He stared at Alesh, his eyes narrowed, daring him to argue. When he didn't, the Lightbringer went on in a lower voice, "I went back downstairs at the inn last night, figuring to get myself a drink no matter what that big bastard Tassin said. I didn't—the son of a bitch was guarding it like it was his only daughter's virtue—but imagine my surprise when a man comes up to me and starts asking if I'd seen someone matching your description? This fella, he told me that the man he was looking for was responsible for Chosen Olliman's death."

"That's a lie," Alesh said, but with little feeling. He doubted that the Lightbringer believed it himself, but he'd no doubt been promised a reward for turning Alesh in.

I'm sorry, Erwin, he thought with something like relief, *I tried.*

"What did you expect me to do, huh?" Garn asked in an angry, defensive voice, "Die for you? You asked me before how I survived when the others were all taken or killed, well, boy, I'll tell you how; I'm a survivor. I'm alive, and I intend to stay that way, and if I have to choose between my life and yours or Merik and those other stupid, stubborn bastards, well, that ain't much of a choice at all is it?"

"You gave them up." Alesh said, knowing it was true as he spoke it. "But how? Why? Lightbringers are supposed to be the bravest of men. They're supposed to be *heroes.*"

Garn snorted and spat disdainfully, "I was trained to fight nightlings not men. Besides, I'd rather be a living coward than a dead hero any day."

"Enough talk," the Redeemer who'd spoken before growled, "Bind him, Lightbringer. We start back to Ilrika immediately."

"Yes, captain. And you'll keep to your end of the deal?" Garn asked, an uncertain, almost pleading tone in his gruff voice.

The scarred man smiled, "Oh yes. Why, I'm sure that the Chosen will have some use for a man as ... *loyal* as yourself."

Garn nodded and withdrew a coil of rope from his belt. "They're going to kill you, Garn," Alesh said in a cold, emotionless voice as the Lightbringer stepped behind him, "You know that don't you?"

"Shut your damned mouth. You don't know a night-cursed thing."

Alesh laughed, but there was no humor in it. "What do you think, Garn? That Kale's going to kill all of the others and, out of the goodness of his heart, decide to spare you?" He shook his head contemptuously, "You are even more a fool than you are a coward."

"I told you to keep your mouth shut!" The Lightbringer growled, striking Alesh hard in the back of the head. It hurt, but he'd taken harder in his training sessions with Kale, and it was what he'd been waiting for. He spun with the blow, turning and planting a fist in the bearded man's stomach. Garn's breath left him in a gasp. Before he could recover, Alesh whipped his hand out and struck the Lightbringer in the throat. Garn stumbled back, clawing at his throat, tripped, and sprawled on the ground in a writhing heap.

"Get him you stupid bastards!" The captain shouted, and the men rushed forward.

Instead of turning to face them, Alesh knelt beside the writhing Lightbringer and dug through the man's tunic. A crossbow bolt whistled by him, close enough for him to feel the wind of its passage. "Don't kill him, you fool!" The captain shouted, "The Chosen wants him alive!"

Not daring to take time to think about what he was doing, Alesh withdrew two massive handfuls of Pralentia—all that was left in the Lightbringer's pouch and many times more than he'd ever seen Garn use—and threw them toward the fire and the single torch that one of the Redeemers carried.

The leaves turned from black to red while still in the air, swelling as they absorbed the light and heat of the flames. Then they burst in a blinding shower of sparks. When the light faded and died, the clearing was left in complete darkness.

Alesh withdrew the Evertorch from his tunic and turned to run, thankful that he'd not left the cylinder with his other belongings for fear of it being damaged. He'd only made it a few steps when something whistled out of the darkness and slammed into his left shoulder. He screamed as pain exploded in his arm, staggered, and only just managed to keep his feet. He reached to his shoulder with his other hand, and his fingers brushed against a thin length of wood. He hissed as the arrow shifted at his touch and sent hot lines of agony through his left side. Apparently, one of the soldiers had decided that Kale would have to be satisfied with a dead traitor to hang from the city's walls.

He shuffled forward uncertainly, the pain making him dizzy. Just a little farther, and he could use the Evertorch to drive back the creatures that, even now, were no doubt skulking forward, surrounding him and the others. He took one step, then another, sweating and growling at the effort. His legs gave out on him on the next step, and he fell to his knees. He wasn't as far away from the others as he would have liked, but it would have to do.

Not thinking, he tried to raise the hand holding the Evertorch, his wounded hand, and a fresh wave of pain lanced through him, making his stomach roil threateningly. Gritting his teeth, he reached for it with his right and gasped in shock. The Evertorch was gone. It must have fallen out of his grasp when he'd been struck. "*Damnit,*" he hissed. Desperate, expecting one of the creatures to come tearing out of the woods any second, he dropped to all fours and began pawing at the forest floor around him with his one working hand.

"Someone make a fire now and get that bastard!" The captain screamed somewhere in the nearby darkness. Alesh noted, even as a part of him shrieked and jabbered in fear, that the calm assurance had vanished from the captain's voice.

"I can't see a thing!" One of the other Redeemers shouted in a terrified voice. There was a loud rustling a short distance away and when the man spoke again his voice quavered like that of a child, "W-wait, what is—" The rest of his words were drowned out by a bone-chilling howl that sliced through the night. Another followed shortly after, then another, and soon the inhuman growls and cries rose in a chorus louder than any thunderstorm. Those hungry cries sent shivers of panic rushing through Alesh, and he tore at the ground with renewed energy, his heart hammering in his chest.

"Oh n-no, Oh g-gods, no," someone whimpered, and Alesh heard the sounds of rushing footsteps as one of the men, mad with terror, bolted into the surrounding woods. The captain screamed at the man to come back, but if the man heard, he gave no sign.

For a moment, Alesh almost ran after him, but he fought down the urge to flee and continued to scrabble at the forest floor, desperately flicking away sticks and leaves. A few seconds later, a scream erupted from the direction in which the man had run, a gut-wrenching, horror-inspiring sound that was, in its way, worse even than the growls and shrieks of the creatures around them.

Alesh felt a flash of pity but pushed it away. If the Redeemers had their way, he'd be led back to Ilrika in chains only to be executed at Kale's leisure. Of course, he might regret his choice if he didn't manage to find the Evertorch soon. Without it, he would surely die and in a way much more horrible than Kale could ever dream of.

Something in the night let out a growl reminiscent of the sounds a dog might make when worrying at a bone, and the man's screams cut off. Silence, deep and heavy, fell on the clearing, and Alesh paused in his search, not daring to so much as breathe lest he draw attention to himself. Then, as if on cue, the forest erupted with the sounds of twigs and branches snapping. He could just make out the vague shapes of creatures gliding forward in the darkness, coming at the clearing from all directions. The Redeemers began to curse or whimper prayers to their goddess, Shira, but she, like Amedan, did not answer and dozens of pairs of yellow and red glowing eyes began to appear in the shadows. Then they were among the soldiers, and the prayers of the men quickly turned to tortured, dying screams.

Alesh clawed at the ground with both hands now, the pain of his wound nearly forgotten in his fear. He was still searching, cursing under his breath, when something exploded out of the darkness to his left. He barely had time to raise an arm in defense before the creature barreled into him with the strength of a galloping horse, knocking him over and sending him sprawling. The nightling was on him before he could rise, and he screamed as dagger-sharp claws traced lines of white hot pain down his sides. He grabbed wildly at the shadowy shape astride him and after a desperate struggle, his hands closed upon two limbs as thin as a child's arms.

The creature's flesh felt oily and scaled in the darkness, like the body of a snake, and despite its thinness, it took every bit of Alesh's failing strength to hold it at bay. Something wet, blood or drool, fell on his face as the creature hissed in frustration and hunger, and he shouted in agony as two claws—those of the creature's back legs—dug into his thighs.

Grunting with effort, he rolled backward and kicked out with both legs, screaming as the claws tore out of his flesh with a sickening squelch. The nightling let out a cry of pain or frustration as it tumbled through the air and disappeared into the waiting darkness. His breath coming in ragged gasps, Alesh struggled to his feet. Shadows began to gather at the corner of his vision, but he shook his head, willing them away. If he was going to die, he was going to die standing. "Come on then, you bastard!" he grated, unable to hear himself over the screams and death throes of the soldiers around him. As if it understood him, the creature appeared a short distance away, its red eyes like pin pricks of blood on a curtain of pitch.

The nightwalker hissed and surged forward, impossibly quick. Alesh braced for it as Olliman had shown him, his hands in front of him, his knees bent, his muscles taut in anticipation. But just before the creature was on him, something slammed into him from out of the darkness. Alesh was flung through the air as if he weighed no more than a child, and he crashed to the earth more than ten feet away from where he'd been standing, his head striking the hard-packed earth. He looked back to where he'd been standing a moment before, but darkness pushed insistently at the edges of his vision, and he could see nothing but a shadowy figure approaching him. *Get up,* he told himself, *You have to get up.* But try as he might, his body refused to obey his commands, and he found himself feeling more tired, more exhausted than he ever had in his life. Why should he bother, really? It was easier to lie still, to stop fighting. He could see them again, all of them. Chorin, Abigail, Olliman. His mother. His father. They were waiting for him. *Torrik,* he thought, blinking, *My father's name*—the darkness rushed forward, and he knew nothing more.

CHAPTER THIRTY-SIX

RION STIFLED A YAWN AS SEVRIN retold the story—was it the third time, now, or the fourth?—of how he'd managed to bed Lady Elisa. The hawk-faced man recounted the events of the previous evening with a dramatic flair, as if it was a feat on par with Amedan granting the people of Entarna the knowledge of fire thousands of years ago. Of course, all of this ignored the fact that Lady Elisa was *known* for such dalliances and that bragging about such a thing was, in Rion's mind at least, like a card player bragging about pulling a trump out of his sleeve.

For their part, Armiel and Bastion were leaned forward in their seats listening eagerly, as if they hadn't just heard the same story no more than an hour ago. The young noble's eyes were wide, his cheeks a bright red, and the fat, future priest's mouth worked soundlessly as if the story made him hungry which, Rion supposed, it probably did. *Everything* did, after all. *Fools all of them,* Rion thought, *but rich fools and that's enough. It has to be.* Still, the thought of sitting and listening to them much longer was an almost impossibly depressing one, and he couldn't stop the sigh that escaped his mouth.

"Oh, I'm sorry, Eriondrian," Sevrin said, running a hand through his slick, black hair as was his habit, "Am I boring you?"

Rion gave him a small smile, "Oh, I wouldn't say I'm bored, Sevrin; I was bored the first time you told the story. I've long since progressed to a comfortable state of discontent."

The nobleman frowned as he motioned to a nearby servant to refill his drink, "Perhaps you would be wise to listen more carefully, Eriondrian. You might learn a thing or two about how to woo the fairer sex—that is, of course, if you *want* to do such a thing. As I hear it, you haven't shown much interest to Lady Allindia, despite her overt advances." He smiled, "Maybe you and that blacksmith are better friends than I've realized."

Rion's expression went blank. Allindia, like many of the noblewomen in the city, was interested in his father's estate, not Rion himself, and the truth was that Rion couldn't stand the childish pouting and simpering so common to most spoiled noblewomen. "Oh, I enjoy the company of women as much as anyone." he said. "The difference between me and you is really no more than a question of standards. For you, it is enough that they have managed to fit themselves into a dress, while I…." he hesitated. The truth was he had no idea *what* he wanted in a woman. He just knew that he wasn't interested in the pampered, face-painted sheep that made up the city's noblewomen.

Sevrin rolled his eyes, "I'm more interested in whether or not they can get themselves out of the dress than into it, friend Rion. Still," he said, waving a hand in a gesture that encompassed the dozens of people dancing in the ballroom as well as the women standing in small groups, servants hurrying to and fro to attend their needs, "Surely, among so many of the city's finest, you could find *someone* that fits your standards. Why, it's been over a year since you courted Lady Marsilla. Too much longer, and people may begin to whisper."

Which means that you already are, you arrogant bastard. It was Rion's turn to frown. He had courted Marsilla for over two months, and for a time, she'd seemed different than the other noblewomen, more concerned with the politics of the city and Chosen Tesharna's latest laws than with dresses or balls. Of course, it hadn't taken long before Rion discovered that she wanted to use a connection with his house as a lever to achieve a position of authority on the city council. That was the problem with being one of the richest, most powerful noble houses in the city—or at least being *thought* to be one at any rate—when people looked at you, they didn't see you, but your name. Thinking of Marsilla, Rion felt himself growing angry, and he patted the handle of the thin, dueling rapier at his side, "Such whispers can be remedied easily enough. Particularly if someone is brazen enough to speak them to my face."

In truth, the swords they all had belted at their sides were more for show than anything, a tradition that was said to have once symbolized the willingness of the nobles to always be prepared to fight for their city and their ruler, but since then the meaning had been lost, and they were worn now merely for fashion's sake. Still, the gesture seemed clear enough to Sevrin, and the black-haired man smirked confidently. *As well he should.* The nobleman was known as being one of the finest duelists in Valeria, which, Rion suspected, was most likely a necessary product of his apparent quest to sleep with every noblewoman—married or not—in the city.

Sevrin was just opening his mouth to reply when Armiel spoke hurriedly, his voice worried, "Come on, friends. There is no need to bicker. Sevrin, there's no question of your prowess both with women," he gave Rion a pointed look, "as *well* as the blade. And Rion, we all know that you've been too busy running your family's estate to spend your time courting. In fact, I'm surprised that you even had time to come tonight."

"Yes," Sevrin drawled in a bored tone, "shocking. Ah," he said, turning to look at a noblewoman dressed in a black dress of mourning that had just entered the ballroom. "If it isn't Lady Anell. I would not have expected her to be out so soon after her poor husband's passing to the wasting sickness. What was it, a fortnight ago?" He turned back to them with a wink, "Perhaps she could use some comforting." This said, he rose and sauntered away in the direction of the distracted looking noblewoman.

Rion frowned as he watched him go. In Valeria, it was custom for a woman or man to wear black for a month after their spouse's passing respect for the dead, and although she was observing the practice of it, the sultry smile Lady Anell gave the approaching Sevrin made Rion suspect that the purpose of the custom had been lost on her. Suddenly, the thought of sitting among the noblemen for a second longer was intolerable, and Rion rose from his cushioned chair. "I'm sorry, friends, but I, too, must go."

"What?" Armiel asked, surprised, "Why, you've only just got here,

Eriondrian. Surely you need not leave so soon."

"I'm afraid I must," he said, standing patiently as a servant brought his sable cloak and draped it over his shoulders, fastening it around his neck with a golden clasp in the shape of a coin. "As you have said, the running of my family's business is a busy job, and there are matters that demand my attention."

The young nobleman's lips turned into a pout, like a child being forced to bed against his wishes, "Very well, but father is hosting a ball at our estate next week. Promise that you'll come?"

Rion nodded, "I will come if I can, Armiel." *If I can stomach the thought of spending my time with a bunch of noble fools with more money than sense that is.* He turned to walk away.

"Oh, and Eriondrian?"

Rion glanced back at the nobleman, raising an eyebrow in question.

The young lord's face had an anxious cast, "You should be careful about how you talk to Sevrin. You know his father has been paying one of the Ekirani Blademasters to train him since he could barely walk; you wouldn't have a chance against him in a duel."

Rion smiled calmly at the nobleman, "Oh, there's always a chance, Armiel. It's what makes life so interesting." He'd only just finished speaking when a man's laughter, loud and deep, rang out directly behind him. He whipped around with a grunt, but no one was there, and the closest of the ball's attendees, a man and woman of minor houses, were far too engaged with each other and their wine to have been the one he'd heard. Besides, he still *heard* the laughter, though it was growing weaker, fading as if its owner were across the room from them and walking away. After another second, it vanished altogether.

"Are you alright, Eriondrian?"

"Hmm?" He turned to see Armiel staring at him, a curious expression on his face. Even Bastion had pulled himself away from his meal long enough to look at Rion with a greasy, uncertain smile on his lips. Rion followed their gazes to his hand and was surprised to find that he'd drawn his sword half out of its scabbard. Coughing, he slid it back and made a show of adjusting it as if it was out of place, "I'm … fine," he said, "but I really must be going. Stay in the light, Armiel. Bastion."

Armiel frowned but nodded, "And you, Eriondrian."

The future priest gave a quick, dismissive nod, his attention once more occupied by the leg of mutton that was, even now, dripping grease and fat onto his chin and white tunic as he took massive, hungry bites out of it. *You may as well put the clothes on a mongrel dog,* Rion thought disgustedly, *they'd stay cleaner that way.*

As he left the ballroom, he watched the other attendees, but no one so much as glanced in his direction, all of them too busy drinking and dining, laughing and flirting. *I just need some rest, that's all,* he told himself with a confidence he didn't feel as he made his way past the tables, *that's all.* Yet, try as he might, he couldn't shake the feeling that someone was watching him. Watching and laughing.

This late in the evening, the streets of Valeria held few people, and the lanterns placed at intervals along the streets did little to fight back the shadows that crept along the street and slithered up the sides of buildings like living things. Rion had always felt most comfortable in the night where a man was only a vague shape in the darkness and no one knew or cared who his family was, when a man was only responsible for himself and no one else. But not tonight. Tonight, he felt hunted.

He took a slow deep breath, telling himself that he was being paranoid, and started toward the *Golden Torch.* He'd traveled this street many times and its familiarity should have comforted him, but it did not. In the darkness, the buildings seemed to huddle around him, to stoop and mark his progress with malevolent stares, and those few people that shared the streets with him were cruel specters, their eyes shining like liquid fire in the orange glow of the street lanterns.

He found himself shying away from them as they passed, wincing at every creaking door or raucous shout from a nearby bar. He passed several city guards going about their nightly patrols, and it was all he could do to keep from running up to them and begging for help; he felt terrified and, what was worse, he felt *helpless.* Helpless in a way that he hadn't felt since he'd been a child, cowering in his bed and staring wide-eyed at the shadows in his room as his mind replayed one of the stories the merchants who sometimes came to his father's manse were so fond of telling. Stories full of swords and blood, nightwalkers and lies. *You're being a damned fool,* he cursed himself, but the feeling of being hunted grew worse with each step he took.

He was only a few streets away from *the Torch* when laughter sounded behind him. He let out a cry of surprise and, gripping the handle of his sword tightly, spun to meet his pursuers. His sword had almost completely cleared its scabbard before he realized that his "pursuers" were a portly man, a noble judging by his fine clothes, and a middle-aged, equally portly woman whose overly-painted face and revealing dress marked her as a professional. The two had just stumbled out of a nearby inn, laughing and nearly falling over each other.

They'd taken several steps toward Rion before noticing him, and the man broke off from fondling the woman's drooping breasts long enough to turn a drunken leer on Rion, "Eh? What'dye aim to do wit' that?"

Rion, heart still galloping in his chest, raised his other hand in apology, "I'm sorry, I didn't mean to startle you."

"Oh, I wouldn't think nothin' of it, hon," the woman said, leering and giving him what he supposed was meant to be an enticing wink, "I've seen bigger, and they don't scare me none." She cackled at her own joke, and the man with her frowned slightly. She leaned closer, eyeing Rion like a horse at market, "Well! But you're a cute one, aren't ya? Tell you what, sweety, you call on me later, huh? Launa will find you a place to put your sword in, yes she will."

Rion coughed uncomfortably and slid the blade back into its scabbard. He opened his mouth to respond but could think of nothing to say. Luckily, he was saved from an overly long uncomfortable silence as the man grunted in anger, apparently only just catching up with the conversation, "Hey now!" He said, jerking on the woman's arm roughly, "I didn't pay, so's to listen to your damned talkin' did I?"

The woman let out a small, obviously feigned cry of surprise and winked at Rion before letting herself be dragged down the road. Rion watched the two go, cursing himself again. He waited for them to disappear down the street before heading out himself. *What's happening to me?* He thought as he walked, *Is this what it's like to lose your mind?* And it wasn't just that he'd nearly cut down a prostitute and a drunk, was it? No, not *just* that. Armiel might be a spoiled child, but he'd been right to worry. Sevrin was a fool who used his family's power in the city like a weapon, beating down those below his station and using it to take advantage of women, but Armiel was right when he said that Rion would stand little chance in a duel against him. So why, then, had he all but challenged the man?

Challenge a man trained by an Ekirani Blademaster since he was a child? It would have been a mistake but, fortunately or not, not one that he would have had to live with for long.

The Ekirani were the people of the small, distant island, Ekiran, the young men of which were trained from birth in what they called, 'The Dance.' Only the very best of these were given the honor of being named Blademasters. Little was known about the Ekirani, taller and thinner than their Entarnan cousins, but their skill and knowledge in all matters of war were unquestioned. The Ekirani were not just trained in sword play, but in battle strategy as well, dedicating themselves to war and battle with a religious fervor. The fact that they were said to worship Paren, God of Conflict, son of the Primes, Shira and Amedan, and twin to Javen, the God of Chance, even above Amedan himself, was enough for them to be declared heretics and blasphemers by the Church of Amedan and the whole of Entarna. Declared quietly, of course, and never around one of the Blademasters themselves.

Blasphemers or not, noblemen paid exorbitant prices to hire companies of the Blademasters for their small standing armies or to make use of them as bodyguards. Only the richest of the noblemen could afford such a thing, but many believed it well worth the price as common belief considered one Ekirani to be worth a dozen regular soldiers or more in a fight, and Ekirani generals were said to be the most brilliant military minds of the age. It was proof of Lord Alrick's fortune that he could afford to hire one of the legendary warriors to train his son in the use of the blade, a tutor that was envied by all of the city's noble houses.

Rion finally made it to his room at the *Torch* and began the process of changing into his ragged clothes and threadbare cloak. Next, he withdrew several daggers from the chest at the foot of the bed and began secreting them in hidden loops and sheaths under his clothing. As he did, Rion reflected that, while Ekirani Blademasters were said to be harsh in their education, the streets of Valeria had their own lessons to teach, and the punishment for failure was nothing so small as a cuff upside the head or an extra mile tallied to the day's jog. The Blademasters, the streets. There were many teachers a man might have, and many ways that he might learn.

CHAPTER THIRTY-SEVEN

ALESH AWOKE IN AGONY. HE tried to scream, but the sound came out as little more than a dry, rattling croak. The memories came back in a rush, memories of the nightlings with their claws like daggers and their hungry, malevolent growls. He forced his eyes open and gasped hoarsely in surprise as blinding light lanced into his vision. It was as if the sun itself, the great torch that Amedan had hung in the sky thousands of years ago when he created his children and gave them the gift of light, had crashed to the earth. Grass rustled beside him. He tried to turn, to rise, but the pain crested, threatening to jerk him back down into unconsciousness.

Suddenly, a figure appeared over him, and the dazzling light grew brighter still. He squeezed his eyes shut but soon realized it did no good and opened them again, squinting. He tried to look away but again his battered body wouldn't move, and he noticed something strange. The light wasn't coming from above or behind the figure but from the figure itself, radiating out as if he or she was some great torch or lantern. *A fever dream,* he thought to himself, *random images in my mind as I die, nothing more.*

And there really wasn't any question that he was dying, the pain was a promise of that much. His skin burned as if it had been set alight, and the wound in his shoulder throbbed with a viciousness that left him short of breath. His thighs, too, blazed where the creature's claws had scored him. *Finish it already, you bastards,* he thought wildly but as soon as he thought it he realized that he could no longer hear the snuffles and growls of the nightwalkers. There was the silence and his own gasping breaths and nothing more. *Your brain's addled. You're dying alright. That's the only way this ends.*

The figure above him seemed to move, a blur of motion as if seen through water, and pain exploded in his shoulder, sudden and violent, and all his thoughts disappeared in a roiling sea of anguish. He tried to scream again and found that he could, after all. He screamed, and he screamed, and then he passed out.

When he awoke again, he was lying on his back. His tongue felt thick and impossibly dry, like a piece of charred firewood in his mouth. His wounds still throbbed, but the excruciating pain had subsided to bearable, and he found that he could think clearly, though he still felt impossibly weak. A steady, rushing, burbling sound came from somewhere close by. *A river? But where am I?* Remembering the painful brightness of before, he opened his eyes slowly. Light spilled into his vision, but it was the normal glow of the morning sun, not the shocking, impossibly bright light of before. *Sunlight?* He thought, *but how? For that matter, why am I still alive?* People didn't survive a night spent in darkness, not anymore. Maybe never again.

Which means.... The priests of Amedan said that the sun always shone in the land of the dead, and that there was no pain. Well, they were wrong—he might not be in as much pain as before, but he certainly wouldn't be doing any dancing anytime soon—but, then, to Alesh's mind, the priests made a career out of being wrong. Was it really any surprise that the same people who believed Amedan was a kind, compassionate being who cherished mankind would also be wrong about the afterlife?

A popping sound came from behind him, and Alesh groaned with the effort of turning a head that seemed to have grown a hundred times heavier in the last few hours. A gray-robed figure knelt in the grass, turned away from him. Alesh tried to speak, but all that came out was a weak cough. He took a moment to steady himself then tried again, "W-who are you?" He rasped and was shocked by how frail his voice sounded.

The figure did not respond, but remained hunched over a small fire. There was something familiar about the scene, the gray robes, the hiss and pop of the fire, something achingly, naggingly familiar. Then, with a shock, Alesh knew what it reminded him of, and he felt his blood go cold. If he'd ever doubted he was dead, there was no doubting it now. For there, knelt in the grass only a few feet away from him, his robes the same dull gray as the smoke that drifted and curled above him, like fingers grasping at the air, was the Keeper of the Dead.

Stories of the Keeper, the soulless creature that was said to escort the recently dead to the afterlife, ran through his mind in a panicked, confused jumble until one half remembered phrase from some old nursery rhyme rang in his head with the finality of a funeral bell.

And the fire's red; he keeps it hot
for those who're dead and those who're not,
if you don't see him wait a while,
he's up ahead, a foot, a mile
waiting, watching, his brand in hand
You may run or crawl, sit or stand,
But no man ever leaves his land.

Gooseflesh rose on Alesh's skin, and he watched the gray robed figure, fear and wonder mingling in his mind. It was said that the Keeper marked the dead with a burning brand, so that they could never again be allowed back into the world of living. *No,* he thought desperately, *I don't believe in the gods.* But believe or not, one was knelt in front of him and there was no arguing with that. Panic seized him, and he tried to lift himself up again. He'd barely risen a few inches when white-hot agony shot through his battered body, and he fell back to the ground, gasping in pain.

The figure went still then slowly began to turn. Suddenly, Alesh wanted anything but to see the figure's face, to look into the eyes of a being who served as eternity's warden, but he found that he couldn't look away no matter how hard he tried. He was frozen, terrified and yet overcome with a sick curiosity. When the figure finally did turn and look at him, Alesh gasped in surprise. "P-Priest?" He asked when he was finally able to speak, "Is that really you?"

The older man smiled, a twinkle in his eyes, and as he walked closer, Alesh realized that what he'd expected to be a fiery brand was actually a steaming bowl of stew. The priest knelt beside him, and as the smell of the stew wafted into his nose, Alesh found that he was ravenous. He tried to reach for the bowl, but his arm wouldn't answer his call, and he cursed quietly at his own weakness.

For his part, the priest only smiled and withdrew a tin spoon from the bowl. "Slowly," he said, his voice soft and kind. Alesh was struck with a memory of how he'd tried to leave the man and his face heated as guilt washed over him in a wave. "It's alright," the priest said, patting his arm reassuringly as if he'd read his thoughts, "but go slowly."

Alesh nodded weakly, and the man began to spoon the stew into his mouth. It tasted better than he remembered anything ever tasting, and he swallowed eagerly, nodding for more, his hunger pushing the questions he wanted to ask from his mind. The priest continued to feed him patiently, but despite Alesh's hunger, he wasn't able to eat more than half of the bowl of stew before his exhaustion overcame him. "Sleep now," The priest said, taking the bowl away "and do not worry. I am here."

For once in his life, Alesh's sleep was not plagued by the snarls and growls of nightlings or the screams of his murdered parents, and he awoke some time later feeling surprisingly refreshed. He was stiff and sore, but the pain, for the most part, was gone. So too, he noticed upon glancing around the small clearing, was the gray-robed man. "Priest?" He asked in a hoarse, sleep-muddled voice.

There was no answer. "Priest, are you there?"

The only answer was the sound of the wind in the leafy canopy overhead and the gentle burbling of the river hidden somewhere behind the thick trunks of the trees. Suddenly, a feeling of dread began to form in the pit of Alesh's stomach. Where could he have gone? Surely, the priest wouldn't have left him without a word. Not unless ... *Unless the Redeemers sent more men. Unless they killed him.*

Alesh slowly started to rise, tensing in anticipation of the pain he'd felt before but when it came he found that, though still bad, it was manageable, and after some effort he was able to sit up. He shrugged away the wool blanket that had been wrapped around him, and saw that he was bare-chested. His shoulder and chest had been bandaged with strips of white cloth and similar bandages were wrapped around his legs where the beast's claws had raked him. He forced himself to remain calm as he surveyed the surrounding woods. He was surprised to see no trace of the Redeemers or the Lightbringer Garn. There was not even so much as a patch of disturbed grass to mark that they had been there. It was as if they'd never existed at all. *One night spent in the darkness and, just like that, they're gone.* It was a depressing thought.

The priest's bed roll lay a short distance away by a weakly-burning, natural fire. If the man *had* left of his own choice, why would he have abandoned his bedroll? "Relax," he muttered to himself, "they couldn't have found you already." But that wasn't true, was it? If the Redeemers and Garn were to be believed, Kale had made finding him a priority, and with the resources of the entire city bent to his bidding, Ilrika's new Chosen could afford to send dozens of troops out to hunt him if he wished.

"*Ha!*" Came a distant shout, and the sound was followed by a loud splash. *They've found him,* Alesh thought, panicked. He glanced around the clearing and was surprised to see his sword lying in the grass. He shuffled to it and bent to pick it up.

They wouldn't catch him by surprise again. He turned and began limping in the direction of the sound. *Hold on, priest. I'm coming,* he thought grimly, clenching his teeth against the shooting pain in his legs. He had to pause after only a few steps to get his ragged breathing under control and helpless anger flared through him. While he was gasping like a sick old man, the priest was out there somewhere, fighting for his life. *Night curse it,* he thought, and started forward again, dragging the sword along the ground beside him.

After what would have normally been a short walk, but what—just then— felt like an eternity, the trees gave way to a river bank. "Priest!" He called, scanning the bank for the old man, "Where are you?"

"Well, good morning!" Alesh turned at the sound of the voice and was surprised to see the priest standing waist-deep in the river. The gray sleeves of his robe were rolled up to reveal thin, bony forearms, and he had a wide, innocent smile on his face.

Alesh swayed, his legs threatening to give way beneath him, as he took a few halting steps toward the edge of the river bank, "Priest," he said, gulping air, "are you alright?"

The man's smile widened—something that, until that moment, Alesh would have thought impossible. "Of course, and why wouldn't I be?"

Alesh sighed and fell to a sitting position. "I thought … never mind what I thought. What are you doing?"

The man gestured expansively at the river, "Getting us breakfast, of course."

Alesh snorted, "Well, good luck. I don't know a lot about fishing, but I do know that you're supposed to be quiet and not disturb them. You've probably scared them all away by splashing around in there like that."

The priest took a minute to consider this, then gestured to the soft, wet soil on Alesh's side of the river. Alesh looked where the man had indicated and was surprised to see two large fish lying still on the ground. "I suppose that those left, then," the priest said, amusement in his tone, "are the bravest, most worthy of their kind. No doubt, they will serve well for food on which to break our fast."

Alesh's eyes narrowed, "I thought that you were being attacked."

The priest looked confused, "By the fish?"

Alesh groaned, "Never mind."

The man nodded and turned away. He held his hands out to either side of him, looking up at the sky with a childlike smile of contentment, as if standing in the middle of an ice cold river was a lifelong dream of his. *Crazy bastard will probably catch cold*, Alesh thought, *and it'll serve him right. Here we are being hunted by soldiers, and he's wading in the water like some country kid when his chores are done.* He opened his mouth to tell the man to hurry up then stopped. The truth was, his legs and shoulder ached, and he didn't relish the idea of walking even the short distance back to their camp, not just yet anyway. It was unlikely that another squad of Redeemers had been sent in the same direction as the others and even if they had, a minute or two wouldn't make any difference. So, instead, he sat and waited.

In the light of the new day, with warm sunlight falling across him and the birds whistling their songs overhead, it was almost impossible to imagine that creatures such as the nightwalkers existed at all and even harder to believe that he was being hunted down by men who sought his life. After a time, Alesh found himself relaxing until, almost against his will, he lay on his back, the grass giving beneath him, more comfortable than any nobleman's silken pillow. He lay there, staring at the sky and listening to the soft, gurgling nonsense speech of the river and the whispery rustle of the trees as they answered. Listening to the sounds of the forest, feeling the warm sun on his skin, Alesh's eyes slowly closed.

"Thank you," a voice said beside him, and Alesh grunted with surprise, jerked up out of a near doze. He turned and saw the priest standing over him, that same smile on his face.

"Thanks for what?" He asked, annoyed that he'd been so lost in thought that he hadn't heard the man approach. He looked at the priest's empty hands confused, "Where are the fish?"

The old man smiled and gestured to the spot on the bank where another large fish had joined the first two and lay unmoving in the dirt. "They are there and, again, thanks."

Alesh looked between the fish and the man again before understanding. "Wait a minute, surely you can't mean for me to go down there and get them? I'm injured, remember?"

The man nodded solemnly, his face a picture of compassion. "I remember. I'll warm the fire." Before Alesh could find the words to protest, the priest had already turned and disappeared into the trees.

Alesh shook his head as he stared after him. The man was crazy—that was certain. His stomach rumbled as if to remind him of the fact that he hadn't eaten yet, and with a curse and a grunt, he levered himself up and started the slow job of working his way down the bank.

Some time and several aches and curses later, they sat on their bedrolls, the cooking fish giving off an intoxicating smell that made Alesh's mouth water. The priest was staring at the fire with a small smile on his face, as if it was an old friend that he'd met after years of absence. "What's your name?" Alesh asked, more to keep his mind off of the cooking fish than anything else.

The man turned to him and shrugged, "If there is anything I have learned about men, it is that they are more than their names."

Alesh rolled his eyes. "I think I liked you better when you didn't talk." He hadn't been with the priest long, but he was beginning to realize that the man had an annoying way of talking a lot without really saying anything. "Well, anyway," he said after a pause, "I need something to call you. I can't keep calling you priest."

The man smiled distractedly, turning his attention to the treetops over head in an expression that Alesh could only describe as wistful, "Priest will do."

"*Are* you a priest?"

The man smiled but did not answer.

"Fine," Alesh said, struggling to keep his patience, "So what happened to the bodies?"

"Bodies?"

"Yes," Alesh said, through gritted teeth, "you know, corpses? Dead men? The Redeemers and that man Garn. What happened to them?"

"Oooh," the priest said, nodding, "*those* bodies. Well, they're gone."

Alesh pinched the bridge of his nose and forced himself to take a deep breath, "I *know* they're gone. I'm asking you where they *went.*"

"Away."

The gray-robed man was too focused on the treetops to notice Alesh's flat look. "They're … gone. Away."

The priest nodded, "Right."

"Alright then," Alesh said, "let's try this a different way. Why did you help me?"

The man finally turned to him then, studying him as if Alesh was the crazy one, "If I hadn't helped you, you would have died."

Alesh bit back a curse, "That doesn't answer my question."

The man raised a bushy gray eyebrow at him, "Doesn't it?"

"Okay fine," Alesh said, unable to keep the annoyance from his voice, "But why were you *here?*"

The old man gave him a puzzled, worried expression. "Where else should I be?"

Alesh grunted in frustration and studied the man. "You can't be ser—"

"The fish is done." The man said with a smile, as if Alesh hadn't been speaking. He rose and began to spoon the hot stew into two bowls, putting a spoon in each. Despite his annoyance, Alesh found himself holding his hands out eagerly as the man handed him his bowl.

He took a bite of the still steaming stew, and his eyes widened in surprise. "Wow. This … is amazing." Then, around a second mouthful, "Can all priests cook?"

The grey-robed man shrugged, a slight smile on his face, "I wouldn't know."

Alesh opened his mouth, paused, thought about it, then shrugged and took another bite of stew.

CHAPTER THIRTY-EIGHT

"WELL? DAMNIT, FOLD OR PLAY already will ya? Some of us got wives waiting at home for us, and if I'm out much later I've a better chance of gettin' stabbed than gettin' laid."

Rion continued to stare at his cards, barely hearing the man at all—what was his name again? Ben? Jim? It didn't matter. What *did* matter was the hand he was holding. A full set of suns and brands, the best possible hand in the game of Brighters, a hand that any gambler worth his salt would be thrilled to see. If, that was, he hadn't just finished drawing it nine times in a row.

He'd always been lucky, always won more than he lost, but this … this was something else. Nobody drew nine branded suns in a row. Nobody. Drawing one would earn a man the envy of the others at his table. Drawing two would earn him their hatred. Drawing three … drawing three would earn him a slit throat in some back alley. He stared at the cards for another second, looked resignedly at the coins on the table, sighed, and folded his hand for the eighth time in a row. "Too rich for my blood by half, Jim."

"I done told you, damnit, It's *Tim.*"

"Right," Rion said, thinking of a night, not long gone, when he'd sat in some other cheap, poor district inn. *He doesn't cheat, Jorin. He's just got a Chosen's own luck, that's all.* He kept looking at his hand, half expecting it to change, the way the coin had. Would it be the smiling nightling this time? Or the torch? The light or the darkness? *Gods, am I going mad?* He glanced up and saw that the man, *Tim*, was scowling at him. "My apologies. Jim's your brother, right?"

If anything, the man looked even more hostile. "I ain't *got* no brother."

Rion started to speak, paused and looked at the other two men at the table, but if he was looking for help, he was wasting his time. Both men, very *large* very *intimidating* men, he noted, had scowls to match Tim's own. Rion sighed and held his hand up, signaling the serving girl to bring him another ale while Tim collected his coins. Normally, he avoided drink—the last thing a man leading a double life needed was to lose his hold on sense—but, tonight, he felt that the drink was the only thing keeping him sane. He was several drinks in now and drunk enough that he kept having to check to make sure his feet were still there—they went numb when he drank, always had. Drunk or not, from time to time, he thought he heard a sound that he would have *sworn* was laughter, ringing in his head.

It was the man next to Tim's turn to deal—gods forbid he even try to remember *his* name—and he watched as the big man handed out the cards. When he was finished, Rion hesitated, staring at them uncertainly.

"Well? Ain't you gonna check your hand?"

Rion looked up and noticed that the three men were staring at him again, and although he wouldn't have thought it possible, their scowls were even deeper than before. Just how long had he been sitting there, staring at the backs of those cards anyway? He cleared his throat, "Yes, of course." He grabbed the cards, wincing as he did the way a man might wince when he's handling a wild animal and expecting to get bit. Conscious of their eyes still on him, he glanced at his cards. Feeling like a man in a dream, he laid them on the table, face down, and slid them into the center. Laughter, loud and clear, rung in his ears. "There!" He said, whipping his head around, searching for the source of the sound, "*there*. Did you hear that?"

The three men glanced at each other as if he'd gone insane, "I didn't hear a damn thing," said one.

Rion's breath felt short and suddenly he thought he couldn't spend another moment in this shitty inn in this shitty part of town. He rose, grabbing his threadbare cloak from the back of the chair he'd been sitting in and pulling it over his shoulders.

"What the fuck, man?" The man, Tim, asked. "Ain't nobody even bet yet."

Rion nodded distractedly, a feeling like he was suffocating beginning to build in his chest and throat. "I'm sorry, but I really must be going."

"Well, you damn sure ain't gettin' your ante back. You can count on that."

"Wouldn't dream of it," Rion said, glancing around the room. His vision was blurry—just how many *had* he drank?—but it was clear enough for him to see that no one was watching him. No one, at least, that he could see. "You gentlemen have a great night." He hurried away before they could respond, his shoulders hunched underneath the unseen gaze he'd felt since that day in the gentlemen's club.

Rion walked on, oblivious of the people he passed, oblivious of the drunken sway that he took with each step. His thoughts were on the coin, on the flickering torch, the smiling nightwalker. Had he just imagined it? He had been telling himself that *of course* he'd imagined it and had even almost managed to believe it, almost managed to convince himself that the eyes he felt following him wherever he went were nothing more than paranoia, a perfectly reasonable paranoia, really, for a man leading two very separate lives. But then the cards. Ten hands in a row. *Ten in a damned, night-cursed row.*

He kept walking, choosing streets at random, letting his feet lead the way. He didn't know how long he walked but, after a time, he stopped, a feeling of vague alarm working its way past his distraction. At first, he didn't know the cause of his unease. Then, he looked around and realized that he was the only one in the street. It was late, but even at this hour there should have been *someone*. Beggars pleading for coins, whores hawking their wares, even pick pockets going about their nightly errands. But there was no one. The street—as much as he could see of it in the poor light cast by the torches ensconced on the walls of several nearly buildings—was empty. A street in the slums was never empty at night: after all, that's when most of its people went to work. Never unless ... "*Damn.*" He turned and started back the way he'd come, his footfalls echoing in the unnatural quiet.

"Not so fast there, Rion," someone said in a rough, gravelly voice. A voice—gods help him—that he recognized. Any doubts he might have had were dispelled as the speaker emerged from the shadows of an alley a short distance up ahead, flanked by two thickly-muscled men. Rion cursed himself for a fool. He'd allowed himself to become distracted, ignoring his surroundings. In the slums, people died for less. Knowing it was useless, he turned and hurried in the opposite direction, but was brought up short when two more men appeared out of the shadows.

Rion glanced back and forth between the two groups. Besides the owner of the voice, each of the others carried a short, cruel-looking club. Bruisers, their malformed noses and cauliflower ears badges of their experience. *Night take it.* Slowly, he reached his hand into his tunic, searching for the handle of one of the blades he had secreted there.

The man who'd spoken smiled, "I wouldn't do that if I were you, Rion. Whiskers over there might get nervous and accidentally let fly with one of those bolts in his crossbow, isn't that right, Whiskers?"

"Yes sir, boss," a voice called from the darkness to Rion's left, "I'm a right twitchy bastard."

Rion forced a nonchalant sigh as he drew his hand out of his tunic, struggling to keep his voice calm and matter of fact, "What do you want, Sigan?"

Sigan grinned, rolling his neck around on his massive shoulders. As big as the bruisers he employed were, the crime lord was bigger. In the orange glow of the torches, the thick, jagged scar that ran around his throat stood out pale and white. It was said that, when he was still climbing through the ranks of the criminal underworld, a fellow criminal had tried to assassinate Sigan; had, in fact, gone so far as to slit his throat. Instead of cooperating and dying, however, Sigan had turned on the man and killed him with his bare hands before going and killing his entire family. Rion supposed that he must have gotten his throat stitched up at some point, but he'd never heard that part of the story. He supposed it wasn't really necessary.

There were thousands of tales in the slums, and most of those were lies, but Rion had always believed that one. Sigan had been an orphan when he was young, with no one to look out for him, and it took a great amount of skill and toughness just to survive in the streets, let alone excel and carve out a place for yourself as one of the city's most powerful crime lords. As for intelligence, well, most people, on seeing Sigan's rough appearance, would have assumed he was stupid, a man of violence who gave little thought to anything beyond his next drink or his last fight. Unfortunately, they would be wrong. "What do I want?" The big man asked, his words returning Rion to the present, his grin stretching the scar on his neck into a smile of its own, "Well, I just want to talk. After all, you haven't come to see me in a while, have you, Rion? Whiskers and the lads are good enough sorts, but not the type for intelligent conversation."

Rion glanced behind him. The bruisers were standing still, watching the proceedings. Apparently, they were in no hurry. And why would they be? They knew they had him. He sighed and turned back to Sigan. The last thing you wanted to do with a man like Sigan was show weakness. That was one of the first lessons the streets had taught him. "I've been busy."

"Oh?" The big man asked, bringing a hand to his chest in mock hurt, "Too busy to come and see your old friend?"

The second lesson the streets had taught Rion was that it never hurt to show a man respect, but it often hurt not to. A good lesson, an *important* one. The problem was, he was angry: angry with a city that let criminals like Sigan prosper while honest people like his mother and father ran a serious risk of losing their home, angry with a world where walking through the woods at night was worth a man's life, and most of all angry with himself for being caught so unaware. He was tired, and he was angry, and, just then, he didn't give a damn about respect. "Fuck you, Sigan."

The crime lord's smile faded, and the thick muscles of his chest shifted like slabs of rock beneath his jerkin. "Fine, enough of the pleasantries. You owe me, and you're late. You do know what I do to people who don't give me what I'm owed, don't you, Rion?"

Rion didn't bother answering. Everyone in the poor district knew what happened to such people. They—or what was left of them—were often found in some back alley or street corner, their worldly concerns far behind them.

"You see, Rion," Sigan said, stalking closer, "I'm perplexed. I mean, the gods know you're a clever bastard, so it seems strange to me that you would put yourself in this position. And then, to make matters worse, when I send Pellam and Darby to give you a friendly reminder about what you owe, you send them back with the shit beat out of them. Night, Darby's hand is so wrecked I don't imagine he'll ever lift a club again. You tell me, Rion, what good 's a bruiser can't lift a club?"

Rion shrugged, "Not much, I guess."

Sigan barked a laugh, "Not much? Yeah, that's about right. The bastard was useless." He shrugged, "So I had one of the boys slit his throat and dump him. He wasn't any good to me, you see? He was a waste of my time, and I think you know what I do to people and things that waste my time. Oh, Rion, I must admit that I'm a bit upset with you. Darby was a fool, true, the kind of man who would piss in the wind and call it rain, but he was *my* fool. Do you understand?"

Rion nodded, "I'm sorry to hear that."

Sigan laughed again, "My but you are a cocky little bastard, aren't you? I like that. Tell you what, Rion. You give me that money you owe me—plus a bit extra for what you cost me in training another bruiser—and maybe I'll let you walk away from here with nothing more than a smashed up hand—a memento to remember Darby by." He held up a hand, forestalling Rion from answering, "Take a moment. Consider it."

Rion took his moment. The truth was he *had* the money to pay Sigan back several times over; his luck at dicing and cards had seen to that. Problem was, his family needed that money. Never mind the fact that—whatever he said—Sigan wouldn't let Rion walk away, smashed up hand or not. He turned back to the crime lord and shook his head, "No thanks."

For the first time, the crime lord looked angry. No, not angry, furious. His face went a deep scarlet, and his chest began to heave with his building rage. "No one steals from me and lives. *No one.* Enough. Whiskers, plug the bastard."

Rion dived to the side, but he was too slow, and he grunted as the arrow struck him like a fist, knocking him to the ground. Hissing with pain, he looked down, expecting to see the wooden shaft sticking out of his stomach. Instead, it lay broken on the road beside him. *How in the name of the gods,* he thought, confused, *it hit me; I know it hit me.* He glanced at his stomach, and sure enough there was a hole in his tunic. Through the hole, he could just make out the shimmer of coins. Apparently, the arrow had struck the leather pouch of coins nestled in his tunic and somehow been turned. *What are the odds?* He thought wildly, as he struggled to his feet.

Again, the knowing, amused laughter sounded in his head, and he fought it down with a will. He couldn't afford to go crazy, not yet. He was still alive, but he wouldn't be for much longer if he didn't do something. He jumped to his feet and sprinted at the man who'd shot the arrow. *"Get that bastard!"* Sigan roared, but Rion didn't take the time to look back. He rolled as the wide-eyed bowman released another shot, and the arrow flew over his head. Before he could load another bolt, Rion was on him, burying one of his knives in the man's chest while the other traced a red line across his throat.

He was leaping over the corpse even before it hit the ground, dashing into the alleyway, his arm clasped tightly around his bruised stomach. *"You're dead, Rion!"* Sigan screamed from somewhere behind him, *"Do you hear me!? You're dead!"* Rion ran on, ducking through alleyways and sidestreets, the footsteps of his pursuers echoing loudly in the still night air, so that it seemed as if he were being chased by an army instead of a four man squad of bruisers.

He flew around a corner, taking it so quickly that he stumbled and slammed into the alley wall, hissed a curse, and ran on. After a few more paces, he risked a glanced behind him, and saw that the men were close behind. *The bastards are faster than they have a right to be,* he thought, gritting his teeth at the pain in his stomach as he rushed on.

He ran faster, his heart hammering in his chest, and managed to put some distance between him and his pursuers. He came to an intersection and stopped long enough to kick open the door of an inn that stood on the corner of the street before darting down the opposite side street. His lungs burned, and his stomach ached as if someone had taken a hammer to it, but he kept going, turning left, rushing down an alley, finally stumbling out onto one of the slum's main streets. He was so focused on putting one foot in front of the other that he didn't see the man standing in the street until he barreled into him. It was like running into a brick wall, and he rebounded with a grunt, hitting the cobblestone path hard. Rion looked up, expecting to see one of the bruisers standing over him, and was amazed to recognize a familiar face instead. "O-Odrick?"

The blacksmith frowned, squinting at the figure in tattered clothing and faded cloak, "How do y—wait a minute," the man said in surprise, "Eriondrian? Is that you?"

Rion glanced at the blacksmith then at the covered cart and horse that he was leading, suddenly suspicious, "What are you doing out here?"

The big man gestured at the empty cart and horse, "I'm just coming back from delivering an order." He said, then he narrowed his gaze on Rion, "What are *you* doing here? And in those clo—"

"There's no time," Rion said, glancing at the alley behind him where, any second, the bruisers would appear. "Listen, Odrick, you have to hide me."

The big man's brow drew down in confusion, and he glanced down the alleyway. Finally he nodded slowly, turning back to Rion, "Hop in, the cover should keep anyone from looking, and no one will suspect anything. They're used to seeing me by now."

Rion hesitated. There was something strange, something suspicious about seeing the blacksmith here, in the slums. Why would a man whose father was one of the city's richest commoners make a delivery to the poor district in the middle of the night? Rion glanced uncertainly between the cart and the alleyway. He was still considering when he heard the sound of nearby shouts. He cursed and dove into the cart, pulling the cloth cover tight behind him. Once he was inside, Odrick clucked to the horse, and the cart began rolling forward.

They'd only gone a short distance when someone shouted, "Hey, blacksmith!"

The cart slowed, then stopped, and Rion tensed, drawing two of his daggers once more. Odrick had seemed like a good friend to him, but if living in Valeria had taught him anything, it was that you couldn't trust anybody, and that everybody, even the rich, no, *especially* the rich, did most of the things they did because of greed. "Yes?" Odrick asked.

Rion peeked out of the sliver of opening the covered canvas afforded, but he could make out nothing except the blacksmith's wide back. "Have you seen anybody running through here?" The voice—no doubt one of the bruisers—asked.

Odrick nodded, and Rion cursed under his breath. "Yeah," the blacksmith said, "I saw him. He ran down that way." The blacksmith turned, revealing one of the bruisers from before as he pointed down a nearby alleyway.

"Shit," the other man cursed, starting away.

"Hey, what's this all about?" Odrick asked. "Is something wrong?" *You damned fool,* Rion thought.

The man stopped and looked back, "None of your damned business, blacksmith," he snapped, "Now get on your way." He didn't wait for an answer before turning and sprinting toward the alley.

Odrick nodded, "Yes sir," he said to the man's departing back. Then he clucked at the horse again, and the cart lurched into motion. Rion didn't dare speak for fear of someone hearing him, so he rode in silence, his daggers clutched in sweaty hands, the only sounds the clip-clop of the horse's hooves on the cobbles, and the rapid thumping of his own heart as they made their way through the city.

After what felt like a lifetime, the cart rolled to a stop. The blacksmith spoke with someone and after another moment, he lifted the covering off the tarp, and Rion winced as lantern light pierced his eyes. "You can come out," Odrick said.

Warily, Rion climbed out of the cart. He glanced around, half-expecting to find himself a prisoner at one of Sagin's hideouts. Instead, he was surprised to find himself standing in a stable. "Where are we?"

The blacksmith turned from where he'd been unfastening the horse from the cart, a slightly amused expression on his face as if he knew what Rion had been thinking, "My father's stables. He doesn't much care for riding, but we need the horses to carry supplies to customers. Why, where did you think we would be?"

Rion shrugged but didn't answer, glancing around the stalls.

"You don't have to worry," Odrick said, "No one's here. I sent Mikhel away."

"Who's Mikhel?"

"The groom that looks after the horses. I thought that maybe you wouldn't want to be seen."

Rion nodded, "Thanks." He studied the blacksmith, searching for any kind of deceit, but if the man's open face hid any, he could not see it. "Why were you in the poor district?"

Odrick shrugged, "I make a lot of trips to the poor district to carry some of my father's goods to his customers. Nails, horse shoes, that kind of thing."

Rion frowned, "Doesn't your father have other people to do that for him?"

The blacksmith began busying himself unhitching the cart, an embarrassed expression on his face. "He does," Odrick admitted after a moment, "but …"

Rion raised an eyebrow at his hesitation and the big man heaved a sigh. "I volunteer to do it sometimes." He said, his voice reluctant but resigned like a murderer that had been caught out and had no choice but to confess.

"Volunteer?" Rion asked, incredulous, "Why?"

Odrick shrugged as he began leading the horse into one of the stalls, "I enjoy it."

"You *enjoy* it?"

The blacksmith nodded as he locked the gate. Then he turned and met Rion's eyes, a challenging look in his gaze, "Yes and so what? The truth is, we don't make much off of the orders in the poor district—people there barely have enough money to eat and don't go about spending what little they do have on elaborate candle holders or swords. While the *rich,*" he said, pointedly looking at Rion, "spend their times figuring out which ball they're going to attend, these people are trying to figure out where their next meal is coming from." *I know the feeling,* Rion thought, but the man wasn't finished yet, "They care about simple things like nails or horseshoes or getting their oxen chain repaired. You may not understand it, but my dad has been dealing with a lot of these people since I was a child, long before he ever gained his fortune. I know most of the nobles think that everyone in the slums is a criminal, but that isn't true. Most of them are just people, good people that work long hours for little pay and try to provide for their families."

Rion nodded slowly, taken aback. He'd known Odrick for years and never before had he heard the quiet man say so much at once. He doubted anyone had. The earnestness in his friend's expression and the sharp look he gave

Rion, daring him to argue, was almost enough to convince him that the man's story was the truth. Almost. "That still doesn't explain why *you* were in the slums instead of one of your father's workers."

The blacksmith shrugged again, "You wouldn't understand."

"Try me." *And if you answer wrong,* Rion thought, grimly crossing his arms so that his right hand rested on the handle of a blade hidden beneath his tunic, *then I think we're both in for a bad night.*

Odrick hesitated for a moment then sighed, nodding, "It's just that ... when I'm at a ball, around nobles, I always know I don't belong. It's like trying to fit a hammer on a sword rack. Sure, the hammer's practical. *More* practical, really, but you don't see people hanging those on their mantles, do you? I know I don't belong, and they know it too. I'm not like them, and they know it, and they hate me for it. Just like the way Sevrin talks—"

"Not all nobles are like Sevrin."

"Aren't they?" The blacksmith asked again, frowning, "They care only about themselves, about their own families and their own concerns without giving so much as a second thought to anybody else."

Rion thought of how, just a moment ago, he'd been ready to kill the blacksmith in order to keep his secret safe and felt his face heat with shame.

"But I can't blame them, really," the blacksmith said, heaving a sigh, "after all, my father always said that money makes men crazy, and the nobles have a lot of it. Who knows, in another year or two, I might be just the same."

Oh, it's not the money, Odrick, Rion thought sadly, *we were crazy long before that. And no ... no, I don't think you will.* "Do you deliver your father's goods a lot?"

Odrick shook his head, "Not a lot. Most of the time I just help him in the shop."

"And do you always go out so late at night?"

"No," the big man said, shaking his head thoughtfully, "I never have before. In fact, I should have been finished hours ago, but one of the wheels broke off the wagon, and I had to fix it. I'd only just finished my delivery when I ran into you. What are the chances, right?"

Rion thought he heard the ghostly laughter again, but it was faint and gone so quickly that he could have imagined it.

"Eriondrian," Odrick asked, "If you don't mind me asking, what were *you* doing in the slums? And what happened to your clothes? More importantly, who were those men chasing you?"

Rion studied the man's face for a moment, trying to decide what to do. He could lie and say that an errand had taken him through the slums, and that he'd been set on by thieves or muggers—a common enough occurrence in the poor district of Valeria—but that would do nothing to explain his tattered clothing. If he didn't tell Odrick the truth, he ran the risk of the man figuring out some other way, and maybe even inadvertently betraying Rion's secret identity to others. The thought of Sagin, a man known for his ruthlessness, finding out his true identity sent chills running down his spine and not just for him but for his parents.

Against all of his instincts, Rion decided to gamble with Odrick's trust. After all, what other choice did he have? He took a deep breath and began to explain everything to the blacksmith, telling of how his father's fortune had collapsed and continuing with his own forays into the slums. The big man listened quietly, not interrupting, and as he spoke, Rion began to feel as if a great weight had been lifted from his shoulders, as if the very act of telling someone else of his struggles took some of the burden away.

When he was finished, the blacksmith stood silently for several seconds, thinking, as was his way. "Are you serious, Erioindrian? This is all true?"

"It's true."

"Why didn't you ask me for help sooner? Business is good—between the nobles and making weapons for the city guard, my father and I have more work than we can handle. I'm sure once I explain to him what's happened, we can help y—"

"*No*," Rion half-shouted, and the blacksmith's eyes went wide in surprise. "No one can know, Odrick," he went on, making an effort to keep his tone calm, "no one. My father worked all of his life to build his fortune, and my mother always stood beside him. Do you have any idea what kind of shame this would bring them? Besides, it's too far gone for that now. That man you saw before worked for Sagin, one of the crime lords in the slums, and he isn't the only one that I owe money to. If they found out that the man they know as Rion was also Eriondrian Tirinian, heir to the Tirinian house …"

"It would be bad." The blacksmith finished, swallowing hard.

"Yes."

"Alright, Eriondrian, I won't tell anyone but … but surely there has to be something I can do."

Rion reached back and drew the tattered hood of his cloak over his head once more, "Do you really want to help, Odrick?" He asked, studying the man's face carefully.

The blacksmith nodded, "Of course. You're my friend, Eriondrian."

He studied the big man's face for several second then nodded. *So I am,* he thought, *you poor fool.* "Call me Rion," he answered as he turned and started toward the door, "and if you want to help me, then forget this ever happened."

CHAPTER THIRTY-NINE

Alesh yawned and reluctantly climbed out of his bedroll, his sore muscles groaning in protest. He and the priest had traveled through the woods, avoiding the roads in case more Redeemers were searching for them. At first, the sprawling hills, forests, and valleys through which they traveled, so untouched by humans, had seemed beautiful, but after three long days spent wading through waist-high undergrowth and being slapped in the face with tree limbs that seemed to attack him out of nowhere, Alesh had had enough of nature.

While he nursed his latest thorn cut or branch lash, the old man walked on like a child in some fairy land, oblivious of the dangers around him, yet managing to never turn his ankle in a hole hidden by leaves or to trip over rocks covered by the undergrowth as Alesh did. He suspected that the priest had saved his life by mending his wounds before he bled out, and he was grateful, but that didn't keep him from daydreaming about tripping the old man or pushing him into a thorn bush. It wouldn't be hard to find one. During his time in the woods, Alesh had discovered that he had a particular knack for it.

"Ah, you're awake. Good morning." Alesh turned to see the priest standing a short distance away, looking bright-eyed and wide awake. Alesh yawned, rubbing at his eyes. How the man always seemed so happy, so tireless was beyond him. If the old priest slept, Alesh had never seen it. He was always awake when Alesh went to sleep and awake when he awoke.

Alesh grunted noncommittally. The priest smiled, "If you will pack the bed rolls and supplies, I'll go and see about getting us some breakfast."

Alesh glanced at the spread out bedrolls and then at the blazing white fire. Although the corpses had been gone when he awoke after the nightling attack—and although he still couldn't get a straight answer out of the priest on something so simple as what his name was, much less what had happened to all of them—the priest had somehow managed to keep the tunic and belt the Lightbringer had carried, a fact that had kept them breathing until now which meant that the man hadn't saved his life once but two times. Still, he'd be damned if he was going to spend another morning playing house maid. "I've packed the camp and put out the fire for the last three days while you wade in a nice cool creek and toss a couple of fish out. How about this time *you* pack our gear, and *I'll* get breakfast."

The priest smiled and nodded as if excited by the idea. The bastard. "Certainly," the old man said, and with that, he set about packing their gear.

Alesh frowned. One of the most infuriating things about the old man was that he was just so damned agreeable. It wasn't natural, and when the man started whistling—*whistling, damnit,* as if there was nowhere he'd rather be than in the woods and nothing he'd rather be doing than packing their bags—Alesh began to suspect that he'd been tricked somehow. He was tempted to let the old man do the fishing after all, but what kept him from it was that he was absolutely certain that the priest would be just as happy with that as well. Alesh didn't consider himself a violent man, but that kind of happy could drive a man to murder.

He glanced at the old man who had stopped packing long enough to run a wrinkled hand gently, almost reverently, over several blades of grass and, frowning, set off toward the creek.

An hour later, he was still standing in the freezing creek, his soggy trouser legs clinging against his skin, cursing and pawing at the water with hands that had long since gone numb. He heard a cough and turned to see the priest standing on the bank. "Would you like some help?"

"No, thank you," Alesh said, his teeth gritted to keep them from chattering.

He took a slow, deep breath, and for what had to have been the hundredth time, began to let his fingertips trail in the cool, bubbling water of the creek as he'd seen the priest do. After a moment, he sensed more than felt something in the water, and, he plunged his hands into the creek sending water showering around him. Something slick, almost oily rubbed against his fingers. He grasped at it, but it slipped from his grip. He pawed around, turning frantically this way and that, but found nothing. *"Night take it,"* he growled. He shot a look at the priest, but the man was pointedly looking away from him, appearing to be studying the bark of a nearby tree.

Smug bastard. Alesh set his feet once more, drew a slow, deep breath, and forced himself to be still. He'd been close that time, damned close. All he had to do was be patient. In another minute, maybe two, he would pull a massive fish out of the water, bigger than any the old man had caught. *See how he likes that.* Grinning at the thought of it, he let his hands sink slowly into the water once more and waited.

Fifteen minutes later, he half-stomped, half-sloshed out of the water to where the priest still stood, shivering with cold. "I'm not very hungry, anyway," he said, scowling, daring the man to say something, "Are you ready?"

The priest smiled, grabbing his own bedroll and handing Alesh his, "Of course."

"How much farther before we reach Valeria?"

Alesh thought he saw the old man's smile falter for a moment at mention of the city, but it was back in another instant. "A few days, no more," the man said, before turning and starting off into the woods.

Alesh nodded and followed after. A few more days. A good thing, considering that the supplies in the Lightbringer's belt were getting worryingly low. If they didn't reach shelter soon, they'd be forced to spend the night with nothing but a plain wood fire to keep the nightlings at bay—not a comforting thought. Ahead, the priest began to whistle as if he was out for a morning stroll, and Alesh gritted his teeth. If they didn't make it to other people soon, he might just give the nightwalkers a try.

CHAPTER FORTY

"*KATHERINE.*" SHE OPENED HER EYES and found herself standing alone in the middle of a grassy field. She turned, looking around her for the sound of the voice, but there was only the dew-covered grass, greener than any she'd ever seen, stretching on in every direction like a sea of emeralds, sparkling and shimmering in the morning sun. Her skin broke out into gooseflesh. How had she gotten here? *You're dreaming, that's all. Just dreaming like you've done a thousand times before.*

And it was true, had to be true, but if it was a dream, it was of a different kind than any she'd ever had. She could feel each strand of grass as it brushed against her bare toes, could feel the heat of the sun and the kiss of a gentle breeze on her face.

"*Katherine,*" someone whispered in her ear, so close that she could feel breath on her neck. She let out a cry of surprise and whipped around, but there was no one there. She was still looking for who'd spoken when, behind her, soft music began to play. She looked at the direction it was coming from and gasped. In the distance, a tree stood where nothing had been only moments before. It was short enough, no more than four or five times as tall as a man, but its trunk was incredibly thick—at least ten feet—and its full, leafy branches stretched out in all directions as if it reached not for the sun, but for the land itself.

Squinting, she could just make out the vague shape of a figure seated beneath the tree, and though she could see only a shadowed outline, something about that figure made Katherine's heart hammer in her chest like a drum. The breeze grew stronger, and on it drifted the sound of a melody so achingly sweet, so *alive* that Katherine felt a tear slide down her cheek.

Unnerved but unable to help herself, Katherine took one step and then another. The world shifted and blurred around her and suddenly she was right in front of the tree and the figure sitting beneath it. She staggered, disoriented, and almost fell before the strength came back in her legs, and she managed to catch herself. Now that she was closer, Katherine could see that the figure was seated in a flawless white throne, so fine and regal that it would have been at home in Chosen Alashia's own castle.

The woman who sat in it wore a golden dress that glowed brilliantly, so that it seemed as if she were covered in sunlight. Her long, graceful fingers plucked the strings of a pearl-white harp, and it was from this that the music came. Katherine opened her mouth to speak but found that no words would come, so she just stood there, listening, carried on the harp's melody, buoyed by it. She had never heard anything so beautiful.

She didn't know how much time passed, but eventually the song drew to a close, and the woman withdrew her fingers from the harp, the last note hanging in the air like the promise of Spring in Winter. The woman glanced up from beneath a thick mane of luscious, golden hair, displaying a face so perfect that it didn't look like that of a living being at all, but the fanciful creation of some master sculptor. "Katherine," the woman said, her voice possessing a lilting, musical quality of its own, "You have come."

"M-mistress?" Katherine asked in a whisper as the last hint of the harp's final note drifted away on the cool breeze, "Please, don't stop playing on my account. It was beautiful."

The woman smiled a slow, almost sad smile, "It was wasn't it? Still, all songs must come to an end, and the time for playing is nearly finished. You know that, don't you, Katherine?"

"Ma'am?" Katherine asked confused, "We don't know each other do we? Surely, I would remember."

"Oh," the woman said, waving a delicate hand in a gesture of dismissal, "you know me, Katherine, and I have known you for a very, very long time.

But let us leave that for now. Tell me, are you going to meet Alashia in Valeria?"

Katherine's shock at the unexpected question must have shown on her face because the blonde-haired woman smiled again, running thin delicate fingers through her golden hair, "Ah yes, I know of your mission, now—" She cut off as thunder, loud and terrible, echoed in the distance. Frowning, the woman gazed over Katherine's shoulder. Katherine turned to look and saw that shifting, black storm clouds had begun to form on the horizon. "Quickly, Katherine," the woman said, her voice tight with what sounded like fear, "There is not much time. You are going, yes?"

"Y-yes ma'am." The words were out of her mouth before she considered. "Mistress Alashia sent me a letter—"

"I know of it," the woman said, waving her hand again, "and it is good that you go. I sense a ... a gathering of sorts there, though for good or ill I cannot say. Perhaps my father could, but light help us he is ...." She paused, and shook her head, "it does not matter. It is enough, for now, that you are going. I ...." Whatever else the woman said was drowned out by the roar of nearby thunder, so powerful that it seemed to shake the ground beneath Katherine's feet.

The woman's frown deepened and worry lines creased her perfect brow. "And so it begins," she said in a soft whisper filled with regret. The clearing grew dark, the gathering clouds blotting out the sun, and Katherine shivered as an unexpected chill came over her. She was suddenly overcome by the certainty that something terrible was coming and a part of her wanted nothing more but to turn and run. Instead, she took a slow breath, watched it plume in front of her face like mist. "Ma'am?" She asked in a low, unsteady voice, "W ... what's happening?"

Lightning lanced overhead, arching and spreading across the dark, roiling sky like grasping fingers, and the woman in gold looked somehow weakened, diminished. "I fear that I do not have the time to tell you what I would," she said, her eyes never leaving the shifting darkness overhead, "for the world of dreams is a place of power, of futures that will be and that might be, of pasts that always have been and never were and we are not the only dreamers. You must go, but remember this, Katherine, things are not always as they appear. Troubled times lie ahead, but do not despair; *He* is coming."

"H-he, mistress?"

The woman turned to her, her eyes a bright shining amber, "You will know him by the mark he bears, for he is touched by light and darkness both and there are none who can know which will claim him or which he will claim. If only ..." she paused for a moment then shook her head, "no, but there is no use in it. The time for planning and orchestrating is done. The song must be played, *will* be played, and we will use what instruments as we may."

"What? Please, mistress," Katherine begged, "I don't understand. What am I supposed to do?"

If the woman heard, she did not answer. Instead, she drew her harp up once more and, studying the unnatural darkness that swam and undulated overhead like some great beast uncoiling from its slumber, she began to play. Though Katherine knew the song was the same as the woman had been playing before, it felt weaker now, incomplete. The woman, too, seemed to notice, and her brow drew down in concentration as she began to play more intently.

In another moment, her graceful hands began to falter on the strings like the clumsy hands of a drunkard. The woman's face took on a pale, pinched look, and beads of sweat began to form on her forehead, "Remember, Katherine," she hissed, "remember that you are not alone and do not forget, things are not always—" there was a terrible, screeching sound from the harp, and Katherine and the woman gasped together, gazing at each other in disbelief.

The woman had missed a note. Katherine didn't know why such a seemingly small thing set her teeth on edge, but it did. The woman was breathing hard now, and she started playing again, her movements jerky and frantic, but no matter how hard she played, the discordant note seemed to hang in the air, a thing of malice and teeth that refused to be moved, and suddenly there was as loud *snap* as one of the harp's strings broke in half. The woman cried out as the wild string slapped her in the face, clawing her like a thing alive and leaving a trail of blood on her otherwise perfect face. Katherine took a step toward the tortured-looking woman, "Mistress—"

"*Go!*" The woman screamed, her fingers never pausing in their desperate clawing at the harp strings. Katherine let out a cry of fear and took an involuntary step back at the rictus of anger and pain that twisted the woman's face. It was a terrible, suffering expression that at once tugged at Katherine's heart and made her skin go cold with fear, but that wasn't the worst of it. The worst of it was her eyes. Where before they'd held a warm glow like that of a summer dawn, now they blazed as if with some inner fire. As Katherine watched, too shocked and terrified to move, the woman's form began to blur and become indistinct, as if she were looking at her through some great curtain of fog. "*Go!*" Came the shout again. Something shoved Katherine with an immense, immeasurable force, and, in the next instant, she was thrown up and into the air. She screamed as she wet spinning end over end, into the seething stormclouds, into the mouth of the waiting darkness.

She awoke with a gasp, sitting bolt upright in her bed and covering her mouth against the scream that begged for release. Beside her, Sonya stirred restlessly, turning over in her sleep, but she did not wake.

Katherine hugged her knees to her chest, struggling to get control of her ragged breathing and thumping heart. It had been a dream ... only a dream. But if that was true, then why had it seemed so real? Why was she, even now, after awakening, still terrified by the memory of those dark, swirling clouds, pregnant with the promise of a terrible storm to come?

And what of the woman that she'd spoken with? She had seemed real. And there had been something so familiar about her, about her face ... about the way she'd played.... Suddenly, Katherine remembered where she'd seen the woman before, and her breath caught in her throat.

Amedan was the first and greatest of the gods, but he was not the only one and although all of Entarna—minus the Redeemers, of course—worshipped the Light Bringer, there were many sects of men and women that also worshipped one of Amedan's sons or daughters, the minor gods. People prayed to Amedan for protection against the darkness, for long life and healthy children, true, but a farmer in desperate need of a good crop took his pleas to Calum, Amedan's grandchild, and the God of Growing Things. Likewise, soldiers would pray to Amedan for ultimate victory in the war, but they would bow their heads and burn sacrifices for his son, the God of Conflict and Warriors, before a battle. And on and on it went.

Gamblers had Javen, scholars Pembrose, the God of Knowledge and Learning, women out to find a husband had Seralina, the Goddess of Temptation and Lust, even the beggars had Alcer, God of the Poor and the Destitute. For Katherine, it was—had always been—Deitra, the Goddess of Art and Music. As a little girl, she'd often accompanied her mother to the Goddess's shrine, offering up her meager skill with the harp in hopes of winning the divine lady's favor. She'd stopped going when her mother had succumbed to her sickness—her untimely death had seemed proof enough of the goddess's feelings toward her and her family—but had started back again after Alashia had saved them from poverty. She'd spent long hours, as a child and an adult, bowing her head beneath the goddess's statue, studying her divine countenance. The woman in her dream did not look like the goddess; she *was* the goddess. The likeness was unmistakable now that she compared the memory of the two, and she was only shocked that it had taken her so long to realize it.

She felt a chill run up her spine. She'd heard stories of people being visited by gods and goddesses before, but they were always important people: kings and queens, priests and champions. What possible reason would the goddess of music have to appear to Katherine? "Don't be a fool," she murmured, "It was a dream, that's all. Nothing more." She was no king of great wisdom, no queen of unsurpassing beauty. She was nothing but a slightly better than average musician only a few years removed from the life of a street urchin. If Deitra really did wish to visit a human, she wouldn't visit one such as Katherine. Instead, she would surely visit one of the Chosen. That was, after all, the whole point of them *being* chosen, wasn't it?

And that was it then, a simple dream. A strange one to be sure, but with all that she'd experienced in the past few weeks, was it really any surprise that her sleep was filled with troubled dreams? She lay back in bed, pushing thoughts of the dream out of her mind. They were only a few days outside of

Valeria now. Soon she would have to meet with Chosen Alashia and tell her what had happened in Ilrika including the death of Olliman, the most powerful of Amedan's High Priests, and leader of the Six. The news would likely cause a war against the city where, inevitably, more innocent blood would be spilled. Yes, she had more than enough to worry about already without trying to borrow trouble from dreams.

CHAPTER FORTY-ONE

IT WAS LATE IN THE afternoon when Alesh shuffled into the city, exhausted after hours spent waiting in line at the gate, the hot sun beating down on him. But as he looked around at the city of Valeria, his exhaustion vanished. During some of his visits to the Chosen's library, he'd read of Valeria's unique beauty, had even heard visiting nobles and dignitaries recounting tales of it, but neither had prepared him for the city—and the people—that surrounded him.

Scholars referred to Valeria as the City of a Thousand Colors, and, standing there, gazing around at the buildings and people around him, Alesh couldn't disagree. The buildings and road of the city were painted in a variety of bright hues and colors that shone brilliantly in the dying sunlight, as if he stood in a rainbow city from some whimsical child's imagination. The men, women, and children were likewise dressed in bright clothes of every color imaginable. "It's … it's beautiful," he said, unable to keep the awe from his voice.

The priest didn't respond and, after a moment, Alesh glanced over and saw that the man was frowning, a troubled expression on his face. "Oh, come on," Alesh laughed, so relieved from finally reaching the city—and what a city it was!—that he'd temporarily forgotten the grim task which had brought him here, "You can't be serious. I've spent the last week or more watching you stare at plants and bugs as if they were made out of gold, and now that you finally have something that's actually worth looking at, you're upset?"

The old man didn't answer, but continued to study the surrounding city as if he'd woken up in some nightling's lair. Alesh sighed and shook his head, determined not to let the man ruin his good mood. He was finally here. His entire body ached from days and nights spent hiking through hills and valleys and sleeping on the ground with rocks digging into his back no matter which way he moved, but he was here. *And,* he thought, *I won't have to suffer through another day of fish for breakfast, lunch, and dinner.* The thought brought back unpleasant memories of the hours he'd spent trying to fish with nothing to show for it but chafed legs and sore feet, and it took an effort to keep the smile on his face.

The priest had been kind, of course, he always was *that,* but Alesh couldn't help feeling as if the man's normal smile grew a little larger as he watched Alesh flail at the water until he finally gave up and stomped away. At such times, the old man would return to camp no more than fifteen minutes later with more than enough fish for them to eat.

"Frown all you want," Alesh said to the priest, not bothering to turn as he watched brightly colored cloths and drapes that were hung on the walls of shops and houses rustle and flap in the gentle breeze like a river of color, "It *is* beautiful."

"A flower is most beautiful before it dies," the man said cryptically, studying the people around him with a sad, troubled gaze.

Alesh rolled his eyes, "What does that even mean? Never mind," he said, holding up a hand, "I don't want to know. Come on, we need to get to the castle."

He set out at a brisk pace, the priest falling in behind him without a word. Smiling merchants stood at painted stalls, boasting their wares, children laughed and ran in the streets, and men and women waved and nodded as they passed. After the hard time he'd had, all of this should have made Alesh feel better, but the priest's words kept replaying in his head. Unbidden, thoughts of Ilrika, the way he'd last seen it, came to his mind. In many ways, Valeria reminded him of the city he'd grown to call his home. After all, had the people of Ilrika not laughed and lived in much the same way before the Redeemers had slaughtered them? He tried to shake the memory of the devastation in Ilrika from his thoughts, but it hung on like a badger with its teeth sank in, unwilling to let loose its hold, and soon he began to imagine that he saw something cruel, something sinister in the smiling, laughing faces.

How fragile it all is, he thought. *They all laugh and joke as if they'll live forever, as if the city will last forever, but it won't. Nothing does.* Not even Olliman, not even the city of Amedan's greatest Chosen. Ilrika may not have been as extravagant as Valeria, but that was no surprise. After all, the city had been much like the Chosen himself: powerful, practical, and, for a time, at least, safe. Despite its lack of ornamentation, the walls had been taller in Ilrika than in Valeria, the guards harder, better trained. It had been believed to be the safest place in the entire realm. People had lived and loved, had grown old and died within its walls, sheltered from the darkness and the dangers it brought. *But never again.*

If each city took after the characteristics of its leader, then Valeria's beauty was no surprise. After all, Chosen Tesharna was said to be the most beautiful woman in Entarna, despite the fact that she was nearly a hundred years old. Age, it was said, never touched her, and that because of Amedan's blessing, she would pass into her grave without enduring the ravages that time wrought on all mortal flesh. That seemed a silly enough thing to Alesh, even if it was true. After all, what did it matter what someone looked like when they were buried in the ground, beneath several feet of hard packed earth? Death came for everyone, sooner or later, and neither wisdom nor beauty could keep it away.

He scowled at the priest, his good mood completely gone. The old man shuffled along beside him, his eyes downcast, his feet dragging with each step, like a man walking to his own execution. Alesh stifled a curse and picked up his pace, not caring if the old man was able to keep up or not. He'd made it; against all odds, he'd made it. He should have felt relieved, but any joy he might have felt was stolen by the priest's dark mood. The brightly clothed people and buildings they passed no longer seemed beautiful. Instead, they put him in mind of a book he'd once read about the Ooramin, a tribe of people that lived far south, across the great ocean. The author had went into great detail describing the strange tribe and had dedicated an entire chapter to the art of what the Ooramin called the *Ulflamen a da Miert* or, as the scholar had translated it, "the concealing of the dead."

According to the book, the Ooramin believed that evil creatures called the Ualikar hunted for the souls of the recently dead, and it was only by disguising them with dyes and herbs used as cosmetics, going so far as to even glue the eyes of the deceased open, that the creatures could be tricked and the souls of the newly dead allowed to travel unhindered into the afterlife. The bright colors of the building and fancy clothes of the people on the street, at first so appealing to Alesh, now felt like nothing more than face paint on a dead woman. A shallow cover, a veil laid over a corpse to hide the grisly truth that lurked just underneath. It was an unpleasant, disturbing thought but one he could not shake, and he breathed a heavy sigh of relief when he was finally able to make out the gates of the castle in the distance.

The towering stone walls of the Chosen's home and seat of power thrust into the sky as if reaching to grasp the sun itself, but it was not their size—impressive, and larger even than Olliman's own had been—that stopped him in his tracks, but their color. Unlike the rest of the city that seemed made of every possible shade and hue, the towers and walls of the castle were perfectly white, shining brightly in the afternoon sunlight as if the castle was the home of the gods themselves.

The white marble castle walls would have been impressive anywhere, but surrounded as they were by the vibrantly painted city, the effect was staggering, and Alesh could understand, seeing it, why many scholars claimed that Valeria's castle was the most beautiful piece of art ever made by man, and why a few had even went so far as to say that Amedan himself had lent a hand in its creation.

"Priest?" He asked, his eyes never leaving the castle walls.

"Hmm?" The man asked in a distracted, worried tone.

"Is it true what they say? That Amedan created the castle for Tesharna as a reward for her service during the war?"

The man hesitated, and just when Alesh was sure he wasn't going to answer, he spoke in a subdued voice, so quiet that Alesh was forced to strain to make out the words, "I once believed that men—because of what they are—were capable of creating things of beauty greater in some ways than anything the gods could ever manage. In them is a capacity for greatness, for sacrifice and kindness, that I thought the gods, as immortals, could never know."

"I'd be careful, priest," Alesh said, smirking wryly, "that sounds remarkably close to blasphemy to me."

The man didn't answer, and Alesh turned to see him studying the castle with a thoughtful, troubled expression. "You said you once believed that."

The man turned and stared at him, his face blank.

"What do you believe now?" Alesh prompted.

"I do not know," the old man said, and although his expression didn't change, for the first time since he'd met him, Alesh thought that the man looked very frail, very tired.

"Come on," he said, "let's go see the Chosen. You'll see, priest; she'll set everything right."

The man said nothing, and finally Alesh heaved a sigh and started toward the gate. Six guards stood at attention in front of the entrance, their white armor glistening in the sunlight, their long white cloaks hanging from their backs like curtains of fresh snow. As the two travelers drew closer, one of the men stepped forward purposefully, his hands clasped behind his back, "Your business in the castle?" He asked, his voice stern, business-like.

"We've come to see Chosen Tesharna," Alesh said.

"The Chosen is giving no more audiences today. Come back tomorrow." He turned and started away.

"Wait," Alesh said. The man turned back, a slight frown creasing his face. "It's important. I *have* to speak with her."

"Oh?" The guard asked, glancing at his grinning comrades before turning back to Alesh, "And what is so important that you demand to speak with the Chosen of Valeria, first among all of Amedan's Six?"

The man's words caused Alesh to frown himself, and he bit back a sharp remark. Everyone knew that Olliman was the greatest of Amedan's High Priests, and that it was he who had led them all during the times of war as well as peace. Still, it would do no good to argue with the man. He opened his mouth, intending to tell the man everything that had happened, but something—he couldn't have said what—stopped him. Instead, he said, "We ... we carry an important message from Chosen Olliman."

The man smirked and looked Alesh and his companion up and down, taking in their travel-stained clothes, worn and frayed from long days on the road, "Is that so?" He asked in an amused voice, "Well, then, by all means, present your papers bearing Olliman's seal, and we can end this matter swiftly."

Alesh gritted his teeth, his patience wearing thin. "*Chosen* Olliman," he corrected, "*greatest* of all of Amedan's High Priests."

The man's expression grew stern, "Chosen Olliman, then. The papers?" He held out his hand.

"I," Alesh hesitated, "I don't have them."

The guard nodded as if he'd expected as much. "Come back tomorrow," he said again, "and, if I were you, I'd wake early. You're not the only one wanting to see the Chosen." He grinned, "The line can get pretty long."

Alesh felt his anger building and forced himself to remain calm. Getting thrown into the castle's dungeon wouldn't do anyone any good. "Come on," he said to the priest through gritted teeth, "We'll come back tomorrow."

The priest didn't respond, and Alesh turned to see him staring at the white walls of the castle beyond the gate, a troubled expression on his face. "It is wrong here," the old man said, his voice little more than a whisper.

"I'll say," Alesh said, frowning after the departing guard, "Come on. There's no use wasting our time; we'll come back tomorrow." With that, he turned and started away.

The old man continued to stare at the castle. At first glance, its white walls seemed to shine in the sunlight, but on closer inspection he could make out the pits and stains that marred their surface. Shadows lurked along the castle's corners, crouched in its many windows and huddled beneath its reaching eves. "It is wrong here," he said again, his voice almost too low to make out. Then he turned and followed Alesh.

CHAPTER FORTY-TWO

"No can do, I'm full up" the barkeeper said gruffly, barely sparing them a glance as he slammed two tankards of beer down on the counter, suds foaming over the cups and spilling onto the wooden surface. "*Nell, two up!*" He yelled.

A harried red-faced woman in a plain linen dress weaved her way between tables packed with people, scooped up the two mugs, and disappeared back into the crowded room without a word. The barkeep grunted and began filling more mugs of ale, ignoring Alesh and the priest.

Alesh rubbed at his temples where a headache was beginning to form. This was the fourth inn they'd checked, only to find it full like all of the others. His feet and legs ached from days spent traveling, and for some reason he couldn't explain, he was growing more and more tense at the crowds of people that seemed to be everywhere. Several times since leaving the castle, he'd been overcome with the feeling that they were being followed. He'd spin around, half-expecting to find someone coming at him with a knife, so strong was the feeling of being stalked, but instead he'd find only the usual crowds, some of the nearest offering him strange, suspicious looks, but no violence. All he wanted to do was to find a nice quiet room to rest but even that seemed too much to ask. "Well," he grated, his patience all but gone, "do you have any suggestions as to where we *might* find some rooms/"

The barkeeper turned to him, frowning, "What am I a damned city guide? How in the night should I know?" He turned away and went about his work.

After a minute, he looked back and saw that Alesh and the priest hadn't moved. "Gods help me you're still here. Fine, try the Golden Pear. Claude's an overcharging bastard, right enough. If anybody's got a room free it'll be him. Now, get out of here. I've work to do."

It was nearly dark by the time they reached the place. Street lanterns, spaced at regular intervals along the sides of the street did little to light the way, their flickering lights giving the shadows shape and form yet too weak to chase them away. Alesh found himself thinking of Ilrika, his home, of those whom he'd loved who now lay dead, butchered like cattle.

Inside of the inn, a warm orange glow came from bright lanterns sat at each table in the center of a variety of colorful tablecloths. Small groups of men and women laughed, flirted, and drank, oblivious of how close the darkness was, of how it pooled outside the door of the inn, waiting to come in. *Fools*, Alesh thought, as he headed for the counter, *don't they know? Don't they understand? All light dies. All beauty fades, and the only thing that is certain is death. Death and darkness.*

"Why hello, good sirs," a portly innkeeper said as they approached, smiling. To Alesh the expression didn't seem like one of happiness but one of hunger. The man's tunic was a patchwork of dozens of pieces of differently colored cloth sewn together in a gaudy outfit that did little to hide his bulk. "And what may I help you with?"

"How much will two rooms cost us?" Alesh asked.

"Ah," the man said, gesturing with a finger as if Alesh had just said something of great magnitude, "well, sir, it will be two Dawns for each."

Alesh frowned, "You've got to be kidding. That's three times more than normal."

The portly man chuckled, patting his ample stomach with a hand, "The good sir would be correct, of course, in normal times. But *these* are not normal times, eh?"

Alesh raised his eyebrows in surprise. Had news of Ilrika somehow traveled so far already? "You know, then?"

The man smiled condescendingly, "Well, of course, master. Everyone knows, and how wouldn't they? Why the Carnival of Lights only comes once a year, doesn't it?"

"The ... Carnival of Lights"

The man nodded, "Of course. Why it is the most—" he paused, staring at Alesh. "I'm sorry, sir, but are you new to the city?"

"We've only just arrived."

"Ah. Well, you have picked the perfect time for a visit. Why, the carnival begins tomorrow. You are in for a wondrous treat."

"Oh?"

The man must have taken Alesh's question for interest. He grinned, gesturing expansively with his arms, "Why, of course, young master. The week of the carnival is a time of celebration and thanks in Valeria, but more than that, it is a chance for the city's people to show the *creatures* that we do not fear them, for without fear they have no power over us."

Alesh barked a laugh. The man had courage enough behind his walls and his lights, but he wondered how brave he would be in the wilderness, when night pressed in and the nightlings prowled in the darkness, hissing and growling in their bloodlust, the only thing keeping them at bay the light of a single fire.

The innkeeper must have misunderstood the source of his amusement because his smile widened further still, "It is truly a blessed event," he said in an eager voice, "one where Lady Tesharna herself, Amedan's favored daughter, travels through the streets and sometimes even graces a lowly innkeeper like myself with her presence. A truly marvelous, blessed time, a time of great fortune."

Alesh grunted, "Well, you're right about that at least. Two Dawns for a room isn't very far from a fortune."

The man sighed regretfully, "Yes, sir. Although I detest the thought of charging so much for a room, the amount of people the carnival brings to the city means that they are in great demand, and I am forced—against my natural inclination, of course—to charge such prices."

"Of course," Alesh said, sighing as he withdrew four of the golden coins from his pocket and handed them to the innkeeper. Luckily, the Lightbringer, Garn, had carried his money in his pack. Alesh remembered thinking, when he'd first opened the small sack of Dawns with a few of the dully colored

Dusks thrown in, that it was a fortune. It didn't seem so now. Still, he was exhausted, and it would be good to sleep under a roof without worrying about the fire going out. He yawned heavily, and gestured for the innkeeper to show them to their rooms.

The man nodded briskly and headed in the direction of the stairs, his wide smile still in place. *As well it should be,* Alesh thought, but he followed after the man, too tired to care.

CHAPTER FORTY-THREE

THAT NIGHT, ALESH DREAMED HE was walking the crowded streets of Valeria. Buildings, colorful and brilliant in the sunlight surrounded him, but as he drew closer to each, he could see that beneath the covering of bright paint, their walls were cracked and in disrepair and a rancid, sickening smell wafted out of their doorways and windows. A sea of colorfully-dressed men, women, and children flowed around him, but there was something strange, something unnatural about their ponderous, shuffling steps. Something else was wrong as well, and, at first, Alesh couldn't think of what it was. After a moment, it hit him. No one was speaking. All around him walked what had to be hundreds, maybe even thousands of people, yet not a single word was uttered. Here and there, he could make out the small shape of what must have been children, but instead of running and laughing as children do, these were silent, their slow unsteady steps matching those of the adults.

Staring around him, Alesh felt a knot of anxiety gathering in his stomach. Everyone wore cloaks of various colors, the hoods of which were pulled up, covering their faces. No matter how he looked at them, Alesh always found himself looking at their backs, or glimpsing a vague, shadowed outline of their profile. It was as if he shared the street with an army of ghosts.

"*Ghosts do not speak as the living do,*" a voice whispered behind him, "*and they have no faces except in their own memories.*"

Alesh felt his blood go cold, and he spun in search of the speaker but found nothing, only the same tide of people flowing past, seemingly oblivious of him, of each other, even of themselves. Finally, unable to stand it any longer, he walked up to the nearest person—a young woman, judging by the figure covered by the slim, sleeveless dress she wore—-ignoring the warning bells that were ringing in his head, fighting an almost overpowering instinct to run, to *get away*. "Excuse me, ma'am?" He asked, but the woman did not answer or pause in her shuffling, weary walk. "Ma'am?" Alesh reached out and gently grasped the lady's arm then recoiled in disgust. The limb had been cold, clammy. At his touch, it had contracted unnaturally, the greasy skin rubbing against his fingers as if he'd tried to grab hold of a water eel instead of a person.

The woman jerked to a stop. Her arms hung lifeless at her sides, and her head dangled to one side like a puppet with its strings cut. "S-sorry," he said, and suddenly, he wished that he'd never touched her, wished that he'd listened to the voice that had told him to run instead, but it was too late. The woman was turning toward him now, her head and neck twitching sharply as she did. Alesh tried to look away, suddenly terrified of what he would see, but the dream held him fast, and as she turned to face him, he gasped in horror. The woman's left eye was milky and unseeing and sitting askew in its socket. Where the right one should have been, there was only a pocked, grisly hole. Her jaw hung slack, and pieces of her cheek and forehead were covered in desiccated, rotting flesh. What little skin was left on her face was covered in white cosmetic powder, her stringy white lips dabbed here and there with dye to make them look a sickening bright red that reminded him of blood.

As Alesh stared at her, too shocked and horrified to move, a plump maggot, the color of curdled milk, crawled from her eye-socket and down her cheek. At the sight of the creature, his feet finally began to obey his commands again, and he took a quick step back, grunting in surprise as he bumped into someone. He whipped around and saw another corpse regarding him with callous, unfeeling eyes. Then he screamed.

His wordless cry of fear resounded and echoed off the buildings and instantly, as if on cue, the sound of shuffling feet stopped, and the silence that followed was louder than any thunder storm. *Gods, don't let them turn*, he thought desperately, *please. I'll go mad if they do*. As if they'd been waiting for just such a thought, there was a loud rustling as each of the people turned toward him, all of them staring at him with dead, cold eyes set in slack, lifeless faces. Then, as one, they started toward him, their wasted hands reaching, reaching, reaching.

Alesh awoke with a gasp, his heart hammering in his chest as if it was going to explode. His body was drenched in sweat, and his hands shook with leftover terror. "J-just a dream," he told himself, "You were dreaming, that's all." But *what* a dream! No, a nightmare, and even though he was awake, Alesh thought he could still feel the woman's slimy arm underneath his fingers, could still smell the odor of rot and decay. "Damn you, priest," he mumbled. Somehow, the man's idiocy had infected his dreams.

He yawned heavily, rubbing at his grainy eyes, then glanced at the room's small window and saw that the sun had only just risen. He still felt exhausted, but after the dream the last thing he wanted to do was go back to sleep, so he rose and began to get dressed.

Finished, he walked to the priest's door and knocked, determined to give the man a piece of his mind. As he waited, his thoughts turned to the dream he'd had of his parents on the night the Redeemers had attacked him, the dream of his father. *Torrik,* he thought, *his name was Torrik.* He'd had the dream since he was a child, but always before he'd blacked out when the wagon tipped. He'd never known who his parents were, or why they'd risked the road at night without the protection of a Lightbringer. All he knew of them was their faces and their screams and now—assuming his dream had been true—his father's name.

And it *had* been true. He didn't know why he knew that, but he did. His father's name was Torrik. The thought filled him with joy and sorrow in equal measure. For years, he'd searched for any knowledge of his parents' identity, but without a name, he'd never had any luck. Until the dream, he'd managed to overcome the desperate yearning to figure out who they'd been that had consumed him during his first years at the Chosen's castle. But now that yearning, that ache, had returned stronger than ever before and it took all his will power to keep from charging to the nearest library in hopes of finding some mention of his parents. *I'll look as soon as I get back,* he promised himself, *once Ilrika is safe.*

A first name of Torrik wasn't much to go on, but perhaps it would be enough. He suddenly realized he'd been standing at the priest's door for several minutes now. Maybe the man was asleep. *Well,* he thought, *it'll serve the bastard right if I cost him sleep. He's cost me plenty of mine.* He banged on the door with a balled fist, "Come on, priest! We have to go tell Tesharna what's happened."

Silence greeted him. A dead, brooding silence so similar to that of his dream that he shot a look behind him, half-expecting to see the woman with the slack jaw and decaying face. But, of course, nothing was there. He turned back to the door and banged again, hard enough to make the cheap wood rattle in its frame. "Get up, damnit, we have to go!" Nothing. Alesh muttered a curse and pushed on the door, surprised to find that it was open. "Listen—" he began angrily, stopping as he realized that the room was empty and had the feeling of having been empty for some time. Frowning, he saw that the bed had been made; there was no way to tell if it had been slept in at all.

The only sign that the priest had been there was a leather pack sitting in the corner that held his bedroll and a portion of their supplies. There was something disturbing about the empty room, the pack left in the corner as if abandoned. Had something happened to the man? Had he been right to be troubled? "Don't be a fool," he told himself, "he's just in the common room, that's all." After all, Alesh had spent enough nights nearby the priest to know that he was a light sleeper.

He turned and headed for the common room. This early, the place was nearly empty. The only people present were two men—merchants judging by their clothes—sitting and talking quietly in the corner, and the innkeeper himself. His sense of unease growing, Alesh walked up to the portly man. As he drew closer, he saw that the innkeeper had dark black circles under his eyes. He couldn't keep the grin from spreading on his face. The man was making a fortune, but at least he was working for it. "Good morning."

The heavy-set man nodded wearily, the wide smile of the night before nowhere in evidence, "Yes, good master," he mumbled, pausing to yawn, "How may I help you?"

"The priest, have you seen him?"

"Priest?" The man asked in a befuddled voice.

"The man who was with me last night," Alesh said, fighting back a surge of impatience, "Have you seen him?"

The innkeeper's eyebrows drew down in thought for a moment then realization finally spread across his face, "Ah yes, your friend. Quiet one, isn't he? I don't mean to pry, master, but he seemed to be … troubled."

Alesh grunted. *Crazy as shit more like.* "Anyway, have you spoken to him this morning?"

The innkeeper shook his head, "No, master, but I have only been up a short while. Ella, my wife, was watching the place earlier, and she's just lain down for a nap. Perhaps he is still in his room?"

Alesh shook his head, "I already checked there. He's gone."

The innkeeper nodded, "I am sorry, sir. Perhaps … would you like me to ask Ella when she wakes?"

"Forget it," Alesh said, dismissing it with a wave of his hand, "it's no problem. I'll just wait for a bit if that's alright with you. I'm sure he'll be back soon."

The man nodded distractedly, "Of course, sir." He said then he walked away and began busying himself with wiping down the far end of the bar.

Alesh propped his back against the counter, facing the common room and the inn's entrance, and began to wait. A half hour passed, then an hour, and a few people began to trickle in from the street, ordering ale or wine and getting an early start on the day's drink, but there was no sign of the priest.

He's gone, Alesh thought, sure of it even as he thought it, *just like in Ilrika before I met Garn.* He waited another few minutes, just in case, then he rose and walked out onto the street and began making his way to the Chosen's castle. *At least I won't have to look after the addled bastard anymore,* he thought, but he was surprised to find that the idea gave him no pleasure. True, the priest hadn't talked much and what little he *had* said had made Alesh want to strangle him, but as unlikely as it was, he realized that he'd grown used to—and in some strange way, dependent upon—the man's presence.

He stopped in the street and glanced back toward the inn. Several people grumbled curses at him as they shouldered past. Perhaps the priest had only gone out to see the city while he'd waited for Alesh to wake up and would be returning soon. Maybe ... *Don't be a fool,* he told himself. The man had seemed depressed, outright scared, in fact, since they'd entered the city. Going sight-seeing would have been the last thing on his mind. Besides, although he couldn't explain why, Alesh *knew* he was gone, knew it as surely as he knew that he would never again joke with Chorin or be lectured by Abigail. He was alone. Again." *The night can have you then,*" he growled, "*I don't need you. I don't need anyone.*"

He stalked through the crowded, unfamiliar streets, each step feeling heavier than the last. Over an hour passed before he finally saw the castle gates in the distance and, breathing a sigh of relief, he made his way toward them. As he approached, he saw that a long line of people wound its way from the gates all the way down to the street. Commoners dressed in simple woolen clothes and nobles dressed in rich silks and embroidered cloth stood together, waiting for an opportunity to speak with the city's Chosen.

Ignoring the frowns and stares of the people in line, Alesh marched past toward a pair of guards in white armor and snow white cloaks that stood near the gate. As he drew close, one of the guards, a man with dark, beady eyes and a nose that looked as if it had been broken too many times to count, stepped toward him, one hand on the hilt of his sword. "Back in line, boy."

"I need to speak with Chosen Tesharna," Alesh began, "it's impor—"

"You going to make trouble, boy?" The man asked in a tone that said he hoped Alesh would do just that, "or are you going to get back in line and wait like the others?"

"There isn't time," Alesh said, unable to hide his frustration, "I have to speak with her—it's important."

"I'm sure it is," the guard said in a bored voice, "but you'll have to wait your turn like all the rest."

"You don't understand, this is really—"

"Important?" The second guard, a thin man with a sunken, emaciated looking face asked with a sneer, then turned and gave the first guard a knowing look before turning back to Alesh, "Yeah, you said that. Now, how about you let me tell you a secret, peasant. *Everyone* who comes to see Chosen

Tesharna believes that what they've got to say's important. Of course, most of the time all they really do is bitch and moan about one thing or another. Sometimes it's that there's not enough food in the city."

"Or the merchants complaining that there's too much and it's driving the prices down," the brute-faced man said.

The skinny guard nodded, "Or that there's too many people or too few, that the streets are too crowded or not crowded enough. Sometimes it's asking for her blessing for a sick child or relative, or the lame and sick coming asking for healing." He snorted, "As if Amedan's Favored would squander her strength on a man or woman too foolish to stay in out of the rain. Shit, I figure the only reason they ain't asked her to make it rain gold is on account of they ain't thought of it yet. 'Course, bitchin's not the only thing they have in common. Want to know the other? They *all* wait in line."

Alesh gritted his teeth, "Would you *listen*. I'm not here to ask for her blessing or to complain. I'm here with a message from Ilrika."

"Wait a minute," the thin man said, squinting his eyes as he stared at Alesh. After a moment, he nodded and barked a laugh, "I *knew* you looked familiar. Why, you're the same fool who spoke to the Captain yesterday, claiming that you'd been sent by Olliman." The man rolled his eyes to show what he thought of that. "Boy, you're a stubborn one, I'll give you that." He turned to the guard beside him, "Isn't that right, Klen?"

"Stubborn or stupid."

The talkative guard nodded thoughtfully, "Stubborn or stupid, huh? Well, boy? Which are you?"

Alesh took a step forward and paused as the bigger of the two drew his sword in a meaty fist. Several people in the crowd gasped. They were too far away to have heard the exchange, but they were plenty close enough to see the naked steel pointing at Alesh's chest.

"You see, boy," The thinner guard said, "Klen here hasn't got a whole lot of patience for folks as don't listen—got a real mean streak in him, that one does. Now why don't you do yourself a favor and get back in line before you end up spending the carnival locked away in a cell or at the healer's?"

Alesh studied the two men, his anger and frustration threatening to overcome his good sense, but the thought of Sonya needing help in the city, counting on him while he lay useless in a prison cell decided him and with a sound of disgust he turned and walked to the back of the line.

He'd only been in line for a few moments when he saw a man, noble by the quality of his clothes and his arrogant stride, walk up to the guards. They spoke briefly, the man handed one of the guards a small coin bag then they opened the gate and let him through. Alesh felt his face flush with anger. He thought of Abigail and Chorin lying dead and broken, thought of Sonya, dead or in need of help and something dark stirred within him. The scar on his shoulder began to burn, but Alesh hardly noticed it just as he didn't notice that he'd started walking toward the guards.

A hand grasped his arm, stopping him. "Easy there, lad," a voice beside him whispered, "Best not to antagonize them."

Alesh turned to see a man that appeared to be in his thirties standing beside him. The man was watching the two guards, so Alesh could only see one side of his face, but it was enough for him to know that they'd never met before. "I'm sorry?"

The side of the man's mouth curved in a smile, but he did not turn to Alesh. "Not yet, maybe, but you will be if those guards decide you mean to cause trouble. You wouldn't be the first person they've taken a disliking to who wakes up bruised and beaten in some alleyway." The stranger regarded him from the corner of one eye, and Alesh was surprised to find that it was completely white, not the foggy, milk white that one sometimes saw in the elderly, but a bright, brilliant white that matched the color of the castle walls.

He's blind, Alesh thought. That was obvious enough, but why, then, did it seem as if the man was looking directly at the two guards? Stranger still, the longer Alesh looked at the man, the more and more familiar he seemed. As if they'd met before but only for a moment, and only that in passing. "Well," he said, remembering the drunk who'd accosted him when Olliman had sent him to find the woman Katherine, remembering the satisfaction he'd felt at knocking the man down, of hurting him, "If they try, they might be in for a surprise."

"And how is being arrested for assaulting guards going to help you deliver the message you bear?"

Alesh was again struck with the feeling that he'd met this man before. "Do I know you?"

The man smiled, "What are the chances of that? No, you do not know me, but perhaps you will come to know me better. Now, relax, lad. You will do yourself no favors by angering men such as they."

"They're bullies and fools," Alesh growled.

The stranger laughed, a deep, sonorous sound, "Sure and what of it? Their swords make up for the sharpness their wits lack, and a man needs little in the way of cleverness to mock peasants or bully commoners."

"But not nobles?" Alesh asked.

The stranger grinned, and Alesh could have sworn that he glanced at him from the corner of his blind eye, "Aye, nobles, too, though most times a man doesn't even need a little cleverness for that. Still," he said, rubbing at his chin with a gnarled hand, "there are one or two that may show promise."

Alesh frowned, studying what he could see of the man's face. There was something strange about him, something *different,* and still that nagging sense of familiarity. "You're sure we haven—"

"Makes a man wonder, thought, doesn't it?" The stranger interrupted thoughtfully. "A position as one of the Chosen's guards … I suspect that there isn't a fighting man in the city or its outlying towns who wouldn't count themselves lucky for the opportunity. Curious, then, that she would choose such men as they, is it not?"

Alesh frowned, not seeing what point the stranger was trying to make. "Well, mistakes happen."

"So they do," the man nodded, "so they do. But, then, one would think that a woman with Tesharna's power and influence would be able to avoid such mistakes. Unless…." He trailed off.

"Unless what?" Alesh asked. "What are you trying to say?"

"Ah," the man said, "it seems that our time is up."

For the first time, the stranger turned to fully face him, and Alesh took an involuntary step back. One of the man's eyes was a bright, almost luminescent white, the other a black so dark it seemed to swallow the light around it. "Be careful, Alesh," the stranger said, glancing over Alesh's shoulder, "and good luck."

Alesh turned and saw the two guards walking toward him. It took him a few moments to realize that the man had called him by his name. "How could you," he began, turning back, but stopped midsentence, shocked to find the stranger gone.

A shiver ran up his spine. Appearing out of nowhere with one white eye, one dark ... he'd heard stories of such a man before, only the stories weren't of a man ... they were of a god. Fighting down a knot of superstitious fear, he tapped on the shoulder of the man in front of him, "Excuse me, sir, did you see where the man I was speaking with went?"

The stranger—a well to do merchant, by his fancy clothes and large paunch—glanced at Alesh then at the approaching guards, "Don't you bring me any trouble."

Alesh started to respond, but the man had already turned away, hunching his shoulders as if expecting to be hit.

"Hey, you!" A voice barked. Alesh turned to look at the two guards. "Come on," the thinner one said, gesturing with a frown, "Chosen Tesharna will see you now." Several of the people in the line grumbled, but a glance from the bigger guard quickly silenced their complaints.

Without waiting for a reply, the two men turned and started away. Alesh hesitated, suddenly unsure. Had he imagined it, or had the men looked at him strangely, almost hungrily, the way a wolf might stare at a wounded deer before it pounced? And what of the stranger? How had he known Alesh's name? He glanced round once more, but the man was nowhere in sight. *It doesn't matter,* he told himself, *you didn't come all this way for nothing, did you? What about Erwin? What about Sonya?* Alesh rubbed at his eyes, heaved a sigh, and followed the guards into the castle.

CHAPTER FORTY-FOUR

He followed the two guards through the sprawling hallways of Valeria's castle, past richly-embroidered tapestries depicting famous scenes from the war, including the fall of Argush. Unsurprisingly, perhaps, most of the paintings showed the Lady Tesharna standing in the front, triumphant and victorious, a vision of a warrior goddess possessed of incredible beauty and strength. Never mind the fact that Alesh knew from his studies, that many of the paintings showed Tesharna in places she had never been, presiding over armies that Olliman—not she—had led. After all, Tesharna was a tactician, not a warrior, and, as far as Alesh knew, she had never directly participated in any of the war's battles.

Soon they came to a large, circular room with walls so white they were almost painful to look at as the sun shone on them through a glass ceiling. In the center of the room stood a life-size sculpture of the Lady Tesharna herself, poised with her nose tilted slightly upward as if in challenge. At her feet cowered what he supposed was meant to be a nightling, but to Alesh there was something terribly human about the wretch's eyes and face and the more he looked at it, the more it seemed to him that it wasn't a nightling at all, but some terribly wounded and scarred man. Several servants busily wiped down the statue, fussing over it as if any speck of dirt or grime on the figure of the Chosen would be the greatest of crimes. *Vanity, it seems, can even befall a High Priestess.* Looking at the statue, Alesh felt an unexplained feeling of fear settle over him.

"Come on," one of the guards said, "The Chosen's not to be kept waiting."

Alesh turned and saw that both of the men were watching him, their hands on the hilts of their swords. *Something's wrong here*, he thought. He didn't feel like a guest being escorted to an audience with the Chosen at all, but like a criminal being led to his execution. *It's your imagination, that's all*, he told himself, *Everything's fine. You'll tell Tesharna of what's happened, and she'll make everything alright. You'll see.*

"Lead on," he said. The men started out again without a word. Alesh followed and although he tried to tell himself that it was only his odd meeting with the stranger and the priest's troubled talk upon entering the city that gave him this feeling of unease, that made him imagine he was in danger, he could not quite believe it.

Stranger or no stranger, he was not imagining the grip both guards kept on the swords at their sides, or the way they kept looking back as if expecting him to run.

"Alesh."

Alesh stopped, unnerved. Neither of the two men had spoken and a quick glance around assured him that the hallway was empty save the three of them. "Wha—" he began, then cried out as a sharp, blinding burst of light exploded in his head, and his entire body gave a vicious spasm as if he'd been struck by lightning. His knees buckled, his legs gave out, and he crumpled to his knees.

As quickly as it had come, the force—whatever it had been—vanished, leaving Alesh feeling drained and exhausted. He realized he was panting and wiped his arm across his mouth, swallowing hard. He glanced up at the two guards. Both men stood, watching him, their swords partly drawn from their scabbards. As he looked at them, his eyes began to itch, and he rubbed at them with the palms of his hands. Instead of subsiding, however, the itching grew worse, turning into an unpleasant burning sensation. Abruptly, his eyes felt as if they were on fire, and Alesh hissed in agony, snapping his eyes shut and pressing his palms against them. After a few moments, the pain faded, and slowly, tentatively he opened his eyes again, letting out a gasp of surprise and fear as he did. Where the two guards had been standing only a moment before now stood two shadowy figures with eyes like small pin pricks of blood.

Alesh backed away across the ground and one of the shadowmen seemed to glide forward, *"Die, you're going to die,"* the creature rasped in a horrible, grating voice that reminded Alesh of snakes and things that crawled in the dark corners of abandoned tombs. *"Kill you, murder you, ki*—lost your damned mind?"

Alesh stared in shock. The last words had been spoken in a normal, human voice completely at odds with the alien one it had first used, but there was no question it had come from the same figure. The figure stopped, and Alesh watched it, something stirring in his chest, as if a drowsing animal was tossing in its sleep, near to waking, and the thought of its awakening at once thrilled and terrified him. He bounced more than rose to his feet, his body suddenly feeling stronger than it ever had before, his muscles and limbs feeling as if they could crush stone and hurtle mountains with little trouble. The shadow that had spoken started toward him again. *If it comes any closer,* Alesh thought, *I'll kill it.* He didn't know how he would—after all, how did one destroy a shadow?—but he knew that he would, just the same, knew it just as surely as he knew his father's name.

The creature took another step forward, and Alesh felt a building of power in him, so strong that it was almost painful, and right as he felt on the verge of some great, some terrible release, the other shadow reached out a hand and grabbed the first one by the shoulder. *"Careful, careful,"* it whispered in that same, alien voice, *"fire, death, pa*—looks as if he's gone mad." It turned back to Alesh, its crimson eyes dancing in the darkness of its face like twin fires on a starless night, "what's gotten into you—*die, must die, protect the*—you to the Chosen. It's what you want—*knows, knows too much, kill y*—it was important, didn't you? Life or death?"

Life or death. An image of Sonya, young and innocent, came unbidden to his mind, and the pressure or force that had been building in him abruptly vanished.

He blinked again, and the two guards were standing in front of him once more. They watched him warily, as if he was a rabid dog that might decide to bite at any moment. *Damn you, priest,* he thought, *it wasn't enough that you were mad, you had to go and make me crazy as well.* "I'm fine," he said, staring at the men, searching for any signs of the shadow creatures he'd seen, "I just got lightheaded for a moment." *A lie. You're far from fine, friend. In fact, I think you're just about as far from fine as one man can be.* Hearing voices, seeing things that aren't there. *But what if they were real?* A small, superstitious part of his mind whispered. *What if the men are the things that aren't there?*

And so what if they are? A part of his mind snapped back. *What choice do I have?* He'd come to tell Tesharna about what was happening in Ilrika, and that is what he would do. "Seriously," he said to the frowning guards, "I'm alright. It was a long trip, and I'm tired, that's all. The sooner we can have this done the better."

The two men glanced suspiciously at Alesh but finally, to his relief, started forward again, though he noticed them glancing back more often than before. Thankfully, only a short time later they came to a large, ornate door and the two guards came to an abrupt halt. Four other men, clothed in the brilliant white livery of Tesharna's guard, stood blocking the entrance. "This is him?" One of the four asked. He was clothed similarly to the rest, but two golden stripes adorned the shoulder of his uniform.

"This is him, Captain."

The captain nodded "The Chosen said that he was to be brought to her immediately. Come, we will escort you."

He motioned to the other men and they turned, swinging the large wooden doors open and following Alesh and his two-guard escort into a massive audience chamber. Rows of richly-furnished tables, bedecked in white tablecloths and silver candelabras with matching silverware filled the room. Women in fancy silk dresses and men in rich doublets and trousers crowded the tables, dining on roast mutton and a variety of sweet meats and cakes, the powerful smell of which made Alesh's already queasy stomach roil threateningly.

Servants clothed in simple, white wool tunics and holding trays of food and bottles of wine stood silently on either side of the room, ready to move forward at a moment's notice. The room was alive with the buzz of conversation when they entered, but as the diners noticed the strange procession making its way through the room, they grew quiet.

Alesh felt his face heating under the scrutiny of the crowd, and his forehead was coated in a nervous sweat by the time the guards came to a halt, dropping to their knees, their absence in front of him revealing a raised dais on which a small, brightly-polished table sat. A woman in an elegant white robe sat at the table, sipping wine out of a golden goblet. Her neck, fingers, and wrists were bedecked in a fortune of jewels of various size and shape, their colors dancing blindingly in the room's light. *Her people line the streets outside, begging to speak with her, and she sits and drinks wine.* He realized, then, how lucky he'd been, as a child, to stumble into Ilrika instead of Valeria.

"*Kneel, fool!*" One of the guards hissed, dragging Alesh down to his knees. Several people in the crowd began to whisper, and Alesh bowed his head, his face growing even hotter with embarrassment.

He'd served Chosen Olliman since he was a child, but he had never been made to kneel. Olliman had never believed in such things; he'd always said that no man was worthy of another's worship and that only the gods themselves were deserving of such gestures. Apparently, Chosen Tesharna felt differently.

"You may rise," the woman said in a bored, slightly annoyed voice, like a host who would like nothing more than to kick her guests out but restrained herself for courtesy's sake. The guards stood, jerking Alesh to his feet, and he waited uncomfortably as Chosen Tesharna studied him the way that a woman might study a particularly revolting bug that had plopped into her wine. The fact that the woman seated before him *was* Chosen Tesharna could not be questioned. Her long white hair fell out from underneath a slim golden crown, and although wrinkles brought on by age marred the space around her eyes and mouth, it was the same face he'd seen on the statue. Older though and, to his mind at least, crueler. *Has time made it so?* He wondered, *or was the cruelty always there and time has only served to unmask it?*

The Chosen's lips were set into a thin line and her blue eyes were cold, hard. Still, there was no denying that even with her age, she was one of the most beautiful women Alesh had ever seen. Hers was a face made for portraits and statues, and aside from the few wrinkles, her light complexion appeared flawless. In several of the records he'd read of the wars, scholars had described

Tesharna's beauty in detail, comparing it to a sunrise or the first day of spring, but neither seemed appropriate to Alesh. To him, hers was not the beauty of spring, not the splendor of birth and regrowth. Instead, it was the terrible, implacable beauty of winter, of heavy snows that destroyed crops and killed the unwary, of the mountain avalanches that sometimes buried unfortunate travelers. It was beauty, true, but it was a beauty that had killed before, that maybe would kill again.

The Chosen frowned as if reading his thoughts, "And who is this that you bring before me to interrupt my dinner, Captain Farrin?"

The big man cleared his throat, "Forgive me, Blessed Above All Others, but you commanded me to bring the ... *messenger* before you as soon as possible."

Blessed Above All Others? Alesh thought incredulously, and had he only imagined the man stressing the word "messenger?" The woman raised one delicate eyebrow, "Oh? This is the one, then?"

The captain nodded, a look of relief on his face, "It would appear so, Brightness, though I cannot be certain."

Tesharna frowned at that, gesturing to dismiss a servant who had come to refill her wine, "I do not appreciate uncertainties, captain. In fact, I appreciate them about as much as a man appreciates a flogging. Perhaps, later, I will make my distaste for them known to you further."

The man swallowed hard, "Y-yes, Brightness."

Tesharna rolled her eyes, "Bring me our esteemed visitor, Captain Farrin, and let us hope that he will prove more capable than yourself."

The captain started to respond, but before he could a voice came from the crowd, "I am already here, My Lady."

Something about that voice was eerily familiar to Alesh, and he, like the others, turned to watch the man approach. *It can't be,* he thought, his body going rigid with shock as he saw the man who had spoken. *It isn't possible.*

Falen Par, the leader of the Redeemers, strode up in front of the dais beside Alesh and the guards. He was wearing a black doublet and black, cuffed trousers instead of the armor he normally seemed to prefer, but there was no mistaking the blood red cape he flourished as he bowed, nor the cold, dead look in his gaze. His smile was a dagger slash in a face that looked as if it had been carved from rock.

"Ah, Ambassador Par," the Chosen drawled, "How good of you to join us. I had thought we would have the *honor* of your company for dinner tonight. If your rooms are too far to allow you to make it in time, I would be pleased to find you closer quarters. The dungeons, perhaps?" Several people in the crowd laughed at that, but they silenced immediately at Tesharna's frown.

If Par was disturbed by the Chosen's words, he did not show it. "I apologize, of course, for my tardiness, Brightness, but certain matters were brought to my attention that had to be dealt with."

"Oh?" The Chosen asked, raising an eyebrow, "and just what matters might those be? I hope that they are not *too* terrible though surely they must be if *I* am made to wait on their behalf."

Either unaware or unconcerned with the peril he was facing, Par only shrugged, "Nothing of any serious note now, my Lady. It seems that a patrol of mine met with trouble near Shyler's Fell." He turned and looked directly at Alesh, and it was all Alesh could do not to recoil at the coldness, the evil, in that stare. "Fools all," he said, turning back to the Chosen, "but fools who will not bother the realm anymore, anyway. You need not trouble yourself, my Lady, for the difficulty is *well* in hand."

"Chosen," Alesh said, finally able to speak past his shock, "this is one of them. He ki—"

He cut off as a hand struck the back of his head hard, "*You will not speak unless asked to, peasant,*" one of the guards growled.

Alesh stumbled forward from the unexpected blow and would have fallen had the guards not grabbed him by either arm. Once he'd gotten his balance back, their grip did not loosen, and the knot of dread in his stomach grew larger.

"Very well," the Chosen said as if nothing had ever happened. She waved a dismissive hand as if bored with the subject, "Correct me if I'm wrong, ambassador, but you were present in Ilrika at the time of Chosen Olliman's," she paused, wiping at her eyes, though from this close Alesh could see that they were completely dry, "you were present at Chosen Olliman's assassination, were you not?" The room broke out into horrified whispers at that, but the Chosen held up a hand and the crowd quieted once more.

The man nodded grimly, "I was, My Lady."

"And tell us," Tesharna said in a voice that oozed regret, "what were the circumstances surrounding this ... this *tragedy?*"

The man stepped back, raising his hands to his sides and glancing alternatively between the Chosen and the crowd as if putting on a show. *And that's exactly what he's doing,* Alesh thought bitterly, suddenly realizing that coming to Valeria had been a terrible mistake, and that, somehow, the old priest had been right. "It was the nightwalkers, Brightness."

Several of the gathered people gasped in horror, and more than one woman went so far as to swoon. "Nightwalkers?" The Chosen asked. Her tone was incredulous, but there was a hunger in her steely gaze that made Alesh's blood go cold, "I must have misheard you, ambassador. Everyone knows that Chosen Olliman was the first High Priest of Amedan, the God of Light and Creation, himself. Surely, he could never be overcome by such unthinking monstrosities."

Falen Par sighed heavily with affected sadness, "It is true, My Lady, and I could hardly credit it myself, had I not seen the evidence with my own eyes." He paused, glancing at the crowd hesitantly, as if dreading what he had to say, but Alesh saw the joy, the satisfaction in those dead eyes, even if everyone else did not. "Still," Par continued, "many believed that Chosen Olliman had grown weak with age. I would normally never subscribe to such foolishness, of course, but it must be said that, for months now, the attacks against Ilrika have grown more and more common. Was it not the famous poet, Arminian, who wrote that all greatness fades with time? I fear that, perhaps, Chosen Olliman's strength was beginning to leave him."

"You *lie!*" Alesh shouted, "It wasn't hi—" His breath flew out of him in a rush as one of the guards struck him in the stomach. He fell to the ground and lay there, gasping for air.

"I will not tell you again, boy" the guard nearest him whispered into his ear, "speak once more, and I'll cut out your bloody, night-worshipping, tongue!"

Alesh barely heard the man, he was too busy struggling to catch a breath. He was still wheezing when the guards jerked him to his feet once more. "Only a fool would have ever thought Chosen Olliman weak, ambassador," Tesharna said in a scolding tone. She hesitated for a moment, looking thoughtful, "Still, it must be said that the war did not leave him untouched. Perhaps, even a man of his greatness could ... but no," she said, shaking her head, "I will need more than one man's word to believe such a thing. Even a man as noble, as *trustworthy* as yourself, Ambassador Par."

"Indeed, my lady," the man said, smiling, "I would expect nothing less from a mind of as great renown as yours, for your wisdom and fairness are well known. It is for this reason that the esteemed City Council of Ilrika—comprised, as it is, of the finest-blooded nobles the city has to offer, not to mention Chosen Kale Leandrin himself—thought it wise to send a letter confirming my words one that, you will see, bears each of their signatures." With that said, he withdrew the mentioned letter from his tunic and held it aloft as if it was the direct word of Amedan himself.

Tesharna, her face an unreadable mask, motioned to the captain of her guard, and the man hurried forward, grabbing the letter and bowing low to Tesharna, presenting it as if it was an offering. The Chosen snatched the letter from the captain's hand and waved him away.

If it had been quiet before, now the room was as silent, as still, as a cemetery. All eyes watched the Chosen open the sealed document and begin to read. Finally, she looked up at the ambassador, "It is true then," she said, folding the letter and laying it on the small table in front of her. "Chosen Leandrin was most wise to send such a letter."

The ambassador nodded once, "Chosen Leandrin is possessed of a wisdom far beyond his years, My Lady, and the only thing greater than his wish to see those responsible pay for their crime is his grief at Lord Olliman's passing."

"Indeed," Tesharna said, thoughtfully, "those responsible ... it was the nightwalkers, you say?"

The man nodded with affected sadness, and Alesh looked around the room, thinking that surely *someone* must realize that he was putting on a show, nothing more. But if anyone noticed, they gave no sign. "Yes, My Lady, the wounds on the Chosen's body—May the gods embrace and keep him—were consistent with those caused by the night's creatures."

The room broke out into quite, disbelieving whispers. Tesharna let it go on for a moment before raising a hand and demanding silence, "There is still something that puzzles me about all of this, Ambassador. I suppose it is possible, *possible* mind you, that Chosen Olliman was no longer able to protect Ilrika from the ravages of the night's creatures, but I still cannot believe that the creatures managed to sneak past the wall, through an entire *city,* and past all of Olliman's personal guards without arousing suspicion. It is true that the beasts—may Amedan curse them to the furthest reaches of the Pit—possess many strengths, but in my experience which is, unfortunately, quite extensive, subtlety may not be numbered among them. Why, I would sooner believe that a thunderstorm had snuck into Olliman's personal chambers than that these abominations managed it without arousing so much as a single shout of warning."

The thin man nodded, frowning, "It is as you say, my lady. There is no possible way the creatures could have managed to infiltrate the city, to assault, unobserved, into the very castle itself. No way at all. Not, that is," he said, waving his hands to the side, his voice booming with theatricality, "unless they had help."

There was a great drawing of breath from the stunned crowd as the man finished, and Alesh watched as the diners began to turn to each other and speak in frantic, terrified whispers. It was one thing, after all, for the nightlings to plague mankind. A terrible thing, true, but at least one they understood, One that they, in their foolishness, thought they could protect themselves against. It was quite another to believe that a person, a man or woman who shared the same sun as them could turn against his people and willingly consort with the nightwalkers.

The Chosen held up a hand for silence, but this time the worried conversations continued, and she was forced to clap her hands loudly before the diners finally grew quiet once more. "If this is a jest, Ambassador," she said in a low, dangerous tone, "then it is a poor one, and one that might as easily end with a hanging as a laugh. Not since Shyler himself," there were murmured curses at this, but they quickly cut off at the Chosen's angry look, "has any man or woman been foolish enough to throw in his lot with the armies of darkness. What possible reason would they have now?"

The thin man raised his hands to the side as if it was the most obvious thing in the world, "Jealousy, Brightness. Jealousy and a deep, seething hatred for those of higher station than one's self."

The Chosen's eyes narrowed, "Perhaps you had better explain yourself, ambassador, and quickly. Amedan has seen fit to bestow upon me many gifts, but I do not count patience among them."

Neither is humility, Alesh thought absently, but the man was already nodding, "As you command, my lady. You see," he said, turning to the gathered people as he spoke, flourishing his hands like a traveling troubadour and speaking in tones more commonly used by street prophets proclaiming the world's coming doom, "the gods—in all of their glory and splendor—sometimes choose to raise above us all a man—or woman," he said pausing to bow his head respectfully to the Chosen, "who is greater than any normal man, whose duty it is to lead and guide us. There can be no question that Chosen Olliman, High Priest of Amedan, the Father of the Gods, was such a man, for it was by his efforts—and those of the other Chosen, of course—that we did not perish to the onslaught of the nightwalker King Argush and his armies."

Several of the people in the crowd made wards against evil in the air and shifted uncomfortably in their seats. "But, alas," the man continued, his face grim, "great achievements often breed great jealousies, even among those to whom the better man has sacrificed so much. It is no wonder—"

"Get on with it, Ambassador," the Chosen snapped impatiently, "do not mince words. The hour is growing late, and we do not have time for your games. We all know well the events of the war—I better than most."

The man nodded indulgently, "Of course, My Lady. Suffice to say, that upon finding the Chosen's body, the Council of Ilrika was as stunned as you. After all, the castle was full of dozens of guards was it not? And these were not just men brought in off the street who fancied the way they looked in a uniform but skilled warriors, hand-picked by Olliman himself. Some, it was said, were more than a match for any Ekirani Blademaster. But even if these men *weren't* vigilant, even if they *weren't* some of the most observant, some of the most loyal and dedicated warriors the world has ever known, they would have needed nothing more than eyes and a mouth to see the creatures as they came and raise the alarm. It would be—as you say—impossible for any of the nightmare creatures to make their way through the castle's hallways to Lord Olliman's quarters unchallenged. Quite impossible."

"By the gods, man!" The Chosen snapped, "Are you wasting our time? You have just said yourself that what you claim is impossible!"

"And so it is, My Lady," the ambassador said, bowing his head in acknowledgment, "no creature could have made its way through those hallways without encountering dozens of people. But there are other, secret ways to the Chosen's chambers. Ways known only by the Chosen himself and a handful of his most trusted guards and servants. Men," he sneered, turning to Alesh, "like this broken, twisted soul."

The crowd broke out into gasps and shouts at that, several men cursing and jerking to their feet as if to charge Alesh. For his part, Alesh's eyes went wide with shock, "That isn't true!" He shouted, but his words were drowned out by the sudden, angry din, "Chosen Olliman was like a father to me, you bast—" he started forward but something struck the back of his head and light exploded in his vision. He stumbled, reeled, and the next thing he knew, he was lying face down on the floor, his head feeling as if it was split in two.

"*Kill him!*" A woman's voice screeched.

"*Yeah, kill the bastard!*" A man's voice shouted, "*String him up!*" Others in the crowd roared their approval, but Alesh could barely hear them. He was too busy hacking and gagging, dry-retching as dizziness and the dull throbbing pain in his head threatened to make him sick.

He tried to speak, to tell them that it was all wrong, that it was a lie, but when he opened his mouth all that came out was a dry, pained croak, easily drowned out by all of the shouting, angry voices. *Oh, gods, priest. You were right.*

"Silence!" Shouted a voice Alesh thought belonged to Captain Farrin, "Silence in the Chosen's court!"

Grudgingly, the crowd grew quiet once more. "These are dire accusations you make, Ambassador," Tesharna said warningly, as if the outburst hadn't occurred, "such things are not to be said lightly."

"I couldn't agree more, My Lady," the thin man said, "and neither could the City Council and Chosen Leandrin which is why the honorable Chosen waited until he was sure. Tell me, Brightness, were you aware that there is a secret underground passageway that can be accessed from outside of the castle proper and that, when taken, will lead a man or woman to an opening that is only a few short strides from the Chosen's quarters?"

Tesharna frowned, "I was not aware of the existence of any such passage."

The man nodded, obviously pleased with himself "And nor should you be, Your Grace. The tunnel is meant to be a means of egress, should the castle become occupied by a foreign force. Only a handful of people know of it— the Chosen's closest guards, of course and perhaps," he paused, glancing again at Alesh, "some of his most trusted servants."

Alesh started to speak but glanced at the guards beside him and thought better of it. It would do no good for him to be beaten to death for talking out of turn. Surely, Tesharna would no doubt give him his chance to speak.

"One of the castle guards found fresh spots of blood along this rarely-traveled corridor," Falen Par continued, "which can only mean that it was used that night. And since only a few knew of its existence," he shrugged, as if the matter spoke for itself. "Still," he went on, glancing between the suddenly still audience and the Chosen, "this was by no means the only ... shall we say, *curiosity*. Further investigation showed that a few of the guard patrols had strayed from their usual path. A path which, without question, would have put them in a position to sound the alarm and alert the castle. As for this *man,*" he said, twisting his mouth in disgust as he gestured to Alesh, "he was witnessed only the day before, idling near a recent break in the city's walls, no doubt searching for an opportunity to betray the city even then." There were several angry murmurs at this, but the man seemed not to hear them, "Curious circumstances to be sure but, as you have said, my lady, a charge of cavorting with nightwalkers is a most serious accusation and not one to be made lightly."

He hesitated, letting the suspense grow before he finally spoke. "With such an accusation, there can be no mistake, and for this reason Chosen Leandrin and the City Council—in their wisdom—decided to begin interviewing *all* of the servants and guards who'd been on duty the day of the Chosen's murder. In fact, it was while Chosen Leandrin was discussing how best to proceed with the investigation with some of his most trusted nobles that this man," he said, nodding toward Alesh, "snuck into the throne room by a little known *servant's passage* and attempted to accost the Chosen himself, charging him like some wild animal or ..." he paused for effect, "something *else.*"

Surely, they have to know he's lying, Alesh thought desperately, *they have to.* But a look at the enraptured faces of the man's audience, and the hate-filled stares that more than a few directed at Alesh, argued otherwise. Even the servants were engrossed in the man's tale, so much so that the Chosen's motion for more wine went unnoticed until she snapped loudly and a terrified-looking servant stumbled forward to fill her glass. "My patience is wearing thin, Ambassador," she said, her eyes narrowed, "finish your story, if you have one to tell and waste no more time on dramatics; we are not children to be moved to terror with a story."

The man bobbed his head, "Of course, My Lady. Anyway, the guards managed to stop the man before he reached the Chosen, and it was decided that he would be interrogated—without force, of course—to find out what, if anything, he knew of the events that had transpired."

"And?" The Chosen demanded, leaning forward in her chair, "What did they discover?"

Falen Par shook his head sadly, "Nothing, my lady, for the interrogation never took place. Four guards were escorting the man you see before you, but one of their own number turned on the others and, with the help of this man, slaughtered them to the last."

A wave of angry and fearful whispers went through the gathered listeners at that, many people's faces going pale white as if they'd just discovered a snake in their food. For her part, the Chosen didn't so much as bat an eyelash. "And what happened then, Ambassador? Tell the rest."

"I'm sorry, My Lady," he said, holding his hands up apologetically, "but that is all there is. The murdered guards were not discovered until several hours later by a maid who is still half-mad from the brutality of the thing. You see, your Grace ... the men weren't just killed. They—or parts of them, at least—were eaten." Gasps of horror rose in the crowd at that, and servants hurried forward to fan several women who'd swooned at the man's words.

"Somehow," Falen Par continued, having to raise his voice over the panicked, whispering diners, "He made his way out of the castle and the city, no doubt by some tunnel or pre-arranged escape plan. As for the traitor who assisted him in this atrocity—a man named Erwin, I believe—two of the castle guards found him, but when they attempted to detain him, he fought like a man possessed, slaying one of them before he was finally taken down." He sighed sadly, "Unfortunately, he succumbed to his wounds before we were able to question him to discover how deeply the plot went."

Alesh stared, stunned. Erwin had saved him when he could have done nothing, and for his kindness, he'd been killed. Despair, great and heavy, settled on him, and he felt himself being crushed beneath its weight. Then the thin man turned to him, his expression blank, but in his eyes a cruel satisfaction, and abruptly Alesh's despair vanished, replaced by a boiling, consuming rage. He hissed in pain as the scar on his shoulder began to burn with a ferocity he'd never felt before but the fury continued to build until, in another moment, even that pain was swept away in the face of it.

He leapt to his feet, his exhaustion, his pain, all distant things, unimportant. One of the guards grabbed at him, but Alesh knocked him away, sending him sprawling with a strength born of fury, and with a bestial snarl he hurtled himself at the ambassador. Fine plates and glasses crashed to the ground and shattered, chairs and tables clattered and fell over as the terrified diners recoiled and tumbled from their chairs in an effort to get out of his path. For his part, Alesh noticed none of this. His eyes saw only the ambassador, the man who had brought death to so many innocents, his ears heard only the cries of his victims. Another guard charged him, his sword raised, and Alesh ducked to the side at the last minute, the blade so close that he could feel the wind of its passage. He growled and kicked the man savagely in the side of his knee. There was a loud *pop* and the soldier screamed. Alesh punched the man in the face, reveling at the *crunch* of something under his fist. The second blow knocked the man unconscious, and Alesh paused only long enough to snatch the handle of the falling man's sword before rushing past.

The ambassador had retreated behind one of the long tables, and, without slowing, Alesh jumped onto the tabletop. Grinning at the fear in the Redeemer's wide eyes, he bellowed in rage and launched himself into the air, the sword raised above his head. He'd made it half the distance when what felt like the weight of a mountain crashed on top of him, smashing him to the ceramic tiles with bone-shattering force. His head struck a tile, cracking it, and the sword's handle came free of his grip, clattering to the floor several feet away.

"How *dare* you?" A female voice snapped.

Alesh groaned and shook his head to fight back the dizziness before finding the strength to look up. The guard he'd struck was being carried from the room by two servants, his leg hanging at an unnatural angle. Chosen Tesharna stood a few feet away, her small dining table knocked to the ground. Her right hand was clasped in front of her in a white-knuckled fist, her hair—perfectly groomed moments before—stuck out wildly. She was breathing hard, her chest heaving as if she'd just run several miles, and through his blurry vision, Alesh thought he noticed wrinkles on her face that hadn't been there before. Then, with a shock, he saw that the woman's eyes had gone completely black.

"Y-your eyes," Alesh grunted, his voice a pained whisper.

Tesharna started at that and jerked her face away from the crowd. When she turned back, her eyes were their normal color once more, though filled with anger. "If he so much as moves again, Captain," she hissed, rubbing a hand across the fresh wrinkles on her face, "you are to cut off one of his feet. Is that clear?"

"Yes, Brightness," the captain said as he and several of his guards crowded around Alesh.

"D-do you see!?" Falen Par shouted, spit flying from his mouth as he finally found his voice. The man's face was blood red, and he was only just sliding what little of his sword he'd managed to free back into its scabbard,

"The man is as bloodthirsty as the beasts that he serves! Why, he should be killed on the spot! Put down like the rabid dog th—"

"*Ambassador Par!*"

The man's rambling cut off at the Chosen's words, and he took a minute to gather himself, his eyes never leaving Alesh, his hand tight on the grip of his sword. "You would be wise, Tesharna," he growled, "to put this monster down before he hurts anyone else." A collective gasp went up from the audience at the man's familiar use of the Chosen's name.

The Chosen's expression grew dark, "I will *not* be told what to do in my own castle, ambassador, and I *will* be shown the proper respect. Am I clear?"

The man's eyes narrowed and, for a moment, Alesh thought that he meant to challenge her. But then he took a deep breath and apparently thought better of it. "Of course, my lady," he grated, "please, forgive me. It was a momentary lapse caused by this, this *man's* violence, nothing more."

Tesharna nodded, "A lapse that had best not happen again, Ambassador. Now, is there anything else, any other proof that you have to offer us?"

The man licked his lips and nodded slowly, "T-there is, Brightness. After the Chosen's death, guards and servants performed an inventory of the castle. Chosen Leandrin conducted the search of the Chosen's quarters personally, and it was discovered that one of the Evertorches was missing. As I'm sure you know well, my lady, the secrets of how to make an Evertorch were lost when Chosen Larin vanished. For this reason, Chosen Olliman has always seen to their care and distribution personally. The Chosen's quarters were searched no more than moments after his death and it was discovered that one of them was missing. Chosen Leandrian had visited the Olliman's quarters the night before for his training, and he remembered seeing it then. The servants were questioned, and they all agreed that no one went inside of Olliman's chambers between Chosen Leandrian himself and the killer's death which can mean only one thing. The killer—whoever he is—stole it."

"And was the Evertorch ever discovered?" The Chosen asked, leaning forward on her throne and studying the man intently.

"No, Brightness," the Ambassador said, "but I have a good idea of where it might be found." He gestured to Alesh, and two of the guards jerked his arms behind him, forcing him to his knees. Falen Par hesitated for a moment then walked forward and began to search Alesh's tunic. In only took him a moment to withdraw the cloth-wrapped bundle from Alesh's tunic, and he unraveled it, holding the artifact high so that everyone could see it before bowing to Tesharna and handing her the Evertorch, "Your Grace, I present to you, Chosen Olliman's killer."

Tesharna frowned, examining the artifact carefully for a moment before making a sound of disgust in her throat and tossing the Evertorch carelessly away. It hit the marble floor with a clatter, rolling across the smooth surface until finally coming to rest at Alesh's feet. "A priceless artifact of immeasurable value," she said, "scarred beyond repair. It would seem, boy," she said, staring at Alesh with narrowed, threatening eyes, "that you have much to answer for."

At first, Alesh didn't understand what she meant. Then he glanced at the Evertorch in confusion, unable to believe what he was seeing. A thin gouge had been made in the runes on the cylinder, severing its magic and making it worthless. *But how?* Since he'd woken up on the morning following the Redeemer attack, the Evertorch had been wrapped and kept safe in his tunic. The Evertorches could be damaged, true, but Chosen Larin had crafted them in such a way as to not make this an easy feat. It would have taken something more than some errant limb to so severely damage the runes carved into its surface. *Something like falling on the ground and being trampled by terrified men and hungry nightlings.*

No, but that couldn't be right, could it? After all, it had been the Evertorch that had driven the nightwalkers away, hadn't it? As Alesh stared at the damaged artifact, his mind whirling with a confusion deeper than any he'd felt since waking after his parents' murder to find himself inexplicably alive. "Very well, ambassador," Tesharna said, "I believe you. Now, you said that you had him followed. What else do you know?"

The man frowned at that, "Not nearly as much as we might have hoped, my lady, but we do know that this man has a compatriot, an older gentleman dressed like a priest, who accompanied him to the city."

Alesh felt a spike of fear for the crazy old man. *Thank the gods you got out while you could, priest. I hope that you are far, far away.* "And I assume that you have this other conspirator well in hand?" The Chosen asked.

Alesh held his breath, looking to the Redeemer, but Falen Par's eyes narrowed as he regarded Alesh cooly, "Somehow, the man has so far managed to slip out of our grasp, Brightness, but I *will* find him."

"This I do not doubt, Ambassador," the Chosen said, "and you will find him all the more quickly with the help of my guardsmen. Once he is in hand, he will suffer for his crimes. I will make sure of that."

The man nodded grudgingly, as if he wanted to contest the right to punish the old man, "Might I ask, my lady, what you propose to do with this one?"

The Chosen considered for a moment, staring at Alesh and tapping her chin thoughtfully with one painted nail, "How many men do you have in the city, Ambassador Par?"

"Twenty five soldiers, not including myself, my lady, all of them as loyal as any man could wish."

The Chosen nodded, a cold smile on her face, "Very well. See that they are ready in the morning. This year, the Carnival of Lights will begin with a show the likes of which this city has not seen in years."

CHAPTER FORTY-FIVE

KATHERINE SIGHED HEAVILY, STANDING UP in her stirrups in a vain effort to see past the line of people gathered in front of her. It seemed that people from all over the realm were seeking entrance into Valeria. Commoners in simple woolen clothing, many of which were shoeless, shared the line with fancily clothed noblemen riding grand-looking horses and noblewomen in brightly-colored dresses who rode in palanquins borne by servants.

Katherine had heard of Valeria's Carnival of Lights before, but she still found herself amazed by the variety of costumes and masks around her. It was said that Tesharna had begun the carnival years ago, and that the people of Valeria wore costumes and masks of strange or hideous aspect in order that the nightlings might be made to feel fear. She'd always thought it foolish—after all, it would take more than decorated hats and paper horns to frighten such creatures—but standing there and looking at the monstrous aspects that surrounded her, she decided that it was more than just foolish; it was unsettling and, if she was honest with herself, a little scary.

The commoners—even the children—carried or wore homemade masks of woolen cloth with stones and beads of various color and shape sewn into them to serve as crude eyes and jagged, cruel slits for mouths. Several had not stopped there, but decided to create a full costume for themselves. A man a few spaces in front of her in the line—at least Katherine thought it was a man, it was hard to tell for certain—wore a black cloth suit. Long, crimson tassels covered the cloth, dancing in the wind like dozens of bloody bandages.

A pair of young noblemen a few places behind her were dressed normally except for the porcelain masks they wore. Both masks had been painted completely black and hateful, painted red eyes stared out of them. The fools had even gone so far as to have cruel, snarling mouths filled with fangs painted into the ebony surface. Even the noblewomen had dawned masks of strange design, though many of these were obviously commissioned with a thought to beauty and attractiveness, not terror, much the same as the low-cut, bosom-exposing dresses they'd taken the opportunity to wear.

She turned to Darl who sat his horse beside her, "This is … strange," she whispered, careful to keep her voice low so as not to wake the girl sleeping in the saddle behind the Ferinan. The dusky-skinned man remained silent, as usual, but she could tell by the troubled, slightly-strained expression on his face that he, too, was uncomfortable. Taken by itself, none of the masks or costumes would have given her a moment's pause, but taken together, at a glance, Katherine felt as if she stood amid an army of nightwalkers, not come to celebrate but to conquer, not come to drink and carouse, but to torture and slay.

She breathed a sigh of relief when they finally arrived at the gate. A short, chubby clerk dressed in fine palace livery stepped forward with four guards following close behind. The clerk stared at them with the haughty arrogance common to those of his profession, squinting despite the glasses he wore. When his gaze reached the Ferinan, his expression turned to one of surprise, and he glanced back as if to make sure that the guards had followed him. The four men frowned and took a step closer, and the clerk took a moment to gather himself, his confidence restored by the four armed men. He jabbed an imperious finger at the spear sticking out of Darl's blanket roll, a sneer on his face as if he'd caught the Ferinan plotting murder, "You *will* relinquish your weapons to the guards," he said in a petulant voice that belonged to a child, "Chosen Tesharna will *not* allow the bearing of arms during the week of the carnival."

Katherine felt her face go red with anger, "Surely, you're joking? You just let those two noblemen through and they were both carrying swo—"

She cut off as Darl's hand fell on her shoulder. She turned and the Ferinan man smiled then shook his head slightly. He turned and began to unroll the spear from the cloth blanket. As he did, the guards fingered the hilt of their swords, one going so far as to draw the blade halfway out of its scabbard. Darl only smiled slightly, offering the blunt end of the spear to the pale clerk who recoiled as if it was a snake. Several tense seconds passed until finally the short, bespectacled man licked his lips and gingerly took the spear.

Disgusted, Katherine withdrew her own dagger from the small sheathe at the waist of her blue dress and tossed it contemptuously in front of the guards who were too busy eyeing the Ferinan to notice. "*Well?*" The clerk demanded of the guard nearest the dagger, and the man started before snatching it up, his eyes never leaving Darl. *Bastard's lucky he didn't cut himself,* Katherine thought. *Too bad.* "Are we going to have trouble out of you, boy?" The clerk asked.

Darl grinned widely, displaying his teeth, and shook his head.

The clerk hesitated but, apparently seeing no way to refuse them entry, waved them through with a reluctant gesture. "*Damn savages,*" he whispered as they passed, and Katherine gripped the reins of her horse tightly, barely suppressing the urge to launch herself from her mount and strangle the fat, pompous little man.

Inside the city, the avenue was lined on either side with merchants and vendors positioned to sell their goods to those entering the gate. Crowds pressed in all around them and although everyone Katherine saw had a mask, many held them in their hands or left them to dangle from strings around their necks. It was still early—even though Katherine felt as if they'd been in line for half a day or more—and the people were content to browse the stalls of the merchants and finish up the final preparations for the first day of the carnival.

A crew of men busied themselves hanging streamers of various sizes, lengths, and colors from the nearby houses and shops. For now, the streamers were secured by long lengths of twine, but later in the afternoon, when the carnival started, they would be set free and them, and the others like them that were hung through much of the city, would flap and twist, making a veritable maze of color and confusion and obstructing the view of the city as a whole for more than a few feet in front of a person's face. The Color Maze, as it was called, was said to be one of the most popular features of the carnival.

The press of bodies forced them to dismount and guide their horses through the crowd. They'd only made it a short distance into the city when Sonya awoke, wiping her eyes and yawning heavily from her place atop Darl's mount. "Katherine?" She asked, in a nervous voice, "Darl?"

"Yes, sweetling?" Katherine said, navigating her mount around a merchant selling pre-made masks of various designs.

"W-where are we?" The young girl asked in a frightened voice, gazing wide-eyed at the masked faces around her.

"It's alright, Sonya," Katherine said, smiling reassuringly, "we've made it to Valeria, that's all."

"I don't like it here," the girl said in a small, scared voice, "can we leave? Something's wrong."

"Soon, sweetheart, I promise. We just have to visit the palace and meet with Chosen Alashia. You'll like her; she's a wonderful woman, and she's excited to see you."

The girl's eyes grew wider still, not with fear this time but astonishment, "One of the Chosen wants to meet me?" She asked, "But why? She doesn't even know me."

Katherine winked, "You'd be surprised how much she knows. She *is* one of the Chosen, after all, isn't she? And I'll bet she'd love to tell you a story." Chosen Alashia had always been good with children. Katherine had accompanied her multiples times on her visits to the city's hospitals where she told the sick children jokes and stories, her grandmotherly manner quickly overcoming their awe at being in the presence of one of the most powerful people in the world.

The girl considered this for a moment. "I *do* love stories, and I'd like to meet her but … but I don't like it here. It's … *wrong*. I think it's … it's *bad*."

Katherine felt the same, but it would do the girl no good to know it, so she smiled again, patting Sonya's leg reassuringly, "It's just a carnival, that's all, sweety. People dressed up in costumes and masks, nothing more. Just like

F—" she paused, stopping herself from saying Fairday. *That's just great,* she scolded herself, *why don't you try to frighten her to death by bringing that up?* "It's just like a party, that's all. Don't you like a party?"

"Y-yes, but...." The girl started, still sounding unsure, but she stopped as Darl clasped her hand gently and smiled. Sonya nodded at the Ferinan as if he'd just spoken, then took a deep breath and turned back to Katherine, "Okay. I'm okay."

Katherine felt a twinge of jealousy at how easily Darl had set the girl at ease without a word, but he met her frown with a smile and a wink.

She fought back a sigh, "We need to find a guard and show them our messenger's seal," she said to Darl. "Otherwise, we'll be wandering around here all day. We'll head in the direction of the castle and look for a guard while we do."

The Ferinan nodded, his expression never changing, but she thought she saw a troubled look in his eyes. Katherine empathized; she wanted nothing more than to find a room in a quiet inn and hide out until the carnival was over. Still, the sooner they made it to the castle, the sooner they could find Chosen Alashia and be sent on their next assignment, hopefully somewhere far away from the city and its oppressive atmosphere.

After an hour of forcing their way through the loud, sweaty people, Katherine began to despair that they'd reach the castle within the week, much less find a guide to help them get there.

She was just about to give up and look for an inn instead—after all, they were all exhausted and surely one day would make no difference—when six men in the white uniforms of Tesharna's personal guards appeared out of the crowd in front of them as if by magic. The six men looked grim, and their hands stayed close to the swords at their sides. *As well they should,* Katherine thought, *this many people would be enough to drive guardsmen insane.* "Lady Katherine Elar?" A man with a golden stripe on his white tunic asked in a deep, gravelly voice. He appeared to be in his mid-thirties, with a face that was hard and sharp enough to cut. He glanced at Darl and, though Katherine wouldn't have thought it possible, his thin lips grew tighter.

"Yes?" She asked, not liking how weak her voice sounded, but the sudden appearance of the guards, mixed with their commander's gruff manner, had unnerved her. She glanced around her but saw that the six men had spread out, creating a bubble of space as the sea of people parted around them like a river current around a boulder.

The man nodded sharply, "I am Lieutenant Ralten, ma'am. We have been looking for you."

Katherine glanced at Darl in surprise then back at the lieutenant, "You have? We've only just arrived in the city."

The man nodded, "We know, ma'am. We were sent by Chosen Tesharna and Chosen Alashia to escort you to the castle."

Katherine was surprised at that. Normally, Alashia was incredibly protective of her agents' identities, so protective, in fact, that Katherine herself only knew of Darl, and she wasn't even sure that he was one of Alashia's agents. What little time she'd seen the two together, Alashia had treated Darl more as an equal than she did an agent. Of course, she seemed to do that with everyone. When Katherine had once asked the Chosen why she insisted that all of her agents use aliases, Alashia told her that an agent whose identity was known was about as useful as a frying pan made of woven grass. Given the Chosen's feelings about retaining the anonymity of her agents, it seemed strange that she would risk exposing Katherine to the entire city for the sake of expediency. Katherine supposed Alashia was just anxious to hear news from Chosen Olliman, but she still didn't like it. Something didn't seem right.

"Ma'am?"

The guard's voice startled Katherine out of her reverie, and she pushed her worries away with a will. Seeing all those people in masks, dressed like monsters and nightlings had disturbed her more than she'd realized. "I'm sorry, Lieutenant Ralten, please forgive me, my mind was wandering. Thank you for finding us, and we are ready when you are."

"We were not told that you would have …." The man paused, glancing at Darl and Sonya meaningfully, *"friends."*

Katherine frowned. Judging from her note, Chosen Alashia had known about Sonya, had, in fact, made a comment about how excited she was to meet her. And, of course, she knew about Darl. Why would she not have mentioned it to the guards? *It probably slipped her mind,* Katherine told herself, *after all, she has a lot to deal with—more than enough to drive most people crazy—who was Katherine to complain if she forgot something so small?* "Darl and Sonya are my companions, Lieutenant," she said, "and Chosen Alashia will want to see them both personally."

The Lieutenant's expression, and those of his men, seemed to grow grimmer at that and, had she not known better, Katherine would have almost thought hostile. Still, it might *be* hostile. After all, people usually showed similar reactions when seeing the Feranin man. If the reaction from the guards was less than perfect, well, they'd no doubt had a busy few days preparing for the Carnival of Lights and several more ahead of them. Still, she would mention it to the Chosen. Darl had saved her life several times, and always treated people with kindness unless forced to do otherwise; he didn't deserve to be scowled at like some common criminal.

"Very well," the lieutenant said, reluctantly taking his eyes from the dark-skinned man, "This way." Without another word, he turned and started away, the crowd parting for him like rats running from a flood. Three of the guards fell in behind Katherine and the others while two remained beside their leader. Katherine realized, as she began to follow them, that she didn't like the lieutenant. It wasn't just his abruptness, though that was a part of it. There was something cruel, something cold in his eyes that set her on edge. But she'd been forced to associate with such men before, and this association, at least, would not last long. Soon, she would be meeting with the Chosen, and she would have to tell her what had happened in Ilrika and about the death of Chosen Olliman. She dreaded the telling, for Alashia had said that she always considered Olliman a brother, and it would break the kindly woman's heart to hear of his death.

As they walked, Katherine tried to make conversation with the guards, but she may as well have been talking to a stone wall for all the response she got, and she soon gave it up, and they pressed on in silence. After an hour spent walking, Katherine was surprised to find that the crowds were thinning out. If anything, she would have thought that the streets closer to the castle would have been more packed not less. And was it just her imagination or did the castle seem farther away than it had? She was just about to ask about this when one of the guards stopped in front of a long, twisting alley that appeared completely deserted. "How about this way, lieutenant?"

The hard-faced man glanced around the nearly empty street in consideration then nodded, "It'll do." He said, starting off down the alleyway. Katherine glanced at Darl and Sonya, suddenly unsure.

"Ma'am?" The Lieutenant asked, turning, "I was told to get you to the castle as quickly as possible, that the message you carried was of great importance."

Katherine felt her face flush with embarrassment. He was right, of course. Alashia had trusted her to deliver a message, the contents of which could affect everyone living on the continent of Entarna, and here she was balking like a child staring into a dark bedroom. "Sorry," she said, starting forward, "We're coming."

CHAPTER FORTY-SIX

Rion was unable to suppress a yawn as he leaned forward and mechanically gathered his winnings. It was a big pot. The biggest of the night, in fact, but he found himself unable to care. He hadn't slept at all the night before—he'd been too busy staring out the window of his room at his family's manse, sure that any minute he'd see Odrick guiding Sigan and a few of his favorite bruisers up the cobbled path. The truth was, he couldn't remember the last time he'd gotten a full night's sleep, and it was beginning to take its toll. At least he'd heard no more of that damned laughter and his luck, though still good, was no longer good enough to get his throat slit. Well. Probably.

"If you's so damned tired," grumbled the bearded man seated beside him—Rion had forgotten his name, if he'd ever known it, "why dontcha go upstairs and catch a few winks, aye? Much as you've won, I 'spect you can spare a Dawn or two for old Hale to fetch you a bed and a bucket. Night, you could buy the whole cursed inn if you had a mind."

A few of the others muttered their ill-natured agreement and Rion smiled, pushing his ratty cloak back over his shoulder from where it'd fallen on his arm, "Hmm ... fall asleep with all this money and no one to guard it?" He paused to consider and finally shook his head, stifling another yawn, "I think not. I'm sure you gentlemen are *quite* trustworthy, but I suspect there are other, far less respectable men than yourselves who would be all too prepared to part me from my coin."

The man frowned at him, the effect only slightly diminished by the way he swayed drunkenly in his seat, "What are you talking like that fer? You sound like one of them highborn bastards thinks they're too good for the likes of us."

Fool, Rion scolded himself, *why don't you just paint "nobleman" on your fucking forehead?* He snorted, forcing himself to remain calm. Any sign of fear in front of such men was as good as asking for a knife in the back. "Me? Noble? Sure, I like the sound of that. Might even get myself a fancy pair of boots. Course, I'll need somebody to keep them real clean like, you know, polish 'em and all." He flicked a coin—one that had been the man's until only a moment ago—at him and raised an eyebrow, "You lookin' for a job?"

The other men at the table frowned at that, but none of them spoke, and Rion paid them no mind anyway. They were like backup singers performing their role while they waited for what the lead—the bearded man in this case—would do. What he did, after the minute it took him to put all of that together, was get very red and very angry. "You've got a smart mouth, boy," he growled, leaning forward, close enough that Rion could smell the whiskey stink of his breath, "and you win more'n you've a right to. Seems to me that's a pretty good recipe for getting your scrawny ass kicked."

Rion shrugged nonchalantly, "I always have been lucky. As for the ass kicking," he said, leaning back and surreptitiously folding his arms, so that his right hand fell where one of his knives was concealed under his tunic, "men have tried before. Most times, they find they're not as lucky as I am." His voice was calm, cool, but his insides were twisting with anxiety. *Gods, just leave it at that,* he thought desperately. The last thing he needed was to start a scene and if the bearded man decided to make something of it....

The man considered this for a moment then frowned, leaning back to fold his own thick arms over his barrel chest, "Maybe you ought to find another game, friend."

"I was just having the same thought," Rion said, struggling to keep himself from breaking into a run as he slowly rose from his chair, his self-assured smile still in place, though inside he cursed himself for his carelessness. The men were all pretty deep in their cups now and several of them still had sizeable stacks of coins sitting in front of them. Coins that *could* have been his, had he not acted a fool. "Good day to you," Rion said, tipping his head, "I hope you enjoy the carnival." To smooth things over, he took a dawn from his coin pouch and tossed it to the big man who caught it out of reflex, "Thanks for the game."

If anything, the man looked madder as he gripped the coin in a massive, hairy paw that wouldn't have been out of place on a bear. A particularly large, particularly ugly bear who was seriously considering mauling some unfortunate soul who'd managed to piss him off. Before the man had an opportunity to speak—or bite—Rion turned and walked away, winding his way around the crowded tables and out the door.

Outside the bar, he winced at the brightness of the afternoon sun and tried to blink the grainy, heavy feeling away from his eyes. Around him, people in costumes and masks capered and laughed, shouted and ran, caught up in the excitement of the quickly approaching carnival. He'd been a fool to stay up for so long. His wits felt dulled, like a blade that's been beaten against a rock, and he was so exhausted that his legs felt as if they had anvils strapped to them. If Sigan or some of his men happened upon him now, Rion would have no chance of escaping, lucky or not. Besides, he hadn't gone home at all last night, and his mother and father would wonder where he'd been. They'd believe him if he told them he'd stayed overnight at the business, but he didn't like lying to them unless he absolutely had to. The gods knew he lied enough. He sighed. If he knew his father at all, there was a lecture about the importance of taking time off from work waiting in his near future.

Rion stepped into the crowded street, one hand gripping the coin pouch under his tunic while the other stayed close to the small knife concealed at his belt. With the crowds that the carnival had drawn, the sneak thieves and cutpurses would be out in droves, and he didn't intend on giving up his hard earned coin without a fight.

"*Eriondrian.*" Rion tensed and whipped around, his hand grasping the handle of his blades, as he searched the passing people for the owner of the voice. Everyone seemed to be going about their own business, paying him no attention. *Eriondrian,* the voice had said, not Rion. No one in the poor district was supposed to know him by that name. Fear clutched at his heart, and Rion started forward again, checking over his shoulder to see if he was being followed. After he'd taken several side streets and doubled back on his trail twice without finding anything, he decided that he must have imagined it, after all.

I'm more tired than I realized, he thought, turning and starting toward his home once more.

"*Eriondrian Tirinian,*" a voice whispered in his ear. He gave a cry of surprise and spun, the knife halfway out of its sheathe.

People passed him on either side, giving him strange, suspicious glances, but none seemed to be the owner of the voice. *I'm losing my damned mind.* He was just starting to turn around when someone in the crowd caught his eye. On the far side of the street, Rion could just make out a man that looked to be in his late twenties standing still among the jostling crowd. The man wore a rich, sky blue doublet, and he was staring directly at Rion. Rion felt a shiver run up his spine. By some trick of the light and distance, one of the man's eyes appeared to be completely white, while the other looked as dark as a starless night.

A large group of drunken, laughing people passed between them and, for a moment, Rion lost sight of the man. He craned his neck, searching for him. After a few seconds, a space opened in the crowd, and he caught a glimpse of him again. The man's mouth was moving as if he was speaking. Considering the distance between them and the noisy street—full of laughter and shouts loud enough to drown out a thunderstorm—there was no way Rion should have been able to hear him, even if the man yelled at the top of his lungs. But, in another moment, he *did* hear him, and his voice did not come in a shout, but in a soft whisper that felt as if it was spoken directly into Rion's ear. "Follow me, Eriondrian Tirinian. For your sake, for your parents' sake, and for that of many others, follow me."

Rion felt a chill run up his spine at the man's use of his real name. He started to turn and run away as fast as his feet would carry him but stopped after his first step. What good would running do? The man knew his name, his *real* name. There were those in the city—Sigan, for example—who would pay good money for that knowledge. *Maybe he's already told him,* Rion thought, a knot of fear twisting his stomach. No. The man hadn't told Sigan, not yet. The fact that Rion was still breathing was proof enough of that. So what then? Why wasn't he, at this very second, being beaten to death by men with names like Slash or Knuckles? There was only one explanation—the man had decided to blackmail him instead.

But how could the stranger have learned his secret? Had Odrick told, after all, or had the man discovered his identity some other way? He decided that, once he caught up with the stranger, he'd have to ask him. Right before he slit his fucking throat. He drew one of his knives and, palming it against his side, started toward where the man had been standing. All of a sudden, it seemed that every person in the entire city, every last damned *one*, had realized they were late for some urgent appointment on the opposite end of the street. He pushed his way against the press of bodies like a man possessed, squeezing between them when he could, and pushing or elbowing them out of his way, when he could not. A trail of angry people shouted curses after him, but their threats were quickly swallowed up in the sea of humanity that flowed down the avenue, and he pressed on without sparing them a second glance.

He lost sight of the man several times, but each time he prepared to give up the chase he'd catch a glimpse of the stranger's bright blue shirt in the crowd. More than once, he saw the man glance back as if wanting to make sure Rion was still behind him.

"Oh, I'm coming alright, you bastard," he whispered fiercely, "but you won't like it when I get there."

This is a trap, a part of him said, *you should be running, not following him. If you hurry, you might be able to get your mother and father out of the city. There may still be time.*

The voice was right, of course, it *had* to be a trap, but he found that just then he didn't care. He'd been hiding and sneaking for a long while—his entire life, it felt like at times—but he was done hiding now. The man might think he held all the cards, but Rion had faced bad odds before, and he had a way of coming out on top.

He was gaining on the man, only a few strides away from him, in fact, when suddenly a fat, drunken man with his arm around what was obviously a recently-rented whore stumbled in front of him, blocking his view. The man let out a snort, "Scuse me there, fella," he slurred, "didn't mean to—"

"*Get the fuck out of my way,*" Rion snarled. He pushed his way past the dumbfounded drunk, ignoring the shouts of outrage from the street woman that he nearly knocked down in his haste, and whipped his gaze around the street. The man was nowhere to be seen. *Impossible.* He'd only been out of his sight for an instant. How could he have gotten away so fast?

Barely containing a shout of rage, gripping his knife so tightly at his side that his hand ached, he kept going. Shortly, he came to an intersection in the road where two alleyways met. Had the man gone down one or continued on in the street? He glanced one way then the other, but there was no sign.

Luck don't fail me now. He picked a direction at random and started down the alley on his right. The empty alley was a relief after the packed street and in a few paces it curved sharply to the right. He went around the corner and nearly ran into the man in the blue doublet who was standing in the alley waiting for him. He stumbled back, grunting in surprise, and barely managed to avoid falling.

"Eriondrian," the man said in greeting, an amiable smile on his face. Rion felt a shiver of fear run through him. This close, he could see that the man's eyes hadn't been a trick of the light at all. One was as white as parchment left to dry in the sun, the other as dark as a nightling's heart. Cursed eyes if there ever were.

"How do you know my name?" He asked, crouching in a fighter's stance.

The man let out a loud, booming laugh that was completely at odds with his thin, almost sickly appearance, "I know all there is to know about you, Eriondrian Tirinian, all about your family's financial problems and your ... *activities* of late. You could say that I have been studying you for some time now."

"Studying me?" Rion snarled, "Why? What do you want?"

The man tilted his head sideways, "What do I want?" He asked as if surprised by the question, "Why, I want *you,* Eriondrian." He winked his white eye then, and for a moment, gazed at Rion with an eye so black that it seemed to fester with all of the world's darkness, all of the quiet, creeping, sneaking things that the light would not, or could not touch.

Rion fought down the almost overpowering urge to turn and run, "Well," he said, his voice hoarse as he brandished the blade he carried, "you won't have me. What do you plan, blackmail?"

The man laughed that disparate, booming laugh again, "Blackmail? Well, I suppose it is that, of a sort, Eriondrian. Of a sort."

"Enough!" Rion growled in frustration, "What is it you want? Money, is that it?"

The man shook his head sadly, cupping his hands behind his back, "I want to help you, Eriondrian. I want to help your parents."

Rion glanced around the empty alleyway, "You made a mistake," he said, circling the man, "You shouldn't have come alone." He rushed forward, the tip of his blade aimed at the man's throat. At the last moment, he stumbled on a small stone he hadn't seen. His arms windmilled as he tried, and failed, to catch his balance. The world spun disorientingly around him, and he crashed to the cobbled alley floor with a grunt of pain and surprise. The blade was knocked from his hand by the impact and he stared, disbelieving, as it flew through the air, tumbling end over end and falling somewhere directly behind the stranger.

The man hadn't moved an inch from where he'd been standing, and as he brought his arms in front of him, Rion saw with amazement that the knife had landed, handle first, in his waiting hand.

"Th—that's impossible," he gasped, crawling backward to put some distance between himself and the stranger.

The man blinked again, this time leaving his white eye open and, for just a second, the eye shone as if every sunset, every flare of a fire or glow of a torch, was contained in that steady gaze, "Oh, not impossible, Rion. Unlikely, perhaps, but there was a chance." He smiled widely, gesturing expansively with his arms, "There almost always is, you know."

For a moment, Rion stared at the man, shocked by that unearthly gaze. When the stranger didn't move, he slowly rose to his feet, eyeing the man warily. "If you're going to kill me, come on. I'm no fool—I know a trap when I see one."

The stranger shook his head as if dealing with a man who refused to see reason. "If it is a trap, Eriondrian, then it is a trap of your own making."

"What are you talking about?" Rion snapped, "You're the one that came to me."

"No, Eriondrian," the man said in a lecturing tone as if speaking to a child, "you came to me. Though you know it not."

"Night take you, I don't even know who you are!"

"Oh? Don't you know me, Eriondrian?" He took a step forward, and Rion crouched low, his hands spread out wide in anticipation of an attack. Instead, the stranger tossed the blade carelessly to the side, not bothering to look where it went. The knife banged against the wall, then rebounded off and flew toward Rion. He tried to leap out of the way but before he could move, it flew past, cutting his tunic and sending his coin pouch falling to the ground with a loud clatter. Coins came spilling out, dusks, dawns, suns, and Rion watched in amazement as all of them, every single one, spun on its side then stopped as if frozen. Not a single one fell over.

Rion gaped, his mouth working soundlessly as he glanced between the man and the coins. "Call it luck," The stranger said, and his rich, full laughter boomed out again only this time it wasn't aloud, it was in Rion's *head*.

"W-who are you?" Rion asked, backing away, "*What* are you?"

"I have had many names in many places, many times," the man said and as he spoke, his white eye seemed to blaze to life, while the black one grew darker still, an endless pit of darkness. "Breaker, the Coinsman, Hashenari, the Youngest, Cutter, bastard, savior. By these names, and many others, have I been known."

"So which are you?" Rion asked. He suddenly felt very dizzy, and it was all he could do to keep his feet under him.

The man smiled, "I am all of them, and I am none of them, but you and your people know me by a different name. To you, I am known as Javen, the youngest of the Elder Gods."

Rion opened his mouth to call the man a liar, but there was something in the glimmer of his inky, black eye that made him think it would be a deadly mistake to do so. He paused, glancing down at the coins and seeing that they were still standing on their side. Every. Last. One of them. "J-Javen?" He said, his voice coming out as little more than a whisper, "You mean you're ... the God of Chance?"

The man nodded, "I am as my father made me Eriondrian Terinan, or, shall we say," he paused, winking, "Rion."

Rion opened his mouth to speak but no words would come. What did a man say to a god? What did he *dare* say? "M-my uh .. my lord," he managed finally, bowing low to the ground, suddenly terrified. Darklings in the night and crime lords after his blood were one thing. A god was quite another. Besides, Javen was known for being a fickle god, for amazing acts of kindness, and shocking acts of cruelty.

The man, no, the *god,* laughed again, "Please, Rion. You are not a man built well for kneeling. Rise."

"B-but ... *why?*" Rion croaked.

"Why you?" The god asked, and Rion nodded. Javen shrugged, "Because there is a chance—however small—that you will be who I need you to be. For now, let us leave it at that." The man glanced up and frowned, though Rion saw only clear skies. "We have little time, so forgive me for skipping the formalities. I want you to be my Chosen, the prosecutor of my will in Entarna, imbued with some portion of my power and trusted with my mission. In return, I promise that I will do all within my power to keep your family safe."

"B-but," Rion stammered, "I ... I thought only Amedan, Father of the Gods, selected Chosen."

Javen nodded, his face suddenly grim, "In normal times, you would be right but, then, these are not normal times. Until recently, my father, the Most High, the Light of the World and Vanquisher of the Darkness, was the only one of us to have ever taken a Chosen. My father has always cared for mankind, and when the Bane showed up, it was his idea to gift certain individuals with a portion of his power and will, so that mankind might not be destroyed."

"The ... Bane?" Rion asked.

Javen nodded, "Such is the name by which we know them, though your kind have other names for them. You would know them as the nightwalkers."

"But ... didn't your father, I mean Amedan ... didn't he *make* them? Why would he want to protect us from them?"

The man's expression didn't change, but his white eye seemed to flash as if on fire, and Rion froze as the heavy, terrifying weight of that gaze fell on him. "My father did not create the creatures," The god growled, his voice deep and threatening, "and you would do well to not speak such again."

"I'm s-sorry, lord," Rion said hastily, "I meant no offense but ... if he didn't make them, who did?"

The anger in the god's eyes vanished, and he smiled again. *Fickle indeed,* Rion thought, swallowing hard. Javen's gaze took on a distant look as if seeing things, or remembering things, that Rion could only imagine, "It is not known from where the creatures come, though I begin to wonder ... Yet surely even she wouldn't—" he paused, narrowing his eyes at Rion as if he'd tricked him into saying more than he'd intended, "never mind that," he growled, waving an angry, dismissive hand, "The origin of the Bane is a matter for the gods, not mortals. It is enough for you to know that my father is not the only thing which creates in this world. There are other forces at work, ones that seek to guide events to their own dark purpose, and there are those among your kind—far more than you would believe—that follow them. If they are allowed to do as they wish, all of the people you love will be destroyed and darkness will once more cover the land as it has not since before the Dawning."

The god's words left Rion feeling terribly alone and helpless. It was not unlike the feeling he'd had when, as a child, he'd listened to the traveling troubadours that often frequented the market square of Valeria. The gaudily dressed men would tell stories of the Night War, describing the darkness that sheltered the nightwalkers as if it were a living thing, one that had lived for a thousand years and would live for a thousand more. A being of cruel, calculating patience possessed of a driving hunger that would never be satisfied until every last light had been extinguished and every last man, woman, or child lay dead.

Toward the end of such stories, Amedan and his High Priests, the Chosen, always came leading armies of the legendary Torchbearers, conquering the nightwalkers and forcing them and the darkness back. But the Torchbearers no longer existed, and the Chosen were old now, no more than shadows of their former selves. If the Darkness came again, who would there be to stand against it? What armies were left to hold it at bay?

"Can't you ... can't you do something?" he whispered, and he was surprised by the note of desperation in his voice, "I mean ... you're *gods*. Can't you stop it?"

Javen shook his head, "Once maybe, but no more. We gods do not possess the strength we once did; to act on the world of the living takes much from us, and if we go too far, sometimes we do not get back all that was taken. Even to appear before you as I am now is a trial. I will suffer for it, later, but the Darkness comes again and with it the Bane. There will be more pain still before it is finished and much of it far worse than what I must endure. Perhaps if we were all together once more, perhaps if it was only the Bane ... but no, it is no use to say such things. The Bane have help—great help—and were I to stand against them, I would be destroyed and be of no use to you or to my father. No," he said, shaking his head again, "it is a chance even I will not take."

Rion's eyes widened, "You could *die?*" He asked, incredulous, "but who could kill a god?"

"Oh yes, gods can die, Rion," Javen said. He opened his mouth to speak again then stopped, cocking his head to the side as if listening to something only he could hear. Frowning, the god turned to stare into the empty alleyway as if expecting to see someone there. When he turned back to Rion, his face was pale and rigid with what Rion first took to be anger. It wasn't until the god lifted his strange gaze to the dark clouds that had appeared overhead as if from nowhere, raising one arm as if to ward off a blow, that Rion realized he wasn't angry. He was scared. The thought sent a shiver of terror up Rion's spine. What could scare a god? "As for who might kill a god," Javen said in a clipped, barely controlled voice, "another god could." And then, in a voice so low that Rion almost thought he'd imagined it, "*What are you planning, mother?*"

His stomach churning, Rion stared at the god, frozen in shock. His *mother?* Surely, Javen didn't mean that Shira had ... had turned *against* the other gods? The Goddess of the Wilderness was Amedan's wife and mother to the circle of Elder Gods. What would possibly make her turn against them? And, more importantly, in a world where the gods battled against each other, what hope did mortals have?

Javen turned back to him, and he must have seen something of Rion's terror in his expression because he smiled slightly as if in reassurance, though the smile did not touch his alien gaze. "Do not give in to your fear, Eriondrian Tirinian. The darkness has come before, and your people fought and won."

Yeah, Rion thought, *but we were fighting nightwalkers, not gods.* "What should I do?"

The god grinned, displaying a big set of teeth, "Are you so eager to begin, Rion?"

He shrugged self-consciously, "It seems to me that from what you've said, I don't really have a choice, do I?"

"There is always a choice, Rion," Javen said, "even a fool knows that. *Especially* a fool. As for—" the god cut off as thunder cracked the sky like some giant smith's first strike on the anvil. "*What, so soon?*" He spun with unnatural speed, and Rion saw little more than a blue blur the color of the man's tunic. In the next instant, he was at least fifteen feet down the alleyway, his head whipping around in every direction. Rion gasped. Of course, he'd *known* that the god must possess superhuman abilities but knowing it and actually *seeing* it were two very different things.

"Father, help me," the god murmured, "It is beginning." There was another blur and suddenly the god was standing only inches away, his expression grim, "Heed me, Rion. The Evernight approaches. My father has faith in his choice, but I am not sure. Darkness and light war in the man, and I fear the dark is growing stronger. Still, the die is cast and none know how it will fall. He will need your help in the days to come; they all will. Protect them. Help them, if you can."

Rion listened as Javen laid out what he was to do, his blood going cold as all of his own carefully laid plans scattered before the will of the god like autumn leaves before a high wind. "I-I will do as you ask," Rion managed when the god had finished, "but ... what of my parents?"

Javen nodded, "I will give them what protection I can. Now," he said, reaching a hand out and touching Rion's forehead, "Close your eyes."

Rion did. "War is coming, Eriondrian," the god said, his voice sounding as if it came from far away, "a war that we *must* win. But to win, we must first survive long enough to fight it." Rion opened his mouth to speak but a sudden force ripped through him, tearing through his body with such power that he was sure he would die. He bellowed in pain and fear, as he swirled in a whirlwind of power so immense that it threatened to rip him apart. Just when he thought he could take no more, that he would go mad from the pain, it stopped. Light and darkness flashed in his eyes, and for a time he knew no more.

CHAPTER FORTY-SEVEN

KATHERINE REALIZED SHE WAS HUMMING and forced herself to stop. It was a habit of hers when she was nervous, and she reminded herself—not for the first time—that she had nothing to fear from these men. They'd come to help her, after all. It wasn't their fault they weren't great conversationalists. From her experience, few men were. She glanced over at Darl for reassurance, but the man's grim expression gave her little comfort. He was watching the three guards in front of him and the way he walked reminded her of a stalking jungle cat on the hunt, ready to pounce or flee at a moment's notice.

Searching for something to occupy her thoughts, she considered the song she'd been humming. It was an old song, one that told the story of a woman trying to evade the unwanted attentions of a man who was desperately, violently in love with her. The truth was, she didn't even like the song—the jilted lover caught the woman in the end and in a fit of jealous rage, killed her—so why, then, was it even now playing in her head. Thinking hard, she remembered the verse she'd been humming, "Run for now, sweet girl, run, and hide until tomorrow comes." *Alright, that's enough.* She swallowed hard and stopped.

"You know what?" She said, as the guards came to a halt, "I just realized that we have to visit a friend first. Chosen Alashia asked me to drop something off before I came to see her." It was a lie, of course, but these men didn't know that, and there was something about their eyes and the way their hands stayed close to their sword hilts that she didn't like.

"I'm sure the Chosen will understand if you come to see her first," the Lieutenant said, glancing at the men, "Come. We will escort you there then you can be about your other errands."

He reached an arm forward as if to grab her, and Katherine took a quick step back, letting out a cry of surprise as she bumped into another of the guards. She righted herself then shook her head, "I would, Lieutenant, and we thank you for the escort, but it is really vital that I deliver the package first. It will only take a short time, and we will head directly to the castle when we're finished."

The hard-faced man stood in silence for a moment, regarding her. Then he sighed and motioned to one of the guards behind her. Suddenly, strong hands fastened around her arms and jerked her back. Darl whipped around, incredibly fast, but not fast enough to avoid a descending sword hilt that smashed into the back of his head with a dull thud. He grunted and stumbled forward, wavering drunkenly. The lieutenant took a step forward and punched the dazed Ferinan with a gauntleted fist. Darl tumbled to the ground, unconscious, and Katherine screamed.

"Run, Sonya!" She shouted, struggling uselessly against the man's grip. She might as well have been a child trying to escape the clutches of a bear for all the good it did, "Get out of here!"

Sonya stared at her with wide, terrified eyes, then turned and tried to run past one of the guards who reached out a thick arm and casually scooped her up. The little girl fought, kicking and screaming, until the lieutenant walked up and slapped her in the face hard, and she fell into broken, gasping sobs. "You *bastard!*" Katherine yelled, "What's wrong with you? What in the names of all the Elder Gods do you think you're *doing?*"

The lieutenant shrugged and when he spoke, his voice showed no more emotion than a man might show when remarking on the weather, "Following orders, ma'am. You can't be allowed to carry your message to the castle. It would ... *inconvenience* some very important people."

"But Chosen Alashia would never—" Katherine cut off, stunned. Chosen Alashia would never allow her and Darl to be treated like this, let alone Sonya.

She swallowed hard. "What have you done to her?" She demanded, "What did you do to the Chosen?"

The man waved a hand dismissively, "Chosen Alashia still lives, or she did, last I saw her, but that is none of my concern or yours."

"Go ahead," he said, nodding to one of the men beside him, "finish it; I want this mess behind us."

The guard nodded and started forward, drawing his sword. The man holding Katherine kicked her in the back of the legs, and she fell to her knees with a cry. "P-please," she said, watching the man approach, "don't." The man kept coming, and Katherine renewed her struggles against the arms that held her, but it made no difference. "Why?" She asked, tears leaking from her eyes, "Gods, *why?*"

The man paused for a second, and she'd just started a prayer of thanks when he turned back to his commander, "What about the other two, sir?"

The lieutenant sighed, shaking his head sadly, "I'm afraid they'll have to be dealt with as well. There can be no witnesses. Now, hurry up. This business has given me a headache, and I could use a drink."

"Yes sir," the man said, turning back to Katherine

"Not the girl," Katherine shouted at the hard-faced man, "She's just a child. She's a *child!*" He turned away, not bothering to respond.

The guard who was to be her executioner stopped in front of Katherine his sword raised. "Well go on then, *coward,*" she snapped, spitting at his feet, "What a big man you are, killing a woman, a child, and an unconscious man. I hope your family's real proud of you."

The man raised his sword then paused as a chorus of raucous shouts and laughter erupted from the far end of the alley. Suddenly, dozens of costumed people were pouring into the alleyway like a flood, dancing and singing in merriment. The guard standing over Katherine looked around uncertainly then sheathed his sword while two of the others picked Darl up and held him between them. As the crowd drew closer, she saw that several of them carried long hand-held streamers of a variety of colors while still others blew loudly into horns made specially for the carnival. Katherine watched them approach, confused. Apparently, some of the city's people had decided to start the carnival early, though why they would have Chosen this small, out of the way alleyway to parade down when they had the entire city to make use of, she couldn't imagine.

Several of the guards held their hands up in warning, but the people were too busy celebrating to notice either the warning or that the man two of the guards were holding between them was completely unconscious. In moments, they were streaming around the guards, joking and laughing, one woman commenting, as she passed, on how real the uniforms of the guards looked and how "lifelike" the blades at their sides appeared.

The guards glanced at their commander as if in question and Katherine saw him frown and shake his head before the crowd blocked him from sight. "*Thank the Gods,*" she breathed. Seeing how quickly the man was hidden in the crowd gave her an idea, and Katherine kicked out as hard as she could, connecting with the shin of the guard holding her. The man's agonized howl blended in with the shouts of the crowd. His grip loosened, and Katherine broke free, charging into the group of celebrants. "Please! Please help me!" She yelled, and several people laughed as if she was play acting.

One of them, a rotund man whose several chins could be seen sticking out from the bottom of his mask, chortled, "Yes, yes, help her! Help us all!" Several of the people in the crowd cheered, and soon took up the chorus. "*Help her! Help us all!*" They yelled, streaming past, their grins wider than ever.

Frustrated and terrified, Katherine grabbed hold of a passing man in desperation. The man turned around, a drunken grin on his face, "W-what are—"

"*Please,*" she said, "You have to help me. These men—" Something struck her in the stomach, hard, and the air left her in a *whoosh*. Her knees buckled, and she would have fallen but hands like iron bands wrapped around her arms and jerked her back. She looked up, fighting desperately, and saw the man she'd asked for help was turning back to the parade, Katherine already forgotten. Suddenly, her arms were jerked up behind her so brutally that her shoulders felt as if they were going to be ripped from their sockets. She tried to scream but all that came out was a dry, rasping croak.

"Move again, bitch," a fierce voice whispered in her ear, "and I'll tear them off."

Hot tears of agony coursing down her face, Katherine struggled to nod, but the man didn't slacken his grip and the sharp, jagged pain in her shoulders was quickly becoming unbearable. Just when she thought she would black out, the man's iron-banded grip abruptly vanished. She groaned breathlessly and would have fallen had hands not grabbed her shoulders once again. She whimpered, struggling weakly to break free. "*Stop that,*" someone hissed in her ear, "or I'll leave you here. Sooner or later, those fools will find a different street to parade down. It would be better for you if you weren't here when they did."

Katherine turned and looked at the stranger holding her. For a moment, she thought she saw his eyes flash white, then black, but she shook her head to clear it of the dizziness, and when she looked again, she saw that they were a plain brown. His face was neither handsome nor ugly, but somewhere in between the two, possessed of sharp, angular features that reminded her of a hawk. His jet black hair was matted as if it hadn't been combed in days and large dark circles lay under his eyes. "Come on," he said, tugging at her arm, "We're getting out of here."

Dazed, Katherine stumbled after the man. She'd only taken a couple of steps when her foot hit something, and she barely managed to regain her balance without falling. She looked down and let out a gasp of shock. It was one of the guards. The man's throat had been slit, and his white tunic was stained crimson. His dead eyes stared at her accusingly, and she gagged, her stomach roiling threateningly. "Wait," she said, tugging back, and the man turned, frowning.

"Look, lady," he said, glancing around them impatiently, "We've been lucky so far, but even my luck runs out eventually. Do you want to get out of here or not?"

"We have to get Sonya and Darl first," she said, shaking her head and refusing his attempts to pull her along, "I won't leave without them."

"It's fine, alright?" The man said, annoyed, "the girl's safe; I got her before I came for you. Now come on."

He started to turn and walk again, "Wait," she said, "what about Darl?"

He shook his head, "Your man? There's nothing I can do. He's unconscious, and I can't carry him. Now stop asking questions and let's go."

"No," Katherine said firmly, "I won't leave him."

The man shrugged, "But I *will* leave you. If you want to live, come with me. This isn't a perfect world, lady, and you can't save everyone." Her expression didn't change, and he gritted his teeth, "*Damnit,*" he snarled, "Do you think this is a game? We can't help him. If you've got a death wish then have at it, but I'm not going to hang around to get my throat cut with you."

***

Rion watched in disbelief as the woman turned and began pushing her way back through the crowd to where the unconscious man—and the guards—waited. *Night take her then,* he thought, turning and starting away, *no one can say I didn't try.* He made it two steps before his feet came to a halt as if of their own accord. "She's a *fool,*" he told himself, ignoring the people that looked at him strangely as they passed, "She's a fool, and soon she'll be a dead fool, and you'll be one too if you go back."

Surely, Javen would understand. What good would Rion be to the god if he got his head chopped off in some back alley? He *had* to understand that, didn't he? But then … Javen hadn't *seemed* particularly understanding. Not at all. More … fickle. He smirked at that. Yeah, the man had been fickle alright. Fickle like a dagger in the fucking throat, maybe. He hesitated for a moment, glancing after the woman. Then, hissing a curse under his breath, he withdrew a slender blade from his tunic and hurried after her.

He made his way back to where the woman crouched over the Ferinan without seeing any of the guards. Apparently, they'd decided that they would be of better use in trying to keep the crowd away or, at worst, hurry it along.

The woman was using a scrap of what appeared to be her sleeve to wipe blood away from the man's face. As Rion approached, she gave him a quick glance before turning back to her ministrations, "You came back."

"Yeah, maybe you're not the biggest fool in Valeria, after all," he muttered, scanning the crowd around them, "Now let's get him up and get out of here."

He was just bending down to help her when something metallic flashed at the corner of his vision. Rion spun in time to see a snarling guardsman swinging a sword down on him. The press of bodies was so tight that he couldn't back away from the blade, and he tensed in expectation of the coming pain.

But instead of slicing into his flesh, the blade struck a large horn that one of the celebrators had just been raising to his lips. The sword smashed the horn, but the man's strike was deflected enough that, instead of splitting Rion's head open, it went directly beside him with only inches to spare. *Lucky,* Rion thought but, then, that's what happened when you were the Chosen of the God of Chance. He took a step toward the guardsman but suddenly the strength seemed to drain out of his body like a bucket with a hole in the bottom, exhaustion sweeping over him. He staggered and would have fallen if not for the press of bodies around him.

He shook his head in an effort to overcome his sudden weariness and looked up to see that the guardsman had been pushed back several feet by the crowd. Rion and the guard locked eyes across the mass of people. "Come on then, you bastard." Before the man could get his sword up again, Rion gave a heavy-set woman that was passing between them a hard shove, and she went tumbling back into the surprised guard.

Rion rushed forward, bulling celebrants out of his way. When he came upon the guard, the man was lying on the ground, struggling to get out from under the fat woman. Before he could free himself, Rion bent down and stuck his blade deep into the man's side. Blood poured from the wound, and the woman screamed. Rion ignored her, plunging the blade in again and again until the man's struggles slowed then stopped altogether, and his eyes took on the glazed, frozen look of the dead. When he drew his hand back, it was coated in blood. The sight made him gag, but he stabbed the man once more, to be sure. Sometimes, it was better not to take a chance.

Satisfied, panting as if he'd run a mile, Rion rose on shaky legs and turned to see that the woman had just dragged the Ferinan to his feet. The man's scalp was coated in blood, and he was wavering dangerously, but he was standing. As he worked his way back to the pair, Rion noticed that the street was fast emptying as the celebrants moved on. At best, they had half of a minute before the alleyway was empty except for the dead and the soon to be. He hurried to where the woman and the Ferinan stood, "Can you walk?" He asked the dusky-skinned man.

To Rion, the man looked more dead than alive, but he managed to nod, his teeth gritted in pain. *Tough bastard, aren't you?* Rion thought. *Well, you'd damn sure better be. We're not out of it yet.* "Alright," he said, "If you can walk, you can run. Let's go."

He led them to where he'd left the girl. She was crying, her face buried in her hands, and she let out a cry of surprise as Rion slung her unceremoniously over one shoulder and pressed through the tail end of the crowd. In moments, they were out on the main road, the passersby eyeing them strangely. Rion looked at the wounded man slumped heavily against the blonde woman then around at the surrounding buildings, "We won't outrun them, not like this. I know a place. Follow me."

CHAPTER FORTY-EIGHT

KATHERINE STARED AFTER THE MAN, unsure. True, he'd saved her life, but who *was* he? And, come to think of it, where had that crowd come from? Darl let out a soft groan beside her. She glanced at him and saw that his eyes were fluttering weakly, and his head was dangling on his neck as if it weighed a hundred pounds. She realized then that the stranger was right. If anymore soldiers came upon them, they were as good as dead. She could worry about who the man was and where he'd come from later. If, that was, there *was* a later.

The man was good to his word, and they'd only traveled a short distance before he went down an alleyway and inside of an inn called The Golden Torch. Inside, a large woman that appeared to be in her forties smiled, nodding at them, and despite their desperate situation, Katherine felt herself flushing at the incredibly low cut of the woman's neckline. The stranger flipped the woman a coin, and she caught it with a surprisingly deft hand before turning and frowning at the bloody Ferinan.

"Is your friend alright, Master Tir—Sir?" The woman asked.

The stranger frowned, glancing at the bloody-faced Ferinan them back at the woman. He raised an eyebrow, "He likes his drink, that's all. If anyone comes, Mistress Aberdine, I'm not here."

"Of course, sir. You never are," she said, but he was already heading up the stairs. Sonya bounced on his shoulders. The little girls' gaze was listless, glazed over, and it hurt Katherine to see it. *Please gods, let her be okay*, she thought as she led Darl after them.

Mistress Aberdine had fresh water and bandages brought up, and Katherine began cleaning and wrapping Darl's wound. Even now, the Ferinan did not speak, but after a time he did seem to regain some of his awareness. He sat in the room's only chair, silent and still, not so much as wincing when Katherine cleaned his wound and wrapped his head in strips of thick, coarse wool.

Sonya sat on the bed silently, staring at nothing. Katherine had made several attempts at conversation, but she may as well not have existed as far as the little girl was concerned. She just continued to stare into space with a blank expression that made tears threaten to spill from Katherine's eyes. Meanwhile, the stranger paced back and forth in front of the window, muttering to himself. Katherine couldn't understand much of what he said, but she thought she heard him say "luck," once before he laughed harshly, cutting off as he noticed her watching him.

"So," Katherine said as she finished tying the strip of bandage on Darl's head, "Who are you?"

The man scowled for a moment then finally shrugged, "I don't suppose it matters. You can call me Rion."

"It's nice to meet you, Rion," she said, "I'm Katherine. This is Darl, and that precious little girl over there is Sonya." Sonya showed no reaction to her name, and Katherine frowned before continuing, "If you don't mind me asking, why did you help us? Not that I'm complaining, of course, but … do you work for Chosen Alashia?"

The man, Rion, barked a laugh at that, "Lady, I do everything I can to stay out of the way of any Ch—" he went silent abruptly, his expression pained then, "No. To answer your question, I don't work for Chosen Alashia. I've never even met her."

Katherine used a fresh cloth to wipe a smear of blood from Darl's face, "Why help us then?"

The stranger, Rion, shrugged, "I have my reasons. Let's leave it at that for now."

Katherine frowned but nodded, "Alright. Anyway, thank you. We're lucky that you came along when you did."

The man snorted, "Yeah, what are the odds? Saddled with a suicidal woman, a half-dead Ferinan, and a child who seems to be about as lively as a statue. My luck must be on a low ebb."

"Alright, look," she said, annnoyed, "I'm grateful that you showed up, and I realize that we'd probably be dead if it wasn't for you, but do you have to be such an ass?"

"Not probably."

"What?"

The man turned to her, a slight smile curving one side of his mouth, "You said you'd *probably* be dead if I hadn't shown up—not probably—you would have." Katherine opened her mouth, but before she could get the angry words out, the man held up a hand as if in peace, "I apologize. That was uncalled for. It's just … it's been a long few months, and it doesn't look like it's going to get better anytime soon."

Katherine nodded, not trusting herself to say anything that wouldn't be rude. The man *had* saved their life, after all.

Rion smiled a rueful smile as if he knew what she was thinking then turned back to the window to gaze at the long stretch of main street below. "Haven't seen them yet," he said, "That's a good si—" he cut off abruptly, craning his neck to peer farther down the street.

"What is it?" Katherine asked, butterflies fluttering in her stomach, "Have … have they found us?"

The man shook his head uncertainly, "I don't … what are they doing?" He pulled on the window, and the wood gave a groan as it slid open. The muffled sounds of shouting drifted up to them from the street. At first, Katherine thought that it must just be people out to celebrate the carnival but after a moment she decided against it. Those voices didn't sound like they were raised in excitement or celebration. They sounded angry.

"Poor bastard," The man, Rion said, shaking his head sadly. "He must have done something truly stupid; I haven't seen a man take The Walk since I was a child."

Her curiosity getting the better of her, Katherine went to the window and looked out. Below them in the street, what looked to be at least two dozen armed men in red and black and one man in the white of Tesharna's guard walked the main avenue, encircling a muscular man wearing nothing but a loincloth. One red-cloaked man walked at the front of the procession, holding a chain that was attached to manacles on the naked man's wrists and ankles. The prisoner limped noticeably, and his body was bruised and battered, much of it covered in blood. People lined the street on either side of the grim procession, throwing rotten fruit and other things Katherine couldn't identify in between the guards to strike the naked man.

Katherine stared at those red and black uniforms in shock. "It can't be," she whispered, "Yhey're here."

Rion turned to her, raising an eyebrow, "You know those men?"

"They're the Redeemers," Katherine said, swallowing hard. The sight of that midnight black armor and those crimson cloaks that hid blood stains so well made her want to run and hide, and it was all she could do to keep standing at the window.

"And they are?" Rion prompted.

"Bastards one and all," Katherine hissed. "They killed hundreds in Ilrika, and I'm all but certain they had something to do with Chosen Olliman's death."

Rion's eyes went wide at that, "Chosen Olliman is dead? Are you sure?"

Katherine nodded, "I'm sure," she spat, "Kale Leandrin, his apprentice, took over the city and put all of the Lightbringers to the sword along with hundreds of innocent men, women, and children."

"*Then he was right,*" Rion muttered in a low voice, staring back out the window, "*It really is coming.*"

"Who wasn't lying?" Katherine asked. In the street, the naked man was just now limping beneath their window. It almost seemed that she'd seen the man before, but that wasn't possible. The Chosen's assignments had taken her to many places, but she'd never been to the City of a Thousand Colors before.

"Nothing," Rion said shortly, "Never mind that. Anyway," he said, turning away from the window, "it's none of our concern. We need to lie low for a while. Once the carnival starts in earnest, we'll slip out of the city; it's not safe here anymore."

"It's Alesh!" A voice exclaimed, and Katherine glanced beside her, shocked to see Sonya staring out the window with wide, terrified eyes.

"Alesh?" Katherine asked. Then she remembered the name. The little girl had been talking about him almost nonstop since they'd left Ilrika. From what she understood, he'd been a servant in the castle with Sonya and like a brother to the little girl, always watching after her and entertaining her with jokes and stories. A kind man, from everything the girl had said, one that Katherine wouldn't have minded meeting. But he was almost certainly dead now, dead and gone like so many of Ilrika's people. "Sweety," she said, leaning down and cupping the girl's face in her hands, "it can't be him, you know that don't you? He's ... he's in Ilrika, remember?"

"He *was,*" Sonya said in an impatient voice as if Katherine was the child and not the other way around, "but now he's here."

"Baby," Katherine said softly, "that just isn't possible."

"Of course it is!" Sonya nearly shouted, "Katherine, it's him, I promise! He can be here. We were in Ilrika too, but we're here now, why can't he be?"

Because he's dead, Katherine thought, *dead with so many others.* She started to tell the girl again that it wasn't possible, but the look in her eyes stopped her. Since she'd met the girl, Sonya had seemed ... haunted. She'd smiled and laughed, true, but there had always been something in her young gaze, a resignation, a cynicism, that was heartbreaking in one so young. For the first time, the little girl's eyes *looked* like those of a little girl. Full of innocence ... full of hope. "I'll tell you what, Sonya," she said, "we'll go down and see if you want, but—"

"Great!" The little girl exclaimed, hugging her, "Thank you, Katherine, thank you so much!"

Katherine hugged the little girl tightly before she pulled her back to arm's reach, "But you have to understand, precious, that it might *not* be him, okay? Those people down there are pretty far away, alright?"

The little girl was nodding before she'd finished, "Can we go now, Katherine, please? Can we go? They're going away."

Katherine glanced at Darl, "Are you up for it?"

Sonya looked at the dusky-skinned man too, and Darl winked at her before nodding to Katherine. "Alright then," Katherine said, rising, "Let's go."

"You can't be serious," Rion said incredulously, as he watched the three start toward the door, "We were very nearly just killed and now you want to go out into the open? We might as well slit our own throats and save ourselves the walk."

Katherine glanced at Sonya as if in question. The little girl nodded and the woman looked back at him, "Thank you, Rion, for all that you've done. It was a pleasure meeting you. Good luck."

Rion opened his mouth to tell them that they were out of their minds, but the door had already closed behind them. He sighed heavily and lifted the loose floorboard from the ground. He withdrew as much of the coin pouches as he thought he could safely carry, muttered a curse, and headed after them.

CHAPTER FORTY-NINE

"*N*IGHTSPAWN*!*"

"*Murderer!*"

"*Gods curse you!*"

The shouts rose up around Alesh as he shuffled forward, a chorus of anger and hate. Faces twisted in disgust and loathing as they stared after him, and the voices came ever louder, demanding justice for his crimes, demanding an answer. But Alesh had no answer to give. All of his excuses, all of his arguments, had been beaten out of him in the night in Tesharna's dungeons, ripped from him between each blow of the guards' truncheons, his pleadings spilled from cracked, bloody lips after each kick of a mailed boot until soon they were as broken and battered as his own body.

No, the only answer he had was one of blood and death, and for that they would not have to wait long. He could feel it, his death, circling above him, studying him the way a vulture studies a dying animal, and that was alright. It was the only answer he had left to give, and if it was not enough? Well, he would not be around to see it, to suffer yet another failure. It would be an end, at least. An end to the doubt and fear, an end to the pain that tore at his body with each shuffling step.

'Gods curse you' the man had said. Had his throat not gone raw from screaming, Alesh would have had an answer for that. *They already have,* he would have told the man, *They've cursed us all. Each breath we take is proof of it. A man's shattered dreams, a child's lost innocence, they hold the truth of that.*

I may be a murderer, but the gods are more than I, for they are the creators of hope, and they are its killers.

A rock the size of a fist flew out of the crowd and struck Alesh in the side of the head. White light exploded in his vision, and he stumbled weakly. He'd almost found his footing when the man holding his chain gave it a jerk, and Alesh crashed into the ground face first, splitting his lip and tasting a burst of coppery blood in his mouth.

Laughter from those in the street, but the Redeemers were not amused. One of them walked up, scowling, "Get up, you piece of shit," he said, kicking him in the side. Alesh groaned, too exhausted and in too much pain to do anything but fold over the mail boot, curling into a fetal position.

Knowing what was coming, Alesh struggled to rise, but he was too weak. "*C-can't,*" he croaked.

The man's eyes narrowed, and he was rearing back to kick him again when a familiar voice spoke, "Enough!"

Captain Farren marched forward, dismissing the Redeemer with a wave of his hand. The red-cloaked man frowned but stalked back to his place.

"Come on," the captain said, kneeling beside him, "It's not far now. Let me help you."

Alesh hissed in pain as the man took hold of his bruised arms and hauled him to his feet. He stumbled forward, catching himself on the man's chest. He jerked away quickly, staring at the crimson stains on the once pristine white tunic. "*Sorry,*" he said, his voice a dry rasp, "*blood. Won't wash out. It never does.*"

"As well it shouldn't," the man grunted, steadying him, "Now come on. It's not far now. Let's finish it."

His vision still blurry from the blow, his chest heaving, Alesh started forward once more as strangers he'd never met screamed for his blood. *And you'll have it,* he thought, *all you can stand.* If what the guards had told him between the beatings was true—and he had no reason to doubt them—he would die slowly, but he *would* die. Eventually. Something to look forward to then. He rasped a hoarse laugh at that, and the nearby Redeemers frowned at him as if he was mad. *And perhaps I am.* He chanced a look at the people crowding the streets, at faces twisted in rage and fury. *Perhaps we all are. And which are the scarier, really? Not nightlings, no. Us. For we do our evils in the day and night alike.*

A face in the crowd caught his eye, and he paused, the breath he'd been taking sticking in his throat as an invisible hand squeezed at his heart. A big dark-haired man stared after him, his expression one of silent fury and accusation worse, in its way, than the shouts and curses of the crowd. "C-Chorin?" Alesh croaked in shock, "how di—" something struck the side of his face, whipping his head around.

He spat out a mouthful of blood, and when he looked back, Chorin was gone. In his place, stood a short, heavy-set woman with gray hair. She wore an apron and one of her hands clutched an iron spoon. "*Gods no,*" Alesh croaked, "*please just let it end.*"

The woman watched him silently, her eyes accusing, until he'd shuffled past. Alesh limped on, tears mingling with the blood on his face, fearing to look at the crowds but unable to stop himself.

He was telling himself that they were just his imagination, these ghosts, telling himself and not really believing. And then he saw her, standing in the crowd, watching him.

"No," he moaned, "oh gods not you." There, in the crowd, stood Sonya, looking as real as she had in life. Alesh's cry was like the tortured wail of a dying animal, and he jerked his head away, shutting his swollen, bloody eyes. If he could have struck himself deaf and dumb then, he would have, he would have cut off his own ears, would have covered them in oil and set them alight if he could, anything to keep from hearing her tell him of how he'd failed her.

"*Sonya,*" he whispered in a harsh voice that barely sounded human at all, "*I'm sorry. Gods, I'm so sorry.*"

CHAPTER FIFTY

"It *was* him," Sonya pleaded through her tears, "Katherine, it was Alesh; I know it was. Why won't they leave him alone?"

"It's alright, baby," Katherine murmured distractedly, staring after the man as the procession went farther down the street. She'd only been able to see him for a moment before the crowd of people came between them blocking her view, but she was struck again by how familiar he looked. Even through the blood that coated his body like a second skin, even past the dirt and filth that mingled with that blood, she'd thought she recognized him from somewhere. She realized, of course, that it had to be the little girl's certainty nagging at her, nothing more. After all, there was no way she'd ever seen the man before and certainly no chance that it was the same man who'd been like a brother to Sonya. It just wasn't possible.

Still, her heart went out to the stranger, and she was astonished by how cruel the people were. No one should have to go through what he was being forced to endure, no matter the crime. She'd asked someone in the crowd—an old man who could have been someone's kind, loving grandfather if not for the bestial rage that flashed in his eyes and the utter hate that had filled his voice. The man had claimed that the prisoner was responsible for leading the nightwalkers to Olliman's personal chambers, that he had come to Ilrika with the express purpose of killing Chosen Tesharna as well. Katherine couldn't fathom why anyone would turn against mankind and do something so unbelievably terrible, but the old man, like the others in the crowd, harbored no doubt of the truth of it.

She and the others followed after the grim procession, pushing their way through the crowd, and for a brief instant, the man turned in their direction, a haunted expression in his bright, fevered gaze so terrible that she felt tears gathering in her eyes. Then, in an instant of revelation, she remembered where she'd seen him before, and her breath left her in a gasp. *No,* she thought, *it can't be him. That man is back in Ilrika. What would he possibly be doing here?* "Sonya," she said, turning to kneel down in front of the girl, "this man, Alesh, you said he worked for the Chosen?"

The girl nodded, wiping at her eyes, "H-he was a servant," she said, sniffling, "just like me."

It's not possible! She thought, her heart thundering in her chest. But never mind what was possible or what wasn't. It *was* him. She knew it as surely as she had ever known anything. The broken, bloody figure that was being dragged through the street in chains was the same man that had delivered the letter from Olliman, the letter that she'd been meant to deliver to Alashia. And what *of* the letter? Might it contain something of the man now being led to his own execution? Something to prove his innocence? She withdrew the letter from her pocket with trembling hands. A letter from one Chosen to another. What right did she have to read it? But, just then, she found that she didn't care. She took a deep breath and, her fingers shaking, broke the seal.

Dear Alashia, it read,

I would have written you sooner, but I wanted to be as sure as possible of my suspicions before I sent this letter to you. Even now, I have far more questions than answers, but that cannot be helped. I fear that I may have waited too long already. Amedan willing, there is still time.

Something is wrong in Ilrika. There have been ... attacks, recently. All evidence suggests that the nightwalkers are the ones responsible yet, in my heart, I do not believe it to be true. I have reason to believe that a group of people are staging these attacks to weaken the people's confidence in me and, thereby, in Amedan himself. I have not been able to uncover their identities, but I feel, I know, that we are at war, one no less important than the one we fought together so long ago.

There is no army camped outside the walls, no men at arms sieging the gates, yet we are at war just the same. I wish that there were an army, for an army can be met on the field of battle, can be scattered, defeated. But how does a man fight shadows and whispers? You may, perhaps, think that I am overreacting. I myself pray that it is so, but I do not believe it. Furthermore, my investigations lead me to believe that, whoever these people are, they are well connected. Some, I am certain, even numbering among the nobles and my castle staff.

As I write this, I am secreted in my rooms, hiding like a sneak thief at the approach of city guardsmen. It galls me that it has come to this, but I do not dare to act against those I believe responsible; I do not know how widespread the conspiracy is and so stealth is the only option left me. If you believe nothing else, Alashia, please, believe this; This group, this army exists, and I fear that it will not be long before whatever they plan comes to pass.

Listen, Alashia, and hear me. I said that I believe that they include nobles and high-ranking officials among their number, but, if I am right, it goes even further than that. Please understand that I would not say this were I not absolutely sure, but I have discovered that at least one of the Chosen are working with them; I do not know which, but there is no question that this is true.

Reading over this letter, I see that it sounds as if I am mad, but I assure you, I am not. Old and tired, yes, but not mad. Not yet. I will do what I can to stop what is coming, but I fear it will not be enough. If I am successful or if I am wrong, then this letter will not matter, but if something should happen to me, then you will have proof of my words. I am sorry, Alashia. I know that it is a heavy burden that I lay upon you, but you are the only one that I can trust, the only one I am sure of. Be careful. I do not believe this group will stop with Ilrika. Even in this letter, I fear to say too much, but I will come to you soon. It has been far too long since we dined together, and there is much I must tell you.

Until then, may Amedan's light guide you through the darkness and see you safe to the sun once more,

Brent Olliman, High Priest and humble servant of Amedan, Our Lord, and yours in love.

P.S. If something should happen to me, find the man who bore this letter. He is young, with the passions of youth, but he is far greater than he or anyone else knows, and he is to be trusted. I ask, for the love that you bear me, that you keep *him safe. He is a good man and like a son to me but there is more than that. I will tell you when we meet only remember. Above all else, Alashia, he* must *be kept safe.*

Katherine finished the letter and wiped at an unexpected tear. She turned and met Darl's eyes, "He brought the letter," she said, and the Ferinan raised an eye as she handed him the parchment.

He scanned it, his normally unflappable expression changing first to one of surprise then sadness and, finally, to what Katherine herself was feeling, a grim, unshakeable determination. She waited until he finished, then he looked at her and nodded once.

"What's going on?" Rion asked, his voice suspicious as he took in the looks on both their faces, "If we were at the card table, I'd say that you two look as if you're preparing to push all your coins forward on a losing hand."

Katherine glanced once more at Darl who nodded again before turning back to Rion. "We have to save him."

"Save who?" Rion asked.

"The prisoner."

Rion snorted, "Sure," he said, "and while we're at it, we can pull the sun from the sky and drive all of the nightwalkers into the sea." He glanced between the two of them, his grin slowly fading. "Wait. You're serious."

Katherine nodded, fighting to keep the fear she felt out of her voice, "I am." She considered handing him the letter but decided against it. True, the man had saved their lives, but she didn't know him and the information in the letter was more than enough for some men to kill over. Instead, she folded it up and slid it back into her pocket.

"You must have lost your night-cursed mind," The man hissed, taking a step forward. Darl took a step closer to Katherine's side, but Rion ignored him, "What is it with you, lady? Nearly getting killed once in a day isn't enough for you? You have to go back and make a better job of it? Why, you'd have a better chance of—"

"Why did you save us?" Katherine asked, interrupting him.

He cut off, suddenly looking uncomfortable, "What?"

"You don't know us from anyone," Katherine went on, "We're strangers.

So why did you save us? How did you even know we *needed* saving?"

He hesitated, glancing between her and Darl, "That uh ... that doesn't matter."

"Fine," Katherine said after a moment, "if you do not wish to tell me, I will not press you on your reasons, just so long as you do not press me on mine."

The man sighed heavily, glancing at Sonya's hopeful expression before turning back to Katherine, "It's suicide. You know that, don't you? And you'll take the girl to her death as well."

Katherine turned to Sonya, "He's right, sweety. It *will* be dangerous. Perhaps it would be better if you—"

"I'm going," Sonya interrupted, her face twisted into a scowl as if she expected an argument and was ready to put it down, "Alesh is my friend, and I'm going. He was always there when I needed him. I want to be there for him too."

Katherine opened her mouth to try to convince the girl that it would be better if she stayed in an inn until it was over then closed it again. Would it be, really? After all, they hadn't been in the city an hour before those guards had tried to kill them. The Lieutenant had no doubt already sent other soldiers off combing the streets and taverns, searching for anybody matching their description. If she left the girl in an inn, alone, then she ran the risk of those men finding her and finishing what they'd started. "Alright," she said finally, and the girl's eyes widened in surprise, "alright, you'll come with us, but you'll have to promise that if things get too bad, you'll let me or Darl take you away."

The girl considered for a moment, finally nodding, "Okay, Katherine, I will. I promise."

Katherine smiled then turned back to the man who was shaking his head in wonder. "You're all crazy." When they didn't respond, he shrugged, "Well, let's go then; if I'm going to get my fool head lopped off, I'd just as soon get it over with rather than stand around talking about it all day."

"You're coming?" Katherine asked, surprised.

"Of course I'm coming," he muttered, "Apparently, I've decided that I'm sick of breathing, and you three seem to be the best cure on offer."

Katherine considered that. There was more to this man than he was letting on. How *had* he known they needed help, and why had he come even when he did? Why was he willing to risk his life, even now, for three people who were all but strangers to him? Still, there was no denying the fact that he *had* saved them—whatever his reasons—and that they would need all of the help they could get.

She caught herself starting to hum a song she'd heard in Ilrika and stopped. She didn't remember the entire song, only that it had told the story of a sheepherder who'd found a suit of armor and joined the King's tournament. He'd lost, of course, but had ended up becoming a knight in the end, eventually saving the king himself from an assassination attempt by one of his advisors. Not an original song—far from it—but the message was clear enough; sometimes, taking a chance paid off. Of course, it also sometimes led to a quick trip to the gallows. *Deitra protect us.* "Alright," she said, "let's go."

By the time they started after it, the procession was no longer within sight, and they had to struggle through the press of bodies in an effort to catch up, "Where are they going?" Katherine puffed, laboring through the crowd with the others.

"The northern gate, I suspect," Rion said, glancing at the sky, "and we need to hurry. There's not much longer until dark, and they'll make sure the gates are closed by then."

Hurrying was easier said than done with the streets as crowded as they were, and it took what felt like a year spent fighting their way through the screaming mob before they arrived at the northern gate. Katherine's heart plummeted in her chest as she noticed that it was closed and two guards stood to either side of it, facing the city.

Rion didn't hesitate, striding up to them as if they were old friends, "Evenin', lads. Why have the gates been closed early? It's not dark yet, and we need to get through."

One of the guards, a thick-chested man with a long, dark moustache and beard, met his eyes and spoke with a bored expression, "By order of Chosen Tesharna herself," he said as if reading from a proclamation, "the city gates are to be closed and barred early for the length of the carnival."

"Why?" Rion asked, "what possible—"

"I do not think to question Chosen Tesharna's decisions, peasant," the guard barked, "and neither will you, if you know what's best for you."

Peasant? Rion thought, *why would he*—it wasn't until he looked down at his clothes that he remembered he was still wearing his disguise. A ratty, homespun shirt, trousers that had more holes than not, and a grimy, frayed brown cloak didn't exactly create an outfit that demanded respect. Distance, maybe, and an eye to your own coin purse, sure, but not respect.

To this man, he wasn't Eriondrian Tirinian, one of the city's most respected nobles, but a street urchin that spent his time sleeping in alleyways and begging for coins. He noticed the guard studying his three companions thoughtfully and there was something in the way he looked at them that Rion didn't like. "O-of course, sir," he said, bringing the guard's gaze back to him once more "So sorry to bother you. Why, forgive me, please, if I've given offense. A fool like me'd never think of questionin' her Ladyship, and that's Amedan's own truth. We'll just be gettin' out of your way."

The woman started to open her mouth to protest, but Rion shot her a look, and, to his great relief, she remained silent, following with the others as he hurried away from the gate at a fast walk. Rion cursed his own foolishness silently, fighting the urge to turn and look back. He glanced over and saw the woman staring over her shoulder at the gate. *"Turn the fuck around,"* he hissed.

She jerked as if slapped, her gaze turning to him, "Where do you get off telli—"

"Those men who tried to kill you, they were guards, weren't they?" Rion asked, trying to ignore the itch that was creeping between his shoulder blades as he walked on.

The woman opened her mouth to answer, but stopped as her eyes went wide with realization. "Surely, you're wrong. There's no way that all of them could be in on it. Chosen Alashia—"

"Could be dead for all we know," Rion whispered harshly. "Now, come on. Walk fast but be natural. The last thing we need is to look anymore suspicious

than we already do." Not that that was very likely. A woman dressed like a wealthy merchant's daughter, a man dressed like a thief, a Ferinan, and a child. Oh no, they didn't stand out. Not at all.

He risked a quick glance over his shoulder and saw that the guard they'd spoken with was engaged in an animated conversation with one of his colleagues. "We *have* to save him," Katherine said beside him, "but how are we supposed to get to him when they've closed all the gates? We don't even know where he *is*."

"Oh, I think I know," Rion whispered, "There's only one place they would have taken him."

"Where?"

He shot her a look, "They call it the Traitor's Tree." He saw the question in her eyes, but the little girl was beside her, her eyes brimming with unshed tears, and she did not ask it. *Just as well,* Rion thought, *you wouldn't like the answer.* The Traitor's Tree was a massive oak with a trunk so wide that five grown men linking hands wouldn't cover half of its circumference. But its size wasn't what it was known for. It was said that beneath its bark, the tree's flesh was a deep red and that, if sliced into, would bleed like a man with his throat cut. Probably all lies, but that didn't change the fact that it had been the place of execution for the land's worst criminals back before there even *was* a Valeria.

Men—even a few women, if the stories his father had told him were true—were taken to the tree in chains where they were manacled to its surface whipped, flayed, and then left to feed the nightlings. The method was so cruel and so rarely used that, according to his father, the last execution had taken place when Rion had been little more than a baby. A hard list to get one's name on; most crimes ended up with a stay in the castle's dungeons or a brief trip to the headsman's block, but, he supposed, if anything would earn a man a spot on the Tree, assassinating one of the Chosen would be it.

They were coming up on a turn in the street, and Rion was just beginning to believe they were going to make it away when he heard the clear ring of drawn steel.

"*Halt!*" One of the guards yelled, and Rion looked back to see the four guards heading toward them, "*Halt in the name of the Chosen!*"

"What now?" The woman asked, her voice tight with fear.

Rion glanced over and saw that the Ferinan had already hefted the girl onto his back and was staring at him, waiting. He nodded once at the man before turning to Katherine, "Now," he said, "we run."

CHAPTER FIFTY-ONE

THE WHIP CRACKED IN THE air like heat lightning, and Alesh screamed a hoarse, helpless scream as it ripped a line of searing agony down his chest. He flailed helplessly against his bonds, but the metal didn't give an inch, and his struggles only served to make fresh blood leak out from under the manacles at his ankles and wrists.

He'd barely been conscious when they'd hoisted him up and secured him to the massive tree—the Traitor's Tree, he thought he'd heard someone call it, but he couldn't be sure. His thoughts were disjointed, incoherent fragments floating in a sea of pain and agony, and the only thing he could be sure of was the terrible, unending pain.

His arms had been secured high above his head, and the pressure of his whole body drug against them, making his wrists and shoulders feel as if they were being wrenched out of place, but he'd long since lost the strength to hold himself up. His legs were spread wide apart, and also manacled. A heavy, long chain connected his bonds and had been wrapped around the impossibly thick tree. He couldn't be sure how long he'd hung there—it could have been minutes or hours—time, in any normal sense, had long since lost its meaning. The only time he could be certain of were the seconds after the whip struck him before he felt its bite again. Those terrible, wonderful seconds.

He watched numbly through dim eyes as the soldier started to raise the whip again, but Falen Par raised a hand, and the man hesitated, a disappointed look on his face. "Where are your friends?" the leader of the

Redeemers asked Alesh in a voice that sounded almost bored, "Where are those you were working with? Why protect them, when they have so easily abandoned you?" Despite the man's words, Alesh dully noted that his men were spread out around the tree, gazing in all directions as if expecting an attack. All of them, that was, except for the man who held the whip. "You will die, boy," the general continued matter of factly, "there is no other way for you, but you need not suffer any more, if only you will tell me the truth."

"I d-don't have any f-friends," Alesh gasped, "Y-you killed them."

"What does he mean?" Captain Farren asked from beside the commander of the Redeemers. The man's white armor and cloak gleamed in the dying light of the sun as if it had been dipped in gold.

"He lies," Par said, waving a dismissive hand, "that is all, captain. It is what his kind does." He turned back to Alesh then, "Last chance, boy. This can all end, if only you will speak their names."

"Night ... take ... you," Alesh managed past his raw, swollen throat.

The thin man heaved a long suffering sigh, "So be it." He gave a curt nod to the soldier with the whip and, for a time, there was only pain.

After what felt like an eternity, the captain stepped forward and grabbed the whipman's arm, "Enough!" Hasn't he suffered enough yet? Just let him die. Let it be over."

"Captain," Falen Par said calmly, "you overstep yourself. After all, was it not the Chosen Tesharna herself—the woman whom you have sworn to protect and obey in all things—that demanded this done? Surely, you do not mean to go against her wishes."

The captain frowned, and gave Alesh a pitying look before releasing the man's arm, "Of course, you're right," he said gruffly, "but I still don't understand why we've got to torture the poor bastard."

The thin man shrugged, "Nor I, captain, but it is not our duty to understand, only to obey."

Farren stared at the thin man for several seconds then finally gave a disgusted grunt and stepped back.

"Now," the leader of the Redeemers said, turning back to Alesh, "will you tell us what you know or must we continue?"

The next strike of the whip didn't hurt as much, and if Alesh had still cared, that would have been cause for worry. The living felt pain, after all. The dead were long past it. But what was there left to care about? He'd failed. Failed Olliman, failed Chorin and Abigail, and Erwin who'd saved him. What a fool he'd been to think that he could make a difference, that he could save Ilrika. He couldn't even save Sonya, a little girl who'd looked to him for protection. Each crack of the whip, each bloody tear it left in his flesh was no less than he deserved, no less than he'd earned. The only thing that he could be thankful for was that, wherever Sonya was, she was far, far away from Falen Par and his humorless smile. His cold, gray eyes that drank in Alesh's torment like a tree drinks in sunlight. A pathetic victory to take to one's grave, that. But it was all he had.

CHAPTER FIFTY-TWO

"IT SHOULDN'T BE LONG NOW," Rion panted, ducking under a hanging branch just in time to avoid ramming head first into it. They'd been running for what felt like forever; his clothes were drenched in sweat, and his legs felt as if they were on fire. The woman, Katherine, looked even worse than he felt, her face twisted in concentration as she stumbled, more than ran, through the dense underbrush. For his part, the Ferinan man was barely even breathing hard despite the added weight of the little girl on his back. Rion had heard that the Ferinan's were part human part beast, but he'd always thought it nothing more than another foolish rumor, one of many that the nobles of Valeria passed around like a used-up whore. Now, he wasn't so sure. The dusky-skinned man jogged ahead of them with a steady, agile gracefulness that seemed to mock Rion's struggles. The bastard.

"I pray that you're right," Katherine gasped, glancing up at the sky with a worried expression on her face and only barely managing to avoid running into a tree herself, "It's … going to … be dark … soon."

Rion didn't bother using what little breath he had to respond to that. He was too busy trying not to pass out and worrying about what they would do once they came to the Traitor's Tree. It was a hopeless mission, trying to free the man from dozens of heavily-armed and skilled guardsmen, but Javen had told him to look after the woman, so he would. He could only pray that his luck would hold out. After all, it had surely been an incredible stroke of chance that had allowed them to evade the guards in Valeria while they made their way to one of the city's secret byways. The dank, damp tunnels were one of the last remaining perks of his father's business. Rion had always thought them a depressing, pathetic legacy, but they'd proved useful enough tonight.

The tunnels had been created during the Night War as a means of transferring goods and food into Valeria even if they were under siege, and knowledge of their existence was only entrusted to a select handful of people. The Chosen, the members of her elite personal guard, and, of course, the merchant and noble who would have been expected to oversee the importing of goods in such a time—namely, Rion's father—and, on the day that he'd taken over the family business, Rion himself.

The tunnels had aided them in leaving the city, but the architects had intended them to be used as a means of escape or as a secret mode of transporting goods into the city. The builders had, apparently, not foreseen anyone wanting a shortcut to the Traitor's Tree. An honest enough assumption, Rion supposed, but just then, with his eyes stinging with sweat, and his chest pumping like a blacksmith's bellows, he would have had some choice words to say to them, had they been present. The kind of words that cut. "*There*," he wheezed in relief, indicating the vague shape of a large hill looming in the distance, "We're close now." He could just make out the enormous shape of the tree, its thick branches reaching out as if seeking to engulf everything around it. Even from this distance, it seemed too large to exist in the world he knew, a remnant of some other world, some long-forgotten time.

"Thank the gods," Katherine said in between ragged breaths, "I pray that we're not—" she cut off as Darl suddenly whipped around and held a hand up for silence. He carefully sat Sonya on the ground, his eyes scanning the surrounding forest, his head cocked as if listening for something.

"What is it?" Rion asked, "I don't hear—"

"Well, well," a familiar voice said, as a dozen men stepped out from the trees all around them, "I'd heard tale that Ferinan savages could hear a man's heartbeat, but I had thought it no more than a story the peasants used to scare their brats. It would seem that I may have been mistaken."

"*Sevrin?*" Rion asked, shocked. The nobleman was dressed in a dark green tunic and breeches as if he were out for a hunt, though the effect was somewhat ruined by the golden lace embroidered on the sides and the golden medallion of his house hanging from his neck. "What are you doing here?"

The nobleman smiled his cruel, oily smile, "I do not like you, Eriondrian. I never have. Did you know?" He laughed then, an arrogant, self-congratulatory laugh, "Yes, I suppose you did. Ah-ah-ah," he said, flicking a lace covered wrist at Darl as the man stalked toward him, "I wouldn't do that if I were you, savage." He indicated the men around him, four of which held crossbows trained on Katherine and Sonya, "I have heard that few are better trackers and warriors than the Ferinan. Your people are known for their speed and cunning in battle, but I doubt that even you are clever or fast enough to stop four crossbow bolts. Wouldn't you agree?

Darl glanced back at Katherine. The woman shook her head once, and the Ferinan took what appeared to be a reluctant step back, so that he stood with Rion and the others. Rion watched him dumbfounded. The man had actually been prepared to attack a dozen armed and armored men with his bare hands. It was a gods-blasted miracle that there were any Ferinan left, if all of the bastards were as crazy as this one. "Why are you here, Sevrin?" Rion demanded, "I don't have time for your games."

"Oh," the man said, smirking, "this is no game, Eriondrian, let me assure you of that. Or would you rather me call you Rion? It is the name you go by these days, is it not?"

Rion froze, stunned. If he knew that name, then he also knew of Rion's activities, but that wasn't possible not unless ... *Odrick,* Rion thought, cursing himself for a fool. He'd thought the blacksmith's apprentice trustworthy, but he'd been wrong.

"Yes, *Rion,*" the nobleman said, exaggerating the name as if testing the feel of it on his tongue, "I know all about what you've been up to of late. You have been acting strangely these last few months, you see, and finally I decided to have one of my men follow you. At the time, it was out of curiosity, nothing more, and always with the hope that I would catch you doing something foolish and be able to sully that sickeningly trite reputation you and your family have for honesty. Imagine my surprise, then, when my man came back to tell me that you'd been dressing up in rags and traveling to the poor district, going by the name of Rion and making deals with crime lords and vagabonds." He tsked like a man catching a child acting out, "I considered letting the truth be known then. After all, such a scandal would ruin your family's reputation and, thereby, do wonders for my own, but if there is anything that jackdaw blademaster my father hired has taught me, it is patience."

"So I waited," he went on, obviously enjoying Rion's surpise, "and I waited, always looking for the best opportunity to show you for what you really are. I had very nearly decided to go ahead with it until one of my men saw you help these three *commoners,*" he gestured to the others with a look of disgust, "escape the City Watch. Even still, I decided to wait, and it wasn't until I saw you try to leave the city by the northern gate that I discovered what you planned." He smiled, obviously pleased with himself, "You see, Rion, you are, perhaps, not so clever as you thought."

What happened to my damned luck? Rion thought angrily. "What do you want, Sevrin?" He asked, "If it's money you're after, I'll give you all that I have, but you must not hinder us any longer."

The man raised his face to the sky and laughed heartily before looking back at Rion, his eyes narrowing in anger, "*Money?* You think I need your *money?*" He spat at Rion's feet, his lip curling, "It is not your money I am after, Rion, but recompense."

Rion frowned, "Recompense? What have I ever done to you?"

The nobleman snarled, "What have you *done?* Surely, you cannot be so foolish as that. Did you think that I would let you belittle my house, let you belittle *me* for years and do nothing about it? Oh yes, you are a clever one Rion, always ready with a quip or a jab to make me appear less in the eyes of the others, but you seem to have none handy now. Why is that, I wonder?"

Rion's mouth hung open in surprise, "You can't be serious," he said incredulously, "You're doing this because … because you're *jealous?* Listen, Sevrin, this is serious; we aren't children anymore. I—"

"*Jealous?*" The man hissed, interrupting him, "of *you?* I am not jealous, you fool, but I will not suffer your jibes any longer. I will see that clever tongue of yours cut from your mouth and nailed to the trunk of the Traitor's Tree."

"Take them," He hissed, motioning to several of the guards. As they stepped forward, he turned to the men with crossbows, "if any of them tries anything, kill the woman and the girl first. They may look innocent, but they are nightling friends and would do anything to serve their dark masters."

Two of the soldiers grabbed Rion roughly by either arm, restraining him as Sevrin stalked forward. "And so, Eriondrian," the nobleman said, drawing his sword, "now we see who is the better man." Rion saw what was coming, but try as he might, he couldn't break free of the hands that held him.

"Sevrin, listen, you don't have to do this," he said, but if the nobleman heard, he gave no sign. Instead, he raised his arm high and brought the hilt of his sword down in a vicious arc and darkness, full and insistent, exploded in Rion's head. *What happened ... to my ... luck,* he thought, and then he fell to the ground, unconscious.

CHAPTER FIFTY-THREE

OVER THE ROARING THUNDER OF his own agony, Alesh dimly heard one of the soldiers shouting in challenge, but he kept his eyes squeezed tightly shut. He'd made the mistake of looking, some time ago—it could have been minutes or hours, he wasn't sure which. The long leather straps at the end of the whip had been coated with blood as if they'd been washed in it, and small pieces of skin had hung from the folds. His blood. His flesh. He had not looked again.

An answering call came from one of the other soldiers, and when another strike didn't come, Alesh tried to open his eyes. At first, the lids refused to budge, but finally the blood caked there gave, and he managed to force them open. He could just make out the thin form of Falen Par, turned to watch the approach of a soldier who galloped toward him on a horse despite the gathering darkness. The sun was beginning to set, and the hilltop was bathed in alternating patches of light and shadow as the trees kept out most of what little light there still was. Already, the soldiers had lit several fires encircling the hillside, though, of course, none so close to Alesh that the nightlings would not be able to have their fun. *They've come,* he thought madly, *it's the nightwalkers. They've finally come for me.* He was at once terrified and relieved by the thought. It would be a terrible, bloody end, but it *would* be an end.

"*Not yet,*" a voice said beside him, and Alesh let out a choked grunt in surprise. With an immense effort, he managed to turn and look to the side where a familiar gray-robed figure stood, staring at him with a deep, abiding sadness in his eyes.

"P-priest?" Alesh rasped, "what—" he hacked and spat out a mouthful of blood, "What are you doing ... here?" *He's not here, not really. He can't be. It's just another one of the ghosts, another of the dead come to taunt me.* "But that doesn't make sense," Alesh wheezed, "You're not dead. You can't be." He shook his head in weak denial, "No, I won't see anymore. I can't. Please gods I can't." He turned away in time to see the soldier who'd been riding up jump off his horse before it had even stopped. The man rushed forward, kneeling before the commander of the Redeemers. There was an excited, eager tone to his voice, though he was too far away for Alesh to hear his words.

"It is not your time, Alesh," the old priest said beside him in a low, sad voice, *"there is much to do first."*

"J-just leave me alone," Alesh said, closing his eyes in an effort to banish the vision, "gods, why won't you all just leave me alone?"

"I cannot," the man said, *"I will not. Open your eyes, Alesh. See. You must see. Do not flee to the darkness. There is no help for you there."*

The man's words floated through Alesh's dazed mind, and his eyes suddenly snapped open as if of their own accord. "I've gone mad, that's all," he said in a dull, lifeless voice, "You're not real. You can't be real."

"You are not the first to say so," the old priest said, his tone one of pity and regret.

Alesh's pain addled mind worked in desperate circles for a moment. The priest *seemed* real enough, as real as he ever had. But ... "The guards," he croaked with some relief, "they would have seen you, if you were real. They would have raised the alarm."

The old priest came to stand in front of him, his form almost seeming to shimmer in the fading sunlight, *"There are many things these men do not see,"* the figure said, glancing around at the soldiers around the makeshift camp. He turned to Alesh then, and by some strange trick of the fading sun, his eyes seemed to glow gold, *"Pity them, Alesh. They are blind, and it is a blindness of their own making."*

Alesh didn't bother responding. What was the point? What pity he'd possessed had been stripped from him in the dungeon, along with his pride, his humanity. He had nothing left to offer to the men who were responsible, nor to a hallucination. Even if—against all logic—the priest *was* somehow real, what was that to Alesh? Night was coming just the same. Night and death, and he had never really known the man.

"*Don't you?*" The figure asked as if reading his thoughts, a small, melancholy smile on his face.

Alesh started at that before he realized that of course the vision *would* know what was in his mind; after all, it was a part of it.

"*They have them, Alesh,*" the figure said, turning to regard the leader of the Redeemers as Falen Par ordered several soldiers into the woods. When the priest turned back, his eyes blazed like a dying sun, "*They have them and only you can save them.*"

Alesh hissed a laugh at that. Vision or not, the man was a fool. "Then th-they're doomed," he rasped, "Whoever they are."

"*Very well,*" the figure said, "*I cannot make your choice for you, but ask yourself a question, Alesh. How did the Evertorch work if it was damaged?*"

It took Alesh's pain-muddled mind several seconds before he understood what the man was talking about. Then it came to him. How *had* the Evertorch become damaged? He remembered wondering about it, in Tesharna's throne room, but beatings had a way of taking precedence over curiosity.

Still, the more he thought of it, the more he was sure that he hadn't damaged the Evertorch after he'd taken it from Garn. The only time it could have happened was when he'd dropped it during the fight, but that was *before* he'd used it to drive the nightlings away. Not a thing he remembered, but a thing that must have happened just the same. He was alive, after all, wasn't he? For a little while longer, anyway.

He told himself that it didn't matter how the Evertorch had worked, that he was going to die soon regardless, but he found his thoughts returning to it just the same. Evertorches were notoriously fragile things, rendered useless at the slightest scratch. So how could it have worked? The answer was close, tauntingly close, but the hot lines of pain on his body made it nearly impossible to think and the answer danced away from his grasp like a leaf in the wind. "It doesn't matter," he hissed finally, "What difference can it make?"

"*It is all of the difference,*" the priest answered matter of factly, "*It is the difference between truth and untruth, between light and darkness. Between life and death.*"

"You're a damned fool," Alesh spat, turning away. But he could not turn away from the uncertainty that the man's question had aroused in him so easily, and he was still pondering it when a group of soldiers appeared out of the dim light at the edge of the camp leading several prisoners behind them.

In front walked two men he didn't recognize. One was a dusky-skinned man who, even chained, seemed to prowl more than walk. Although his expression was unreadable, the man's eyes roamed ceaselessly, taking in everything around him as if searching for any opportunity. An opportunity that would not come, Alesh could have told him, had he cared enough.

The other was a lighter-skinned man with the pronounced, aristocratic features common to the nobility. He was stumbling drunkenly, one of his hands pressed against his bloody forehead and the look of desperate resignation in his eyes showed that he, at least, knew what was to come. Behind him walked a woman with long, blonde hair. Even in the dim glow of the surrounding blazes, Alesh could see that she was strikingly beautiful with eyes like the brightest emeralds he'd ever seen. With a start, he realized that he had, in fact, seen those eyes before, and in another instant he remembered where. She was the woman he'd met in Ilrika, the one who Chosen Olliman had sent him to find. Katherine, she'd said her name was. But how could she be here?

Then he saw the last prisoner in line and all other thought vanished from his mind. Alesh gasped, his heart lurching in his chest. "S-Sonya?"

"Alesh!" The girl screamed upon seeing him, "Oh, Alesh!" She started to run toward him, but the chains around her ankles caught her, and she tumbled to the ground in a sobbing heap.

"What is this, Ambassador Par?" Captain Farren asked, glancing between the four prisoners, "What have you done?"

"These four came to rescue him," Falen Par said in a calm voice, nodding to Alesh. He turned to a haughty looking man with black, grease-slicked hair who appeared out of the group of guards, "You will be rewarded for your dedication to the Light, Master Alrick," the general of the Redeemers said, "I will see to it personally."

The man grinned in a smug, self-satisfied way that made Alesh hate him on sight, "It is enough to serve Chosen Tesharna in all of her glory."

"Sir?" One of the soldiers asked, "What would you have us do with them?"

The leader of the Redeemers sighed as if with regret, "I fear there is only one thing *to* do. They have tried to rescue a man who is known to consort with the creatures of the night. Gentlemen, we have found the co-conspirators that we have been searching for and, for the sake of all of Entarna, they will suffer the same fate as their compatriot. Stake them to the ground, and make sure their bonds are tight. Oh, and be quick about it," he said, glancing at the darkening sky, "Night will be here soon."

"Yes sir." The soldiers led the prisoners to a spot a short distance away from where Alesh hung. Then they drove metal stakes into the ground and fastened the chains of the prisoners to them with practiced precision.

"You can't be serious, Ambassador!" Captain Farren exclaimed, stepping forward, "Why, there is a woman and a *child* among them!"

"So there is, captain," the leader of the Redeemers said, "and it is perhaps one of the greatest tragedies of this world that darkness corrupts not only old men, but the fair and the young alike."

"No," the captain said, shaking his head, "I will not allow this. The Chosen would not appro—"

"Captain, captain," Falen Par said, laying a hand on the man's shoulders, "I know that you are upset, but you must understand that, despite our personal feelings, we must do what is best for Valeria. And sometimes that means," he leaned forward, as if to whisper something into the captain's ear, and in one smooth motion, withdrew a dagger from his belt and thrust it under the man's breastplate, deep into his side, "*Sacrifices must be made.*"

The captain's body went rigid, and he grunted in shock, staring down at the blade plunged into his side with wide, disbelieving eyes. He grasped weakly at Par's arm, but the leader of the Redeemers ignored his feeble efforts, withdrawing the blade and sticking it in again and again until the captain stopped struggling altogether, his hands on Falen Par's arms the only thing keeping him on his feet. Finally, his hand and wrist coated in blood, the thin man ripped the blade free with a sickening *squelch* and took a step back, leaving the captain to fall to the ground. The captain lay on his side, staring up at Falen Par, his mouth working silently as a crimson stain spread over his white tunic. "You are a fool, Captain Farren," the leader of the Redeemers said, "a fool and a coward, and the world can afford neither now. There are big changes coming, captain, great changes, and I'm afraid you were in the way."

"B-but … the Chosen will not stand—" The captain started, but cut off in a coughing fit that left his mouth and chin coated with blood.

"Fool," Falen Par said, shaking his head, "It is by the Chosen's order that you die."

"Take him out of my sight," He said in disgust, motioning to two nearby guards who leapt to obey. Alesh watched, stunned, as they carried the dying man away.

"You *bastard,*" Alesh growled, staring at Sonya, "She's just a child, damn you! Let her go!" He struggled against his bonds, heedless of the pain and fresh blood that began to flow from his wrists and ankles as the manacles dug into them, but no matter how hard he tried, they metal would not give.

"If he speaks again," Falen Par said to one of his soldiers in a cold, emotionless voice, "Kill the girl." He flashed his cruel smile, "Let them be chained so that they might look upon the man who brought them to this, the man who they came to save." Alesh was forced to watch in silence, trembling with rage, as Sonya and the others were gagged, and their chains were tied to the stakes in such a way that they were made to kneel, facing him.

Alesh felt a wave of despair wash over him, mingling with his impotent fury. He'd been given Sonya back only to lose her again, and there was nothing he could do. What chance did the world have against such men? Men who would kill anyone who got in their way without a second's thought. What hope was there in a world when even Tesharna, the Chosen of the gods, turned against mankind?

Once it was finished and the others were secured, Falen Par strutted up close to Alesh where he hung, smiling widely. "How did you think this would end, boy? The time of men following the Chosen meekly, of being slaves to Amedan is coming to an end."

"*Night take you,*" Alesh rasped, "You ... had no reason ... to kill him."

Falen Par laughed, "The captain?" He shrugged, "The man asked too many questions. Besides, I would worry more about myself and my friends, were I you." He glanced at the darkening sky, "I wonder, how do you think the creatures will make it to you, past your friends?"

With a shock, Alesh realized why the man had spaced them out in front of and around him. Fires had been set behind him, so that the nightwalkers would be forced to come from the other direction, through Sonya and the others. The leader of the Redeemers had made it so that Alesh would be forced to watch the others be torn apart by the nightwalkers before he, too, was finally killed. He looked desperately to Sonya. The girl watched him with wide eyes, scared, but full of what appeared to him to be hope. *She thinks I'll save her,* Alesh thought, his heart aching, *somehow, she thinks I'll be able to protect her. But I can't protect anyone. I can't even protect myself.* "You ... bastard," he growled, his anger making his mind clearer than it had been in over a day, "I'll kill you."

A distant, hungry howl tore through the darkness sending shivers up Alesh's spine, and Falen Par laughed, "We'll talk after." He winked at him then turned and headed to the safety of one of the fires, leaving Alesh and the others in the gathering darkness.

"I'm so sorry," Alesh croaked, looking at those gathered around him, "Gods, I'm so sorry."

The four other prisoners stared back at him, and though he could not see them well in the darkness, he thought he saw accusation in those stares. And he deserved no less. He had failed, had failed Olliman, and Chorin, and Abigail, and now even Sonya. He had tried, had done all that he could, and it had not been enough. Not nearly. "I've failed you all." He hung his head, unable to look at them anymore, and waited for the darkness to come.

A growl sounded from the nearby trees, then another, and despite himself,

Alesh found his head raising, his eyes searching the distant treeline. The leaves rustled and branches cracked and snapped as shadowy forms flitted through the dark forest. Strangely, Alesh found himself thinking of the Evertorch, and of what the priest—or his vision of the man, at least—had said. How *had* the Evertorch worked if it had been damaged?

"*Why did they not kill you on the road that day?*" Alesh turned, only half-surprised to find the priest standing beside him again. Somehow, the man's eyes seemed to glow even brighter than before, though there was no light to reflect in them now except that of the distant fires.

"W-what?" He asked, "What do you mean?"

"*When you were a child,*" the priest said, his gaze never wavering from Alesh's own, "*when your wagon was tipped and The Bane came, why did you survive?*"

Alesh had asked himself the same question hundreds of times since that day, had spent countless hours in Ilrika's libraries researching everything he could about the nightwalkers in search of some answer to why he had lived while his parents had died, but he had found nothing. "Someone must have ... must have saved me, that's all." He said, confused and more than a little disconcerted by the man's golden stare.

The old priest nodded, his expression serious, "*Yes. Someone did.*"

Alesh closed his eyes. Why could it not just end? He had suffered, and he had failed. When would it be enough? "It doesn't matter," he said, "It's over now."

"*There is nothing that matters more,*" the priest said, walking to stand in front of him, "*It is time, Alesh. It is time for you to wake up. Time for you to come out of the darkness. How did you survive? How? How did the Evertorch save you, when it could not work? How, Alesh?*" The apparition demanded, "*How?*"

"I don't know!" Alesh screamed, his rage, his fear and his self-hatred pouring out in his voice, "I *don't know!*"

The creatures were close now, so close that he could hear their snuffling, hungry growls and grunts, yet despite the darkness that had settled on the world like a sable coverlet, he could see the priest's face clearly. "*It is time, Alesh,*" the man said again in a sad voice, "*It is time.*" With that, he reached out a hand that Alesh could have sworn was glowing and touched him on the forehead.

At the man's touch, a force with the power of a thousand lightning strikes, with the strength of a hundred whirlwinds, smashed into Alesh. He cried out and blood flew from his ravaged body as his back arched under the invisible force rushing through him, his hoarse incoherent shouts drowning out even the sounds of the nightlings. Power, raw and hot as if the sun itself had been placed inside him roared through his body, and he felt as if he was burning alive. Then, as quickly as it had come, the feeling vanished but, in its wake, it left an answer. Suddenly, without knowing how or why, Alesh knew the answer to the old priest's question. How had a damaged Evertorch driven the nightlings back? It hadn't. Who had saved him on the road that day? *He* had.

He stared around himself at the fires dotting the hillside, and he saw that fire, that light, in a way that he never had before. It seemed to him that he could speak to it, that, if he did, it would hear. Abruptly, not knowing why he did it, but feeling that it was right just the same, Alesh breathed out, and in that breath there was a question, and in the question, a command. It drifted out from him, carried on the wind and through the flickering orange light on the hill, to each fire burning there, for where light was, the question was asked. It asked its question of the fire, and the fire heard. And then, the fire answered.

Streamers of light and flame, thin at first but growing every second, began to extend out from the blazes toward Alesh, so that it looked as if thousands of bright fingers were reaching toward him. Then the questing fingers of light found him and when they touched him, power, strength unlike anything he'd ever felt before flooded into him. "Enough!" He roared, and his voice reverberated across the hillside like the crack of thunder. Men gathered at the fires waiting for the bloody spectacle stopped their conversations and turned to him, their expressions ones of shock, of awe. Growling in fury, Alesh flexed the muscles of his body, and the iron bonds enclosing his wrists and ankles shattered and fell away.

He dropped several feet to the ground and landed on one knee, his body trembling with want, with *need*. He raised his head and stared out into the darkness and the creatures it contained with eyes blazing like twin suns. Then he rose, his chest heaving, and strode toward the treeline, "*Remember me!?*" He roared to the darkness, "*Do you know me? You do, and you will know me better yet!*"

CHAPTER FIFTY-FOUR

IMPOSSIBLE, RION THOUGHT WILDLY. HE watched in shock, his ears still ringing from the stranger's bellow, as the man screamed a challenge into the darkness like a mad man. Streamers of light from all of the fires on the hillside trailed toward him, the blazes dimming as they gave over their light. Rion blinked, sure that he had to be imagining things, but when he opened them again, the streamers were still there, and the man was actually *glowing*.

The stranger stalked toward the shadow of the treeline, apparently oblivious of the injuries he'd taken, injuries that should have killed him on their own or, at the very least, left him a mewling, cringing thing of pain and torment. The stranger paused and glanced back, and a superstitious shiver ran up Rion's spine as those blazing eyes locked on him. Then, to Rion's dismay, he began to come closer.

Rion tensed as he approached, and he seemed to feel the fury radiating off of the stranger in waves of heat. Suddenly he felt that he'd rather risk the nightwalkers than this *thing* with its glowing skin and eyes that blazed in their sockets like funeral pyres. The man knelt down, and Rion cringed as he reached forward, but the stranger grabbed the bonds holding him in both hands and tugged. The chains gave a tortured creak then snapped apart, and the stranger tossed them carelessly to the side. "Free the others," he grated, in a deep voice filled with barely contained rage.

Something growled hungrily nearby, and Rion and the stranger turned to see a nightwalker emerging from the trees. The man turned back to Rion, and his eyes flashed like a lightning strike, "*Now!*" he shouted, and before Rion could find words through his shock, the stranger was up and charging toward the nearest creature, bellowing a bestial cry of rage and, unless Rion had gone mad himself, something that sounded very much like eagerness.

He watched in disbelief as the stranger tackled the creature and both went flying into the darkness. *What have you gotten yourself into, fool?* He thought wildly as he turned and began fumbling at the bonds of the others with trembling fingers, *Just what in the name of the gods have you gotten yourself into?*

CHAPTER FIFTY-FIVE

KATHERINE STARED, SHOCKED, AS ALESH hurled himself at the shadows and the creatures that waited there. *He'll be killed,* she had time to think, a knot of fear constricting her throat, and then he was among them. She winced, expecting to see him fall at any moment, cut down by claws like daggers, expecting the nightwalkers to pile on him and tear into his flesh. But they did not.

She could see little of the creatures but the various colors of their malevolent stares in the darkness and, from time to time, the vague form of their bodies as they hurled themselves at the man. A creature the size of a large wolf pounced at him, but Alesh snatched it out of the air, seemingly with no more effort than a man might give to catching a ball. He shouted in rage, and the muscles of his arms rippled and flexed as he held the creature by one arm and its throat. The nightwalker screamed, an inhuman wail of agony and fear, and the sickening smell of burning flesh and hair drifted to Katherine on the wind. Alesh's arm tensed and the creature's cry abruptly cut off. He tossed the lifeless body behind him, and it tumbled into the torchlight, a mass of claws and razor-sharp teeth and dead, burned flesh, its eyes melted as if it had been cooked from the inside out.

Katherine glanced back at the man, transfixed, and saw that anytime his glowing skin touched the nightlings, their bodies sizzled and popped like grease in a fire, and they screeched in agony and rage. *What are you?* She thought, as she watched him tearing at the creatures, bellowing his own fury in answer to their cries as he waded among them, his arms, twin beams of sunlight, shattering their bodies beneath his heavy, lightning-fast blows. It was as if he didn't fear them at all. No, that wasn't quite right. It was as if he was filled up with a bursting, insane rage so complete that it left no room for fear.

Even as she looked on, a creature reared at him, raising its massive front claws to rake at him, and the man caught it by its arms, holding it at bay. The nightling snapped at him with a mouth filled with long, salivating teeth, its red eyes gleaming hungrily, but the man swatted its head aside almost contemptuously, wrapped both hands around its neck and broke it with an audible *pop*.

What in the name of the gods are you? Katherine thought again.

"A crazy bastard, that's what," a familiar voice answered, "now stay still."

Katherine started and craned her neck to see Rion working at the clasps on her ankles with a thin dagger. She hadn't realized she'd spoken out loud. "*Free the others,*" he grumbled as he twisted the dagger this way and that, his hands shaking, "*as if anyone can just snap iron as if it were nothing.*"

Katherine waited anxiously for him to finish, forcing herself to keep still despite her nervousness. The nightwalkers might be busy fighting Alesh, but the soldiers around the hill wouldn't be content to just watch forever. Sooner or later, they'd get over their shock and fear and decide to finish Katherine and the others the old fashioned way. She was just about to tell the man to hurry when there was a loud *click* and the manacles on her wrists came free, falling to the ground. "There it is," Rion said, a satisfied tone in his voice, "I think I've got the knack of it now."

Indeed, seconds later, Katherine's ankles were also free, and she rose, rubbing at her tender wrists. The man, Rion, went to work on the others and soon they were standing together, their bonds lying useless on the ground. Katherine hurried to the crying Sonya and pulled her into a hug, "Are you okay, baby?" She whispered.

"He's g-glowing, Katherine," the girl sniffed, "Alesh is *glowing*."

"I know, sweetheart," Katherine said, "I know."

"He won't be able to hold out like that for long," Rion observed in a tense voice, "I don't care who he is. Whatever he did, it looks to me like it's wearing off."

Katherine glanced back and saw that Rion was right. Alesh's skin still glowed, but it no longer carried the shocking brightness that had been painful to look upon. Instead, it had taken on a dull, somber glow like fire embers that were almost out. She thought she knew all too well what would happen when it vanished completely. "We have to help him," she said, struggling and failing to keep the fear from her voice.

She looked at Rion and the man glanced between her and Darl, sighing, "Why not? If the nightlings don't get us, the soldiers will. Alright then," he said, producing two thin blades from the inside of his tunic, "Let's help him."

CHAPTER FIFTY-SIX

ONE OF THE NIGHTLING'S DARTED FORWARD, opening its wide jaws and displaying a row of needle sharp teeth, but before its mouth could close, Alesh caught one side of the creature's jaw in each hand, grunting with the effort of keeping the creature's jaws stretched apart. The creature made a guttural sound of pain, struggling helplessly as its jaws drew wider, then wider still, until they snapped with an audible crunching and tearing of sinew and muscle. The nightwalker's frantic struggles intensified, but Alesh gave a mighty wrench of his hands, screaming, lost in his own unquenchable rage, and black blood and ichor showered over him as the creature's jaw ripped apart.

He cried out as razor sharp claws raked bloody furrows down his back and threw what was left of the nightling into several others that were charging at him and spun to face his newest attacker. The creature that had struck him was vaguely man-shaped, but its body was much too thin for any human and covered in what appeared to be interlocking black scales. Its jaw was twice as long as a man's and full of sharp, needle-like teeth, its arms so long that the claws of its hands would have scraped the ground when it walked. The nightling lashed out, and Alesh barely managed to catch its wrist before its talons tore out his throat. He growled, squeezing with all of the newfound power that filled his muscles and the creature screeched in pain. There was a violent ripping and the creature's thin wrist tore free from its body in a shower of blood as black as oil. Alesh threw the severed limb away with disgust and kicked the creature in the stomach, sending it flying back into the surrounding horde.

He risked a glance back in the opening this provided and was relieved to see that the man was just now finishing freeing the other prisoners, but the distraction nearly cost him his life. Instinct, more than anything else, caused him to dive to the side, and he narrowly avoided being skewered by a nightling's darting tail. The appendage was as thick as a man's arm and ended in a wicked, spiked projection at least six inches long.

Before the creature could retract the sinuous limb, Alesh grabbed hold of it and, with a grunt of exertion, spun in a circle, heaving it into the crowd. *Please gods let them escape,* he thought. Then the creatures charged toward him in force, and all thought vanished as his body responded with instincts ingrained in him from countless hours spent training with the Chosen.

Had it not been for Olliman's lessons, he would have been dead in moments, powers or not. Even still, he suffered several deep cuts to his back, sides, and arms that bled freely, but he fought on anyway as he sought to fill the emptiness inside him with the blood of the creatures who'd created it. *Here* were those who had slain the Chosen, *here* were those who had murdered his mother and father. He waded into them, an avatar of death, searing their flesh with his touch, glorying in each scream of agony, each wail of death. But even as he fought, he realized that he couldn't keep this up for much longer. The strength that had filled him before was slowly beginning to ebb, and each sidestep, each dodge became a little slower, a little more sluggish than the last.

Something struck him hard in the side, staggering him, but he turned the motion into a lunge, lashing out with his fist and striking one of the nightspawn that screamed as it tumbled backward, its face bursting into flame. Another creature the size of a large dog pounced on him from behind, digging its claws into his already wounded back, and he fell to one knee under its weight. He felt the inhuman strength leaking out of him through his many wounds, and he growled with the effort and pain of ripping the beast free and heaving it away.

He started to rise to his feet, but suddenly his legs were impossibly heavy, and his head felt as if someone was going to work on it with a smith's hammer.

Nausea swept over him in waves as he struggled to one knee. The creatures closed in around him, sensing his weakness, uttering grunts of hunger and hate as they drew closer.

Alesh watched them come, his teeth bared, "*Come and get it, you bastards,*" he snarled. The creatures drew closer, then closer still, and they were almost within touching distance when fire rained down from the sky. The nightwalkers hissed and cried out in pain as the light struck them like a blade, and they collided with each other, snarling and biting in their haste to get out of its deadly orange glow. Confused, Alesh just had time to register that the ruddy light was coming from several large pieces of burning kindling before someone was on either side of him, helping him to his feet. "You're a heavy bastard, I'll say that much," someone said, and Alesh looked over to see the prisoner he'd freed. The man's face was pale, ghostly in the dim glow, but his eyes were hard, determined.

Alesh grunted in response, suddenly too tired to speak. He felt more exhausted than he'd ever felt in his entire life, far worse, even, than after a long training session with Olliman. On his other side, he saw the woman, Katherine, her face straining with the effort of holding him up, her wide eyes watching the creatures surrounding them. "Thanks," he croaked, noting the half a dozen burning brands that lay scattered in a circle around him, "but you s-should have ran. Those pieces of wood won't burn long and then…."

"Just don't you worry about that," the woman said, "We shouldn't have to wait long."

Around them, the creatures growled and hissed in anger, several of them tentatively reaching limbs into the light only to jerk them back again. "Wait?" He asked, "for wha—" he cut off as the Ferinan man appeared, holding several makeshift torches that blazed fitfully in one hand and guiding a terrified little girl with the other.

"Alesh?" Sonya asked, "Is it … is it really you?"

Seeing her alive, Alesh fell to his knees, "It's me, Sonya," he said, "I'm so sorry I didn't—" he cut off, grunting as the girl rushed into his arms, nearly knocking him down. "It's me," he whispered, not caring about the tears that wound their way down his cheeks. She was alive. Sonya was alive.

Alesh laughed with the pure joy of it, and soon Sonya was giggling too. "I don't know who you are, strangers," he panted, grinning widely at the girl, "but thank you for protecting my sister. I owe you a debt I could never repay. My name's Alesh, by the way."

"Katherine," the woman said, "We've met."

Alesh stared at her for a second then laughed again, "I remember. You nearly got me killed."

"Yeah," she coughed, glancing at the Ferinan man, "Uh … sorry about that."

If the Ferinan man noticed her look, he gave no sign. Instead, he surprised Alesh by dropping to his knees. The dusky-skinned man bent and touched his forehead to the ground before looking up to Alesh's eyes, "I see you, Son of the Morning. I am Darl-asheek Binakrala, Chief of the Palietkun tribe of the southern deserts, First Witness of the Dawn Whisperers, Seeker of the True Light. Long have my people awaited your coming."

Alesh glanced uncertainly at the pale-skinned man at his side, but the man only frowned and shook his head, apparently as confused as Alesh.

For her part, the woman's mouth fell open in surprise, and her eyes went wide. "*Darl*," she breathed, "you *spoke*."

The dusky-skinned man smiled widely, revealing a set of bright white teeth, "Yes, my friend. I have found the Son of the Morning, the Bringer of the Light and Destroyer of the Darkness. The oath is ended."

"I knew you could talk!" Sonya exclaimed grinning.

The man nodded, "You are wise beyond your years, little one," he said solemnly, but the effect was ruined somewhat by his wide grin and the wink he gave her.

"Yes, yes," the other man said impatiently, "the Ferinan can talk, this one can glow like a firefly, the woman's suicidal, and I'm a fool. Now then, how about we save the friendly conversation for a time when we don't have nightwalkers and soldiers drawing lots for who gets to kill us first?"

Alesh frowned, his relief at seeing Sonya and confusion at the Ferinan's words evaporating as hate, fresh and hungry and insistent, flooded through him. He could make out Falen Par standing at one of the distant fires with what looked to be four or five Redeemers. The man had tried to kill Sonya, had—with Kale's help—murdered Abigail and Chorin and Chosen Olliman. He would pay. They all would.

"You're right," He said, gently setting Sonya down. He turned to the Ferinan man, still crouched in the dirt, "Get up, man. I don't know what you're talking about, but there'll be time for it later."

"As you wish," the man said, nodding and rising to his feet with a cat-like grace.

"What now?" Katherine asked, staring with wide eyes between Darl and Alesh.

"Now," Alesh said, his voice as sharp as the edge of a sword, "I will speak with General Par." He sat off without a word, and the others fell in beside him as he stalked toward the fire at which the leader of the Redeemers stood. "Falen Par!" Alesh yelled, his voice echoing in the night, rising above the hisses and growls of the creatures around them.

The general of the Redeemers turned from where he'd been whispering to one of his men to take in the group with wide, terrified eyes, "Don't you come another step nearer, you monster!" He shouted, but Alesh ignored him, stalking forward with deadly purpose, his anger and hate at all that had been taken from him crying out for release.

***

Rion watched the stranger head for the firelight as if there weren't half a dozen armed men standing in it. The man could barely stand, what in the name of the gods was he thinking? He glanced at the others, but they were already moving forward and, muttering a curse, he reluctantly followed after them.

In moments, he and the others were within the firelight where the thin man and his small group of Redeemers stood, staring at the man, Alesh, as if he was a nightwalker himself. Rion didn't blame them for that. "Kill him," the thin man hissed, and Rion tensed in anticipation, producing two of the thin blades from his sleeves. But he needn't have bothered. The soldiers didn't so much as move an inch. Instead, they continued to stare at Alesh with wide, terrified eyes. "I said kill him, you cowardly bastards!" The thin man shouted.

Two of the men backed away instead, and in their haste to get away from Alesh, they strayed too far out of the light. Claws shot out and grabbed them, lightning quick, and the men disappeared into the seething throng of darkness. Their tortured, terrified screams lasted only for a moment.

Rion swallowed hard, staring off into the shadows where the men had gone, but Alesh didn't spare them a second glance, "You killed the Chosen," he said, staring at the leader of the Redeemers.

"N-no!" Falen Par blurted, his face going pale as he shot looks at the men, woman and child gathered in front of him, "I only did what they told me—that's all, just what they told me, I swear!" He'd drawn his sword, but his hand trembled so much that it looked as if he'd drop it at any moment.

"Who?" Alesh asked, his voice deadly quiet.

"Kale Leandrin," the man blurted, "a-and Chosen Tesharna. I just did what she told me, that's all. Please, have mercy."

Rion felt his blood go cold. Tesharna was behind the death of Olliman? Surely, the man had to be lying. Rion glanced at Katherine and Darl and saw his own surprise mirrored in their faces. For his part, the man Alesh only nodded as if he'd been expecting as much. "I believe you," he said in a voice so cold and seething with hate that it sent shivers up Rion's spine, "but as for your mercy, you will not have it. Come forward, Falen Par, and accept the fate that has been waiting for you all your miserable life."

The thin man stumbled back, his head shaking in terrified denial and snatched a burning beam of wood from the fire. Then, screaming, he turned and ran into the sea of nightwalkers, sending the creatures scattering before the light with howls of pain and frustration. The two remaining soldiers looked after their commander, then at Alesh, and finally at each other before grabbing up makeshift torches of their own and charging off after their master.

Rion looked after them in surprise, "Are they insane? Surely, they won't get away ... will they?"

"It's alright," Katherine said, her own tone cold, "We can always get them later."

"No," Alesh said, staring after them, "Falen Par has left the light. He has chosen the darkness instead, and so *he will have it.*"

Alesh took a long, deep breath, and his eyes flashed a bright, brilliant gold. Then he closed his hand tight, and the light of the distant torches vanished as if they'd been doused with water.

In another moment, the night was split with the wretched death screams of Falen Par and his two men, and Rion stared at the man in awe, "Wha-what was that?"

Alesh glanced at him, a cruel smile on his face, and Rion felt a shiver run up his spine. There was a hunger in the man's face, in his eyes, that was as bad as any that could be found on the face of the nightwalkers. "Justice," the man growled. "That was justice."

In the orange glow of the fire, the man's face looked almost feral, the teeth his smile revealed those of a creature before it ravaged its prey. Rion swallowed hard. Oh yes, he was crazy alright. There was no question about that. He glanced over at Katherine and saw her studying the man with a troubled expression. "So … so it's done then," she said in a voice little more than a whisper.

"No," Alesh grated in a harsh voice that barely sounded human at all, "It's just begun."

"What do you plan to do?" Katherine asked.

Alesh thought of Abigail lying butchered in the street, of Chorin propped up against an alleyway, dead for trying to save a woman and a child. He thought of Chosen Olliman, the closest thing he'd had to a father, lying in his bed, his chest ripped open, the sheets soaked through with his blood. "I plan to find every last person responsible for what happened in Ilrika," he said. "I plan to find them, and I plan to kill them. I'm going to kill them all." Something inside of him, in the darkest part of him, rejoiced at that, and a smile that didn't feel like his own spread over his face.

Katherine stared at the man and pulled Sonya closer to her. There was something dark in the man's face that she didn't like. "Y-you can't be ser—"

He held up a hand, and she winced out of reflex, half expecting him to strike her. He saw her recoil and frowned, turning back to the darkness, "Wait." Katherine and the others turned to follow his gaze, and she gasped as the nightlings fled as if in terror, creating a large opening from which a figure approached out of the shadows. As the figure stepped into the light, it resolved itself into an old man in faded gray robes. The man's face held no expression, but his eyes seemed to be smiling.

"*You,*" Alesh hissed. He took a threatening step forward, and Katherine was alarmed to see his hands knot into fists at his sides.

Katherine watched, tense, but the old man either didn't notice, or chose not to respond to Alesh's threatening posture. Instead, he continued forward until he was only a few feet away. "It is I," he said, nodding, "I have returned."

Alesh spat, "You've a habit of turning up when it's too late to do any good, priest. Or should I say *Amedan.*"

Katherine felt a wave of fear wash over her and glanced at the man to see if he was joking. But he didn't *look* like a man telling a joke. He looked angry. No, that wasn't right. He looked furious, like a man ready to do murder. *But it can't be*, she thought, *It's just an old man, that's all, not the God of Fire, the Bringer of the Flame and creator of mankind. Just an old man.*

Sure, another part of her thought, *just an old man who spends his time walking through fields of nightwalkers with no more fear than a child skipping through her family's gardens.* She realized that her hands were trembling. No, not just her hands, her whole body. She shot a glance at Rion and saw that the man was staring back at her with wide, terrified eyes. He'd gone so pale that he didn't look like a man at all but some disembodied spirit, floating in the darkness. Darl was on his hands and knees, his head bowed so low that his forehead touched the ground. After a panicked moment, she dropped down beside him, and Rion followed a second later.

"How long have you known?" The priest asked in an amused tone.

"Never mind that," Alesh growled, "you nearly got me killed." He gestured to those behind him angrily, "You nearly got my friends killed. Why didn't you help? What good is a god who won't help his people?"

Katherine's breath caught in her throat. The man must be completely mad. Who else would dare to talk to the Father of the Gods in such a way? She waited in tense anticipation, expecting them all to be struck down by the god's wrath at any moment, but when he spoke, his voice was calm and comforting, like the soft gurgle of creek water over stones, "I did send help," Amedan, the Bringer of the Light and creator of mankind said, "I sent you."

Alesh flinched at that, as if struck, and suddenly he didn't look angry anymore. Instead, he looked tired, tired and lost like a man who has been set on a task that he finds himself unable to finish. "Why me?" He asked, and Katherine was shocked by the utter anguish, the torment, that filled his voice and twisted his normally handsome face, "I'm nobody. Just the son of a dead commoner. A servant who was taken in by a great man and treated better than he deserved."

Amedan smiled, and Katherine was suddenly overcome with a peaceful, contented feeling that reminded her of sitting in front of a warm fire in the dead of winter. He walked up to Alesh and put a hand gently on his shoulder, gazing at him with impossibly blue eyes that seemed to Katherine as if they could look into a person's soul. They were the blue of the sky on a summer day, the blue of an ocean when the morning sun danced across it. *No*, she thought, *that's not right*. The man's eyes didn't look like those things, those things looked like his eyes, imperfect copies of the depths, the majesty that lay in that gaze. "You are what you are," he said in a soft, comforting voice, "and that is more than you know. You are the Son of the Morning, and it is up to you to stand against the Darkness that is coming, a Darkness worse than any that has come before it."

"And you?" Alesh asked in a whisper, "What will you do?"

Thunder crashed a short distance away, and the old man stared up at the sky, a grim expression on his face. He closed his eyes and when he opened them again, they were full of such deep, abiding sadness that Katherine felt an unexpected tear fall from her eye. It was a sadness that spoke of innumerable hurts. It was, she thought, a sadness that no human could bear, one that would crush any normal man or woman under its weight. "I will do what I can to help you," the god said, "but I have my own battles to fight, the Light help me."

Alesh opened his mouth to speak but stopped as two shapes appeared out of thin air behind Amedan. The first was a young man with one eye as black as pitch, the other so white that it hurt to look at, and Katherine felt herself stunned anew as she recognized Javen, the God of Chance, dressed in white armor that glowed brightly, and a cape as dark as the night around them. Beside him, graceful even with the fear that was plain on her face, possessed of a beauty to make the world's greatest poet lose his words, to make the realm's strongest man weep, stood Deitra, Goddess of Music and Art. Her dress was the same that she'd been wearing in Katherine's dream and Katherine noticed that there was an almost hair-thin scar running down one of her cheeks. *The string of her harp,* she thought with a shock, *the scar is from where the string of her harp struck her.*

Javen, the God of Chance, was said to have a twisted sense of humor, and he was most often immortalized in busts and sculptures with a wry smile on his face, but his smile was nowhere to be seen now as he stepped toward Amedan, "Father," he said in a deep, grave voice completely at odds with his appearance, "We have to go. She is coming, and you cannot meet her, not in your weakened state."

"In a moment, Javen," Amedan said, turning back to Alesh, "You must protect them, Alesh. Please, for me, save them. Save my people."

Alesh's mouth moved for a moment but finally his face grew hard, "I will do what I can, but not for you. I will do it for them. I will not be your slave."

Javen frowned, stepping forward, "You will not sp—"

"Peace, Javen," Amedan said, holding up a hand, his gaze never leaving Alesh's. Immediately, the lesser god fell silent. "I would not have you be," Amedan said, "nor anyone."

Alesh barked a harsh laugh, "Strike me down if you want, but do not lie to me. I know better. Chosen Olliman spent countless hours on his knees, praying to you, seeking your favor."

A genuine expression of surprise came over the god's face for a moment then he raised his head to the sky and laughed a deep, hearty laugh that echoed across the hilltop. "Praying, you call it? Well, I suppose you *might* call it that, though yelling would be far more accurate and, I can assure you, it was not something I enjoyed. Brent had … quite the temper."

"Father," Deitra said. The goddess's voice was melodic, possessed of a harmony all its own, but Katherine could detect the worry in it, "we really must—"

"A moment, daughter," The god said. He turned away from Alesh, and Katherine froze as those blue eyes locked on her, "Ah, Katherine Elar," he said, "rise and be at peace."

Terrified, Katherine rose to her feet on wobbly legs. "My daughter has told me about you," Amedan said, smiling, "I see that she has chosen wisely."

Chosen? Katherine thought, confused, but she bowed her head in response, "T-thank you, my lord."

Amedan nodded, then turned to Rion, "Eriondrian," he said, humor in his voice, "We are well met. Please, rise and be seen." Rion did so, his face as pale as a man attending his own execution. "My son, Javen, has told me about you as well," the Father of the Gods said.

"Y-yes sir, err … Amedan, ah, my lord," Rion stumbled.

Amedan laughed then, "Be at peace, Eriondrian Tirinian, and carry my blessing. You are a man who likes to gamble, are you not?"

Katherine would have thought it impossible, but the man's face paled further, "Ah, yes, my lord. That is—"

"It is well," Amedan said, "for we will be taking the greatest gamble there has ever been and we stand to win—or lose—more than we ever have before." The god glanced at Darl, and Rion breathed an audible sigh of relief as the god's attention turned away from him.

"And you," the god said. "Chief Darl-asheek Binakrala. Long have I known your Fathers. May the sun be always at your front and the waters always at your feet."

"I-I am unworthy, My Lord," Darl said, planting his forehead in the ground.

"No, my friend," The god said, leaning down and gently pulling the dusky-skinned man to his feet, "You have given much for the light and your people have not forgotten the old ways as so many others have. There is none worthier."

"Yes, my lord," Darl said, bowing his head, "and may your own drink be sweet and plentiful in the land."

Amedan nodded then turned to Sonya. If anything, the little girl looked far less terrified than the rest. He smiled at her, and she smiled back, a bit shyly, but no more than that. "Ah, daughter," Amedan said, kneeling down so that he could look her in the face, "it is well with you?"

The little girl smiled, hugging Alesh's leg, "Yes, sir. Thank you."

The god smiled then rose, turning to Alesh, "A man could not ask for greater allies, I think, and that is well. You will need each other in the days to come."

A sudden gust of wind sent leaves flying around them and lightning crashed nearby, lighting up the world in a flash of brilliance. "Father!" Javen yelled, having to shout to be heard over the rising gale, "We must leave now. She will bring the others with her!"

Amedan nodded grimly and turned back to Alesh, "There is much that I would tell you, but it seems that we are out of time. My wife is coming. Javen is right; she has grown powerful in her hate and, as I am now, I could not protect you from her. We must go, but know that I will send you what help I may." He turned to the lesser gods and nodded, holding out his hands toward them, "Come Javen, Deitra, attend me. Oh, and Alesh," he said, turning back, "you are a lot like him, you know."

"Olliman?" Alesh asked incredulously, "Chosen Olliman was the wisest, kindest man I know. He was a hero."

"So he was," Amedan said, smiling. He put a hand on Alesh's shoulder, and it shone with a blinding brilliance for a second then was gone, "and he, too, was a poor fisherman."

Alesh opened his mouth to respond, but the gods vanished into thin air without a trace. The five of them stood, staring at where they'd been, each considering what they'd seen and heard. Finally, Rion cleared his throat, "Uh ... what now?"

Alesh turned to them and in the torchlight Katherine saw that one of his shoulders held a deep puncture scar with black lines radiating from it. The other, the one Amedan had touched him on, was marked by a golden handprint that looked remarkably like the sun. Staring at it, the words in Chosen Alashia's letter ran through her head, *And he will be marked with the light and the darkness both.* "Now?" Alesh said, eyeing them each in turn, "Now, we prepare. The night cannot last forever." He looked at the dark sky, his jaw set, "The morning comes."

Stop by and say hi!

And so we've come to the end of *The Son of the Morning*. We truly hope you've had as much fun hanging out with Alesh and the others as we did. The second book in The Nightfall Wars will be coming to you as soon as possible. To get a **FREE** copy of *The Silent Blade: A Seven Virtues Novella*, sign up for Jacob Peppers's newsletter at www.jacobpeppersauthor.com

Alternatively, feel free to try out ***A Sellsword's Compassion***, Book One of the Seven Virtues. If you've enjoyed the book, we would really appreciate you taking a moment to leave an honest review. They make a tremendous difference as any author can tell you and there are few things cooler than hearing from readers.

If you'd like to reach out and chat, you can email Jacob at JacobPeppersAuthor@gmail.com or visit his website at www.jacobpeppersauthor.com

About the Author

Jacob Peppers lives in Georgia with his wife and three dogs. He is an avid reader and writer and when he's not exploring the worlds of others, he's creating his own. His short fiction has been published in various markets, and his short story, "The Lies of Autumn," was a finalist for the 2013 Eric Hoffer Award for Short Prose. He is also the author of *A Sellsword's Compassion* and *The Silent Blade*.

Note from the Author

So here's the thing—books are kind of like clay. No, seriously, this works bear with me. See, you start with an idea, a rough, simple thing with little or no shape to it at all, just a blob of a beginning, really. Then you go along molding it into what you assume—or, at least, *I* assume—is an incredibly accurate and flawless representation of what you intended.

You take some pieces out, put some pieces in (and if you're anything like me, you put in about three times as much as you took out, seriously it's a problem) and eventually you're holding it in your hands. Your little creation, your perfect little masterpiece. You do a little dance, drink a lot of beer, probably do a lot more dancing, and then you bestow it upon those lucky souls we know as "beta-readers."

"Hey, look!" You say, with wide, expectant eyes, "Look what I made!"

There are appropriate oohs and aahs. "That's great!" They say, "Very awesome." You glow and beam and accept your much deserved accolades. Then, of course, comes the inevitable question; "No, really, it's great but…What is it?"

Worlds shatter, puppies let out mournful calls of grief and abandonment, and thinking of Prufrock and how this is not what you meant at all, you throw your hands in the air. You go back to the computer armed with the possibly unwanted but certainly *needed* understanding that you are no Shakespeare. That, in fact, your creation is a (cue ominous music) monster.

You probably drink some more beer, but you *certainly* don't do any dancing. You moan and sigh, and you put in the time, paying close attention to the notes you took grudgingly from each beta reader. And, to your surprise, the shape of what you're trying to create becomes clearer. All of a sudden, you don't have to look at your creation with squinted eyes to see what it is. All of a sudden, it's there, looking back at you. Alive or, at least, as alive as you can make it. After that, well. I won't go into the details, but let's just say there's a bit more drinking involved, alright?

As always, I want to thank those who have taken their time and energy to beta read this book for me and to put up with my … well, let's be kind and say hyper sensitivity. Thank you to my many friends whose kindnesses in helping me with this book (as with all the others) are too many to list here.

Thanks to my mom for being even more excited about the book than I was myself and to my dad for helping me to stay motivated to sit down at the computer and just *write*. Thanks to Josh for being a great sounding board for ideas and concepts during the writing of the book and thank you to my wife, Andrea Peppers, for her tireless and unflinching support.

And what about you, dear reader? You didn't think I forgot you, did you? Oh no, I saw you there, noticed you as soon as you set foot in my little workshop. Thank you, as always, for visiting me here and taking a look at my latest project. I do hope you've enjoyed yourself. As for the workshop? Sure, it may be a little grimy, a little dirty, but we don't mind that, do we? Sometimes, when you wipe away the dust and cobwebs, you find treasures. And speaking of, what what are all those things covered with tarps, you ask? Well, I can't say as I know all of them myself. But hey, why don't you hang around for a little while? We'll find out together.

Made in the USA
Las Vegas, NV
02 July 2023

74163457R00197